"Original, vibrant, and intelligent; the characters leap from the page thanks to authentic settings, nonstop action, backstabbing villains, and rough justice. These novels are tough as nails, written by a pro who knows what he's doing."
—STEVE BERRY, *New York Times* bestselling author of *The Last Order*

"Tougher than William Johnstone, grittier than Louis L'Amour, Jackson Cain writes as if he were the illegitimate love child of Sam Peckinpah and Cormac McCarthy."
—WILLIAM MARTIN, *New York Times* bestselling author and winner of the Samuel Eliot Morison Lifetime Achievement Award for historical fiction

"These novels have amazing narrative command. Everything is strong: storytelling and characterization as well as pace and tempo. They're Technicolor and widescreen combined. Jackson Cain has written both a thriller and a western."
—RICHARD WHEELER, winner of Western Writers' Lifetime Achievement Award and five other major awards

"This is the Wild West—as vividly re-created as has ever been done on the page or screen. Hits with the force of a Winchester '73 bullet and the kick of a wild horse.
—RALPH PETERS, *New York Times* bestselling author of *Judgment at Appomattox* and winner of three Boyd Awards and the Hammett Prize

DEAD MEN DON'T LIE

An Outlaw Torn Slater Western

JACKSON CAIN

PINNACLE BOOKS

Kensington Publishing Corp.

www.kensingtonbooks.com

PINNACLE BOOKS are published by

Kensinton Publishing Corp.
119 West 40th Street
New York, NY 10018

All Kensington titles, imprints, and distributed lines are available at special quantity discounts for bulk purchases for sales promotions, premiums, fund-raising, educational, or institutional use. Special book excerpts or customized printings can also be created to fit specific needs. For details, write or phone the office of the Kensington sales manager: Kensington Publishing Corp., 119 West 40th Street, New York, NY 10018, attn: Sales Department; phone 1-800-221-2647.

PINNACLE BOOKS and the Pinnacle logo are Reg. U.S. Pat. & TM Off.

ISBN-13: 978-0-7860-4627-0

ISBN-10: 0-7860-4627-9

First printing: October 2020

10 9 8 7 6 5 4 3 2 1

Printed in the United States of America

Electronic edition:

ISBN-13: 978-0-7860-4628-7 (e-book)

ISBN-10: 0-7860-4628-7 p(e-book)

To Maribel Gutierrez,
To whom we all owe so much . . .

Pity poor Méjico, so far from God, so close to the United States.
—EL PRESIDENTE PORFIRIO DÍAZ

DEAD MEN
DON'T LIE

PROLOGUE

A bullet always knows.

High up in the San Carlos mountains in southern Arizona, a woman with shoulder-length auburn hair sat cross-legged. She was studying the cliff face in front of her. Dressed in a blue close-fitting denim work shirt and Levi's, she sported an old, worn, light brown, scoop-brimmed work Stetson and hard-used riding boots, which were heeled with large steel rowels. She looked fit, and she was. Her long tresses, full mouth, flaring cheekbones, and expressive green eyes still drew stares—even from men a fraction of her thirty-five years. A pair of saddlebags were casually spread out on her lap; a black-and-white Appaloosa with a mottled rump was rein-standing beside her.

The woman stared fixedly at the three circular points embedded in the cliff face. Each of them was approximately two inches in diameter—two on top, one below, each approximately eighteen inches from the other. Pale as old ivory, these disks were considered by her godmother and legendary Apache war shaman, Lozen, to be sacred.

The woman needed something sacred at this moment. True, she and her husband, Frank, owned the largest ranch in the entire Arizona territory as well as several extremely profitable silver mines, but now, it seemed, her wealth no longer mattered. For the past twenty years, the woman's life had gone from marvelous to monstrous. Her two headstrong children—nineteen-year-old Richard and eighteen-year-old Rachel—were continually running off on "adventures." Their hair-raising exploits had always frightened the woman out of her wits: Richard's rock-climbing, high diving, and heavyweight boxing drove Katherine to distraction, and she was convinced that Rachel's obsession with breaking wild mustangs would be the death of her only daughter.

But now the two had topped themselves. They had set out on another "adventure" in the dead of night, without warning, leaving only a letter of good-bye. In it, they explained that they were hopping a freight train down to Mexico. Traveling in peon garb, they intended to explore Sonora and Sinaloa—two of Mexico's most lawless states. Sinaloa was especially frightening. Brutally tyrannical, its titular head was a dimwit named Eduardo. His shockingly psychopathic stepmother—known throughout Mexico as "La Señorita"—really ran it, and she had brought back the torture chambers of the Spanish Inquisition and the sacrificial pyramids of the Aztecs, on one of whose summits her faux-Aztec priests cut the hearts out of anyone who crossed her. In short, her political systems—which Porfirio Díaz privately and whole-heartedly supported—were derived from the worst excesses of the Spanish Inquisition and the Aztec Empire. Since the Señorita was also Díaz's most generous personal benefactor and political contributor, her power throughout Méjico was surpassed only by that of El Presidente Díaz.

For the past decade she and Méjico's vicious dictator, the same Porfirio Díaz, had embarked on a path of conquest and had subjugated almost everything and everyone in Mexico. Only the state of Sonora had fought them off and remained free. But Sinaloa and Chihuahua, under Díaz and the Señorita, had allied themselves against Sonora, and that state's days seemed to be numbered. The Señorita let everyone know that after Sonora she also planned to come north and reclaim the Arizona Territory for herself and Díaz.

The Señorita had spouted that theory one too many times, and Katherine's children decided it was time to stop speculating on Sinaloa and its empire from hell and find out what was really going on. In the letter they had characterized their expedition as "a reconnaissance mission and fact-finding operation." They quoted Sun-tzu's dictum: "Know thy enemy." They believed they would return with "indispensable intelligence, which will determine the survival or the extinction of El Rancho del Cielo."

As Frank had once observed, the two young people "suffered the curse of Odysseus—incurable curiosity."

"Which will lead only to Cyclopes, sirens, Scylla, Charybdis, and witches who turn people into swine," Katherine had added.

"Then why are they doing it?" Frank had asked.

"They like living close to the bone, on the razor's edge . . . on the hair trigger's trembling touch."

"In other words, they're like their mother was when she was their age," Frank had answered.

Katherine had been abducted by the Apache as a child and Frank believed the experience had left her with a wild, rebellious streak, and there was some truth to his theory. But contrary to much rumor and false report, Katherine was not made of stone and was not impervious to fear or anxiety.

And now Katherine was facing something more unbearable: Frank had always been a dynamo of indefatigable energy. Not only was he the foremost surgeon in the entire American Southwest and not only was he running that region's most modern, scientifically advanced surgical hospital, he was also indispensable in running and expanding the ranch and their mines. Now, however, he was constantly in bed and devastatingly exhausted. Even worse, over the last several months he'd begun experiencing intestinal pain.

Then came the diagnosis: terminal abdominal cancer.

And her children were down in Mexico—incommunicado.

Katherine secretly feared that all she and Frank could do was hope that their children were safe and wait the disease out—until finally Frank's suffering came to its inevitable end.

Katherine, however, was not good at "waiting things out," which was why she'd come up to the San Carlos mountains to meet with her lifelong friend and mentor, Spirit Owl.

* * *

Seated earlier that morning in his heat lodge—a brush wickiup filled with aromatic smoke and scorchingly hot steam—Spirit Owl had spoken to her of her children:

"Everyone is an individual with a different destiny. You have to learn to leave people alone—Frank as well as your children. You have to learn to let them choose and follow their destinies. You have to stop manipulating everyone."

"If I had adopted that attitude twenty years ago, there would be no Rancho del Cielo. It has survived and thrived precisely because I have, when necessary, told people what to do, even when they resisted. It's survived because I have run it with an iron hand."

"But you run the lives of those you love with that same iron hand even when they need kindness and understanding."

"I can't help interfering in their lives if they are hurting themselves and those around them. Noninterference in such situations isn't love."

"You came to me because you're depressed. That's because, in truth, you don't do good deeds for their own sake. You do good works because you live to control people. Now you feel that control slipping through your fingers. Frank is ill, your children are in Mexico, you can't manipulate them, and you mourn the loss of your power."

"Richard and Rachel went down to Mexico and into the heart of hell. You're saying I shouldn't have tried to stop them. I should have let them go—let them get tortured and killed?"

"Did it ever occur to you that they did the right thing? The Rancho knows nothing about Sinaloa. It was time you learned what you're up against."

"But our spies are my children."

"Oh, I get it. It's okay to send someone else's children down there but not your own."

Katherine buried her face in her hands. "Spirit Owl, I'm losing my grip."

"You mean you're losing your control."

Katherine raised her head and stared at the Owl angrily. "Richard and Rachel kept their trip a secret from me. Had I known, you bet I would have 'controlled' them. I would have locked them up and tied them down till the insanity passed."

"That's because you're a miserable person, Katherine, and you aren't happy unless you're making those around you miserable. Grow up and learn to stop meddling."

His advice depressed her even more. She'd brought her Colt .44 army-issue pistol, ostensibly to fight off pumas, javelinas, and diamondbacks, but as of late she had increasingly considered another use for it. A little voice said inside her head:

I'm sorry, Frank, Richard, Rachel, Owl, I just can't take it anymore.

She put the pistol to her temple.

And after a moment of silence pulled the trigger.

Suddenly she saw Spirit Owl in a vision. She said to him: "Am I dead?"

"No," the Owl said. "Just in Arizona."

"I'm supposed to be dead."

"You're supposed to stop feeling sorry for yourself."

"I don't care. Everyone else gives up," Katherine said. "Why shouldn't I?"

"You have to care," Spirit Owl. "You have work to do. Anyway it's not your time."

"How do you know?"

"Because I'm the Owl."

* * *

The vision faded and she heard the hammer dry-snap on a dead round.

"Click!"

The Owl was right.

The bullet told her.

And a bullet always knows.

PART I

How about un abrazo*?*
All you gringos like the abrazo.
—Major Mateo Cardozo

Chapter 1

Rachel Ryan stood at the Hermosillo cantina bar, staring into her glass of tequila. Glancing around the crowded *taberna,* she absently noted the two dozen tables with their quartets of straight-backed chairs. Coal oil lamps were bracketed against the walls, and twenty or so hung randomly from the ceiling.

In a corner, a mariachi band played all the great plaintive Mexican songs—"Corrido," "Dormir Contigo," "Te Desean," "La Incondicional," "Mi Terco Corazón," "El Son de la Negra," "Algo Tienes," "La Cárcel de Cananea," "Tu Amor," "Vive el Verano," "La Paloma" as well as hers and Richard's personal favorite, "La Golondrina." The band included a trumpet, an accordion, a violin, a high-pitched, round-backed vihuela guitar, and its big, bulky, bass counterpart, a *guitarrón.* The cantina featured a large dance floor. Since Sonora's main fort was nearby, half the clientele were soldiers in gray uniforms. A dozen or more cavalry officers had on brown, roweled riding boots, which clinked on the wood floor when they walked.

The other half of the clientele were civilians. White cotton shirts and faded Levi's were popular among the civilian men, white cotton dresses among the women. Since La Paloma was an upscale cantina, even the *putas* sported white cotton dresses.

Fluent in Spanish, Rachel and her brother, Richard, both understood the song lyrics around them. After three months in this country she was even dreaming in Spanish. Rachel listened to "La Golondrina," absently taking in the song's words:

> *A donde irá*
> *veloz y fatigada*
> *la golondrina*
> *que de aquí se va*
> *por si en el viento*
> *se hallara extraviada*
> *buscando abrigo*
> *y no lo encontrara.*

Ever the clown, Richard mockingly warbled the English translation:

> *Where can it go*
> *rushed and fatigued*
> *the swallow*
> *passing by*
> *tossed by the wind*
> *looking so lost*
> *with nowhere to hide.*

"Sort of summarizes our whole trip, doesn't it?" Rachel said.

Richard let out a long sigh. "Are you questioning the wisdom of our venture?"

"Maybe."

"Don't let Mom hear you say that," Richard said. "She'll never let us live it down—sneaking off like we did in the dead of night, then coming back broke, our tails between our legs, admitting we screwed up."

"I'm starting to wonder why we came here at all," Rachel said.

"We wanted to know if Sinaloa was as bad as we'd heard, and if it posed a threat to El Rancho, which it does."

"I wanted to hook you up with our Lady Dolorosa," Rachel said. Now it was her turn to mock.

"Yeah, right, pimp me out. Maybe I could earn us train fare back."

"From what I hear her lovers do not find her generous," Rachel said.

"She's built an Aztec pyramid behind her main hacienda. She's installed Aztec priests and brought back their rituals. Her priests even conduct human sacrifices atop those temples."

"That's where she sends the lovers who disappoint her," Rachel said.

"After her Grand Inquisitor finishes with them in his torture chambers," Richard said.

"That's when her Aztec priests take over," Rachel said. "After flaying them whole, they cut out their hearts atop those pyramids, then bleed their remains out into troughs, like stuck pigs."

"That's only because they failed to satisfy her in bed," Richard said, thumping his chest, "which in my case could never happen."

"You're different, Virgin Boy?" Rachel said, taunting him with her favorite nickname for him—and the one he hated the most.

"'My strength is as the strength of ten, because my heart is pure.'"

"What's that from?" Rachel asked.

"Tennyson," Richard said. "*Idylls of the King,* but don't bother reading it. You wouldn't get it."

"Why?"

"It's literature."

Rachel gave her brother a condescending frown.

Six rurales in gray, silver-trimmed uniforms and dark brown riding boots, heeled with razor-sharp buzz-saw rowels, bellied up to the bar on their right. They had .44 Colt revolvers on their hips and bandoliers crisscrossing their chests. They all wore broad-brimmed sombreros with triple-creased steeple crowns, which matched their uniforms. The tallest of the six pounded on the bar with his palm. Eléna, the woman who owned the cantina and served the drinks, didn't take anything off anybody, and she glared at him. An attractive widow, her hair was as black as a crow's wing, and her tight-fitting red cotton dress showed her figure off to her considerable advantage. She was a successful, good-looking businesswoman. Men vied for her attention and tried hard to stay on her good side.

"Mateo," she warned the officer, "keep it up and Antonio will break a shotgun butt on your thick skull."

Major Mateo Cardozo grinned widely. Under his black, downward-sweeping horseshoe mustache, his white even teeth shone brilliantly. Mateo and Eléna were both playing a favorite game.

"A thousand pardons, señorita," Mateo implored,

"and a compliment on your *belleza* [beauty]. Also a bottle of tequila for my men and myself, *por favor.*"

"I can see you hombres have already had a bottle somewhere else."

"Two bottles," Mateo said.

"You have to make five a.m. roll call, not me."

She gave him a bottle and six glasses. He gave her the money.

"Who knows, señorita?" Corporal Rinaldi said. He pulled himself up to his full five feet, six inches of height, his forehead furrowed but his dark eyes glittering. "Tomorrow, we may not even be in the army."

"That is a fact," Mateo concurred.

"What's wrong?" Eléna asked, polishing a glass.

"We have to figure out those goddamn howitzer trajectories," Sergeant Enriqué—the big, bearded guy—muttered under his breath, "and until we do, those damn guns won't hit shit."

"General Ortega is madder than hell at me," Mateo admitted. "Díaz and the Señorita are planning another attack, and if we can't get our artillery up and running, we're screwed."

"We're all screwed," Eléna said softly, nodding.

Rachel gave Richard a quick hard look. "I'm going to the *excusada* [the restroom]," she said, "then let's slope on out of here. I've had it with Méjico Lindo. This whole trip was a bust. As much as I hate to admit it, Mom was right. We'll figure out how to find our way back to Arizona tomorrow."

Richard nodded his agreement. "*Verdad.*" ["Truth."]

Mateo was still complaining about his cannons. "That's 'cause those cannons are old Napoleons, and no one has fired them in a decade. The generals can't expect us to learn this shit overnight. We don't even know how to aim the damn guns."

"I don't even know how much powder to use," Rinaldi said.

"Or how to make the right kind of *hideputa* [son-of-a-whore] powder," Mateo said.

"We're using the same mix of sulfur, charcoal, and saltpeter that we use to load rifles," Enriqué said.

"Except those howitzers aren't saddle rifles," Mateo said.

"They aren't handguns either," Enriqué said.

"Why'd the general give us the job anyway?" Enriqué asked. "We're cavalry. We ain't no artillery."

"Someone has it in for us," Rinaldi said.

"He gave the job to me," Mateo said, "not to you hombres. You won't get blamed. I will, and Ortega will be right. I was supposed to figure out how to make those guns work. I let him down."

"It's not our fault that Sonora doesn't have real artillery officers," Rinaldi said.

Richard had just graduated at the top of his class from West Point as an artillery officer. He was so young though, only nineteen, that they asked him to take a year off before the army gave him a field commission. Emboldened by three shots of tequila, Richard tore a sheet of writing paper from his knapsack pad and began filling it with ballistics equations. He then tapped Mateo on the shoulder.

"You have three basic problems," Richard said. "You need someone from your university who knows integral calculus to compute your trajectories. He'll understand these equations here." Richard wrote out a glossary, defining the symbols. "He then has to find a good book on the chemistry of explosives. He will then be able to tell you how to mix the cordite you need to power your shells."

"Cordite?" Mateo asked.

"None of the European Great Powers are using black powder for their artillery and their other high-powered weapons," Richard said. "Not anymore. America is phasing it out too. You'll need nitroglycerin, if you want to manufacture nitrocellulose and nitro-guanidine, both of which you really need if you want to produce the cordite necessary for really high-quality howitzer powder. It's not easy to make though."

"I can't even make a shell go a hundred yards," Mateo grunted, eyes downcast.

"Aim the guns at a forty-five-degree angle for max-imum range," Richard said, "and then—"

Stopping in midsentence, he looked up from his paper full of equations and saw the troopers were all circling around him, staring at him, fixedly, fascinated—a little too fascinated. Mateo was sud-denly putting his arm around his shoulders.

You had to show off, didn't you? Richard cursed silently. *How in living hell do you get out of this one?*

Rachel came back. Hearing Richard's last remarks and seeing the paper full of equations, she instantly realized how badly Richard had screwed up. She re-moved Mateo's arm from Richard's shoulders.

"Richard, we are out of here."

Chapter 2

A woman in a black robe stood with a youthful captain of the guard on the third step of the Great Pyramid of Quetzalcoatl. The widowed stepmother to the governor of the Sinaloa, she was that state's true ruler and now ran Chihuahua as well. She was also the wealthiest woman in all of Central America. She had made countless enemies over the years, and if she truly wanted to go out in public, she was wise to do it incognito. The black robe effectively disguised her appearance. With the hood up, most people mistook her for a priest.

She wanted to stand next to the young *capitán* during the next few minutes and watch his reaction when the enormity of his fate finally and irrevocably sank in.

She had commissioned this particular pyramid almost fifteen years before. She had overseen its construction and had visited it countless times. Still it never failed to impress her. Close up, it was so vast that no one could fathom its dimensions. It was as if it encompassed the entire universe.

Its square base was three hundred yards along the edges. Its sloping sides were lined with hundreds of steps—so numerous they seemed to reach the sun. At its top, off to one side, was the sanctuary of Quetzalcoatl—the god-king. Many mejicanos *viewed him as the Aztec Jesus Christ. Quetzalcoatl was the only god in their firmament who had once lived and walked among them and who actually liked the* mejicano *people. Hanging on the sanctuary wall atop the temple was a stunning representation of Quetzalcoatl, an immense mosaic rendered in gold, silver, and turquoise.*

But on the flat summit also stood several gesticulating priests, brandishing machetes and obsidian carving knives. Before them was a limestone altar, four feet high and six feet long—the infamous stone on which countless victims had been, as the Lady Dolorosa liked to mockingly put it with a sly sneer curling her upper lip, "heartlessly sacrificed."

Shrouded in human skins, crowned with gleaming headdresses of elaborately woven eagle plumes, gemstones, and glittering strands of finely spun silver and gold, the bloodstained holy men harangued the roaring throng, shaking their big gore-dripping obsidian knives at the howling masses below.

The pyramid was cordoned off and federales kept the surrounding mob approximately a hundred feet from the temple's base. The Señorita needed federales to control them. The crowd numbered in the thousands, and they howled continually: "Blood for Quetzalcoatl!" She still could not believe how popular her human sacrifices were with Sinaloa's populace.

Four hulking novitiates appeared at the pyramid's base with the terrified wretch in hand. Partially flayed by the Grand Inquisitor, he was almost too weakened to resist. But one glimpse of the priests—their knives, the stone—and he was a raving madman with the strength of the demented.

The Señorita had chosen her spot on the pyramid well. Her ex-lover was about to be dragged, kicking and screaming, past her on his way up the terraced steps to the sacrificial stone. In fact, he was so close she could discern his whip welts, burns, knife slashes, his missing teeth and fingernails, to say nothing of large swaths of stripped-away skin. From the way his right arm was bent and pressed against his chest, she inferred that her Inquisitor had dislocated that shoulder, probably on the strappado or the rack.

There. They were dragging him up the first step less than ten feet from her.

"Ey, hombre!" she yelled at him.

Recognizing her voice, he abruptly turned his head and stared straight into her eyes. The shock of recognition shook him to his core.

"Why are you doing this to me?" he shouted at her. "What did I do to you?"

She quickly crossed the short distance between them. The priests, sensing who she was, quickly stopped on the fourth step. Mounting that step, she leaned toward the captain, her mouth and eyes bursting into a blazing sunburst of a smile. When the two of them were nose to nose, eyes locked, she said:

"You were a truly terrible fuck." The Lady Dolorosa spoke softly, her smile still grand and glorious. Looking back at her new major—a man whose name she also could not, did not, remember and would never remember—and staring him straight in the eye, she grinned condescendingly and said: "Got the picture, *puto*? You *comprende*? That's what happens to hombres who can't cut it between the sheets."

Chapter 3

The big man in the black Plainsman hat with the flat crown and broad uncreased brim stared into the campfire. Dropping to one knee, he fed several dried-out cottonwood branches into the blaze, warmed his hands, and then drank some more mezcal out of the neck of the bottle.

"We gonna take that bank, Torn?" the man on his right said.

Slater passed the bottle to his friend and nodded slowly. He'd done time with Moreno in the Sonoran Pit—arguably the worst of Méjico's many despicable slave-labor prison mines—for three long years, and he trusted him. They'd been through hell together, and Luis did every minute of it standing straight up. If he couldn't rely on the man here on the outside, he couldn't rely on anyone, and Slater couldn't take down major banks and payroll trains all by himself. Even worse, since Slater was wanted in thirteen states and territories, as well as the states of Sonora, Sinaloa, and Chihuahua, and had the same $20,000 price on his head in both the U.S. and Méjico, trust was a luxury he couldn't usually afford.

But for three years, he and Moreno had survived that prison hellhole together, and afterward they'd robbed banks and trains together. Yes, Moreno was a man you could ride the river with.

Their third man, Alberto Segundo, sitting on his saddle blanket by the staked-out horses and finishing his dinner, was another story. His older brother, Roberto, had been Moreno's oldest friend, and that man had proven himself in the Sonoran Pit as well. He'd finally died there—trapped in a cave-in. Before he'd died, however, he'd convinced Moreno to take his little brother on a job, if they ever got out.

And it turned out they needed Alberto. They were short a man, time was running out, the payroll was about to arrive at the bank, and so they'd taken him on. None of which meant they could rely on him. His appearance alone reeked of lifelong failure and bad mistakes: He was missing half his teeth and one eye. There was nothing anyone could do about that, but he was also a drunk, and he stank. They had to force him to wash himself, his clothes, and his long, straggly, stinking hair in the occasional stream. He couldn't stop his almost insane boasting about how tough he was—how many federales he'd killed, how many banks he'd knocked over, and how many trains he'd robbed. Any man who bragged about such stuff to Outlaw Torn Slater was clearly . . . *muy ignorante y muy maníaco.*

But they didn't have time to find anyone else.

"Think Alberto'll hold up his end?" Slater asked.

"All he has to do is guard those remounts for us up the trail."

"I wouldn't trust him to carry a dozen tamales across the street."

"He'll do it," Luis said. "He'll be there. If he isn't there, he won't get his end."

Slater stared at him, silent.

"If he's not there, Torn, we'll hunt him down and kill him."

Torn Slater was still silent.

"You want me to kill him, amigo? Now. Just say the word."

"Not yet. Maybe he'll do his job."

"Stranger things have happened," Moreno said, nodding his head.

Slater looked away.

"Ey, compadre," Moreno said, smiling, hoping to lighten Slater's mood. "What you want to do with your end?"

Slater shrugged. "Same as always."

"What's that?" Moreno said, genuinely curious.

"Hard liquor, fast women, slow horses."

"And waste the rest?" Moreno said, finishing the rest.

"*Verdad.*"

"Then what?"

"Rob every bank, fuck every woman, and kill every swingin'-dick, lawin' sonofabitch that gets in my way."

"You left out trains," Moreno said. "We blow them *también.*"

"Trains too," Slater said.

Moreno shook his head sadly.

"What's wrong?" Slater asked.

"Is that all you think about? *¿Pesos, gatito y muerta?*"
["Money, pussy, and death?"]

"What else is there?" Slater said. "We rob banks and trains for a living. We don't live lives of fine distinction."

"But blood and *putas*, pesos and death, that ain't no life for us—not *siempre* [forever]."

Slater allowed him a not-unfriendly smile. "We got tequila too."

Now Moreno looked away, shaking his head, unamused.

"So what you wanna do with all this money?" Slater asked. "Invest it with El Presidente Porfirio or J. Pierpont Morgan? The Señorita? Try that and she'll put us in one of her prison mines."

"I got nothing against mines. I got a mine up in the Sierra Madres—very remote. We take that bank money and head on up there. We pick up provisions along the way, and, when we get there, we bury the money nearby. We work the mine, sluice the streams, and when we get bored, we hunt game and we fish. They got deer, antelope, trout, and bass like you ain't never seen in your life. In the nearby *indios* villages, they got *muchas buenas indias puras* if we want *chiquitas*. And who knows? Maybe we also take a fortune in *oro puro* [pure gold] out of that mine. Main thing is we don't come down off that mountain till the federales forget who we are, forget what we did, and forget we'd ever been. Then we get ourselves a real life—one with no more banks to hit, no more trains to rob, and no more lawmen dogging our trail."

Slater stared at his amigo, silent.

"*Verdad?*" Moreno finally asked.

"*Verdad*, but, amigo, we got one more bank to rob—tomorrow morning."

"But still, think about that mine, amigo, the hunting and fishing, the *chiquitas*? How long has it been since you relaxed? You interested?"

"I'm interested in that next bank," Slater said.

"I know, amigo. We got one more bank to rob. Always one more bank and train to rob. But after that, we back off for a while, no? Promise me you'll think about it?"

Slater slapped his friend on the shoulder. "*Sí, mi amigo*, I'll think about it. Why not? Why the hell not?"

Chapter 4

In the cantina Rachel politely removed the major's arm from her brother's shoulder.

"He's not going with you," she said to Mateo.

Major Mateo Cardozo did not seem upset. Treating her to an affectionate grin, he said: "*Sí*, I understand completely." Mateo picked his military hat up from the bar and placed it over his heart. "But on the other hand, there are some *hombres muy malos y muy duros* in this benighted land, and when two gringos, such as yourselves, come here so far from home, they have need of amigos such as us, no?"

"We have *muchos buenos amigos* here already," Rachel said. "We aren't alone."

She and Richard both hesitated to say who their parents were. Their ransom would be worth a fortune.

"I am sure you are not, *guapa* [beautiful]," Mateo said.

"And you aren't taking him with you," Rachel said, standing her ground and holding Richard's arm.

"I really don't know much about artillery anyway,"

Richard said, still trying to backpedal. "I was only spouting off."

"Richard," Rachel said. "Shut up."

Mateo gave them both another captivating smile. "What can I do to prove I love you, that I am a man of trust? How about *un abrazo*? All you gringos like the *abrazo*."

Mateo was a big man—at least six-two—with broad shoulders, and under his tan army shirt, his biceps bulged. Richard, however, was a good six feet four, and had the muscles of a seasoned rock-climber, which was what he was. He'd also boxed, wrestled, and done high-platform diving at West Point. Still, when Mateo wrapped Richard in his big burly arms, Richard felt as if he'd been embraced by a grizzly bear.

"See," Mateo said, "I give your brother the *abrazo*. We are amigos—now, *siempre* [forever]. I will never go back on that."

A crowd was gathering around them now, which not only made Rachel even more nervous, it seemed to bother Mateo.

"Tell you what," he said to Rachel. "Let's you and me go outside and discuss this. Too many ears in here. We'll work something out. We won't shanghai anybody. We're *soldados* not *hombres malos* [bad men]."

Apprehensive but still wanting to hear what he said, Rachel followed Mateo out the side door and into the alley.

"Those hombres back there, they aren't as *simpático* as me," Mateo said. "They get ahold of you, they'll drag you into this alley and rape you so *malo-duro* you'll never fuck again. Not me. I'm *uno mucho bueno hombre.*"

"And I'm *una mucha buena mujer* [a very good woman]. But you take my brother, and I won't stop till I kill you. You die, and I'll carve my name on your tombstone. I'll harrow hell for your *excremento*-stinking soul."

Suddenly, Rachel saw a blur, and Mateo's big right hand slapped her temple hard enough to ring temple bells and hang stars. Slamming her head against the adobe wall behind her, Mateo grabbed her throat and whispered:

"You watch your mouth, *puta.* I'll drag you out of here in shackles and leg irons. I'll sell your *gringa* ass into a *casa de puta dura bruta* [a rough whorehouse]. You'll die there turning *muchos tortuosos* tricks [many torturous tricks]."

But Rachel wouldn't back down. Shaking loose from Mateo's grip, she began beating on his chest with her fists, ripping his cheeks with her fingernails, kicking his shins with her heavy boots. She about to shout her mother's name—she was so angry she didn't care what happened.

"We have connections!" she shouted. "We're not nobodies. Our mother is one of the most powerful people in North America! We'll come after you with police, politicians, whatever it takes. Our mother will—"

But she never got it out. In a blind, red-eyed rage, Mateo thundered:

"PU-TA!!!"

Then he hit her in the left temple, not with his fist

but with the shot-loaded, whip-spring buttstock of his wrist-quirt—a makeshift blackjack.

She didn't pass out immediately. She stared at him in what seemed to be wide-eyed wonder.

"What the fuck?" was all she said.

Then her eyes slowly closed. Passing out, she slid down the cantina wall. Rubbing his torn cheek, Mateo stared in shock at her, at what he'd done.

"Lo siento, chiquita," ["I'm sorry, baby"] he said to her sadly. "I think I maybe killed you, but you got me *muy loco.*" He studied her for one more long, hard moment. "Aw, fuck it," he finally said with a head-shaking shrug. *"Así es como sucede a veces."* ["That's the way it happens sometimes."]

Heading back into the cantina, he grabbed Richard and dragged him out to their mounts, which were tied to the cantina's hitchrack. When his men came out with his hat and jacket, he commandeered one of the cantina patron's horses and told Richard to mount up. Instead Richard started to turn around and look for his sister, but before Richard could go into the alley and find her, Mateo laid the quirt's leaded stock over the top of his head. Catching Richard on the way down, Mateo hoisted him up face-first and belly-down across the saddle of the confiscated bay. Using a coiled saddle rope to secure Richard, Mateo grabbed the horse's mecate and swung onto his big horse. Dallying the mecate around his pummel, he led his men and Richard—trussed up, unconscious, and belly-down over the mount—toward the army fort.

"Amigo," Mateo said to the unconscious Richard, "welcome to the Sonoran rurales."

PART II

What's more important?
Pesos in your saddlebags or notches on your pistola?
—LUIS MORENO, outlaw

Chapter 5

Lady Dolorosa and her new *capitán* watched the four novitiates drag the Lady's ex-lover up the temple's stepped slope. She was giving him a shy, demure wave.

"Yes, I shall almost miss you, whatever your name was. We did have some fine times. We must have. I kept you around for over a month." She looked at her new prospect. "To tell you the truth, I don't remember much about any of my lovers. When I try to recall their faces and features, it's as if their memories seem to vanish without a trace. In my head they all blur into a single, generic, composite male."

She turned to her "prospect." "But every day is a new beginning, and now I have you. Any questions?" she asked, giving him her most endearing smile.

"I was curious why we're here," he said nervously.

"Think of this as motivation. That's what I try to instill in all my eager young boys: the passion to serve and excel."

"To serve and excel in the service of Madre Méjico?" he asked, confused.

Lady Dolorosa broke into a series of mocking, mean-spirited giggles.

"No, silly. I'm talking about fealty to my bed and body, of course! I thought you knew. I can't sleep nights and one of the few things that distracts me in those dreadful nocturnal hours is really good . . . *sex*. You able to excel in that department? You better be."

"Of course, My Lady. You're the most beautiful, irresistible woman I've ever seen, and you're my ruler."

"Funny, that's just what who's-it up there on the pyramid used to say. Flattering words, however, are no substitute for action and endurance. Stamina—that's what I require from my willing young men—juggernaut stamina. I do hope you're up to the task—unlike what's-his-face."

An almost preternaturally shrill and piercing scream ripped through their conversation like a thunderbolt.

"Ah, the pièce de résistance!" Lady Dolorosa shouted to her new *capitán* above the crowd's ear-cracking cheers.

Her former lover—up on the altar—was still alive, and the Señorita's head priest was covered with the man's gore as he stabbed and hacked his way into his chest cavity. Reaching deep into it, the priest slashed the aortas and yanked out his victim's still-throbbing heart. After shoving it straight into the man's hysterically screaming face, he lifted it high overhead for the crazed congregation to see. He then tossed it into a huge ceramic crock filled with the hearts of those previously immolated.

His assistants hung her ex-lover by the heels over a nearby edge, along which a gutter ran all the way down into a ground trough. As thoroughly as any slaughtered steer, the man was finally exsanguinated, his blood filling a huge ceramic crock below.

When she looked back up at the summit, the head priest was hacking at the man's neck with a black, razor-sharp obsidian blade. When he cut through, the man's head slipped off the altar and hit the stone summit with a sickening *crack!* The priest picked up the head by the hair and flung it down the terraced slope. It hit every one of the hundreds upon hundreds of steps on the way down.

"Good-bye, Pancho," she muttered half aloud, "or whatever the hell your name was."

"Do you wish to go anyplace else?" the *capitán* said, looking a little queasy.

"No, this has been amusement enough. I have to get back to the palace before my colossal joke of a stepson burns the place down. You can do whatever you have to do. My bodyguards here will take me back, but I must see you tonight at ten p.m. sharp. Don't be late."

"I'm looking forward to it."

"That's what they all say."

"Until then?"

"Until then . . . El Dopo."

She pinched his cheek so long and hard that his squinting eyes teared, and the bruise quickly turned garishly, sickeningly livid. Studying her handiwork, she could not resist pinching it again. And again. And again.

Turning abruptly, she headed toward her team of bodyguards, which had remained a discreet twenty or so feet behind them. When she reached them, she paused for just a second to look back at her new lover.

"Just one more thing, *Capitán.*"

"Yes, My Lady?"

"Do not ever disappoint me. I am the last woman in the world you want to disappoint."

Chapter 6

Two hardcase strangers in black frock coats, matching broad-brimmed hats, and white shirts with black dangling bow ties rode up Culiacán's main street. With two huge bulging carpetbags strapped to each of their saddles, they easily passed for two ranchers arriving at the bank to make a deposit. Even the pack mule following them, laden with panniers, crossbucks, and more carpetbags, would not have raised suspicions. El Primer Banco Nacional y Fiduciario de Sinaloa was the biggest bank in the state, and Culiacán was that state's capital and its biggest city. The bank was used to large deposits and withdrawals.

Dismounting, the men each gave their reins two quick turns around the bank's hitchrack—two turns guaranteed that the horses' bits would injure their mouths if they tried to bolt—but they weren't tied up tight enough to slow the men's escape.

They entered the bank, Moreno first, then Slater. It had just opened and behind the cashiers' windows stood three men. They wore green forehead visors, white boiled shirts with black elbow garters—to prevent them from shoving money up their sleeves and into their shirts—and celluloid collars. As of yet, there were no customers. It was still too early. Moreno spoke to the security guard in a dark blue policeman's uniform, asking for the manager's office.

"To the left," the man said, studying the two strangers carefully. All the while, the guard, with studied nonchalance, rested his right hand on his holstered pistol.

"We're here to make *uno gran depósito*, señor," Moreno said to the manager, entering his office and pointing toward their six valises and smiling. *"Uno muy magnífico depósito."*

Entering the manager's office, Slater studied the bearded, dark-suited manager seated at his big dark wood desk. He immediately stood to greet them. Three dark wood armchairs faced his desk and behind him a small couch was flush against the wall. A portrait of El Presidente Porfirio Díaz hung behind the man's desk. A placard on the desk read, MANAGER: JUAN HIDALGO. Rounding his desk, Hidalgo said, smiling, his hand out:

"What's this I hear about *uno depósito gran y magnífico?"*

"Here, my friend, let me show you," Morena said, putting his two valises on the couch behind him and shaking his hand.

Placing his two valises on the floor, Slater quietly slipped out of the office. Reaching into the bag, Moreno pulled out a sawed-off twelve-gauge Greener and shoved it into the manager's crotch.

"I'm gonna blow your cojones to kingdom come, if

you don't open that safe and deposit all that gringo gold you got this morning in these satchels."

Catching the blur of motion, Moreno glanced sideways just in time to see Torn Slater whip a thin stiletto out of his sleeve and backhand the guard's throat hard enough to sever his trachea, his jugular, and carotid. Stepping to the right, Slater narrowly ducked the deluge of blood geysering out of the guard's throat. He then kicked the pistol, which the guard had just drawn, out of the man's fist. Picking it up, Slater shoved it in his belt.

"*¡En el piso!*" ["On the floor!"] Slater shouted, pulling his own pistols and pointing them at the three cashiers standing at their open windows.

The three men dropped to the floor, facedown and shaking, as if they'd been shot. There were still no customers.

"That money's not worth dying for," Moreno said to the manager, "which is what you'll all do if you don't open that safe *ahora* [now]."

The scattergun was still crowding the manager's crotch, so for emphasis Moreno eared the double hammers back to full cock.

"You don't want those pesos to cost you your co-jones," Moreno added to the manager. "You and your family don't mean squat to Díaz. Start to doubt that we'll kill you and take a look at that guard back there bleeding all over your floor. That's what happens if you try to stop us."

Head down, the manager nodded his acquiescence. Pointing toward his right-hand desk drawer, he said:

"The key, señor. In there."

Moreno nodded. "Get it, amigo, and then let's get them pesos."

Hidalgo removed the big brass key. "It's down here," he said, pointing toward the heavy black wool rug covering his office floor.

"A floor safe?" Moreno asked, surprised.

"*Sí, señor.* Understand though, you are stealing a personal loan from the United States government to El Presidente Porfirio Díaz—a hundred fifty thousand dollars in newly printed one-hundred-dollar bills. El Presidente will have to pay that loan back personally if Méjico is ever again to borrow money from foreign investors. Díaz will not rest until he hunts you down. He will move heaven and earth until he sees your souls in hell."

When Moreno looked into the open safe, he saw it was packed with countless stacks of banded, fresh-printed one-hundred-dollar bills.

"*Hideputa* [son of a whore]," Moreno was finally able to mutter. "What the fuck have we got here?"

Chapter 7

Eléna Vasquez sat on the edge of Rachel Ryan's bed. Emiliano Pérez, the elderly, white-haired family doctor, sat across from Eléna on the other edge of the bed. He wore wire-rimmed glasses and a pale gray suit with matching shirt, socks, and pants. Only his shoes were black. His eyes were warm but tired, and he was putting cold compresses on Rachel's hot, shattered temple very, very gently.

Eléna's close friend Antonio sat in the corner. His clothes were also white *mejicano* garb, but he wore leather shoes, not rope sandals. He stood six feet three, and even under baggy clothes his muscles seemed massive. His neck was as thick as a telegraph pole. He said nothing. Antonio seldom said anything, but it was common knowledge that he would follow Eléna into the grave.

"Eléna," Dr. Pérez said, "the woman has suffered a fracture of the left temple, which happens to be very dangerous. It's one of the thinnest areas in the skull and quite susceptible to shattering when struck with a blunt instrument. Additionally, it has an artery riding right under the area of the fracture and through the cerebrum. It's called the midcerebral artery. Indispensably vital to the cerebrum's blood flow, it has been severely compromised. The temple bones are fragmented, and bleeding between the skull and the dura mater, which covers the brain, can result in a subdural hematoma. In other words, she has an extremely serious, extremely life-threatening concussion."

"That *hideputa* [son-of-a-whore] Mateo did that to her," Eléna said.

"And you feel compelled to help?" Dr. Pérez asked Eléna.

"*Sí.*"

"She's not your responsibility," the doctor pointed out.

"She entered my house, and *mi casa es su casa*. I was responsible. I am responsible."

"You can't protect everyone," Dr. Pérez said.

"But she's so young, has so much to live for, and they did *this* to her. And then they abducted her brother. *¡En mi casa!*"

"I can do nothing, Eléna."

"You're a doctor, no? You can operate on her."

"I would have to do a craniotomy, then assess both the condition of the brain and its dura—the protective tissue covering it. Afterward I would have to remove the skull fragments and then reassemble them, putting the single piece of patchworked cranium back into place. There's no way I can do any of that. I don't have the skill, the equipment, or the trained personnel to assist me."

Dr. Pérez rose, picked up his bag, and gave Eléna a

polite bow. She walked him out of the room, through the cantina, and to the door. After telling each other *"Buenas noches,"* he disappeared into the night, bag in hand.

Eléna returned to Rachel's room.

"Antonio," Eléna said, "this woman and her brother came by themselves to our country, unescorted, unprotected, trying, as she told me, to understand Madre Méjico, what I call this Land of Perdition."

"Her brother was something special," Antonio agreed, nodding. "He understood artillery—modern warfare. You saw how fast those *diablos* kidnapped him."

"Inside her backpack," Eléna said, "she will have identification papers. Maybe we find out who her relatives are. Maybe we can notify them."

"You better just hope she has money to pay you," Antonio said, "for room and board."

"It happened in *mi casa*. She owes us *por nada*." Eléna spat out the last two words angrily.

Rachel's bag was on the floor near the foot of the bed. Going through it carefully, Eléna found nothing. "Her papers must be in her clothes."

She had removed Rachel's clothes before putting her to bed. She'd worn a money belt under her pants. Going through it, Eléna found an ID, stating that her name was Rachel Hendricks. She also had enough money to get her and her brother home. Still it wasn't much to go on.

Going through Rachel's pants, Eléna found a second hidden pocket, directly behind the left-rear button-down pocket, sewn into the back of the pants. The outside pocket contained the decoy wallet; the real ID was in the hidden pocket. She pulled out the real identification papers, stared at it in blank astonishment, and read the ID aloud.

"Rachel Lydia Ryan. Brother: Richard Francis Ryan. Parents: Katherine Jane Paxton and Frank Herbert Ryan.

"Her mother is Katherine Ryan," Eléna said, "known down here as Gobernante del Mundo [Governor of the World]. She owns and runs El Rancho del Cielo in Arizona. She is the richest woman in the American Southwest. Rachel's father is also one of the most gifted surgeons in the Western Hemisphere, and the man who possesses the finest hospital and medical equipment in the Arizona territory. I've read all about them. They're famous. Dr. Pérez might not have the equipment to treat Rachel but her father will—if we can get her there in time."

Madre de Dios, Eléna was sick of Mexico.

"Antonio? How would you like to take a long *jornada* by train?"

"To where?"

"El Rancho del Cielo—Rachel's parents' place."

"Why not?" Antonio said. "They can't hurt us any worse than Díaz and the Señorita."

Chapter 8

When Richard came to, he was flat on his back on an iron cot in the Sonoran rurales' stockade. His head throbbed unbearably, and his pulse was hammering audibly in the high hundreds, as if someone were inside his skull, banging a gong or a bass drum. His cell was small, and the door was open. Security was obviously lax. Outside at a table, three bearded, uniformed guards sat smoking cigars, playing cards, and drinking what looked to be tequila. One of the card-players made eye contact with Richard and shouted:

"Ey, Mateo, Sleeping Beauty just opened his eyes."

Major Mateo Cardozo entered. He paused to take a swig from the neck of a mezcal bottle.

"Young Ricardo, you took some nap there. You must have been tired."

"How long was I out?" Richard asked.

"A dozen hours."

"Feels like you ran my head through a hammer mill."

"My fault. I gotta be more careful swinging with *cuarta*'s buttstock."

"Maybe it's just your nature to break skulls."

"Just so!" Mateo roared with laughter. "But here, I got something for your pain, something to put hair on your chest." He handed Richard the mezcal bottle. "Take a good swig. *Muy bueno* for the cojones too. Make you *mucho hombre* [much man]."

Richard needed something. He took a swig and almost spit it out. It burned both his throat and his stomach; still he kept it down. Within a few minutes, however, his head felt better.

"My young amigo," Major Mateo said, "we got off to a bad start, and I wanna make it up to you. You will see I am not *uno hombre malo* [a bad man]. I don't want you to spend your life in this brig, not even in the rurales. I just want you to join us for a little while. Ey, you can move into the officers' quarters. You teach me how to make gunpowder for his artillery, then show me how to load, aim, and figure the tra-jec-to-ries of them *puta* guns. When we no need you, you can leave and go back to Gringo Land."

"You want help with your howitzers?"

"Those *chingo-tu-madre* howitzers."

"What makes them so important?"

"Sonora's the only state in Mexico left that can stand up to Sinaloa—to Díaz and the Señorita. They stomp all over everyone else."

"So those two are as bad as everyone says?"

"Those two are *demonios del infierno* [fiends from hell]. They torture and dismember people for laughs, and so far only we can stop them."

"It's not my fight."

"It's everybody's fight, *mi amigo*. If they get past us, your home—wherever that is—will be next."

Richard nodded, silently noting that he and his sister—wherever she was—were of the same opinion.

"And if you do help us," Mateo said, "you will be given *mucho dinero*, and even more important, you know what?"

"*¿Tequila y buenas mujeres?*" ["Tequila and beautiful women?"] Richard asked with mocking derision.

"And something much, much better—*¡libertad!* [freedom!]"

"And if I say no?"

Mateo gave Ricardo his widest, most charming smile. "My young compadre, that is not a possibility you wish to contemplate. All our survivals are at stake, yours too. If we do not make those guns work, we will all suffer the tortures of the damned and die a thousand times."

"We will suffer a Sinaloan Inquisition?"

"I will, but not you. You, young muchacho? I will see you die a thousand times long before I do. I will see to it personally." For once Mateo wasn't smiling.

Chapter 9

That night Slater and Moreno rode into Alberto's camp behind the clump of boulders up in the Sierra Madre foothills. He was sitting in front of a blazing fire, drunk on tequila, shoving hot beans and tortillas into his mouth.

"You got the pesos?" Alberto asked with an inebriated grin.

"You got anything in your head except *tamales y frijoles*?" Moreno asked, swinging down from his horse.

Alberto put down his beans. He stood and, lowering his hand onto his holstered pistol, he said:

"You really wanna fuck with me?"

"Nobody wanna fuck anybody dumb as you," Slater said. "Anyway we got the pesetas—more than you can ever imagine."

Alberto still had his hand on his gun.

"Ey, amigo," Moreno said, slapping Alberto's back, giving him his widest, most ingratiating grin. "What's more important? Pesos in your saddlebags or notches on your *pistola*? Come. Bring the tequila. We got to celebrate. You are now a wealthy man."

Turning around toward his mount, Moreno unhooked a valise, opened it up, and tossed it at Alberto's feet. Bound-up packs of hundred-dollar bills spilled out in front of the drunken man.

"Ah, I knew you was *simpático*," Alberto said. "We will have *mucho bueno* times, you, Señor Slater, and me, no?"

Hypnotized by the riches strewn in front of him, he knelt down and opened up money bag after money bag after money bag on the blanket in front of the fire.

"It is *mucho bueno, muy bueno*," the inebriated outlaw whispered.

"No," Slater said. "It's no good, no *bueno*."

The two bandits stared at Slater. Alberto was confused.

"There's too much money in them bags, Moreno. Didn't you hear the banker? We didn't hit any federale payroll. We intercepted a money shipment straight from the U.S. Treasury to El Presidente Díaz himself. We got us over a hundred fifty thousand fresh-minted yanqui hundred-dollar bills. How many brand-new, hot-off-the-printing-presses hundred-dollar bills you ever seen in Méjico? Spend one of those—take one into a bank, a hotel, take one anyplace, even into a dirt-poor Chiapas cantina—and you'll have Díaz, his federales, his rurales, the U.S. Army, every bounty hunter south of the Rio climbing up our asses."

"What you suggest we do?" Moreno asked.

"I'm taking my share and going to ground. I'll stash

it and live off the land till I can figure out how to spend it. It may take me years to dig it up."

"You sayin' we got a fortune, but we can't spend it?" Moreno asked.

"Not one bill of it. It's so hot, it's smokin'."

"Es verdad," Moreno said softly, half to himself, finally understanding their problem.

"You just ain't got the cojones to spend it," Alberto said, his hand, once more, hovering over his sidearm. "I'm taking my share right back to my village. I left it like a thief in the night, but I'm comin' back rich as Don Porfirio himself. I'm livin' like a grandee from here on out, and any hombre says different, he's havin' it out with me."

Slater cross-drew a pistol out of his belt in a smooth, single motion and shot the intoxicated man just above his right eye.

"Had to be done," Moreno said, slowly nodding. "He was a threat to both of us."

They paused only to eat the rest of the beans, washing them down with black coffee. Quickly, emptying the rest of the blackened pot onto the campfire, they kicked dirt over the rest. Unsaddling their horses, they walked to the remuda, threw the saddles onto their new mounts, and cinched them up. They threw a pad, crossbucks, and panniers onto a fresh mule. They then meticulously loaded the gear and money bags on it.

They cut the exhausted stock loose.

We got fresh horses, a strong pack mule, mucho dinero, *and a head start,* Slater thought bleakly. *That's all I ever asked for.*

Chapter 10

Eléna spread a thin gray mattress on the floor of the flatbed train car and covered it with a sheet. Seating herself at the head of the mattress with her legs spread out and a dark pillow on her lap, Antonio gently placed Rachel on the mattress, easing her head onto Eléna's pillow. Rachel's face was flushed with fever. Eléna wiped her brow with a cool wet washcloth.

"You sure you want to ride on the flatcar?" Antonio asked.

"The air will be better here than in the boxcars," Eléna said.

"If we catch a rainstorm or banditos attack, the boxcars will provide more protection."

"Then we'll carry Rachel into a boxcar."

Eléna looked down at Rachel and emitted a long, slow sigh. She was even more worried about the skull fracture than she had been back at the house. The fractured temple was depressed, which meant, according to Dr. Pérez, that it was putting pressure on the brain. A surgeon, he had said, would need to do a craniotomy to inspect the condition of both the brain and the protective tissue enveloping it. The surgeon would then have to remove the skull segments, re-assemble them, and put the jigsaw puzzle pieces of patchworked cranium back into place. Eléna and Dr. Pérez only knew of one doctor and one hospital within a radius of a thousand miles that could conceivably perform the operation: Dr. Frank Ryan at El Hospital del Rancho—Rachel's father.

No way it could be done in Mexico.

Eléna glanced at her pocket watch. She had inherited it from her grandfather. A B. W. Raymond, it was a big railroad watch with a white face and roman numerals marking the minutes. She'd especially loved the anachronistic IIII, which represented the numeral 4. Since it was a railroad watch, it was the right timepiece for their trip. In fact, it was time for the train to pull out. As if on cue, the wood-fueled locomotive, which stood four cars ahead of them, screeched three long whistle bursts. Slowly but with increasing frequency its engine chugged, lurched, and strained, black smoke billowing out of the diamond-shaped stack. Gradually, the wheels rotated, and the cars jerked into motion.

The train was thankfully taking off on time—something of a miracle in Mexico. Eléna took that as a good omen. She needed the train to depart on time. The clock was running out on Eléna and her patient. In thirty-six hours the train would hopefully pull into a rail stop, which was a one-hour wagon ride to the Ryans' rancho. She would contact Katherine Ryan when she got there. She had been afraid to wire Katherine, telling her that she was bringing her daughter home, for fear that prospective kidnappers might intercept the message. Rachel would bring a queen's ransom down here.

All Eléna could hope was that she'd find a wagon and horses at the train station.

Time was so precious she'd sold her cantina in under three hours—in the same amount of time Antonio needed to book their train, then borrow a wagon and horses in which to drive them to the train station. She had packed hers and Antonio's rucksacks, two large canvas bags, and three two-gallon water bags. She did it as quickly as she could, since they were desperate to make the two p.m. train to the Arizona Territory.

Her brother-in-law, Alfredo, had been trying to purchase her cantina for years, and now she'd sold it to him. He was stunned that she would pull up stakes, abandon virtually all of her possessions, and leave Sonora in such a hurry. She knew she was selling her establishment at fire-sale prices but she told Alfredo that she did not care. He was so insulting that it took every ounce of self-control to keep from shouting at him:

"Chingo tu madre, puto. *I'm going to Rancho del Cielo.*"

But she and Antonio could not tell their destination to anyone.

Now her only fear was that they wouldn't get to the Rancho in time to help Rachel. She wanted to scream at the fireman and engineer to throw more kindling into the firebox and get that damn train moving.

PART III

Chapter 11

After a breakfast of *carne de cabra*, frijoles, and tortillas, Mateo took Richard outside. The sun was at zenith and burned in the cloudless sky like a white-hot poker. The temperature was over 105 degrees, and the air was as dry as a cinder block. Before them lay the fort's huge square parade ground. Three hundred yards on edge, it teemed with companies of rurales, seemingly frenzied but actually engaged in disciplined activity. Dozens of companies of soldiers—over five thousand men in all—in sweat-stained gray uniforms and matching forage caps practiced close-order drill. Under the stern, unblinking eye of obscenity-bellowing drill sergeants, they shouted out their sweltering cadences. Companies of recruits in sweat-soaked fatigues were performing interminable push-ups, jumping jacks, knee bends, sit-ups, and leg lifts—roaring out the numbers of their repetitions. Other companies practiced field-stripping and re-assembling their rifles. Whenever a company finished, the drill sergeant ordered them to take a half-dozen laps around the field.

Surrounding the parade ground were a score or more of huge, whitewashed, four-story adobe buildings. Half of them, Mateo told Richard, were barracks in whose bunk beds the base's soldiers slept each night.

"Each of those barracks," Mateo said, "holds hundreds of enlisted men. At night, we stack them like cordwood—in triple bunk beds."

"And you dragoon all of them into your army like you did me."

"We practice universal conscription in Sonora, and, yes, if the men resist, we enlist them by force."

"I've died and gone to hell," Richard muttered.

"No, we just walked past the guardhouse. That's hell."

"Lovely," Richard said.

"Off to the right are two mess halls. The men eat there three times a day."

"Eat what?"

"The enlisted men live on frijoles and tortillas. The latrines and showers are out back."

"The enlisted men must need a lot of showers the way you work them," Richard said, glancing at the perspiring soldiers on the field.

"Amigo, that is not possible. We suffer serious water shortages."

"Beans and body stink," Richard said. "Great."

"We ride 'em hard and put 'em up wet," Mateo said, a grin flickering under his black, downward-sweeping mustache.

Mateo pointed out offices, the dispensary, the officers' quarters.

"What are those buildings like?" Richard asked. "The ones where you and the officers sleep?"

"Private rooms, all the showers you want."

"The food?"

"*Pollo, carne,* and *queso frijoles, arroz,* mangos, *café, cerveza,* and tequila."

"And women?"

"*Muchas mujeres.* You can even bring them into your rooms for the night."

"And the enlisted barracks stink really bad?"

"The smell could drive a *zopilote* [buzzard] off a shit wagon."

"You suggesting I should enter Officer Candidate School?"

He shrugged. "It's a thought. But come, amigo, let us take a take a brief stroll."

Chapter 12

The Lady Dolorosa stared up at her bed's canopy. Its alabaster satin top and sides were fringed with matching lace. Reclining against a small mountain of fluffy white silk pillows, she casually surveyed her room. Everything was white—from the bedposts to the walls, from the thick rugs and carpets to her silk dressing gown.

Once, when one of her court ladies asked her why she favored the color, she'd responded: "It's the color of virgins."

Their laughter had been immense.

Flinging her arms out, she emitted a huge, heartfelt sigh. After a night of desperate, almost demented debauchery, she felt sleepily, dreamily at peace. Still all that exertion had given her a voracious appetite, and as soon as she had awakened, she'd shouted to no one in particular that she wanted her usual breakfast. Five of her ladies-in-waiting now entered, armed with breakfast trays—chile rellenos, *pollo con mole poblano*, tortillas, sliced jalapeños, dishes of scorchingly hot salsa, all backed up by a large, ice-filled pitcher of tequila, tomato juice, and Tabasco sauce—imported from the state of Tabasco—as well as six bottles of Pila Seca, a highly regarded *mejicano* beer, which their Lady greatly favored, all of the drinks chilling in ice buckets.

Her ladies placed a tray in front of her, containing a beer and her first tequila, tomato juice, and Tabasco. Taking a healthy drink, she quickly washed it down with an even thirstier gulp of beer.

"That tastes like life itself!" she shouted happily.

Her ladies-in-waiting laughed nervously. The Señorita was happy, and their job was to make her even happier—to provide amusing conversation, excellent food, to take her horseback riding, if she so wished, and to buy her pleasing clothes. When their Lady was forced to compose letters or memos, they took dictation. They retailed salacious gossip, including tales of their own erotic exploits; fanned and massaged her; inundated her with the most unbelievably fulsome flattery—anything and everything to keep her entertained. Desperate to make and keep her happy, they understood that the consequences of displeasing their Lady were almost too painful to contemplate.

Each year her majordomo dispatched scouts to examine the daughters of the country's wealthiest families, and from them she chose her new crop of court ladies. They were invariably the most talented, beautiful daughters in all of Sinaloa. And often the most spoiled. For such daughters, serving their Lady could be an ordeal.

She tolerated no insubordination. Those who rebelled, she did not send to the Rack and the Stone.

Those ladies, she handed over to her priests, who promptly pitched them into el Volcán de Colima, a fire-belching, smoke-billowing volcano in Tabasco. Consequently, none of her court ladies dreamed of discomfiting their lady, let alone defying her.

She devoured her chile rellenos and *mole poblano*, and gulped down her drinks with breathtaking alacrity and a resounding belch. She *was* in a good mood. Her ladies continued their pleasant, playful banter.

"Our Lady had a good time last night?" Rosalita asked. "A night of wonder and revelation?"

Rosalita was dressed in a sheer red close-fitting toga, scarlet lipstick and nail polish, as well as matching riding boots. Her obsidian-black hair hung down to her waist. She was the most beautiful of Lady Dolorosa's court attendants. She also was a skilled pianist and had an exquisite singing voice.

"Wonder and *fornication* is what you mean," her Lady answered. "Talk about commitment. What's-his-name actually wore *me* out."

The Lady Dolorosa could never remember any of her lovers' names.

"He performed all night?" Rosalita asked.

"When I woke up this morning, I needed every ounce of strength to make it to the bathroom. It was all I could do to wash up and brush my hair, which looked like a hawk's badly ripped-up roost."

"Your beauty inspired him to such exalted heights," Roberta said. A shy, demure blonde in a black dress and matching heels, she wasn't as much fun as the others but was a superlative harpist and also had a melodic voice to match.

"Stark terror inspired him to such ecstatic heights," the Señorita said, shaking her head.

"I find that hard to believe," Roberta said meekly, her eyes downcast. "It had to be Our Lady's radiance."

"Really?" Lady Dolorosa said, treating Roberta to an earsplitting thunderstorm of lurid laughter. "You should have seen the look on the idiot's face when the High Priest ripped out the heart of my previous lover. Or when that old fraud of a witch doctor bled the guy out over the downward-sloping gutter and chopped his head off. You should have seen the new guy's mouth gape when that moron's head went banging down the pyramid's steps. No, I taught him the meaning of fear."

"But he was inspired last night, no?" Catalina asked.

"When I was done with him, his knees, elbows, even his chin and nose, looked like they'd been worked over with a wood rasp. I've never seen so many third-degree bed-burns on a man in my life."

Her ladies chortled melodiously.

"Did you talk at all?" Gabriella asked. "Did he have anything interesting to say?"

Gabriella wore a toga of the sheerest yellow lace, her dark hair shoulder-length. The Señorita Dolorosa viewed her as naively romantic and kept her around primarily because she liked baiting her.

"*Nada.* The boy is dumb as a box of rocks. I could barely stand to listen to him. Also half the time he was too frightened to speak."

"Still he performed heroically," Rosalita said.

"Indeed. That is beyond cavil, and in the future, I shall subject all of my prospective lovers to the spectacle of the temple-pyramid. I shall also take them into our torture chambers and show them how my Grand Inquisitor treats those who fail me here in my boudoir."

"It worked for you last night," Catalina said. "The new one performed admirably. You can't argue with success."

"No, you can't. Rosalita, please make a note that I am changing protocols. I will take the new ones to the Inquisitor's chamber first. Then afterward I shall allow them to witness blood-sacrifice of my previous inamorato atop the temple."

Rosalita quickly took a red leather notebook from her person and jotted down the instructions. "What do we call this new protocol, My Lady?"

"Motivation, Inspiration, and Instruction."

"If only I could train my lovers so . . . *effectively*," Roberta said.

"If you're nice to me, I might let you bring one of them along for our next . . . motivational lesson," Lady Dolorosa said with a mischievous grin.

Chapter 13

Slater and Moreno sat under the lean-to over the front of the mine. The year before Moreno had buried a cache of mining tools and fishing gear near it. This time they'd buried the money they'd stolen—almost $150,000.

Twenty miles away was a Yaqui village, where Moreno could purchase provisions with no questions asked. On the way up, they'd bought bags of beans, dried tortillas, chili peppers, and a dozen quarts of tequila. They'd used their old pesos.

The first week they spent chopping wood until they had stacks of shoring timbers and firewood near the opening to the mine. They had also killed a deer and an antelope, and one of the venison quarters was now hanging in a makeshift smokehouse. Made out of a pole tripod wrapped with deerskins, it looked like a crude tepee. The green-wood fire at its base was smoking the haunch that hung above it.

A large slab of antelope was hanging on a green-wood spit over the fire. Periodically Slater or Moreno turned it over. Off to the side, a pot of corn, beans, rabbit, wild turkey, and venison, tomatoes, and red chilis boiled, as did a fire-blackened pot filled with coffee. Mostly, however, the two men focused on the mess cups of tequila.

"Well, amigo," Moreno asked. "Is this place not the paradise I promised?"

"The game, the fishing, the *indias chiquitas* if we want them," Slater said. "It's everything you said."

"So why are you grim? What is so *malo* [so bad]?"

"That damn mine you're so obsessed with. It's snakebit."

Moreno stared at Slater, silent.

"The rock is too brittle to tunnel through," Slater explained. "Shoring timbers don't help. Look what happened to *los indios* help we hired. They died under cave-ins."

"We can always find more *indios*," Moreno said. "Méjico's got plenty of *indios*."

"Not at the rate that mine is killing them."

"Torn, we get some gold, we can take all the time in the world figurin' what to do with that bank's money."

"Remember what happened when Ojo Serpiente [Snake Eye] went in two weeks ago. He died in a cave-in, buried alive."

"One accident."

"Then, El Mustang. The methane got him. When that damn gas isn't poisoning us, it's catching fire and incinerating everything in its path. How many mine fires have we had?"

"But we got a fortune in gold in that mine. I saw the main vein—*oro puro* [100 percent gold]—the real thing."

"Tell that to Cuervo Rojo [Red Crow]."

"Fuck him."

"And what happened to him?" Slater asked, grimacing.

Luis looked away, silent.

"Trapped under a ton of deadfall, a whole mountain's worth of rock."

Slater even shuddered at the thought.

Still Moreno leaned forward and fixed his friend with a tight stare.

"But you ain't listenin', amigo. I just told you I seen the vein. A drift of solid gold a foot thick and running only God knows how far and long. Enough *oro* to buy Sinaloa *and* Sonora. We could own Méjico!"

"We already got seventy-five thousand dollars apiece. We don't need any more."

"And if we spend one centavo of that money, we get all the armies of Méjico and Norteamérica coming down on us like rockslides. That's Díaz's money we stole."

"That ain't a mine, Moreno. It's an open grave. You go in it, it's your grave."

"I'm going back in. I'm not walkin' away from a fortune in gold."

"Then you're goin' in alone. I tell you that hole is cursed, and I'm takin' off. I'm not hangin' around here to watch you die."

"Then *adiós—vaya con Dios,* old friend."

"*Y diablo* [and the devil]," Slater said.

Luis Moreno turned his back on Slater, picked up his pick, and headed into the mine.

Without looking back.

Chapter 14

For hours on end, Eléna sat on the flatbed car with
Rachel's head cradled in her lap. The car banged and
bounced so hard it was the only way she could protect
the woman's cracked head. Occasionally, Antonio
would spell her, but for the most part, she did not
want Antonio tied up. He was their protection, and
this was bandit country.

But most of all she worried about Rachel.

They had packed four pistols, two knives, and a
sawed-off shotgun in their rucksacks. The guns were
all rechambered to take cartridges, and Antonio kept
them loaded and close at hand. They had three two-
gallon water bags, which Antonio had hung on the
vertical ladder bolted onto the end of the adjacent
boxcar. Dried beef and mangos, tortillas, and some
soft cornmeal mush, which Eléna had packed specif-
ically for Rachel, made up their rations.

She had no appetite but forced herself to eat;
Rachel, who was unconscious, could not ingest food,

not even the mush, and came to only when she was thirsty enough to drink.

Otherwise, Eléna's sole job was to sit upright on the hard floor of the car and keep the woman's head immobilized.

There were a dozen *soldados* on the train, but they mostly stayed in the boxcars or up on the boxcars' roofs. So as the train roared through the waterless wastes of the great Sonoran Desert, she preoccupied herself by studying the various flora—the endless stands of yucca, the bushy forests of mesquite, fields of maguey, which her people raised for its fiber, which they wove into cloth, and its fruit, from which they made tequila and mezcal. Ubiquitous prickly pear cactuses, bent sagebrush, creosote, and stunted salt-bushes rolled into sight, while hot winds blew through the chaparral.

As the train rumbled through the desert, she un-thinkingly observed the animals as well. Scrawny jackrabbits, scrawnier coyotes, and dark ugly javelinas with their downward-curving tusks, which foraged and hunted along the track bed. When the train pulled up onto the sidings for water and kindling, Eléna studied the procession of reptiles—the side-winders, diamondbacks, and speckled rattlers. She noted snakes as well—whip snakes, king snakes, red racers, and gopher snakes. Then there were the usual innumerable varieties of lizards—horned lizards, whiptail lizards, desert spiny lizards, long-nosed lizards, side-blotched lizards, the zebra-tailed and leopard lizards.

In her boredom, Eléna almost unconsciously cata-logued insects—the assassin bugs, the talapai tigers, thread-legged bugs, wheel bugs, which, when they tried to board her car, she smashed instantly. She deliberately watched out for the twiglike, two-inch walkingsticks, otherwise known as the devil's darning needles, which stripped the leaves from trees and sprayed poison at their enemies. She actively disliked the praying mantis, which eats its mate whole. She cringed at the tarantulas, yellow jacket wasps, jewel wasps, and stink beetles, which direct a noxious-smelling spray at their enemies. She even spotted a reclusive scorpion or two from time to time and re-minded Antonio to check his boots for them before putting them on each morning. Eléna's personal favorite were the ant lions, which hunted ants like predatory cats.

She didn't sleep and wasn't sure if she ever would again. They not only had Rachel to worry about, they were now in the middle of bandit country. Armies of them roamed and plundered this wasteland, and a gang of them, pouring out of a nearby barranca, could shatter their boring tranquillity in a heartbeat.

How did the old saying go?

There was no law in Veracruz, no Sunday in Sinaloa, and no God south of Ciudad Juárez.

Chapter 15

On and on Richard and Mateo walked. By now physical training was in full swing, and over six thousand soldiers were drilling. Not on the sidelines though. There, the army's disciplinary problems—men who failed to follow the army's draconian orders—suffered. Some were hung by the wrists, even by the thumbs from a seven-foot-high cross-pole. Four were spread-eagled on caisson wheels. Several more were spread-eagled upside down.

The sun beat down on them like hell's furnace itself.

For a long time Richard and Mateo walked in silence.

"Why did you join the rurales?" Richard finally asked Mateo. "There have to be easier ways to earn a living."

"What do you know about Díaz and the Señorita?"

"That they're fiends from hell who cloak themselves in human flesh."

"*Es verdad*. They also killed everyone in my family."

Richard stopped walking and studied Mateo, silent.

"My father was a Sinaloan cavalry officer," Mateo continued. "I grew up on their military bases, and, believe me, what you see here is God's Peaceable Kingdom compared to that hell on earth."

"What made you come here?"

Mateo looked away. The story came out of him slowly, haltingly:

"I had an older brother, named Carlos, who was not quite right in the head, but all eighteen-year-olds are conscripted into the Sinaloan Army. He was no exception. He hated it and got drunk as thoroughly and frequently as he could. He was hilarious too—*mucho cómico.* A great comic, he was full of wisecracks and a natural mimic. He would have the entire barracks rolling around on the floor, clutching their bellies. He was especially uproarious when he ridiculed the Lady Dolorosa, her stupid stepson, even her terrified lovers. He would act out the parts, doing frightening imitations of each of them. In one routine he pretended he was summoned to her bed. He acted out all the lurid things they said and did to each other, twisting his face into different masks of horror and ecstasy while delivering the appropriate punch lines.

"He even did skits of her torturing loved ones in the Inquisitor's dungeon and assisting the High Priest in a human sacrifice at the summit of the temple-pyramid. He ridiculed the Señorita's sadism in the most hilarious ways imaginable.

"My brother was a clown but he was also a fool. He had no sense. His fellow soldiers loved his routines. But one was an informant and told the Señorita of my brother's mockery of her would-be Aztec priests, and she turned him over to her Inquisitors. She summoned several of his fellow *soldados* into her throne room, and she made him do his routine. My brother was *brillante*, funny beyond all understanding, beyond all restraint, and he held nothing back. She laughed the whole time. Soon they were all laughing.

"Afterward, wiping tears of hilarity from her eyes, she said to us: 'You think that was funny? Oh, that's a hand I can call and raise. I'm going to give young Carlos here comedy lessons that will have him screaming into the night. I'm sending him to our Inquisitor and telling him to spend an excruciating amount of time teaching Carlos the meaning of real . . . *comedy*. Then I'm sending him to the Stone. Your whole regiment will attend that extravaganza. I shall be there myself. I will laugh at him just as you all laughed at me. Anyone I spot not laughing will take follow-up comedy courses on the Rack and at the Stone.'

"The Señorita feared familial retaliation after such extravaganzas, however, so after she'd killed one of her citizens, she routinely killed all that person's family members. She left no one behind who might seek revenge on her. So she immediately killed all my blood relatives."

Mateo stared at Richard a long time, silent.

"How did you escape capture?" Richard finally asked Mateo.

"My family raised horses, and I grew up breaking them on a rancho with an uncle in Sinaloa. We then sold them to the military. I was adopted, and the state of Sinaloa had few official records on me, so the Señorita's secret police were slow to learn of my existence and discovered too late that Carlos was my brother. One night after they murdered everyone, my uncle gave me two horses and provisions, and I fled for Sonora. I had information to trade on the Sinaloa military, that Carlos had imparted to me—tactics, strategy, strengths, weakness—and I was motivated to fight against the Señorita and Díaz. The state of Sonora gave me citizenship and accepted me into officers' school at age sixteen. So, *sí*, I understand why many people—you included—are critical of our discipline here and of our recruitment methods. I agree, at times, we are overly harsh. But Madre Méjico is not Norteamérica, where life is gentle and fair and just. This is Díaz's and the Señorita's Méjico, where people are branded, shackled, jailed, enslaved, even castrated, and ruled by the whip. I have experienced their Méjico on my bones and blood. We are at war with Sinaloa and Chihuahua both and must fight them with everything at our disposal."

"You want to destroy them for what they did to your family?"

"For that—and for much, much more. Still, while we need discipline, we never want to be like them. We must not be like them."

Richard stared at Mateo, silent.

"Come with me to our Intelligence Center," Mateo finally said, giving Richard a forced smile, "and you will learn what else Sinaloa does to its subjects. It isn't just to me."

PART IV

The Señorita's laughter rang through the
chamber like the bells of hell.

Chapter 16

Decked out in a white silk dressing gown, the
Señorita Dolorosa lounged in her bed, sipping
Madeira. For two centuries, that wine—*vinho da roda*,
as the wine had been called in the Portuguese
Madeira Islands, which had produced it—was highly
sought after worldwide, particularly in the United
States. There, the Founding Fathers had drunk it day
and night. Luckily for the Señorita, Mexico's former
dictator, General Antonio López de Santa Anna,
had been especially fond of Madeira. In fact, he had
purchased several dozen Madeira "pipes"—the massive 112-gallon casks, in which the brandy-fortified,
famously long-lived wine was shipped. Mexico's rulers
and wealthy elite had been partaking of those "pipes"
ever since. Maximilian had been especially enamored
of the wine.

From the Señorita's perspective, Santa Anna's
importation of it had been especially fortuitous. In
1851, a grape blight had destroyed Portugal's Madeira

Island vineyards. Consequently, only two or three dozen of the "pipes" remained in all of North America. Several years ago, the Señorita had bought them all up—or in some cases forcibly commandeered them. She kept them safely locked away in her hacienda's wine cellar. She had now convinced herself that she owned and was consuming the world's last casks of the wine. That knowledge vastly increased her enjoyment of the wine, and she shared it with no one, not even Díaz, and least of all with her court ladies.

In fact, they were now circled around the Señorita, watching her enjoy her wine. Keeping the Señorita happy was always wise, since the penalties for not amusing her were . . . *unendurable.* The beautiful, dark-haired Rosalita had recently fallen out of favor and she was now desperate to redeem herself in the Señorita's eyes. Dressed in a sheer black nightgown, Rosalita was smiling and waving enthusiastically at the Señorita, hoping to get her permission to speak. Finally, the Señorita called on her.

"My Lady," Rosalita said, "I've heard that you lived in America for several years and that you learned to speak English in that country. Could you tell us about your experiences there?"

They knew that their Lady enjoyed reflecting on her life, particularly on her past triumphs and accomplishments:

"When I was twelve, my father did business with the governor of Sinaloa. The man was named after the Spanish conquistador, Hernán Cortés, who first subjugated and sacked Méjico. The governor's full name was thus Hernán Cortés Castenado. Like his namesake, he was obsessed with conquering a kingdom and carving out an empire. My father was an arms merchant who had supplied him with guns and ammunition during his early years. Both had prospered through their association, and my family was wealthy— one of the wealthiest in Mexico.

"As a child I noticed that Castenado was fond of me. He was always making me sit on his lap, even when it was no longer appropriate. When he became the governor of Sinaloa and was now all-powerful, he ordered my father to hand me over to him. I was only thirteen, and my father hated *'abuso sexual'* [child molestation] with special vehemence. His own mother had been raped when she was thirteen, and my father, Fernando, had been the illegitimate issue of that assault. He knew that the governor had no intention of marrying me. He simply wanted to take me by force. When the novelty wore off, he would then discard me, which had been his practice with every other *mujer joven* [young woman].

"When my father refused to hand me over, the governor had his rurales abduct and torture him. He told him if he didn't sell me to him he'd frame us on charges of sedition, then convict and imprison us. He also said he'd have me anyway, that he was too powerful to resist or deny. He then sent my father home to sign the papers and to deliver me to the governor the next day. Instead my father put me on a night train to El Paso, Texas, where a fellow arms dealer would raise me *en secreto* as his daughter.

"When the Sinaloa governor learned I was gone, he put my father through hell in an attempt to learn my whereabouts. My father died on 'the Parrot's Perch,' one of the most agonizing of all the tortures."

Their Lady paused, while her court ladies stared at her in stunned silence. This was one story they had never heard before.

"What happened next?" Roberta finally asked.

"I grew up in El Paso. I was not particularly grateful or obedient. In fact, I was wild, headstrong, even resentful of my adopted parents. Sneaking away at night, I'd run the streets with the tough Mexican gangs. My foster father tried to reason with me, and when reason failed, he took a razor strap to me, which only incited me to further rebellion.

"And all the while, the Sinaloa governor, Hernán Cortés Castenado, never forgot me. He circulated wanted posters with my photo on them, offering a reward for my apprehension. He claimed I was a killer and a thief. He sent bounty hunters looking for me, several of which came as far as El Paso.

"I did not care. I was rowdy, angry, and promiscuous even then. Finally, my foster father had had enough. He sold me to the governor for the reward. That night I arrived at the palace, the governor had the court ladies bathe and scrub me till I was raw, then deliver me to his bed. He never knew that on El Paso's mean streets, I'd been having sex since age thirteen. Instead he thought he was getting a seventeen-year-old virgin. I played along with the lie, sharing his bed and biding my time.

"During those years, I studied the power structure in Sinaloa. The most powerful man was with the commanding general. Our leaders have always ruled through violence and terror—going back to the Aztecs and beyond—and the commanding general was the one who put down our people's periodic rebellions and who defeated our enemies abroad. His military strength far transcended that of the governor.

"By this time my reputation as the most passionately beautiful woman in all of Sinaloa—in all of Mexico really—had spread, and I was increasingly popular with the masses, far more than our governor was.

"I was, the governor told me, *muy magnífica* in bed. When I saw my chance, I poisoned his ugly shrew of a wife, and by then he was so smitten with me that he took my hand in marriage. However, I now needed him *por nada*, so I seduced the commanding general, Ramon Osorio. I gradually planted the notion in his head that if my husband, the governor, were eliminated, he and I could take over the throne. Since women could not legally rule Sinaloa, I'd bring the governor's son—my idiot stepson, Eduardo—in as figurehead. He was a coward, a moron, and I could make him do anything. Ramon and I could easily intimidate, subjugate, and then circumvent him. As for Ramon, he would have riches beyond dreams of avarice and *el poder de los dioses* [the power of the gods]. Delusions of grandeur aggravated by his delirious desire for me caused him to suggest that I poison my newlywed husband, Sinaloa's governor, Hernán Cortés Castenado.

"I did so happily and became the de facto governor of Sinaloa. By then, however, I'd met a rising star in the *mejicano* army, a young general named Porfirio Díaz, and we'd secretly joined forces. We decided that since Ramon was blocking Díaz's final rise to power, that I should get rid of him. So one afternoon, when

Ramon and I were out by ourselves, having a picnic in the desert, I injected him in the neck with diamond-back venom. His demise was inconceivably painful. To make matters worse, the whole time he was dying, I knelt over him till we were nose to nose. Gazing into his eyes, I gave him my widest, most loving smile, all the while stroking his cheek, kissing his lips, and whispering, 'There, there. There, there.' He found the combination of my betrayal, the radiance of my smile, the tender sensuousness of my caresses, and the excruciating agony of his death throes . . . *shatteringly unbearable.* I had destroyed his body, his mind, and, I honestly believe . . . *his soul.* I have to admit it was one of the most thrilling experiences of my life.

"Afterward Díaz assisted me in my conquest of Chihuahua, which I now rule along with Sinaloa. Díaz and I have been closely allied ever since."

Her ladies stared at her in astonishment.

"My Lady, do you always get what you want?" Catalina asked.

"Siempre." ["Always."]

"You now have wealth, power, fame. Is there anything in life you miss or crave?" Roberta asked.

Their Lady shrugged, then looked away.

"Does anything even bother you?" Rosalita asked. "You always seem so confident, so fearless, so sure of yourself."

"I wish my nights were better. My days might be filled with excitement and amazement, but tedium tortures my nights. Only exhaustive, nonstop, strenuous fornication can relieve me. But no man has ever proven up to that task—not in the long run, not month after month after month—and so that relief is only transitory. Most of the time, my nights are an agony of boredom, which leads to insomnia, which produces a melancholia that I find infuriatingly . . . *intolerable.*"

"What would improve your evenings?" Catalina asked.

"I've had fantasies from time to time of a wondrous lover who would please me not only in bed but who would lighten my soul and enthrall my heart and mind. But to do so he would have to be smarter, wittier, more knowledgeable, and more sexually insatiable than . . . *I.*" The Señorita smiled wistfully at the sheer absurdity of the idea.

"Have you ever found a man who came close to fitting that bill?" Rosalita asked.

"Of course not," their Lady said.

"Never?" Catalina asked.

"How could I? Such a man clearly could never exist."

Chapter 17

Slater had saddled his mount, a big, broad-chested roan. He was taking nothing but a two-gallon water bag, beans and tortillas, jerked antelope, and ammunition. He wore a large black broadcloth shirt loose and over his pants. Under the shirt, two double-sided, black, oiled-silk money belts crisscrossed his back and chest while a third was buckled tightly around his waist just above his gun belt. He was taking only what was his and what he needed. He was leaving the tools and everything else for Moreno, who had become clearly obsessed. He had been laboring in that damn mine like a madman. He even worked nights by torchlight, napping down there. Searching for that drift lode had driven Moreno *muy loco*, and now his obsession was driving Slater *muy loco* as well. He couldn't stand it any longer. Slater had told Moreno he was going to leave, and he was finally doing it. He'd dug too much ore in Díaz slave-labor prison mines, and this mine was too goddamned dangerous.

I rob banks and trains, the outlaw said to himself. *I don't tunnel through rock and dirt like a goddamn mole.*

Most of all Slater couldn't bear to wait here and watch his friend die, crushed under a collapsing mountain of rock.

"Hasta luego, maníaco," Slater said to himself under his breath. "You want to kill yourself, you're doin' it on your own time and by yourself. Maybe someday I'll catch up with you again—probably when I see your soul in hell."

He swung onto the roan, leaned back in the saddle, and lifted the reins. He was wheeling the big horse around when he heard the slow-building *boom-boom-boom-boom-BOOOOOOM!Boom-boom-boom-boom-BOOOOOOM! Boom-boom-boom-boom-BOOOOOOM!*

The roan was up on his hocks, spinning around, crow-hopping, whinnying insanely, the mountain's roar echoing in his ears, each reverberation bouncing and banging off the surrounding mountains, canyon cliffs, and vertiginous chasms, each sound reproducing itself in an infinite progression. Sooty black smoke was billowing and mushrooming out of that hole, while hell itself thundered out of that mine shaft like a portent out of Revelation and detonating death and destruction all across Sonora.

"Well, that's that," Slater said softly. *"You put it to him coldcock and country-simple, but the man wouldn't listen. He went in anyway. So, Moreno, you done it to yourself. You brought that whole goddamn mountain down on your ass. I can't do nothin' for you now, not nohow. Time to slope on out of here."*

But somehow he couldn't do it.

He sat there frozen immobile in his saddle.

Goddamn it to hell.

He swung down off his heaving roan and slowly quieted him down. Taking him to a patch of mountain grass under a pine, he staked him out and pulled off the saddle. Putting on an old torn shirt, he attached a canteen to his belt and wrapped his bandanna over his mouth and nose. He roped together a dozen precut shoring timbers, to brace and prop up the collapsed tunnel in front of him. Picking up a two-foot pickax, a half-dozen candles, and matches, he crawled, bent over, into the mine. He dragged the shoring timbers behind him.

He was determined to save his friend.

Chapter 18

Mateo led Richard to a massive three-storied building of immaculately whitewashed adobe, which housed the army's main headquarters. Heading him down two hallways, he took him into the Military Intelligence Center. In a large bullpen surrounded by filing cabinets, intelligence officers, clad in gray uniforms, manned eight desks. They worked by the light of coal-oil lamps, sifting through mountains of paperwork, occasionally pausing to write down notes on foolscap. Refugees from Sinaloa and Chihuahua provided Sonora's analysts with endless transcribed interviews and depositions, which the analysts used to assess that country's threat potential. The men at the desks worked relentlessly, heads down, funereal as death. Given that country's propensities for violence, terror, and imperial aggression, the analysts had every incentive to take their work seriously.

"The general and I are old friends, and I asked him for a few minutes of his time," Mateo said. "He knows more about Díaz, the Señorita, Chihuahua, and Sinaloa than anyone I know."

Taking Richard into the corner office, he sat him down on the leather couch. In front of them was an oval-shaped oak coffee table and the desk where the chief of army intelligence, Major General Rafael Ortega, sat. Both desk and coffee table were stained oak. Mateo introduced Richard to the general.

"Ricardo will be indispensable in developing our artillery," Mateo said, "which we sorely need. He is from Arizona in Norteamérica, however, and he's not pleased at our recruitment and disciplinary procedures. Our world seems harsh to him—perhaps because he does not understand our enemy. I want him to know what we are up against. ¿*Uno poco momento, por favor?*" ["A small moment, please?"]

The general shrugged. "As you wish, Major. I have something new to show you anyway, which young Ricardo might want to look at as well."

General Ortega sent a sergeant to get what he'd referred to, and a minute later the sergeant returned with a half-dozen file folders. He laid them out on the coffee table.

"On a regular basis, we receive drawings and even photographs depicting the Señorita's atrocities. One source of these over the years has been the Señorita Dolorosa's own staff. Her ladies-in-waiting and everyone else around her hate and fear her with a passion. Every so often one of them will sneak out of her palace and escape to Sonora. They know we are always looking for intelligence, so they will, if possible, steal some of the Señorita's photos before leaving. Suffering from severe insomnia and nocturnal depression, she amuses herself by studying photographs of different atrocities occurring in her torture chambers and in her country's penal system. She has boxes of them. We've collected quite a trove of these photos and drawings over the years."

"Tell him how these victims end up in the Señorita's and Díaz's prisons, slave-labor mines, and torture chambers," Major Mateo said.

"Méjico, under Díaz, has no system of justice," General Ortega said simply. "No real courts of law, no real laws, in fact."

"How are people sentenced?" Richard asked.

"There are no trials as such, and often those who are sentenced aren't criminals at all but people whom someone in authority has a grudge against. Such people are often sent to Díaz's and the Señorita's stone quarries, slave-labor mines, and ranchos. There is no real parole in those places, and the *prisioneros* are worked to death in them."

The major handed Richard a folder filled with photographs of men in huge dust-choked quarries, breaking rocks with sledgehammers. Some of the quarries held thousands of men.

"Many victims, however, never make it to a prison mine, a quarry, or a slave-labor hacienda," Major Mateo said. "Some people they simply torture and execute."

He got out a folder filled with pictures of torture chambers. The first picture Mateo showed Richard in the general's office was of a large dark dungeon, which contained a variety of torture instruments. A black-robed Inquisitor stood beside each one.

"Recently," Mateo said, "one of the court ladies escaped Sinaloa and made her way here to Sonora. When we debriefed her, she told us how Señorita Dolorosa had given her ladies and a prospective lover a tour of her Inquisitor's dungeons and her Aztec-style ceremonies atop her pyramid. The Señorita frequently brings the court photographer along to photograph the atrocities. The Señorita keeps boxes of them in her bedroom for late-night viewings. Recently, a young woman smuggled out some of the photographs and gave them to us. She later reconstructed notes on Lady D's monologues in her torture chambers and atop the pyramid, and the woman gave these notes to us. I have the transcript here."

The major handed Richard a photograph—a close-up of a thick oak bench. Beside it was a huge pile of heavy stones. The major then showed them the photo of a man on a thick wood rack, groaning under a high pile of stones, his face, a red twisted mask of pain.

The major read to Richard and Mateo from the transcript.

"Margarite, the lady-in-waiting, wrote, 'Our Lady seemed especially fond of the *peine forte et dure*, depicted in these photographs. The victim's body, neck, arms, and legs are lashed to a rack. Boards are placed on top of him, and stones are piled one at a time on them. The person is eventually crushed under a small mountain of rocks. The Inquisitor may want the person to confess to a crime . . . or not, since there's frequently no crime to confess to.

"'Our Lady liked the fact that each stone, as it was piled on top of the man, increased his agony. The Señorita laughingly called it *agony on the installment plan*.'"

The major produced a photo from the folder of another man, who was being waterboarded.

"'Our Lady lovingly regaled us on the theory and

practice of waterboarding, explaining: *It's simulated drowning, which is as horrible a torture as there is. Some survivors say that afterward rainstorms and baths frightened them half to death.* The Señorita's laughter then rang through the chamber like the bells of hell.'"

The next photo was of a pulley bolted into a steel hook sunk into an overhead beam. A thick rope was run through the pulley. A young woman with long black hair was about to be strappadoed. Her face was turned to the wall, so she was unrecognizable. Her wrists were tied behind her back and affixed to that rope was the end of the pulley rope. A hooded, black-robed priest had hoisted her up off the ground. A basket was tied to her feet. Next to her was another pile of rocks. Another photo showed the Señorita dropping rocks into the basket.

The major read from Margarite's transcript:

"'Our Lady's favorite trick is to raise the rocks high above her head, then drop them into the poor wretch's ankle-basket. She described their subsequent screams to us as . . . *sublime.* After one such act of cruelty, Our Lady rolled her eyes back until only the whites showed. Heaving a stupendous sigh, she raised her head as if toward the heavens and shouted at the ceiling:

"'*God, I feel good!!!*

"'The victim's screams merged with the Señorita's hilarious howls.'"

Last but not least came a photo of the rack. A rectangular wood bench, it resembled a wooden bed frame with a roller at each end. Cranks turned each of the rollers and a ratcheted lever froze the rollers in place. Around each of the rollers wound ropes that were tied to the victim's wrists and ankles. A man was stretched horizontally on the infernal machine, his face writhed with unspeakable suffering.

The major read from the manuscript again:

"Listen to what the Señorita tells her court ladies about the rack: 'I love putting my former lovers on the rack, then taking the crank away from the presiding priest and turning it myself until the tendons creak and crack. I love hearing the imbeciles beg for mercy. Imagine someone asking . . . me . . . for mercy.

"'The Señorita then burst into gales of derisive laughter.'

"She goes through legions of lovers," Mateo explained, "and, as a parting gift, sentences each of them to the Rack and the Stone. She is sometimes referred to as 'the Black Widow,' after the female spider, who notoriously eats her lovers whole after sex. Clearly, the Señorita is the last woman in the world a man should ever want to go to bed with."

"Even though she is reputed to be genuinely . . . *beautiful*," Richard said.

"She most assuredly is," Major Mateo said.

"Now do you see what we're up against?" General Ortega asked.

"We're up against the horde from hell," Richard said.

"Led by the satanic Señorita," Mateo said.

"You're saying defeat for us is not an option?"

"Especially from your point of view," the major said. "If they destroy us, New Arizona will be next."

"In other words, Sonora is the Alamo, Thermopylae, and Horatius at the Bridge," Richard said.

"And we need you and our big guns to stop them," Mateo agreed.

"They're throwing everything at us this time," the general said.

"We don't stand a chance without that ordnance," Mateo said.

"The last three battles seriously depleted our ranks," the general explained.

"And you expect me to make up the difference?" Richard asked.

"Whether you like it or not, you're in the army now," Mateo said.

"If Major Mateo is right, you *are* the army," General Ortega said.

Richard looked away from both the photos and the two officers.

What have I gotten myself into? he thought with terrible foreboding.

Chapter 19

Their train was in a waterless waste in the middle of nowhere when Eléna heard the whistle blow and the train slow. Not a good sign. She shouted at Antonio:

"Go see what's happening."

Climbing the nailed-on ladder, he mounted the adjacent boxcar and jogged along the boxcar roofs to the tender, which was piled high with kindling, to the locomotive. Just around the bend, he could see a big lightning-smitten cottonwood tree lying laterally across the tracks. Its thick, massive trunk branched out into a dozen large dense limbs heavy with countless branches.

The engineer and fireman looked up at him. They both wore gray canvas pants and dark cotton shirts. Their hair was black, their skin and clothes were stained by smoke and soot.

"Does that trunk look like lightning hit it to you?" the engineer, a big man named Carlos, asked.

"You could bore a hole in the tree," Antonio said, "fill it with blasting powder, and blow the trunk in two.

We'd do that in the army when we were too lazy to chop the trees down. You'd achieve the same look."

"I don't like it," the engineer said. "It's too big a coincidence."

"And I don't see signs we had a lightning storm here either."

"We still got to move that *hideputa* [son-of-a-whore] log," Fernando, the fireman, said, "whether we like it or not."

"You gonna help?" the engineer said. "You're big enough to move the tree yourself."

"I got two women to look after, one of them hurt and sick. Anyway, you got a bunch of *soldados* on the train. They need to come out of their boxcars *también*—in case we are attacked while we're moving that tree."

"That's why they're here, *¿verdad?*" the engineer said.

Eight rurales *soldados* were already climbing out of the boxcar nearest to Antonio's flatcar and were walking down the track toward the fallen tree. They wore gray uniforms, sombreros with broad brims and high crowns with four side-creases, and brown horseman's boots. They all had big black mustaches and had sidearms strapped to their hips. Canvas bandoliers filled with shiny brass cartridges crisscrossed their chests. Several of them carried slung rifles from their shoulders.

"I didn't think those *soldados* would leave that bullion safe alone in the boxcar," Fernando, the fireman, said.

"I thought they'd stay in it forever," Carlos said.

Madre de Dios, *we're on a bullion train*, Antonio suddenly realized.

"Them lazy *bastardos*'d rather have you removing that cottonwood for them," the engineer said.

"I have to get back to the two women," Antonio said.

"Well, that log ain't movin' itself," the fireman shouted to the *soldados*.

"Have them scout the nearby arroyos *también* before they start moving that tree," Antonio said. "Banditos could be hiding nearby—maybe in an arroyo or behind those rocks. They'll be sitting ducks once they get it off the ground."

Antonio pointed to a cluster of large boulders on a ridge overlooking the fallen cottonwood.

"How do you know that?" Fernando asked.

"Scouted several years in the Mexican army."

"Why did you quit?" the engineer asked.

"A bullet through the knee."

"I wouldn't mind trying something different, amigo," Fernando said. "Is the army all right? You like it before you got shot, I mean?"

"It's okay if you're *loco-estúpido.*"

"Speaking of *soldados*," Carlos said, "they're up by the tree."

"We better help them," Fernando said.

"Have them scout that terrain first," Antonio repeated.

"We'll be lucky if we can get them to move the tree," Carlos said.

By that time, Antonio was jogging along the boxcar roofs, heading back toward Eléna and Rachel.

He didn't like this stop at all.

PART V

You and I are going into the war business.
—RICHARD RYAN to Major Mateo Cardoza

Chapter 20

The Señorita Dolorosa entered the palace ante-chamber, where she was to meet her stepson, Eduardo, and El Presidente de Méjico Porfirio Díaz. She was the first one there, and took a moment to study the room. The walls and ceiling were almost blindingly white—in fact, every wall inside and outside the vast palace seemed to sparkle. She'd ordered her workers to grind the gypsum, which blanketed the edges of so many of the region's riverbeds, to a fine powder. After mixing it with water, they then gessoed the adobe walls of all her buildings, whitewashing them to a dazzling alabaster.

The sala was also filled with polychromatic light, which flowed through a dozen leaded, stained glass windows. At least six feet high, four feet wide, and five feet off the floor, the multicolored panes cast iridescent designs on the walls, ceiling, and polished hardwood floors.

She casually reviewed the room's layout. She wanted

everything right for El Presidente. In the palace, even
the antechambers were grand halls—this one had
eight chairs spread throughout the middle of the
room in the shape of an octagan. Their arms, legs,
and tall narrow backs were made of exquisitely carved
teak and upholstered with rich Moroccan leather.
In between the chairs were small round tables of
the finest teak. Underneath all of the tables were
varguenos. These ancient chests contained seemingly
countless drawers—some with secret compartments—
tastefully inlaid with ivory, gold, and silver. To one side
was a vast fieldstone fireplace almost forty feet across.
Above its granite hearth thick, soot-blackened fire
tools hung from its huge maw. Off to the side was a
long, narrow teak table set with silver goblets and decanters. She knew from past experience the decanters
would be filled with fine wines, cognacs, and champagnes. Still no one except the Señorita was allowed
to sample her private stock of Madeira.

Catching her reflection in a gilt-framed wall mirror,
she paused to observe her short, close-fitting tunic of
scarlet silk. A black tasseled cord tightly cinched her
waist. Today, she favored black stockings and black
shoes with three-inch heels.

El Presidente Porfirio Díaz entered next. A stocky
man with a square frame and a huge head, he sported
one of those heavy, downward-turning Mexican
mustaches. He wore gray trousers, a matching military shirt and jacket, heavy brown boots, and a big
holstered .45 caliber Remington on his hip. Crossing the
room, he took the Señorita in his arms and attempted

to kiss her on the mouth, a maneuver she artfully parried.

"Ah, my *guapolita* [little cutie], you look ravishing as ever."

"And you, my *oso mucho malo* [big bad bear], you look mean enough to murder God."

"Only because you mock my love."

It was a game they played. It delighted El Presidente no end and bored Dolorosa to distraction.

"I almost forgot how much I missed you," he said.

Again, he tried to take her in his arms.

Again, she decorously deflected his advances.

"My moronic stepson is late again," she pointed out.

She walked over to the table and filled a goblet to the brim with her scrupulously hoarded Madeira.

"I need something to get me through this hideous meeting," she said with a painful grimace.

"He'll be here soon."

As if on cue, her stepson walked through the door.

"Ah, your sainted stepson honors us with his presence," Díaz said with a transparently fulsome smile.

"Dishonors us, you mean," the Señorita said.

"How is our wicked *araña* [spider] today? Still spinning her murderous webs?"

"¿*Araña*? What do you know, Porfirio? El Idioto learned a new word. Could it be he's trying to read books again? His lips and fingers must get awfully tired trying to follow all those words."

El Presidente gave them a broad smile, put an arm around each of them, and pulled them both together. "Come, children, can't we all be friends—one big happy family?"

"I have no friends," the Señorita Dolorosa said curtly, extricating herself from his arm, "least of all with *abyectos retardos* like El Imbecilio here. Anyway you said we were here on business."

"Just so. Let us sit."

The dictator got himself a large crystal goblet of Napoleon 1811 Grande Reserve cognac, and they each took one of the straight-backed chairs.

"We are preparing a new offensive against Sonora," Díaz said. "We will combine both our Sinaloan and Chihuahuan forces and crush them in an overpowering frontal attack. I thought you might be interested in haranguing our multitudes the night before our assault—something to raise their morale. You know they do love and revere their Señorita."

"You mean fear and loathe her," Eduardo said.

"Nonetheless, many will die that morning, and afterward we shall be doubling their taxes. There will be serious unrest . . . even after our inevitable, overwhelming victory."

"Of course, any unrest will be forcefully, terminally . . . *put down*," the Señorita said, yawning.

"Of course. That is why God gave you so many slave-labor ranchos and prison mines," Díaz said. "You are in constant need of replacement prison labor, and our political opponents supply us with endless quantities of such fodder. It is my honor to hand them over to you. Still our people will not be pleased with all the death, destruction, and destitution that the coming conflict will force upon them."

"And I'm supposed to care, why?" the Señorita said.

"Because you do not want pandemic revolution

and ubiquitous uprisings such as the French endured in the late eighteenth century," Díaz said. "Violent anarchy racked that nation for a dozen years afterward and cost their leaders and many of their aristocrats—people such as us—their heads. And anyway what do you have to lose except a few minutes of your time? Who knows? If you lift their spirits and let them know what our men are fighting and dying for, you won't turn them into cheerful givers, but perhaps they won't shoot your tax collectors on sight."

"Last year we did have a rather bloody revolt on our hands," Eduardo said.

"We taxed them into a truly terrifying famine," the Señorita noted with a pleasant smile.

"And this year we plan to tax them even more severely," El Presidente said.

"*Bueno,*" the Señorita said softly.

"I will harangue the multitude if my stepmother can't do it," Eduardo said.

El Presidente and the Señorita looked at him and . . . *laughed.*

"What's so funny?" Eduardo said. "I'm their governor, not you, Stepmother!"

Now the room rocked with their raucous guffaws.

"The last time you 'harangued the multitude,'" the Señorita Dolorosa said, "half the crowd walked away in less than five minutes."

"They thought it was about to rain," Eduardo explained.

"It was a clear, warm, cloudless day," the Señorita said.

"The other half stayed because they were entranced," Eduardo said.

"The other half couldn't leave because they'd fallen asleep," the Señorita said.

"My dear Eduardo," Díaz said, struggling to promote a truly charming smile, "you aren't the most animated speaker I've ever seen."

"What he's saying, El Dopo, is that you're a stupendous . . . *bore*!!!"

Eduardo stood and stamped out of the antechamber.

"You think inviting him here was a mistake?" Díaz said.

"He is the governor," the Señorita Dolorosa said, "if in name only, and he had to know the offensive is coming. Now tell me about it."

"Our intelligence says that they have acquired and are learning to master heavy artillery. They've been tough enough without it, and I fear if they ever do master those big guns, we'll never defeat them."

"They are rumored to have workable Gatlings as well."

"We hear that rumor before every one of our wars with them," Díaz said. "As you know, however, their highly inferior black powder clogs and jams their firing mechanisms with their residue. Their Gatlings have always been useless after the first thirty or forty shots."

"Where do you plan to hit them?" the Señorita asked.

"There's only one strategy and one front that will allow us to destroy Sonora for once and for all: a full-frontal assault on their main fort."

"To move that many men and that much matériel

will not go unnoticed," the Señorita said. "They will have time to dig breastworks and trenches."

"We'll have a fight on our hands, true, but we can and should prevail. If we don't delay."

"How soon can we launch such an attack?" the Señorita asked.

"In two months," Díaz said.

"I'll prepare my speech."

"You write such stirring speeches, My Lady."

"I am gifted," she shamelessly conceded.

Chapter 21

Slater was over two hundred feet up-tunnel when he found Luis Moreno. He was on his back, his head near Slater's outstretched candle, the lower half of his body buried under a ton of rock. The deadfall appeared to have broken every bone in his friend's body from his short ribs down to his toes.

Raising a lit candle, Slater could see two heavy canvas ore sacks near the top of Luis's head. He looked inside the two bags. In the candlelight he saw dozens of solid gold nuggets, several the size of his fist, none of them smaller than a .50 caliber rifle round.

Slater checked for a pulse in Luis's throat. It was surprisingly steady. He dripped some canteen water on Luis's mouth, and miraculously, Luis's eyes fluttered open.

His friend was still alive.

"Ey, compadre," Luis said, giving Slater a small, brave smile. "You came back for me. I knew you wouldn't let your compadre down. I told you *también*

we'd hit it big, and we did. That gold is for you now—
because you came back for me. Take it and *vaya con
Dios* [go with God]. This tunnel is not safe."

"I'm not leavin' without you."

"Then you will die in darkness and dust under a
Sierra Madre of rock. Just like me. With me. Only you
aren't going to die, because I'm asking you to leave me.
Por favor. You were right. I never should have come
back here. Nothing can save me now."

"But—"

Then they heard it—up-tunnel. The hysterical
shrieking and frantic scurrying of mine rats—an army
of them.

They smelled Moreno's blood, and they were coming
toward him.

That froze Moreno, and the machismo ran out of
him in a nerve-racking rush.

"Still, amigo," Moreno said, "don't let them *bastardas
ratas* [rats] eat me alive."

But what could Slater do? Luis was the best friend
he'd ever had. The man had saved his life and
watched his back a thousand times over for three go-
dawful years in that Sonoran hell pit. Luis never complained, never backed down from a fight, and never
turned his back on his friends. You knew who he was,
what his word was worth, the things that count.

But Luis hadn't listened to him, had come back in
to dig out that gold, and now Slater couldn't save him.
If Slater stayed they both would die. In less than an
hour.

Sooner.

The army of scurrying, shrieking rats was getting
closer and closer.

Slater slipped his double-edged Arkansas toothpick out of its belt sheath. Covering his friend's eyes with his left hand, he said:

"Don't worry, amigo. I won't let the rats eat you alive. I am your compadre—now, always, to the end. You are so lucky to have such fine a compadre as me."

"*Muchas gracias, mi amigo.* I know you would not let me down."

Slater knew there should be words at a time like this. If they had been back in the civilized world, there might have even been a Christian service and a sermon filled with meaningful words. Over the years, Slater had heard some of those words—sermon-words about how "dust we art and to dust we shall return" and about "men who riseth up like the grass in summer and are cut down in their prime." Slater knew that hymns often came before the words and followed afterward. Then there were the burials in the churchyard, which began with hymns, followed by more words and more hymns, even as the bodies were lowered into the grave. Potluck dinners frequently followed. Slater had eaten a few of those too. He remembered the food was goddamned good.

But Slater was running out of time, and the rats were closing in. Their shrieking and scurrying—along with the creaking of shoring timbers, the jolting crack of the collapsing deadfall, and the dripping of the mine water—were the closest things Luis would have to a church choir. Screeching rats would serenade his unceremonious demise.

Still there had to be words.

"Luis, you were *mi amigo—mi amigo bueno.* Whatever we done—robbin' banks or blowin' trains or stackin' time—you held up your end. You were always there. But that ends now. *Adiós, compadre, y vaya con diabla.*"

Placing a hand over Luis's eyes, he quickly slit his friend's throat from ear to ear.

Grabbing the big ore sacks, he began crawling backward, making his way out of the mine, careful not to knock down any of the shoring timbers, laboriously dragging the two thick bulging sacks full of gold behind him.

Chapter 22

Like Mateo, Richard was now attired in gray fatigues and a matching military shirt and cap. They both sat at a dark, dirty workbench in a corner of one of the Sonoran rurales' black powder factories. A former warehouse with thirty-foot-high ceilings, its hundred-foot-by-fifty-foot concrete floor was now covered with other filthy benches and worktables as well. Men and women sat at the tables grinding wet gunpowder.

"We have a fairly elaborate gunpowder industry in Sonora," Mateo said. "We've been battling Sinaloa and Chihuahua for so long we always need industrial quantities of the stuff."

"Fine," Richard said, "but you have a couple of problems with all this black powder. It's not potent enough to power your artillery pieces, and it's so dirty it quickly fouls all your pieces, especially your Gatling guns. You need a cleaner, better explosive if you want to stop a broad-front offensive by two combined armies, which is what your intelligence says you're about to confront."

"What do you suggest?" Mateo asked.

"Do you keep a tally of all your military equipment?"

Mateo nodded.

"I want to see your lists," Richard said, "including all the equipment you currently have in storage but have considered useless. I want anything and everything you have related to the manufacturing of guns—all kinds of guns—and I don't care how old the ordnance and the component parts are. This is arid country. Those things won't corrode quickly. They're probably in good shape. Maybe you have old, forgotten factories that once manufactured components and ammunition."

Mateo stared at him, curious.

"Here in Sonora can you get me nitric acid?" Richard asked.

"That is one thing we have not figured out how to make."

"Sulfuric acid?"

"We have that."

"We're also going to need other things—a lot of brass shell casings, as many as we can locate. I know you have percussion caps for your black powder cartridges. We're going to need a hell of a lot of those."

"May I ask why?" Mateo said.

"You told me your forces are so depleted they cannot repel another all-out Sinaloan-Chihuahuan combined attack without adequate weapons. I intend to get them for you."

"How?"

"We're going to deploy land mines and Gatlings."

"Didn't anyone tell you our black powder jams our Gatlings? It's too dirty. It clogs the breech, barrel, and auto-feeders. Our weapons jam almost immediately."

"So I'll make you powder that won't foul their feed-loading mechanisms."

"How?"

"Let me worry about that."

"But I do worry."

"You got no problem." Richard gave Mateo a hard, ebullient slap on the back. "You and I are going into the war business."

Chapter 23

When Antonio returned to the flatcar, he found two *soldados* dragging their Gatling out of the back of the boxcar. Sonora's biggest, most profitable company, the Conquistador Gold Mining Consortium, was shipping the train's gold, and they had brought the gun along to secure their gold shipment. Antonio smiled to himself. It was a weapon he knew well. You had to fire it in short bursts or else the black powder would foul the breech. Still it was an overpowering weapon if used properly. Antonio knew how to use it properly.

Weighing only sixty pounds, it was less than four feet in length, so the *soldados* had little trouble hauling and hoisting it up to the roof of the boxcar. Aided by a man inside, they quickly bolted it into the roof through predrilled holes.

Antonio felt a little better. The Gatling would provide some cover for Rachel, Eléna, and himself.

He climbed the neighboring boxcar's end-ladder and helped the *soldados* lock down the big gun. The gold company's Gatling was in good shape—clean and well oiled. It fired its rounds through a cycle of eight one-inch-diameter revolving barrels, arranged in a circle. The gunner turned a crank, the barrels revolved, and when one came under the hammer, it fired. The shell casing was instantly ejected, and another bullet—from a hopper full of rounds—was dropped into the receiving mechanism, which fed the round into that barrel's empty chamber. The next loaded barrel then came under the hammer. The entire operation was automatic—untouched by human hands—save for the gunner's turning of the crank.

Everything was in order. After checking the weapon out, Antonio was finished. He climbed down the boxcar's end-ladder onto the flatcar below.

"How does it look?" Eléna asked. She was still sitting on the bed of the flatcar, cradling Rachel's head.

"The Gatling's in good shape," Antonio said, "and the men up there seem to know what they're doing."

"Why do they need two men up there?" Eléna asked.

"Reloading the Gatling is fast and simple, but having a loader working alongside you speeds up the process," Antonio said, glancing around the side of the boxcar, trying to get a glimpse of the men in front of the locomotive, struggling to clear the fallen cottonwood from the track.

He turned to Eléna and handed her the first weapon.

"If they come at you, start with the twelve-gauge double-barrel Greener."

He handed her the shotgun first.

"You kept it behind the cantina bar," Antonio said, "and you know how to use it. Sawed off just above the breech, it's chambered for shells and fully loaded. Each twelve-gauge shell has nine lead balls, a third of an inch in diameter. You have a short barrel and a big spread pattern. At close range, you'll take out lots of banditos with it."

"You look concerned," Eléna said.

"Neither of us knew we were on a bullion train, and now the train is stalled on the track. We have to be ready, is all."

Eléna nodded.

Suddenly, shots rang out. Antonio glanced around the corner of the boxcar in time to see six of the eight men dragging the cottonwood go down. They did not look like men diving for cover. They went down like felled trees, and they were bleeding profusely.

Up ahead, the track had a slight bend. The fallen tree was far enough ahead of the locomotive that the Gatling gunner had clear aim at the bandits swarming the falling men, and it tore them to pieces. Unfortunately, the gunner's friendly fire tore up his surviving comrades as well and now the banditos had spotted them. The bandits quickly picked off the man behind the Gatling.

Antonio was already scaling the boxcar's end-ladder and going for the big gun. Straightening up, but keeping Rachel's head squarely in her lap, Eléna raised the Greener to her shoulder. Sighting down the double barrels, she slipped her finger around the double triggers.

And waited for the attack to come.

PART VI

*Maybe you redeemed past sins
by redeeming the future . . .*
—MAJOR MATEO CARDOZA

Chapter 24

The Señorita Dolorosa awakened her court ladies from their middle-of-the-night slumber. When they arrived, she sat alone on her bed—scowling.

"What is wrong, My Lady?" Catalina asked.

"Captain whatever-the-hell-his-name-is failed me tonight—failed me so miserably I had to kick him out of my bedroom."

"That's terrible, My Lady," Roberta said.

"They all fail me in the end—inevitably!"

The Señorita was, of course, right. The pressure to perform sexually, the horrific fear of failure combined with heér furious rants against the male sex, with which she continually assaulted her lovers, eventually unmanned the hardiest of her paramours.

"The male of the species ought to be wiped off the face of the earth" was one of the more maniacal mantras with which she hammered her lovers, often during the act of *amor*. "The insuperable stupidity and maddening misogyny, which they have visited on the feminine gender time immemorial, time out of mind, are simply too much for any sane woman to bear," she would roar into their trembling faces. "Every man jack of them should be castrated and racked, drawn, and quartered."

Still the desire to survive and to postpone what they knew would be an inconceivably agonizing end inspired even the most frightened of them to try their best. They all wanted to please her for at least . . . *a few days*.

But not Captain whatever-his-name-was.

So the Señorita was now in a blind rage, delivering a demented diatribe against all men everywhere.

"Take the Spanish Inquisition and that pervert of a priest, Torquemada. His child-beating mother was Jewish, and the woman who jilted him was a Moor. So what did he do? He tortured, robbed, and killed every Jewish and Moorish woman he could get his sick, twisted, loathsome, self-abusing hands on, plundering their prodigious estates after he was done. Then he split the take with Spain's king and the Vatican, keeping a third of the proceeds for himself and his sadistic priest buddies. Can you imagine anyone today torturing their fellow human beings so hideously? Can anyone imagine—?"

She suddenly stopped in midsentence and peered out into nothingness, slack-jawed. For a long moment she simply stared and scratched her nose, lost in thought.

"Well, er, uh, come to think of it . . . maybe I can. You see, we have our own version of the Inquisition right here in Sinaloa, and I guess I do kind of . . . *run it*. Except I've changed the focus of the old Torque-madian auto-da-fé. I send relatively few women to our

Inquisitor's chambers; mostly I send him men who fail me in the sack. If they fail in their amorous duty to me, I then give to them what Torquemada gave to those Jewish and Moorish widows and the Aztecs gave to their human sacrifices. What's wrong with that? After all, it was mankind which created this little game. I see nothing wrong with giving the male of the species a taste of his own malicious medicine."

"Hanging the *bastardos* by the thumbs is too good for them!" Roberta shouted furiously.

"Send them all to the rack!" Catalina thundered hysterically, terrified herself but also offering moral support to her frightened friend.

"Cut out all of their hearts!" Rosalita roared.

Suddenly, however, the Lady Dolorosa seemed strangely anxious. She shook her head slowly, as if there was something she wanted to explain to them.

"You have to understand, Roberta," she finally said, "I'm not a complete bitch. I don't just torture them in dungeons and rip their hearts out on a stone altar. I do plenty of nice things for them. Among other things, I . . . I . . . I . . ."

She seemed genuinely stymied, at a loss for words. But then she howled at her ladies at the top of her lungs:

"I fuck their brains out first!!!"

Her ladies stared at her in mute shock.

"Eh, that's something Torquemada never did to his terror-stricken widows, right?" the Señorita said.

"Right," Roberta whispered weakly.

"Right!" Catalina echoed meekly, frantically nodding her head.

"Still I must confess that Torquemada and I have

both done some truly amazing things. We've hung our subjects from crosses—the four-armed crux immissa, the three-armed crux commissa, and the X-shaped Saint Andrew's cross—frequently upside down. Then there's the rack, the strappado, the iron maiden, the wheel, the skull crusher, thumb and toe screws, hot pincers, and tongs. I've had my Inquisitor use all of them on men whom, of course, I order gagged, blindfolded, and earplugged. Torquemada and I have been known to sequester our subjects in coffins for months on end, allowing them out only to excrete, hydrate, and consume food."

The ladies-in-waiting stared at her in horrified silence, but she had her wind up and was oblivious to their trembling.

"But then I always do it for their own good," the Señorita Dolorosa continued. "It's 'the path of pain.' Did you know one of the first Inquisitors wrote that 'pain alone leads to salvation'?"

"He called it the Via Dolorosa [the path of pain]," Roberta said, barely able to find her voice.

Their Lady gave the ladies-in-waiting a demure, almost saintly smile. "Bravo, Roberta! Bravo! You must be remunerated for your attentiveness. Virtue such as yours should not be its own reward. Also I like to think that I, the eponymous Señorita 'Dolorosa,' was named after that unenviable 'Via.'"

Chapter 25

Slater sat on his saddle blanket on the hill above Nogales, on the U.S.-Méjico border, studying the city through his sniper scope. It was evening but the sky was clear. By the full moon, the desert-bright stars and the lights of Nogales's many cantina/brothels, he could see the main street clearly.

Slater had just exchanged Luis's gold for $15,000 in hundred-dollar bills, and he now had them in his silk money belts under his shirt and in his canvas saddlebags. He was going to give it to Moreno's surviving family. Still it was enough make men to want to trail, kill, and rob him.

Just after dark, he had sneaked out of his hotel room, leaving a dummy made of pillows, trash, and old rolled-up grain sacks filled with dirt and soiled clothes under the blankets. Nogales was a hell town, and Slater was expecting company.

By the time he'd reached his hilltop, four rough-looking men in gray uniforms and sombreros were in front of the

*El Presidente Hotel. Pulling Winchesters out of their saddle
sheaths, they worked the levers and checked their firing
chambers. Barrels resting on their shoulders, they entered
the El Presidente.*

*Five minutes later, a half-dozen pistol and rifle shots
cracked in the hotel and light flashed in the windows of
Slater's room.*

*In his mind's eye, he envisioned his bed dummy, riddled
with black, charred, smoking holes. He knew they'd be on his
trail now. There had been no way for him to sneak out of
Nogales; even now, too many people had seen him ride out
of town.*

Crawling forward, Slater worked his way to the
rim of the hill and down into his shallow firing pit,
the forward edge of which was surmounted by rocks
and hard-packed dirt. In the middle of the barricade,
he'd opened a groove for his Big Fifty Sharps, which
lay beside the firing pit along with a dozen .50 caliber
shells. The men were a mere four hundred yards
downhill, so Slater was not even bothering with the
sniper scope. He had his ladder-style, vernier-scale
peep sight adjusted for elevation, distance, and
windage. He was ready for them.

Within minutes, the four men reached the base of
his hill and were peering up the gradually sloping
trail. He could start shooting them now, but the question was: Which way would the survivors flee? If they
headed downhill, they could return with more men.
If they fled uphill, they'd be out of sight for most of
the way. They could dog his trail and blindside him
whenever they wanted. He sighted in on a narrow

curve a hundred yards farther up the incline from them.

Leaning forward in their saddles, peering up the trail, the men slowly worked their way forward. When their mounts entered the downward-sloping turn in the trail, Slater eared back the Sharps's hammer. Even if he only winged them, it would be with .50 caliber rounds, designed to kill four-thousand-pound bison at eight hundred yards, so he did not need to nail the men between the eyes—not unless he wanted to. And anyway in times like this, it was usually better to wound your pursuers. The sight of a shot-up compadre tended to slow the other men down, and it typically took at least two of them to look after a wounded friend. Pressing his eye against the peep sight, he bracketed the lead rider's torso.

Your first look is your best look, Slater reflexively repeated to himself.

He let the hammer down, and the rifle bucked against his shoulder. The booming recoil rocked his head.

Without thinking, he automatically pushed the trigger guard forward and extracted a shell casing. Setting the hammer to half cock, he quickly sleeved in another round and pulled back the trigger guard. He also engaged the rear trigger, which lightened the primary trigger's touch.

Staring into the peep sight, he lined up a second target. The man was mounted and staring uphill, trying to spot the sniper. Suddenly, he was staring straight at Slater. He might have even spotted the whitish cloud of black powder smoke emanating from Slater's Sharps. Dispersing the smoke-cloud with his left hand, Slater sighted in on the man's chest and squeezed off a round. The bullet hit his lower sternum, lifting him off his saddle and dropping him behind his horse.

Slater was working fast. He had to kill the two survivors before they could return for reinforcements. Easing back the hammer to half cock, he slammed the trigger guard forward and extracted the shell casing from the chamber. Slipping in another, he pulled the trigger guard all the way back. The hammer was still on half cock, so he set the primary for the lighter touch. One man's horse was up on its hind legs, circling, insanely spooked at the sight and scent of blood. Slater went for the rider's chest, but rushing the shot, he hit him instead in the throat, effectively decapitating him. The man's head went bouncing down the trail.

The fourth man's horse was now bucking wildly, so much so Slater couldn't get a shot at the man, who was whipping up and down in the scope.

Fuck it.

He frantically set the hammer at half cock, slammed the trigger guard forward, ripped out the shell, pulled the lever back, and without bothering with the second trigger, sighted in on the crazed, jumping mount. Shooting the horse in the side of his chest and through his heart, Slater knocked the big bay onto his side, pinning the rider's leg. Bracing his free leg against the saddle's cantle, the man pushed frantically to free himself from the fallen animal.

Setting the hammer at half cock and levering the trigger guard, Slater removed the spent, smoking shell casing. Now he had all the time in the world. He inserted a fifth round and pulled the hammer back to full cock. Returning to the peep sight, he was staring straight into the howling man's face.

As he depressed the trigger, the rifle once more hammered his shoulder, the whitish black-powder smoke mushroomed up, and again his ears rung. Waving away the dense, blinding haze, he again studied the scene below.

The pinned-down man lay twisted on his side, the back of his head blown all over the ground and the dead, bloody bay.

Chapter 26

At night, Mateo brooded. His clubbing of Rachel outside the cantina still haunted him. He hadn't been ready for the ferocity of her assault. In defending her brother, she had attacked him like a demon straight out of hell, and in a moment of anger and perhaps even panic, he'd laid her out with the weighted buttstock of his *cuarta*-quirt. He'd felt something crack and then realized he'd hit her too hard.

Why had he hit her in the temple? He now secretly feared he'd killed the girl.

He felt bad enough about it that he'd approached General Ortega one night in his office.

"The important thing," the general had said to him, "is that her brother didn't witness it. He doesn't know how badly you hurt her. According to the man who took the cantina over, the sister and Eléna, the former owner, took a train north, and that's all anyone knows. And who knows? Maybe the sister made it. Stranger things have happened. We've all seen

*men who were wounded severely in battle survive. Whether
she lives or dies is in the lap of the gods and should be of no
concern to you. It's nothing you can affect. In all probability
no one down here will ever know, her brother included."*

*"She was just a kid, and I really hurt her. I don't know
what came over me."*

"We're soldados," *the general said with surprising
gentleness. "We aren't trained to pull our punches."*

Mateo stared at him, silent.

"My friend," the general said, "it can't be undone."

"Still . . ."

*The general put his hand on Mateo's shoulder. "You're a
soldier—a professional, and the hard truth is we have a war
to fight. You can't let anything distract you. Look at it this
way: In any war there is collateral damage. Maybe Ricardo's
sister was just in the wrong place at the wrong time."*

"General Ortega, she was only trying to help her brother."

"Sí, mi amigo, but that's the way it happens sometimes."

The general was right, of course. Mateo could not
rewrite the past. What was done was done. The blow
to her head—no matter how bad he felt about it—was
on his backtrail. He had to move on. He was also right
that at this moment their real problem was defeating
Díaz's and the Señorita's troops, and the survival of
Sonora—of all of them—was at stake. A drunken
mistake—no matter how tragic—had happened, but
that was over now. It could not be altered or recalled.

It was over.

Still he suffered—as did the woman.

Assuming she was even alive.

However, he could conceivably affect the future.

Maybe that was the key. Maybe you redeemed past sins by redeeming the future and helping—even saving—those you cared about.

Maybe he could keep the girl's brother alive. After all, he'd played a dirty trick on him—dragooning the poor boy into the Sonoran rurales. Furthermore, he was starting to like the kid, something he hadn't counted on, since he was not a man with *muchos amigos*. Throughout his hard life he'd found compadres to be an unaffordable extravagance. Still almost against his will he was starting to like, even admire, the young man.

Sorry I got you into all this, Ricardo.

Oh well, the past cannot be undone.

It couldn't, but Mateo could fight for the future. He could fight for Sonora. The girl's brother would help him, and, in turn, he would watch the boy's back. Maybe that would help to make up for what he'd done to the young man's sister—and to Ricardo.

He hoped in his soul it would.

Chapter 27

Bandits were pouring out of the south end of the barranca and charging up the trackbed toward the locomotive. The Gatling had a five-hundred-yard range and was chewing up most of the bandits as soon as they exited the arroyo. Those who made it to the train attempted to press themselves along the sides of the boxcars and position themselves outside the big gun's line of fire. Only when they spread out from the flatcar were they again in range, and the *soldado* on the Gatling had a shot at them.

Several of the banditos were squeezing between the boxcars. Scaling the end-ladders, they were crawling over the roofs and sighting in on the two *soldados* manning the Gatling. One of them shot the *soldado* manning the big gun. Antonio pushed the gunner off the boxcar and took over. Several bursts from his Gatling sent the bandits scrambling back down the ladders or leaping over the side.

In the meantime two bandits jumped off their horses onto the far end of the flatbed. Close together, they attacked Eléna. With Rachel's head still in her lap, Eléna eared back the double hammers. She and Rachel were a dozen feet from the banditos, the twin barrels were sawed off at the breech, and their pattern was immense. Eléna blew the two off the car with the first barrel. Seconds later three more took their place. They were twenty feet away, and close enough together that again a single barrel killed all of them.

Breaking open the shotgun, Eléna quickly shook and shucked out the shell casings. Cramming two more into the barrels, she'd eared back the hammers just in time to blow a nearby pistol-waving bandit off his horse, then another, even as additional bandits charged. All the while bodies piled up outside her car and on both sides of the trackbed. When she ran out of shells, she raised her old .44 caliber U.S. Army Colt, a sidearm powerful enough to knock a man off his feet, and it sure as hell did that—knocking bandits off the car as they clambered aboard and off their horses, all of them piling atop the rising sprawl of dead men below.

When the Colt was empty, Antonio tossed her his long-barrel .36 caliber Navy Colt, which she caught two-handed. After emptying the Navy, she had no cartridges for it, but she had time enough to attempt to reload her .44. Flipping open the loading gate, she was ejecting shell casings and shoving rounds into its wheel as fast as she could.

She'd just closed the loading gate when a tall, raw-boned bandit in a straw, floppy-brimmed sombrero, a gray collarless shirt, filthy denims, rope sandals—and with a stench that could make a javelina give up a dead buzzard—swung down off his mount and onto

Eléna's car. Kicking the Colt out of her hand, he was standing over her and pointing a cocked pistol directly into her face. Bending over her until they were nose to nose and she could smell his foul breath and wince at his filthy mouthful of broken, missing, and rotten teeth, he said:

"Tell me what hell looks like, *puta*."

A pistol rose up under the bandit's chin and fired so close to Eléna's head that her ears rung and its side-flash scorched her neck. Covered with the bandit's blood, Eléna looked down and saw Rachel wide awake, her eyes locked on Eléna's and the Army Colt smoking in her fist. She had come out of her coma long enough to grab the .44 up off the flatbed and shoot the bandit under the jaw.

And save Eléna's life.

Then Rachel's left arm relaxed, and her head settled back onto Eléna's lap. Her right fist, which had shoved the gun directly under the bandit's jaw, dropped back onto the flatbed. The pistol remained rigidly locked in her unconscious grip.

Prizing the .44 out of Rachel's still-clenched fist, Eléna quickly pivoted her head, glancing at both sides of the flatbed, looking for bandits to shoot. To her surprise, there weren't any.

Then she noticed the silence.

Antonio wasn't firing the Gatling.

"Everything okay?" she yelled up to him.

He had run up to the next boxcar to get a glimpse of the barranca's north end and the front of the train. He was back up above the flatbed.

"A couple of bandits took off," he yelled down to

Eléna. "They looked pretty shot up. They were trying
to haul away some amigos who looked even worse."

"Are they coming back?"

"Naw, they're in bad shape."

The engineer was jogging up the trackbed toward
them.

"Where were you?" Eléna asked.

"Hiding under the locomotive," he said without
shame.

"*Muy bueno,*" Antonio said. "I'm glad you're still
alive. We need you to take this thing north."

"To Nogales?"

"No, El Rancho del Cielo," Eléna said. "We got a
very sick woman here who's going home. You get us
there, you'll have *mucho dinero.*"

She looked down at Rachel then. To her surprise
her eyes were open again. She was staring at Eléna
fixedly.

"*Gracias,*" Rachel whispered. "*Muchas gracias, mi
amiga.*"

PART VII

She had to save Rachel.
—ELÉNA VASQUEZ

Chapter 28

The Señorita Dolorosa led her court ladies into her palatial bedroom suite.

"I have a special treat for you," she announced. "A new lover. He's going to be here in a few minutes. When he comes in here, you have to watch."

The Señorita loved terrifying and humiliating her lovers in front of her ladies. They put on a good front and pretended to enjoy the spectacle. Their survival often depended on appearing happy and cheerful, even when they were frightened half to death.

Today, however, they were more sanguine than usual. The night before their Lady had presented them with new clothes. This was the first time they had a chance to try them on. Catalina was wearing her new toga of crimson silk, which played off her red hair, matching nail polish, and high-heeled sandals. Rosalita's outfit was an ebony toga, and it perfectly matched her long raven tresses and sandals. Isabella was attired in bright canary yellow, which complemented her long blond hair, while Roberta's turquoise robe, sandals, and necklace almost seemed to reflect the deep lustrous blue of her sapphire eyes.

None of her ladies favored white, knowing that it was the Señorita's favorite color.

"Is this new one gifted in bed, My Lady?" Catalina asked. "Is that why you want us to meet him?"

"Oh, I don't think it will get that far," the Lady Dolorosa said. "I plan on having a different kind of fun with him."

"What kind of fun?" Roberta asked.

"He is the most craven man I've ever seen. You should have seen him when I took him into our Inquisitor's chambers. When he saw the Inquisitor thumbscrew a man—who was already moaning, sobbing, and hanging from a strappado—the new man's bladder released. He started crying at the temple-pyramid when the High Priest ripped out the heart of another of my former lovers. I had to summon my guards and make them force him to watch. I've never had one so bloody sensitive before. Usually my paramours are more . . . *manly.*"

"What will you do with him, My Lady?" Isabella could barely choke out the words.

"I thought you'd guess. I'm going to terrify him out of his wits and then have him tortured half to death."

"My Lady," Catalina said, secretly sick with dread, "it sounds *so* delightful."

"Oh, we'll have some fun with this one."

Then the Señorita's eyes flashed with a merriment so macabre and her smile blazed with a malevolence so feral that her ladies visibly shook involuntarily, even as they struggled to suppress their trembling.

Her ladies of the court could not imagine what unexpected horror the Señorita Dolorosa planned to perpetrate next.

Chapter 29

Dressed in dark work clothes, Richard explained to Mateo what Sonora needed to defeat the Señorita's and Díaz's combined Sinaloan and Chihuahuan armies:

"The key to victory is in your ammunition. All our weapons at West Point and at the Rancho fire smokeless, cordite-based powder because it doesn't foul our weapons after repeated use—especially the Gatling's firing mechanism. It also doesn't billow up smoke clouds that obscure your view of the battlefield and prevent you from sighting in on the enemies."

"How do you make this smokeless powder?"

"Usually, we would make a mixture of two parts nitrocellulose, otherwise known as guncotton, to one part nitroglycerin. We don't have the time or expertise, however, to make nitroglycerin in the huge quantities we'll need. Instead we're going to use single-base powder—nitrocellulose colloided with ether alcohol."

"And where do we get nitrocellulose?" Mateo asked.

"It's just cellulose exposed to nitric acid."

"First, what kind of cellulose do we use?"

"Cotton or wood pulp will work."

"Secondly, you said you knew how we could make nitric acid?" Mateo asked. "You sure we can do it? We can't."

"Sure, you can. Find a big porcelain crock, then you boil sulfuric acid and saltpeter in it. Distill the steam, and you'll have nitric acid. You next soak the cellulose with nitric acid, then colloid the resulting powder with ether alcohol, which will stabilize it and keep it from spontaneously combusting in your faces."

"It's that unstable?"

"Not in colloid form. In fact, you use the same technique to make dynamite—you mix nitroglycerin with sawdust, and it will be safe to handle."

"We also have tons of black powder. What do we do with it? Throw it away?"

"Oh, you'll use it. You'll dig fire trenches a hundred yards in front of your main trenches—where you'll deploy your Gatlings—and man those breastworks with your riflemen. If the Sonoran *soldados* start to overrun them, instead of charging them with bayonets, your riflemen'll drop back and deploy right beside your machine gunners."

"What about our mortars?" Mateo asked.

"We'll also use the black powder to power your smooth-bore mortars. The mortar shells will be filled with black powder but instead of projectiles, we'll use thin metal cans packed with shrapnel. The cans will be sealed, airtight and watertight. They will have a trajectory of about three hundred yards, after which the heat and blast will disintegrate the shrapnel-filled can. When it hits, each one will blow scores of *soldados* to bits—depending how densely they're clustered around the explosion. The Díazistes will have never seen anything. The Lady Dolorosa and her stepson will never know what hit them."

Mateo gave him a mock salute. "Anything else, *mi general*?"

"I looked at your inventory book. You have a lot of high-speed fuses. We're going to use them to set off land mines. Again, big cans filled with shrapnel, backed by black powder, and sealed tight. Put them an inch underground except for where the fuses attach. When the troops hit the line of mines, you light those high-speed fuses. They'll burn through water, through dirt, through anything. Those Díazistes will get the surprise of their lives."

Chapter 30

Eléna, Rachel, and Antonio were in the engine compartment of their eight-wheeler Baldwin locomotive. Eléna was sitting on the floor; Rachel's comatose head lay faceup on her lap. Eléna was glad the engineer and the fireman had made it. This was bandit country, and they needed people who could run the train.

The engineer fired up the locomotive, and they were on their way. Sitting on the floor of the engine compartment was not as pleasant for Eléna as riding on the flatcar. Up here, the train was a black, thundering monster. Smoke, embers, and sparks continually erupted out of its diamond-shaped smokestack, and the engine roar was deafening. Steam was ubiquitous, floating up from everywhere, including up from under the wheels. In the fuming compartment's twilit gloom, the brass fixtures gleamed incongruously, while the whistle shrilled in Eléna's ears, throbbing in her, through her, like the mournful wailing of the damned.

None of which had any effect on Rachel, who was, once again, unconscious. Staring down into her face, Eléna could see Rachel deteriorating before her eyes, spinal fluid leaking from her nose and ears, her fever dangerously high. Perhaps it was a blessing that shock and the coma kept her oblivious.

Eléna tried to cool Rachel's forehead, cheeks, and neck with a wet rag, which her two-gallon water bag kept moist. Occasionally, she sat Rachel up and put the bag to her mouth in an attempt to cool her lips and trickle some water down her throat. Eléna tried to keep Rachel as hydrated as possible, which wasn't easy.

Nogales would be an ordeal, and she dreaded that Nogales crossing, as if they would be thundering straight into Hellmouth, which that borderline could well turn into if things went bad. Sonora was in rebellion, but Díaz still controlled the blood-drenched border town, and he did not like any of Méjico's citizens fleeing his ruthless regime. He'd ordered Nogales's federales to shoot on sight anyone attempting to cross that border without authorization.

The engineer had warned her that, when they reached Nogales, a wagon filled with ballast would sit laterally across the track. It was always there, he said, and he could not breach it. In Nogales, he would have to drop off Eléna, Antonio, and Rachel. Eléna promised him Katherine Ryan would handsomely reward them if they got them to her rancho, but the two men still believed it couldn't be done.

Forcing the engineer and fireman to crash through the Nogales border blockade would take some doing. Antonio would definitely back her. Among other things,

Díaz and the Señorita had killed everyone he had ever cared about—torturing them hideously, working them to death in their prison mines or shooting them against a wall. He wanted out of Méjico as badly as she did. She and Antonio still had their pistols and the Greener. Eléna kept them beside her on the locomotive's floor. They would make it over that Nogales border or die trying.

No, Eléna would not let the two men stop the train no matter what. She had to get Rachel to Rancho del Cielo as fast as possible. Eléna knew in her soul Rachel would die if a Rancho surgeon did not operate on her soon.

If the engineer and the fireman resisted, she would kill them both, then, holding the throttle wide open, highball the locomotive herself over that border with Antonio feeding the firebox.

She had to save Rachel.

Chapter 31

The Señorita Dolorosa's new lover slowly entered her bedroom suite. He wore a capitán's uniform. Tall, lanky, well built, his hips were narrow, his shoulders broad. He had prominent cheekbones, large dark eyes, and a strong jaw. When he smiled, however, his upper lip trembled, his jaw quavered, and his eyes darted back and forth. He clearly wished he was somewhere else.

Nor did the Señorita do anything to allay his concerns. She did not even acknowledge his presence. Instead she continued lecturing her ladies on the erotic behavior and misbehavior of the male of the species in the animal kingdom.

"God, I love rats!" the Señorita roared. "In most of the animal kingdom, females are forced to couple with one mate at a time, despite the female's obvious sexual superiority, demonstrated by her ability to have almost unlimited orgasms. In the rat kingdom, the female's sexual stamina is even more overwhelming. The female rat—known as the doe—is uniquely orgiastic, typically having four hundred to five hundred orgasms during coitus; consequently, no male rat can satisfy the female. Therefore each female rat has legions of lovers—hundreds at a time. They line up to fornicate with her. In that regard, rats are utterly unlike their mammal cousins, the rabbits. In the rabbit world, a doe only gets one buck, and the strong bucks capture and enslave as many does as they can control. They hoard and torture the does into submission. The bucks run a reign of terror in rabbit warrens, and the does, who are forced into their personal harems, suffer horrifically.

"Up and down the biological scale," the Señorita histrionically declaimed, "the males are monsters. They not only abuse the females, they eat their young. Tigers, lions, and panthers famously devour the cubs when they take over a new pride. You know why?"

"Why, My Lady?" Roberta asked.

"So they can get laid!" the Lady Dolorosa roared.

"Really?" Catalina asked in shock.

"Absolutely. When the female is lactating, she can't go into estrus, and the males can't rut."

"You mean the males cannibalize the cubs so they can have sex?" Catalina asked, feigning anger. "That's monstrous."

"Men are the same in all species—murderous swine," Rosalita concurred.

"Yes," the Señorita agreed, "although that statement is probably a slander on pigs."

"Speaking of men," Roberta said, staring at the Señorita's prospective lover.

All the court ladies turned and fixed Immanuel with resentful stares. He could not meet their eyes. He looked scared out of his skin.

"It's universally true," the Señorita said, continuing her monologue. "The males—whether they are a tiger, an ape, or a monkey; a rodent, fish, bird, lizard, snake; whether he is a squirrel, wild dog, dolphin, baboon, langur, chimp, gorilla, orangutan, gull, kangaroo, crow, vulture, eagle, osprey, cormorant—are insanely obsessed with raping the females of the species and devouring her young. One of the reasons the female of the species is so motherly, so defensive of her infants, is because she has to protect them from all males everywhere, particularly their own vile, cannibalistic fathers."

"Are there any good males in the animal kingdom?" Roberta asked, indignant.

"There are some in some insect species," the Señorita said. "When a male spider has sex with the female—a black widow, for instance—he allows the female to devour him whole afterward. Thus, he sacrifices his body to nourish both the female and his offspring. Same thing with the praying mantis. You know that big locust-looking thing with the front legs bent as if in prayer? The male's sexual brain is in his gonads, not his cranium. So the mama bites off his head at the beginning of the act, causing him not to stop but to boff her harder, longer, and ejaculate even greater quantities of sperm. Now that's one hell of a man, if you ask me. Why can't our men be more like their praying mantis counterparts? That male not only propagates the species with his imbecilic brains, his cretinous cranium provides the mother and her progeny with their sustenance."

"Tell me, My Lady," Isabella asked. "In your next life, if you could come back as any creature, it would be a female black widow or a female praying mantis, would it not?"

"How perceptive, Isabella," the Lady Dolorosa said. "I'd be hard pressed to choose which. I admire them both so much. Those females are the true heroines of the animal kingdom. We could all learn from them. We should all strive to be more like them."

"Are there any males in the biological world who don't murder each other rampantly and cannibalize their offspring?" Catalina asked.

"Yes, the male chimpanzees don't devour their young," the Lady Dolorosa answered.

"Why?" Roberta asked.

"They're bisexual," their Lady explained. "If a male chimp wants to get laid, he doesn't have to devour his young to make the mother go into heat. He can just bang another male."

Their Lady then got a wicked glint in her eye and turned to the young, trembling Immanual Imanez.

"You there," she said, sternly. "You aren't going to go all ape on me, are you? If you do, you know, I'll have my priests rip off your heart. Who knows? Maybe I'll eat it. It might be good with some chilis, mole sauce, frijoles, and an excellent Madeira," the Lady Dolorosa said cruelly.

Her teeth flashed like feral fire. Her lip was pulled back over her teeth in a supercilious sneer, half grin, half grimace. She looked as primally wicked as original sin, inscrutable as the abyss, mean enough to murder the universe.

Her prospective lover's jaw dropped in stone horror. With a hideous shriek and a throat-wrenching sob, he fled her bedroom, as if all the demons in the Aztecs' hideous-beyond-belief Netherworld were escaping and clawing at his back. The thunderous laughter of the Señorita and her court ladies rocked her boudoir.

"Don't worry," the Señorita said, "the poor *guapito* won't get far. My guards will round him up in no time."

"And then what?" Isabella asked.

"The usual," the Lady Dolorosa said. "They'll bring him back to me. I'll sit him down on the bed, tell him all is forgiven, that I will love him forever. Then I will send him back to his quarters and shower him with presents. When I'm sure he's gotten over his terror and trembling, I'll have the guards drag him out of bed and haul him to the Inquisitor's chambers. There, he will get the full treatment. Everything!"

"After that?" Catalina asked, grinning lasciviously.

"What I give them all in the end," their Lady said. "The Sacrificial Stone. After all, it's only what they deserve."

Señorita Dolorosa's up-from-the-gut, roll-out-the-barrel, knock-me-down, drag-me-out belly laughs combined with the terrified chortling of her court ladies reverberated through the palace like echoing death knells out of hell.

PART VIII

Soon not only the rivets but the boiler's bolts were ricocheting through the engine compartment like rounds fired from Antonio's Gatling.

Chapter 32

Richard stood on the testing range—a broad, flat plain, whose unobstructed field of fire ran a full 1,500 yards. Beyond it lay nothing but parched desert arroyos. Only life-size replicas of men populated the kill zone—white man-shaped targets at 200-yard, 300-yard, 500-yard, 600-yard, 700-yard, and 800-yard intervals. Each of the targets was six feet tall.

Richard was about to test his new smokeless cordite powder. When the combat started, the Gatlings would have to fire many thousands of rounds without getting clogged, and the new cordite had to radically increase the power, range, and accuracy of their artillery. In truth, Richard had no idea whether his newly fabricated explosive would do the job. He knew the theory behind mixing and producing this kind of powder, but he'd never made any that had been put to practical use on such a spectacular scale afterward. Now he had enough for Mateo to test several hundred Gatling rounds. He hoped and prayed they passed today's exam.

All their lives depended on it, his in particular. He

hoped and prayed that the Gatling gun, which he was about to fire, didn't blow up in his face.

"You ever shoot one of these before?" Mateo asked.

Like Richard, Mateo was dressed in fatigues, brown army boots, and a plain gray forage cap. Both men had long-barreled revolvers holstered on their hips and crisscrossed canvas bandoliers, whose loops were stuffed with shiny cartridges.

"Many times. At the Rancho, by age fourteen, we had to get checked out on all our weapons, which was of every kind imaginable. We liked to think of ourselves as 'citizen soldiers.'"

General Ortega walked up to them. He was wearing the same fatigues, gear, and guns.

"You really think you can make our Gatlings fire hours on end without fouling their breeches?" the general asked. "You think you can actually make our cannons hit something?"

"If this powder works, they will," Richard said.

"Es mejor trabajar," ["It better work"] the general said.

"Failure is not an option," Mateo added.

"If you fail, we're fucked—all of us," the major said. "Our intelligence says that Díaz and the Señorita are throwing everything they have at us. They're shanghaiing every peon and convict they can get their hands on. They're going to hit us with innumerable, interminable, human-wave assaults."

Richard met his gaze, unblinking.

"How is the ammunition fabrication program progressing?" the general asked.

"Pretty well," Richard said. "We're producing rounds as fast as possible. We'll need a lot of them though."

"Then let's see how good your powder is," the

general said. "The Gatling too. *Vamos a ver cómo se come al perro grande.*" ["Let's see how the big dog eats."]

"It'll devour a few of those targets," Mateo said.

"The question is," the general said, "how many rounds can we pump through these guns before they burn up, clog up, and wear out?"

"Or explode in front of us like bombs," Mateo said.

"Maybe I should step back," the general said.

"Not a bad idea," Richard said. "No one has tested these guns beyond, say, twenty or thirty consecutive rounds. We're going to fire a lot more than that."

"How many more?"

"I want to see if this gun can take two thousand rounds without jamming or overheating," Richard said.

"I think I'm stepping back," General Ortega said, stepping back sixty feet from the Gatling.

"*Uno hombre inteligente,*" ["A smart man"] Mateo said.

"You can step back as well," Richard said.

"For a man of Mateo's machismo," the general said sarcastically, "an exploding Gatling is nothing."

"What about me?" Richard asked.

"You made the powder, no?" the general asked.

"So?" Richard said.

"You're on the gun," Mateo said, grinning.

"So if its breech blows up," the general said, "it'll hammer *your* cojones into pinole."

"Ey, why not?" Mateo said. "You made this shit, not us."

Grabbing his crotch, Mateo stepped back, as did the general.

Richard had no choice but to man the Gatling.

Chapter 33

The Lady Dolorosa was bored. Not that her newest
lover wasn't physically attractive. He was as handsome,
physically impressive, and as exceptional in bed as any
she'd ever known. He was so infuriatingly stupid, however, that she'd ordered her Grand Inquisitor to
remove him from his chambers that very night and
give him the full treatment—immediately. Simply because she wanted to go down to the chamber and hear
his screams.

Her rage was understandable, but nonetheless the
suddenness of her fury bothered her. She had always
been more calculating in her vindictiveness. In her
worldview, timing was everything; it was not enough
for her to merely hurt those who displeased her, she
had to shatter their universe, lay their souls bare, and
leave them baying like moon-mad wolves for the rest
of their desperate, despairing days, praying to their
gods that this earthly dispensation would mercifully
come to a close . . . *immediately.*

That was the way she had always done things. She

didn't torture people capriciously, putting little or no thought into it; she studied on revenge. She treated vengeance as if it were an art form, as if she were Michelangelo and her victims cunningly turned-out oeuvres, a Sistine Chapel of exquisitely rendered . . . *pain and suffering*.

She took her works . . . *seriously*. She didn't just throw people at her Inquisitor, willy-nilly. She put thought, care, and effort into it.

Until now.

What was happening to her?

Her midnight melancholia was the problem. It made her nights a living hell, and God help the man or woman who displeased her when that all-enveloping black madness consumed her soul. In those moments she was capable of doing . . . *anything to anyone*.

Still she hated capriciousness—destroying people on a whim, which is what she'd just done. It showed sloppiness, carelessness, and carelessness was a vice she could not afford. Dimwits, like her stepson, could live lives of carelessness. They were men who were blind to consequences and therefore never considered them. The Señorita, on the other hand, had never indulged in such recklessness. She had always plotted three, four, five steps ahead—a hundred steps ahead—and planned for the consequences accordingly. She had never shot at anyone from the hip. She had never been out of control in her life.

Until now.

That black nocturnal despondency was doing it to her. She needed some new endeavor, some mission, some vision that would excite and inspire her. But nothing worked. She was a woman without a purpose, without a dream.

And what was life without a dream?

More and more, she took it out on men. They were supposed to be the panacea to a woman's woes, a silver bullet for depression and boredom, not monuments to imbecility, which they inevitably turned out to be. At times such as these, in the bottommost pit of her heart's abyss, she wondered whether she ought to take a woman into her bed instead.

No-o-o-o-o!

Deep down inside she knew they were just as stupid as men, and they weren't as much fun to torture. It was more amusing breaking a man. Make him think you're eternally in love with him, that he's the only thing in your universe, that you'll live, you'll cry, you'll laugh, you'll die . . . *for him.*

Then break him on the rack.

Rip his heart out on the sacrificial altar.

Then get nose to nose, eyeball to eyeball with him—and laugh in his face!

That's what she should have done to that moron she'd bedded tonight, but she didn't. She let him off easy. She had not deceived him as to her affections. All he knew was her hate and rage.

But to tell the truth, she didn't care. She no longer cared about anything, and that scared her.

She had to find something that thrilled and enthralled her soon—or she was going to lose it big-time.

She had to tighten up her game.

Chapter 34

"Well, what do you think of our new cordite powder?" Richard asked General Ortega.

The general stared at him, speechless. He wasn't sure what he thought. He raised his binoculars and looked up-range again, meditating on the test he'd just witnessed.

Large white six-foot-high man-shaped targets had been erected at 200-yard, 300-yard, 500-yard, and 800-yard intervals. With all five targets, Richard had fired a few test rounds, just to get the range. Mateo had studied where the rounds impacted through his own binoculars, and told Richard where they had struck. The young man then sighted in on the targets.

And obliterated them.

The last three had been so far away, they were barely visible with the naked eye, yet when they studied those targets

*through telescopes, they saw that the Gatling had shredded
them into sawdust and splinters.*

*Just as amazing was the fact that they could view the
obliterated targets at all. Black powder would have shrouded
them in impenetrable clouds of thick whitish smoke that
would have blinded the entire field. All Ricardo's cordite
powder produced was an attenuated, easily dispersed haze.*

*Two thousand rounds later the smoke was still relatively
thin, still not blinding them, and the Gatling operated as
smoothly as it had when it was firing its very first rounds.*

Mateo was again studying the disintegrated targets
through his binoculars.

"You know we put a lot of effort into constructing
those targets," Mateo said.

"We stuffed them with sawdust and even painted
faces of Díaz and the Señorita on them," the general
added, "encircling their likenesses with bull's-eyes."

"Now it's like they'd never existed," Mateo said.

"Pretty inconsiderate, wasn't it?" the general said,
nodding.

They were all silent awhile.

"Those Gatlings sure make a mess of things." Mateo
finally spoke up.

"Are you thinking what I'm thinking?" General
Ortega asked Mateo.

"That the Sinaloan-Chihuahuan army will never
know what hit it," Mateo said, nodding.

"You know we have to try to keep this test secret,"
General Ortega said.

"Ricardo here," Mateo said, "made the same point.

He said whether the test succeeded or failed, we did not want the Sonorans to know about it."

"That's why you ordered all our soldiers and workers away from the firing range?" General Ortega asked.

"No witnesses," Richard said.

"It's going to be hard to keep it quiet," General Ortega said.

"Almost impossible," Mateo said. "We've rounded up every brass shell casing we could scavenge as well as commandeered more workers to assist all of the tens of thousands that we had already sent to that old ammunition factory. We've also built a plant where we're putting percussion caps on the casings. We've recruited ten thousand workers to fabricate the smokeless powder and to fill those fifty-thousand-plus one-hundred-caliber brass shell casings and pack the shells in boxes."

"Then we're going to have to train our Gatling teams to load their guns," Richard said. "Spotting their targets, they'll have to know how to calculate their guns' range and trajectory."

"And then cut the enemies to pieces," General Ortega said.

"This gun should cause serious panic when the Sonora troops charge it for the first time," Mateo said.

"It'll cut them down like a scythe," General Ortega said.

"Like Death's sickle," Mateo said.

The two men nodded their agreement, but Richard noted that their mood was surprisingly glum despite the overwhelming success of the test. They all understood that the war against Díaz and the Señorita would not end here. The test's success had served only to underscore the bloody enormity of the future battles and foreshadow the catastrophic carnage to come. The men charging these guns would be flesh and blood, not sawdust and pine.

"The poor babies will never know what hit them," the general said.

"We're going to kill a lot of men," Richard concurred.

"Look on the bright side," Mateo said. "Díaz and the Señorita Dolorosa will be madder than hell."

Chapter 35

Now Eléna's train was approaching Nogales, snaking precariously around its steep arid foothills and brush-filled arroyos. The distant sierras to the southeast trembled in and out of focus in the heat haze.

Carlos and Fernando had not been pleased when an hour earlier Eléna and Antonio told them the bitter news. They were going to crash through the Nogales border crossing, full throttle. When the two men said they'd refuse, Antonio had responded by clambering up the boxcar's end-ladder and manning the Gatling, which he'd moved up to the roof of the first boxcar. Lowering the angle of fire, he sighted in on them.

When they lowered their eyes, they saw Eléna sitting on the compartment floor, staring up at them. The cut-down, double-barreled, twelve-gauge Greener in her hands was pointed straight at them.

Rachel's head was still in her lap.

"You don't hammer through that crossing," Eléna yelled

at them, red-faced, "you'll murder this young girl as surely
as if you shot her in her head. You try that, even think about
it, and—madre de Dios—*I'll empty this buckshot into your*
muy estúpido cojones, *assuming you even have any."*

They bleakly nodded their assent . . .

The surrounding desert—arid and scorched as sun-
bleached bones—was hotter than Hellgate with the
hinges melted off. Prickly pear, yucca, and mesquite—
that was all that grew. A buzzard wheeling high overhead kept a solitary vigil. Gradually, falling-down adobe
shacks and ramshackle jacales materialized on each
side of the trackbed—the first sign that the city of
Nogales lay ahead.

Carlos, the engineer, reached up to yank the
whistle's rope.

"Not yet," Eléna said, shaking her head. "We're
going in full speed, no warning. Fernando, start throwing wood into that firebox just as fast as you know
how—*muy rapido, mucho pronto.*"

"You heard her," Antonio also shouted at them,
sighting the big Gatling in on the frightened fireman.

Carlos and Fernando were completely miserable.
For a half hour now, Antonio and Eléna had forced
Carlos to tie down the throttle and assist Fernando in
hurling kindling into the firebox, as if their lives
depended on it, which Antonio assured them that
they most definitely did. Between the sweltering
desert sun, their physical exertions, and the heat
rushing out of the blaze that they were so fanatically
compelled to feed, they were soon drenched in sweat
and black with soot. They crammed so much fuel into

the firebox that it was now a shaking, roaring blast furnace. The diamond stack had become a kind of choke point for the belching, billowing smoke, and it was working overtime, pumping embers and ashes into the sky like a demonic chimney protruding up out of the Infernal Pit.

Nor was Eléna all that happy. Looking at the steam gauge, she saw the needle was off the dial, deep in the red, so lifeless and inert, it looked as if it had died. Still she and Antonio yelled at the fireman:

"*¡Darlo todo!*" ["Pour it on!"]

Every so often, Carlos and Fernando grew tired and their refueling of the firebox slowed down, but that was not an option. Antonio and his Gatling were motivational experts. A few short bursts of one-hundred-caliber—one inch in diameter—Gatling rounds fired into the woodpile directly behind Fernando, and the two men were, once again, feeding the firebox like *hombres locos* [madmen].

Then they were in Nogales. Donkeys, carts, huts, and shacks, then bigger buildings—cantinas, hotels, restaurants, banks, offices, more elaborate homes. People, horses, donkeys, and dogs shot past them in a blur, and the engine compartment was a protracted ear-cracking . . . *bo-o-o-o-o-o-om!* Sweat poured off all of them from the desert sun and the engine compartment's murderous heat. Eléna estimated the temperature in that compartment to be over 130 degrees.

When the crossing was a mile or so away, the boiler made its displeasure known. Eléna thought it sounded like a satanic screech from beyond the grave, from beyond the farthest reaches of darkest hell, the death cry of a wounded beast gone mad with feral suffering.

Then it got even worse. The boiler's rivets started to pop. At first, the rate was erratic but then it became increasingly incessant, until finally the popping was a steady, relentless, buzzing, singing . . . *WHA-A-A-NG!!!* Soon not only the rivets but the boiler's bolts were ricocheting through the engine compartment like rounds fired from Antonio's Gatling.

But all Eléna could think about, all she cared about, was that border crossing. Her double-barreled twelve-gauge still leveled at Carlos and Fernando and Rachel's head still in her lap, she shouted at the two terrified men:

"*¡Mas madera! ¡Mas madera!*" ["More wood! More wood!"]

Now they were into Nogales proper, and Antonio was pumping his arm up and down, gesturing to Carlos to pull the steam-whistle rope. It was time to let everyone know they'd arrived. The whistle shrilled and echoed through Nogales like the demented wailing of the doomed and the damned. As they approached the crossing itself, soldiers opened fire on them, but one taste of Antonio's hundred-caliber rounds and their opposition was diving for cover.

Then Eléna saw it—their own personal Armageddon. Up ahead was the track's barricade: a heavy wagon standing athwart the track, piled high with . . .

with . . .

with . . .

avocados!!!

The vegetables didn't bother Eléna as much as the wagon. It wasn't exactly as huge as a house, but it was sturdy enough to derail a Baldwin eight-wheeler, hammering through Nogales with the highball up and the throttle down.

Eléna suddenly realized that Carlos and Fernando might have been right and that they might all very well die. She would be the one murdering Rachel. Still she saw slamming over that border and escaping Méjico as Rachel's only real chance at survival. They had no other choice.

By then Antonio was opening up with the big Gatling. Cranking hundred-caliber rounds into the big cart, he was shredding it like a meat grinder, but he just couldn't destroy it quickly enough. Despite his efforts, the torn-up, bullet-smashed remains of the vehicle were now rushing toward them with frightening rapidity, growing closer, closer, and closer with every second.

The engine compartment's din was beyond deafening—thunderous boilers, whanging rivets, Carlos's ear-piercing hysteria. Suddenly the big Baldwin locomotive was drowning in splinters and wood fragments, and the green squashed pulp of smashed avocados was plastering them all with . . . *guacamole.* The shattering of the wagon added to the decibels as did the screeching of metal against metal as the train fought to hold the rails. The whistle— powered by enough steam to blast it in half— reverberated through the compartment and the streets of Nogales with mind-shattering fury.

Then they were through the city, past the *soldados*— who had unceremoniously fled Antonio's Gatling. All of the people around Eléna—except the comatose Rachel, whose head still lay peacefully on Eléna's lap— now had the eyes of lunatics, which they all were, every one of them stark-staring mad. Finally Eléna, Carlos, and Fernando all lost it, whooping and braying as if all the demons in hell were inside of them, scratching and clawing and fighting their way out.

Only Antonio remained calm. Miraculously alive, he was still atop the boxcar and manning the Gatling, even though the shattered wagon had battered him badly. But why shouldn't the others scream? he thought to himself. They had a lot to yell about.

After all, they had beaten the bandits.

They had beaten the *soldados*.

They had beaten the barricade.

They had beaten the border.

But most of all, they'd beaten Díaz and the Señorita— and escaped the hellhole that they had made of Méjico.

When they were well out of Nogales, Eléna finally told Fernando to stop feeding so much wood into the firebox, but by now the man was a machine run amok and could not stop. Antonio had to shriek at him that they were in Arizona Territory and on their way to Rachel's Rancho and that they did not want that boiler to blow.

Now that they were safe.

Now that they were almost . . . *home.*

Chapter 36

Midnight in the hacienda.

The Lady Dolorosa could not sleep, but she was not in the mood for a lover or company. Instead she donned a black-hooded robe and went for a walk, her bodyguards trailing her at a discreet distance.

As usual, she ended up once more at her favorite spot in the city: the Temple of the Sun. Because it was a cloudy, moonless night, the priests were not performing human sacrifices to the gods on the pyramid's summit-altar. The great *plazula* in front of it was empty, and so the Señorita could gaze on the great pyramid, brightly illuminated by lanterns and watch fires, in solitude and peace.

She decided to climb its forbidding slope.

What did she want out of life? she wondered, taking the first steps toward the top.

Men? They meant nothing to her—disposable pleasures, which she used, abused, and discarded at will—nothing more than a black joke, a ludicrously laughable distraction.

She loved confronting them at the base of the pyramid after their nights in her bed and their days and nights in her Inquisitor's chambers. She especially delighted in greeting them as they began their arduous ascent up the temple's stepped slope, where they would keep their bloody liaison with the High Priest and his razor-sharp obsidian blade. The look of hurt, fright, betrayal, and confusion in their eyes was, for the Señorita, profoundly prurient, a tsunami of titillation, a truly transcendent moment.

But was that all there was?

Did she not want more?

What else did she seek?

Sensory pleasure? She'd had more lovers than any other woman could ravish in a hundred lifetimes. Material luxury? She possessed towering mountains of jewels, the world's most expensive haute couture, and palace-homes as ostentatiously imposing as any in the Western Hemisphere.

Conquest? She loved the sense of omnipotence that obliterating and subjugating an enemy conferred on her, but knew in her soul that that sense of fulfillment was an illusion. Her power already transcended mortal understanding. She and Díaz had conquered almost every inch of Mexico worth conquering. Except for that thorn in their side, the state of Sonora, they owned Méjico in fee simple.

And Sonora's days were numbered. After she and Díaz sacked that miserable state, she and Díaz would next set their sights on Arizona—El Rancho del Cielo, included—and return that territory to Méjico, its original and rightful owner.

Now El Rancho del Cielo—that was something worth the conquering. According to every report, it was a veritable heaven on earth, not only rich in livestock, corn, cotton, and forestry but in silver and gold mines.

But suppose she did conquer it? What then? She was already rich in gold, silver—and everything else she desired.

Did she really wish to conquer the world?

What was the point?

She was torn. To rule the world sounded enticing, but in truth she was lazy and jaded. Why shouldn't she be? She had everything the world could offer her in extraordinary abundance. What would be the point of further acquisitions, further exertion? She had read enough about empires to know that once you established an imperium, you had to incessantly defend your borders. You either waged continual war on those peoples beyond your borders or you were crucified by them.

It sounded like a lot of work.

So she was ambivalent.

Her mind drifted back to men as it so often did. Suppose she found one with whom she could willingly and gratefully share her empire's throne? He would have to be a veritable Caesar or Alexander. He would have to be an emperor and conqueror of Olympian dimensions, an almost preternaturally gifted lover, and a man so witty and wise, so learned and diverse, so mesmerizingly entertaining, that he would never, could never . . . *bore her.*

To rule Méjico with such a man she would of course have to kill her idiot stepson, but that was of no consequence. She'd already done the same to the previous emperor and performing that deed had meant no more to her than kicking a clod of desiccated dung off her shoe.

But, in truth, she knew in her soul that such a man could not exist, and in her perpetual quest for the perfect man and lover, she was doomed eternally to a never-ending cycle of transitory lust, followed by interminable tedium, followed by her lover's inevitable banishment to the Inquisitor's chambers, culminating in that long, agonizing climb up the temple's stepped slopes and his terror-filled, pain-racked immolation on the stone altar.

His last impression of the Delectable Dolorosa would be meeting her at the pyramid's base, glimpsing her cruel smile and hearing her wickedly derisive laughter.

No, she was destined to rule alone.

She finally reached the top, impressed that she was in no way out of breath. Staring overhead, she gazed at the full moon, the billions of brilliant stars, and the blazing swath of the Milky Way. It seemed as if she could study the universe from this summit with resplendent clarity and sublime omniscience.

Yet she could not find a man who came close to suiting her.

Would she ever find him—the man would always

amuse her, never bore her, and, most important, always prevail over her in bed?

No.

She just had to face facts—the man brave and smart enough to master the Señorita did not exist.

Chapter 37

Richard's room wasn't much—a ten-foot-by-ten-foot windowless cubicle with a desk, chair, and two foot lockers for his personal items. A clothing rod for hanging his uniforms was connected to two corner walls. Richard was grateful for it though. Compared to life in the dormitories with their triple bunk beds and three hundred people to a barracks room, his existence in the officers' quarters was paradise.

As he lay there on his bunk, unable to sleep, he couldn't help but worry about his sister. After Mateo had taken her out of the cantina and into the alley, Richard had never laid eyes on his sister again.

Oh, he'd asked Mateo about her. He claimed she'd caught the train back to El Rancho del Cielo, swearing she'd return with help to fetch Richard back. Lots of luck with that one, Richard thought.

His thoughts drifted idly to his mother and father. He loved and admired them both beyond measure, and he'd never doubted their immense, unqualified love for him and his sister. Rachel continually complained that he was Katherine's favorite—a complaint he did not understand. His mother was always mad at him and Rachel both. She had a very dark sense of humor and always referred to them as her "Scylla and Charybdis." She threw so many allusions to Homer's *Odyssey* that he'd finally read it. To his astonishment, he loved it.

Well, you're on an odyssey now, kid.

But when do you find the Pallas Athena, who will guide you through it back home?

She was nowhere in sight, but he did know who the Cyclops was. His name was Díaz, and his partner was Circe—the Señorita Dolorosa. She did not turn men into swine but something perhaps just as hideous— she seduced men into her bed in order to torture them to death later. She also delighted in sending them to her slave-labor prison mines. The most infamous of them was El Infierno de Plata—the Señorita's answer to Odysseus's Land of the Dead, which the gods compelled him to visit before allowing him to return to Ithaca, to his home.

Was it his fate to suffer the wrath of Díaz, the Señorita Dolorosa, and, heaven forbid, sojourn in her own hellish Dead Land—El Infierno de Plata?

If Sonora lost this war, a lot of people would face that fate.

Well, he'd try to stay off her island and out of her lascivious lair.

And if my smokeless powder works, maybe I can stop you from raping and pillaging Sonora.

And prevent you from coming north and plundering Arizona and El Rancho del Cielo.

Aw, hell, Richard said to himself, *things could be worse.*

You're not in El Infierno de Plata yet. Or in one of her torture chambers. Or atop her Temple of the Sun with a would-be Aztec priest hacking your heart out of your chest.

And with those cheerful thoughts, he closed his eyes and finally, restlessly, attempted to fall asleep.

Chapter 38

Eléna's battered, bullet-pocked, smoke-belching train pulled into the Rancho del Cielo's train station. She was back on the flatcar again, sitting on its edge, holding Rachel's head on her lap. She watched as the water tank and hose, as platforms piled high with kindling and coal, each with an adjacent feeding chute, came into view. A red station house was a hundred feet off to the side, and a platoon of armed cavalry soldiers in blue uniforms was turned out to meet them. They did not appear hostile.

Eléna and Antonio let Carlos and Fernando leave the train just outside of Nogales, and Antonio was running the engine. He gave the whistle three hard yanks as they pulled up alongside the station house.

A woman stood at the head of the greeting party. In her midthirties, she had reddish-blond hair, flaring cheekbones, a generous mouth, and hard eyes. Arrestingly beautiful, she carried it with such relaxed casualness that, it seemed to Eléna, she was utterly unaware of it. Businesslike, unsmiling, she exuded an air of intrepid readiness and cold command. This was a woman used to getting her way, a woman one did not trifle with. A woman made of stone.

Then it hit her like a ton of bricks.

Eléna was staring at Katherine Ryan—Rachel's mother.

The woman was inspecting the locomotive. She'd no doubt heard about the Nogales border crossing and was obviously asking what had happened. Antonio climbed down the from the engine compartment. Eléna could see him approach Katherine and, saying nothing, point to Eléna and Rachel's flatbed car and shake his finger. The woman stared at Antonio a moment, then shrugged and started walking toward the flatbed. Antonio clearly had not told her about Rachel.

When Katherine reached them, Eléna was wiping Rachel's face with a wet cloth, Without saying a word, Katherine looked at Eléna, then Rachel, then did a double take. Staring at her daughter, in shock, she was unable to credit, let alone comprehend, what she saw.

Both Eléna and Rachel were sweat stained, dirty, and splattered with blood from the battle with the banditos.

"We brought your baby back to you, Mama," Eléna finally said. "She's hurt bad. We gotta get her to a doctor. Her skull's cracked *muy malo*. You got doctors here at the Rancho, no?"

"GET FRANK!" the woman suddenly roared at the top of her lungs down the platform toward the men she'd rode in with. "Someone get on a horse and ride like hell back to the Rancho. Get Frank off his sickbed, off his deathbed, raise him from the fucking dead. I don't care how you do it. You tell him Rachel's here, and he has to help her. He's going to have to open her skull."

Katherine finally looked at Eléna. For a long time she was speechless.

"Who in God's name are you?" she asked.

"It's a long story. I'm not sure you'll believe it."

"Oh, I'll believe it, and I'm going to hear it. I'm going to hear every goddamn word."

"You won't like some of it, but Antonio and I, we got your daughter out of Sinaloa—away from Díaz and the Señorita."

"And you brought her back to me."

"*Sí*, but I'm afraid to move her. So we wait here till the doctor comes, no?"

"That's right. You hold her just like that. We'll both wait till he tells us what to do."

"I hold her good, Mama," Eléna said. "I been holding her like this for three days, for over a thousand miles. Antonio and I killed a lot of men along the way to get her here, but I never let go of her—not once. I'm not lettin' go of her now either."

Stepping back, Katherine stared at the two blood-covered, sweat-stained women—and at the sawed-off double-barreled shotgun and .44 Army Colt lying beside them—still incredulous, but unable to deny the reality in front of her. When it finally sank in, her jaw dropped. Her chin trembled in and out, and her eyes began to blink. She clambered up onto the flatbed and sat next to Eléna, her legs dangling over the side.

She took one of Eléna's hands with her right hand and squeezed with a grip strong enough to crack acorns.

Then the stone woman broke. Then tears ran down her cheeks, and her body convulsed with sobs.

Part IX

The sun was turning a brilliant crimson as it languidly descended through the dust and gun smoke toward the distant rimrock in the west. The haze of battle hung over the field below like a miasma out of Dante's *Inferno* or Homer's Dead Land, the shrieks of the wounded still agonizingly audible. A score or so of vast vulture-swirling vortexes were spiraling above the dead and dying—the largest assemblage of carrion birds the Señorita had ever heard of, let alone witnessed. Quite frankly, she would have found the pectacle stirring—even physically arousing—were it not for the fact that those were *her troops* shattered and destroyed before her. Even worse, they'd been blown to bits by a force one-tenth their size. It now seemed that Sonora had ordered her dreams of new riches and a radically expanded power along with the tens of housands of her dead *soldados* that they'd sent to hell today.

Chapter 39

The Lady Dolorosa was in her palace, seated on a tall, straight-back, carved-teak chair. Upholstered with crimson leather, it was fringed with matching silk and was almost painfully uncomfortable. Her stepson had disastrous taste in decor, which was only one of the innumerable things that she deplored about him.

An antechamber, the room was still huge—at least a hundred feet long and half as wide. Several sets of tables and chairs were spread throughout. They were all of the same carved, narrow-backed teak and leather upholstery, and they all had accompanying varguenos—ancient chests inlaid with gold and silver, containing countless drawers, which were invariably filled with nothing. She found the varguenos contemptible as well.

On the end table next to her was a glass of 1811 Grande Reserve Napoleon cognac, which El Presidente Díaz imbibed continually. In fact, he was already in midharangue, glass in hand, holding forth on the virtues of the brandy.

"The 1811 Château d'Yquem Flaugergues Comet Grand Reserve Cognac is without doubt the world's finest."

"The champagnes from that year are also quite good," her brain-dead stepson chimed in.

"Exactly so," Díaz said, nodding enthusiastically. "The 1811 Cuvée de la Comète is still preeminent. It was the first year that Veuve Clicquot used remuage to rid its sparkling wines of all those bitter carbonated dregs."

"So 1811 was also the first year for the truly great champagne vintages as well as the greatest year for French cognacs?" Eduardo asked the dictator.

"The greatest year of all," Díaz said. He then added softly, placing a hand over his heart, "In my humble opinion."

Díaz's false modesty almost made the Señorita throw up. The man not only presented himself as a connoisseur of European wines, cognacs, and even English whiskeys, he believed himself to be an expert on every other stupid subject as well.

The Señorita suddenly realized that she would not

rest until she'd had El Presidente and her dimwitted stepson both . . . *killed*. Yes, the sands of time were running out on both those assholes.

Still the Señorita did enjoy her alcohol—everything from beer to wine to far stronger spirits. Given a choice, she preferred the increasingly rare and extortionately expensive Madeiras or a really old Spanish Brandy de Jerez. She was perversely nostalgic about the cheap, almost painfully harsh Sinaloan mezcals of her childhood—the kind that burned all the way down—but she drank the mezcals only in private. She understood that men such as Díaz or that loathsome stepmoron, Imbecilo Idioardo, viewed such predilections as . . . *déclassé*.

She also decided that since today she wanted something out of Díaz, she would actually try to humor him. The Señorita had heard some rather disconcerting rumors about a new Sonoran army weapons program, and she wanted to get the best intelligence on it from Díaz, not the usual palace gossip. So she would pretend to enjoy his pretentious 1811 Year of the Comet Premier Grand Cru Classé Cognac.

El Presidente and her stepson were standing next to a long, narrow teak table, which was set with silver goblets and decanters. They were pouring decanters of the illustrious cognac into sterling silver goblets, while Díaz continued to drone on and on about the brandy's "indubitable preeminence," saying that the 1811 Napoleon horse piss was "nonpareil—the cognac of the gods."

She had heard these mindless monologues hundreds of times and could no longer feign even bored half interest in his dopey disquisitions.

She felt her mind detaching—about to disappear into the ether and the astral. To slow down its drift and rein it back in, she tried to concentrate her mind and vision on her surroundings. It was a trick she'd discovered decades ago, and it usually helped her focus. She started by observing El Presidente. He seemed a little older than when they first met. She attributed the aging to the stress of running a country as backward, violent, and cretinously corrupt as Madre Méjico. Still he seemed to be in shape. Built like a concrete blockhouse, he had a incongruously large head, a big bushy mustache that reached all the way down to the sides of his chin, a broad, rather flat nose, and skin as dark and tough as old saddle leather. He wore dress grays and knee-high black boots, and a holstered, nickel-plated .44 Colt was strapped to his hip. His cartridge belt was stuffed with .44-40 ammunition, the brass shell casings gleaming with an almost mirrorlike gloss.

God, was she bored. Looking away, all the while attempting to suppress a yawn, she caught a brief glimpse of her own sartorial splendor in the wall mirror—a tight ebony tunic, cinched at the waist, and matching riding boots, heeled with three-inch sterling silver buzz-saw rowels. Her lipstick was a sinfully scintillating scarlet, her waist-length hair black and shiny as polished onyx.

"My esteemed Porfirio," she said politely, turning to the dictator and distracting him from his cognac mania, "I understand you have me bankrolling a rather large army, which you plan to throw against Sonora."

"Our timing is *muy perfecto*, Señorita," Díaz said. "Our repeated offensives have ground the Sonoran army down to nothing—fewer than ten thousand troops," Díaz said. "One massive, full frontal assault will utterly overwhelm them."

"Then why do I keep hearing rumors about Sonora producing some sort of miraculous weaponry, guns and ammunition that will mow down our men like a McCormick reaper?" the Señorita asked.

"I questioned our generals about the same thing," her stepson, Eduardo, said, "and they have assured me that those rumors are part of a systematic Sonoran deception campaign designed to scare us out of the next offensive."

"Dear Porfirio," the Señorita said, stepping in front of her stepson, turning her back on him, and blocking his view of Díaz, "if my dullard of a stephalfwit, Eduardo Dullard-O Retard-O, rejects these stories out of hand, they must indisputably, inconvertibly be . . . *true.*"

"A loathing for your inestimable stepson," Díaz said, "is hardly a substitute for sound strategic thinking, My Lady."

She ignored his sarcasm. "The rumors further say that Sonora has acquired a military mastermind, a youthful prodigy, and that he is developing these weapons and training Sonora's rurales officers in their use."

Her stepson snorted condescendingly. "I have run those stories to ground. They are all rumor and false report."

"One of my ladies," the Señorita continued, keeping her back turned on her stepson, "recently removed from Sonora, dated a *soldado* who told her that the

Sonoran rurales were alleged to be developing and testing Gatling guns."

"Oh, they might very well be testing Gatlings," Díaz said. "They might even fire some in battle. But not for long. Their powder is too hopelessly foul. Their black powder will jam them—quickly and thoroughly. It always clogs up their firing mechanisms and always will."

"Suppose the prodigy was helping them manufacture the smokeless cordite powder, which is all the rage on the continent and increasingly in Norteamérica?" the Lady Dolorosa asked. "I understand the U.S. Army is having it mass-produced."

"Sonora can't make smokeless cordite powder," the general said. "No one in Méjico can. Our benighted land lacks the plants, infrastructure, and the munitions chemists necessary to fabricate it in quantity."

"Certainly not in the industrial quantities that Sonora would need for the battle to come," the stepson said.

"But suppose Sonora has found a way to do it?" the Señorita asked Díaz.

"You're dreaming," her stepson said, interrupting Díaz with a supercilious certitude that made the Señorita's flesh crawl and blood boil.

"Señorita," Díaz said sweetly, smoothly, "do not fear. I'm starting to think this disinformation campaign represents real panic on the part of Sonora. I think they're scared out of their minds and that we should attack at the earliest possible opportunity."

"Sonora is ready to fall," her stepson said emphatically. "Timing is everything in war, and the quicker we begin our assault, the quicker and more decisive our victory will be. All we need is commitment and cojones."

And suddenly the Lady Dolorosa knew in her bones that hers and Díaz's combined forces were facing inevitable, irrevocable defeat.

Where did these two buffoons come from? she wanted to scream. If she left matters in their hands, they would bring down her whole empire down around her ears.

She knew then she had to watch the battle in person and find out how dangerous Sonora truly was. Afterward she would know which course to take—and what to do with this so-called boy-genius mastermind if he truly existed and was a threat.

Chapter 40

General Ortega, Major Mateo Cardozo, and Richard stood on a high hill overlooking the flat arid plains of southern Sonora.

"The terrain below," Mateo said for Richard's benefit, "is the only ground on which the Sonora forces can attack. The rest of the terrain is either mountains or swamp."

"Which is part of why we've been able to hold out for so long," General Ortega said. "Over the years, we have spent an inordinate amount of time digging and fortifying our fire trenches, reinforcing our barbwire aprons, and sighting in our cannons."

"Still a decade of nonstop war has taken its toll on us," Mateo said to Richard. "We can't hold out much longer."

"And if our Gatlings and artillery don't work," Richard agreed, "none of us will survive the battle to come."

"You included," General Ortega said, fixing Richard with a tight stare.

The young man understood that the general meant that statement as a factual assessment, not a threat.

Richard turned to study the ground below them through his field glasses. It was not an inspiring sight. In the distance lay the vast peon horde that constituted most of the Sinaloan-Chihuahuan force. Dragooned from all over Méjico, Díaz had subjugated and impressed a vast slave army into his service and was forcing them on pain of death to attack the state of Sonora, with whom they had no quarrel. Behind that slave army was a smaller contingent of officer overseers armed with *cuarta*-quirts; revolvers; sawed-off, double-barreled, buckshot-loaded shotguns; and lever-action rifles. The officers behind the peon *soldados* would drive that force with barbaric cruelty, spurring them toward the miles of zigzagging trench lines defending Sonora's artillery and Gatlings. Between the two armies lay over a half mile of bare, waterless desert, pocked with countless shell craters—the kill zone that the Sinaloan-Chihuahuan army had to cross.

"Díaz's snipers are so numerous and accurate," the general said, "many of our men won't stir much beyond our earthworks."

"You'll want to keep your head down as well," Mateo said to Richard.

"We also have snipers," the general said. "The enemy will keep their heads down too."

"Until, that is, they launch their first humans of their wave assaults," Mateo observed.

"Then they will come at us like hellhounds," the general explained, "roaring as if all the demons in hell were behind them."

* * *

But Díaz and the Señorita's army had never charged into crisscrossing, intersecting Gatling fire, Richard thought. Nor had Mateo and the general seen what these one-inch-diameter, one-hundred-caliber automatic rounds—powered by their new high-velocity, cordite powder—do to human flesh, especially when the men are ensnared and trapped in the toils of Sonora's heavy-gauge barbwire aprons.

Ah, what the hell. In this world it was either victory or the untender mercies of Méjico's sadistic dictator, Porfirio Díaz, and those of his prodigiously rich, femme fatale psychopath, who was bankrolling him and helping him run the country.

The Señorita Dolorosa, they called her. Lady Pain, in his own tongue.

True, Richard was engineering the mass slaughter of tens of thousands of guiltless men but perhaps that was better than capitulating to Díaz and Dolorosa. Better to die on this battlefield than to labor, suffer, and succumb in her torture chambers, on her faux-Aztec altars, or in her prison mines and hacienda slave-labor fields.

Still, in the pit of his soul, Richard knew he was about to become a mass butcher on an incomprehensible scale. He wondered what his mother and father would think of him now. His mother was so tough she'd probably respect him for what he was doing. His father, who was a doctor, heavily invested in saving lives, would be less impressed. But his father would always have his back. Richard knew that too.

Still Richard was heartsick at what he was about to accomplish. In that regard, he was more like his father. He hated and dreaded the carnage to come.

* * *

"How have the new ammunition plants turned out?" General Ortega asked Richard, pulling him out of his reverie.

"We're all working round the clock, cranking out all that cordite-powder ammunition," Richard said.

"You conscripted one hell of a lot of women, children, and grumpy old men into those ammunition plants," the general said, "over thirty thousand in all. Most of them aren't real happy to be working those jobs."

"But they're getting paid and getting fed. They also know they could be slaving in rock quarries and hell-mines for the Señorita Dolorosa," Richard said. "And they know the work isn't forever."

"They also know it's for the battle to come," Mateo said, nodding slowly.

"You still dragooned a lot of people for those munitions plants," the general said. "You've conscripted a lot of forced labor yourself."

"We all did it," Mateo pointed out.

"And you've seen the math," Richard said. "You know how many workers it's taking to fabricate and load enough shells to stop an army as huge as the one that Díaz and the Señorita are deploying."

"And their combined force is growing larger," Mateo said. "Intelligence tells us tens of thousands of slave-soldiers are en route here even as we speak."

"If we don't stop them on this field," the general said, "we'll all meet again in the Señorita's infamous slave-mine, El Infierno de Plata [the Silver Inferno]."

"Or in hell," Mateo said.

"Whatever happens," the general said, "your ammunition plants are our last best hope, our only chance to defeat them."

"How do you like being a merchant of death?" Mateo said, laughing sardonically.

"I don't," Richard said under his breath, shaking his head.

"I never thought I'd have to help Richard run an ammunition plant," Mateo said. "That I'd have to help train technicians to distill nitric acid, turn cellulose into guncotton, and turn it all into high-powered smokeless gunpowder."

"And find the men and women to fill all those hundreds of thousands of old used Gatling shell casings with Ricardo's new smokeless cordite powder," the general said.

"Or put together all the buildings and the benches, the techs and the foremen, the equipment and materials," Mateo said.

"Maybe we've all become captains of industry," Richard observed.

"Captain of industry?" General Ortega asked. "What is that?"

"A turn of phrase," Richard said.

"Who originated it?" Mateo asked.

"Someone in the New York press, if memory serves," Richard said.

"New York's a long way from Sonora," Mateo noted.

"It might as well be on another planet," the general said.

"In another universe," Mateo added.

"The same New York reporters also coined the expression *merchants of death*," Richard said.

"I like that phrase better," Mateo said, smiling. "I plan on selling those Díazistes *mucho muerte* today."

"*También,*" the general said.

Richard studied the killing ground before him, clearly dispirited. "None of us ever knows what the future holds," he said quietly.

"Look on the bright side," Mateo said. "It's better than our enemy's murderous ministrations."

"Maybe this is preferable," Richard said, "but that doesn't mean I have to like what we're doing."

"Then welcome to the club," the major said.

The three men started back down the hill.

They had work to do.

Chapter 41

The hospital room had immaculately white walls and floor, and a bright coal-oil lamp hung over the comatose woman lying on the examining table. From the neck down, her body was covered by a white sheet.

Frank feared sepsis like the wrath of God and made everyone dress in clean white hospital gowns, even masks. Everyone and everything was swabbed with antiseptic.

Abdominal cancer is a painful, crushing disease, but when Frank learned that Rachel had returned to the Rancho and needed brain surgery, nothing and nobody could have held him back. He was soon palpating Rachel's head. Katherine, who had worked with Frank many times as a surgical nurse, was at his side.

"Clearly, the bones of Rachel's left temporal region are broken," Frank dictated.

An assistant, Judith Peters, was also dressed in a white cap and gown. She had a pad of paper and was taking notes on the operation. It would be complicated and Frank wanted a written record, which they could refer to when determining follow-up procedures and when they needed to retrace their steps. Among other things, they'd have to reassemble the pieces of skull they'd be cutting out and put everything back into place.

"The technical description for this area," Frank dictated to stenographer, "is the *temporal squamous portion of the skull.* We usually refer to it as the temple. As it so happens, this a very dangerous spot for the trauma to occur for a couple reasons. It is one of the thinnest areas in the skull and quite easy to fracture with a blunt instrument.

"Now some of the bone fragments," Frank continued, "are protruding out of the skin, making the break, by definition, a compound fracture. The fragments have torn the outer epidermis, and we have to assume that the dura mater covering the brain is also damaged. Given the power of the blow, it is also prudent to assume the brain itself is bruised.

"Additionally, it has an artery that rides immediately under the temporal bone known as the *middle meningeal artery.* The danger here is that when somebody fractures the skull with a blunt instrument, they often tear that artery, which can cause acute bleeding between the skull and the membrane that covers the brain, the dura mater. This bleeding coalesces into a rapidly expanding blood clot, which is called an *epidural hematoma,* which quickly becomes life-threatening.

"People with an epidural hematoma often have a moment of lucidity after the blow. Blow followed by *Damn, ouch, that really hurt* . . . then they quickly trail off into a coma. Once they slip into a coma, they often have a 'blown pupil.'" Frank lifted her left eyelid.

"The left eye is on the side of the injury. Note it is severely distended." He then lifted the right eyelid. "The right pupil, meanwhile, is normal. The reason for this is that the blood clot—the technical term for it is *hematoma*—is expanding. It's also pushing the temporal lobe—the specific part that is known as the *uncus*—against the third cranial nerve. This so-called oculomotor nerve is responsible for controlling our pupillary diameter. When it gets damaged or pressed up against the eye, the pupil goes to its default position by becoming widely dilated and points out laterally and down."

While Frank was still lifting the eyelid, he held a small, thin candle up to the eye, then moved it side to side, up and down.

"The eye cannot move vertically or horizontally," Frank said. "Instead it stares down to the left. This is due to impaired muscle functioning. The musculature, which opens the eyelid—known as the *levator palpebrae superioris*—is also impaired, causing the upper eyelid to droop. This is called *ptosis*. This condition is known as third nerve palsy, which means the patient is very close to death."

For the first time since he'd begun the examination, Frank looked up. He stared at his wife, Katherine. His eyes were sad, but his gaze told her he was in control.

Chapter 42

Richard stood in a fire trench staring out over the battlefield toward the distant specter of the Sinaloan-Chihuahuan army. All night the Sonoran artillery had hammered their enemy's big guns. Because they had their range bracketed and because of their new, more powerful and more efficient cordite powder, they had pounded the enemy's cannons to pieces. Díaz and the Señorita's much-vaunted artillery was a thing of the past.

The Sinaloan-Chihuahuan army, however, had been deeply bunkered in and had survived. As the sun started its flickering ascent above the eastern rim-rock, it was out of its trenches and dogtrotting over the first leg of the 900-yard battlefield toward Ortega and Mateo's dug-in force. Monument-size white concrete blocks, scattered across the field every 100 yards—marked 8 for 800, 7 for 700, all the way down to 1 for 100 yards—boldly enumerated the ranges for Sonora's artillery and their Gatling gunners.

As the first line of troops approached the white 800-yard blocks, Mateo barked out the order:

"EIGHT HUNDRED YARDS!"

"*¡LISTO!*" ["Ready!"]

Then: "*¡APUNTAR!*" ["Aim!"]

Then: "*¡FUEGO!*" ["Fire!"]

The orders echoed and were repeated up and down the Sonoran lines, as cannon and Gatling gun-fire exploded in one deafening sequence after another. Even though their so-called smokeless powder produced far less smoke than the previous, now-antiquated black powder explosive, it was not completely pellucid. It shrouded the Sonoran trenches in a light, whitish haze. So, through his scope, Richard could still study the effects of the barrage: The first ten rows of Díaz and the Señorita's soldiers walked into high-velocity Gatling fire, compounded by spectacularly accurate, shrapnel-filled, exploding artillery shells, blowing them all to kingdom come, their heads, arms, legs, weapons, the very ground beneath the soldiers' feet, spinning high into the air. Nonetheless, the officers behind them drove their suddenly diminished front ranks forward, dropping stragglers and mutineers with pistol shots and rifle rounds as well as blows from their wrist whips.

Meanwhile Sonora's cannoneers and Gatling gunners had reloaded and were preparing another coordinated fusillade.

At the 700-yard markers Mateo again shouted his orders:

"SEVEN HUNDRED YARDS!"

"*¡LISTO!*" ["Ready!"]

Then: "*¡APUNTAR!*" ["Aim!"]

Then: *"¡FUEGO!"* ["Fire!"]

More explosions. More smoke clouds. More re-loading.

Through his scope, Richard watched in horror as row upon row upon row of men were obliterated in stunning unison, as if they'd struck a trip wire. More body parts and more bloody earth were catapulted high above the field, even as the men behind them continued their juggernaut march into the omnivorous death machine, which Richard had designed, constructed, and was now helping to implement.

Again, Sonora's gunners reloaded.

Again, Mateo shouted the orders.

Again, Díazistes died.

Six hundred yards.

More orders.

More death.

Five hundred yards.

More orders.

More death.

Four hundred yards.

More orders.

More death.

Then Sinaloa's and Chihuahua's much diminished ranks were reaching the 300-yard range markers.

"LIGHT FUSES!" Mateo shouted.

The order thundered up and down the Sonora ranks.

The high-speed fuses to the first series of shrapnel-packed, half-buried bombs were lit, and Richard watched as the fuses flickered quickly up the field toward the approaching horde. The Sinaloa troops were now tightly packing the area between the 300- and

400-yard concrete markers, not realizing that they were standing atop one vast, massive minefield.

To trigger the entire field required only that the first line of mines were set off. The rest of the minefield detonated sympathetically, and so the entire field of mines—a hundred yards wide and a half mile long—went off, igniting an almost simultaneous series of blasts, the emerging sheets of flame swelling into a series of red-orange fireballs. Those quickly converged into one rising, immensely distended dirigible of wildly furious flames, sucking up smoke, tons of earth, endless fragments of soldiers, guns and clothing included, levitating high above the battlefield. The thermal energy emanating off the firestorm engulfing the enemy's forces, was overwhelming. Richard felt it so intensely, it seemed to him as if all the furnaces in Satan's hell had exploded. The consequent conflagration was one massive force-twelve hurricane of heat. Roaring out of that Hellmouth in one blazingly hot *WHOOSH*, it hit Richard in a single overpowering rush, almost knocking him and his fellow gunners to their knees.

Slowly, the flaming debris fell from the sky, seemingly in slow motion, and the whitish smoke began to clear. A third of the Sinaloan army had survived, but now they stood stock-still, as if frozen in place, paralyzed by sheer, irresistible terror. Even the officers to the rear were immobilized by shock and horror. Turning in their traces, the troops finally fled the field at a dead run, the officers behind them too frightened to stop them. They turned and were running as well.

At which point Mateo shouted: *"¡FUEGO A DISCRE-CIÓN!"* ["Fire at will!"]

The Gatlings and cannonry opened up with a vengeance, firing as fast as the officers and their men could keep the guns loaded. The fragmentation mortar shells were now dropping on the Sinaloa troops in the front of their escape route, while the Gatling gunners ripped through those at the rear.

Mateo was thrilled beyond belief. He clapped Richard repeatedly on the shoulder, forcing an *abrazo* on him, all the while screaming:

"YOU DID IT, YOUNG RICARDO! YOU DID IT!"

But Richard was thunderstruck by the violence, blood, and savagery of his assault. All he could do was stare at that field of death and think over and over:

What have you done? What the hell have you done?

Chapter 43

Richard was not the only one who'd studied the battle in dismay. The Señorita Dolorosa stood on a high rocky hill behind the Sinaloa lines. She'd witnessed the slaughter through a telescope, as did her three comrades—Méjico's illustrious El Presidente Porfirio Díaz and his two newest patrons and investors, the ultrawealthy but shockingly ruthless British billionaire James P. Sutherland and his equally rich, equally violent, yet gloriously gorgeous consort, the flaming-haired beauty Judith McKillian.

The Señorita, who'd been outspokenly skeptical of the battle's outcome, had opposed inviting foreign guests, and she'd clearly been right. Sonora had utterly extirpated her and Díaz's forces, and their annihilation was clearly demoralizing their guests. Díaz had hoped to amaze them with a transcendent victory over Sonora and then fleece these foreign financiers out of as much of their ill-gotten lucre as he knew how. And Méjico needed investors as unscrupulous as these two. Most magnates, no matter how mercenary, were loath to sink their capital into economies fueled almost entirely by bloody oppression and barbaric slavery. If nothing else, they viewed such economies as "unstable."

Unfortunately, the massacre they had just witnessed would discourage any sane person from funding any projects presented by Díaz or the Lady Dolorosa.

Still the Señorita continued to avert her gaze from the smoking killing-ground in front of her and instead studied her companions, hoping that if she ignored the fiasco that might somehow, miraculously, make it . . . *go away*. Against her better judgment, the Señorita had allowed Díaz to invest some of her vast fortune in that battle, so she had in part underwritten this macabre nightmare.

Well, those were pesos she'd never see again.

So instead of contemplating past mistakes, she tried to focus on her surroundings—on those around her, including Díaz. It was a technique she'd worked on for decades, and she'd found it relieved stress.

She casually noted Díaz's broad, sweeping mustache and sharply pressed generalissimo's uniform, sagging under a battalion's worth of heavy, gold-and-gem-encrusted decorations—the most meretricious medals the Señorita had ever seen. She wondered whom Díaz thought he was impressing with those tedious trinkets. Did he think anyone really cared about Méjico's laughably ludicrous wars?

Her eyes drifted over to Judith McKillian, whose long, flowing, dazzlingly red hair hung down past her waist. She had the purest buttermilk skin the Señorita had ever seen, and her emerald eyes twinkled with malicious mischief. She had on black riding britches, shockingly tight around her posterior, her pants legs tucked into a matching pair of high-heeled, thigh-high, brilliantly burnished riding boots. She wore a jet-black blouse of sheerest shantung. She casually but fiercely cracked the tops of her boots with a hippopotamus-hide, ebony horsewhip.

The Señorita decided that she liked McKillian. She understood her intuitively. This was a woman she could do business with.

She then turned to Sutherland. She already knew him by his reprehensible reputation. He was, as in his photographs, flamboyantly attired in black twill riding breeches, which were tucked into matching, thigh-high Wellington boots. A ruffled silk shirt and a bowler felt hat, both blazingly bloodred, completed his ensemble.

However, he possessed one anomaly. The left side of his head, instead of hair, was composed of a bone-white swath of slick, shimmering keloid, the densest scar tissue known to humankind.

The Señorita knew the history behind that garish disfigurement. Everyone did. It was widely reported, often in the international press, that the financial titan had once hired a gang of bounty hunters and had attempted to hunt down and kill Torn Slater for the sake of fame, glory, and filthy lucre. He'd intended to impale the outlaw with his longbow and his quiverful of steel, tri-bladed broadheads. After decapitating him, he'd planned to tour the world and perform his murder of Slater before millions of adoring fans. He planned to make millions more—except now his name would be up in lights and he'd be celebrated in all the royal courts and best establishments.

It was not to be. Instead, Slater had turned the tables on the billionaire. After killing his men, Slater had half scalped Sutherland and all but burned him alive.

According to much rumor and legend, Slater had now become Sutherland's idée fixe—so much so that he'd promised Díaz and the Señorita unlimited funding for their slave-labor haciendas and prison mines if they would assist him in capturing the outlaw and then help Sutherland exact his revenge on the outlaw.

Well, today's battle was finally over. The sun was turning a brilliant crimson as it languidly descended through the dust and gun smoke toward the distant rimrock in the west. The haze of battle hung over the field below like a miasma out of Dante's *Inferno* or Homer's Dead Land, the shrieks of the wounded still agonizingly audible. A score or so of vast vulture-swirling vortexes were spiraling above the dead and dying—the largest assemblage of carrion birds the Señorita had ever heard of, let alone witnessed. Quite frankly, she would have found the spectacle stirring—even physically arousing—were it not for the fact that those were *her troops* shattered and destroyed before her. Even worse, they'd been blown to bits by a force one-tenth their size. It now seemed that Sonora had murdered her dreams of new riches and a radically expanded power along with the tens of thousands of her dead *soldados* that they'd sent to hell today.

"Looks like you backed the wrong horse, ducks," Sutherland was saying with snide cynicism in fluent Castilian Spanish to the Señorita. "Maybe I should be bankrolling Sonora instead. As you may have heard, I desperately want to apprehend a notorious brigand named Outlaw Torn Slater and need some assistance.

Well, he's wanted in that state too. I'll bet Sonora would help me bring him to bay—in exchange for a few well-greased palms and a well-placed investment or two."

"Never fear. We have only begun, my friend," Díaz said with a truly spectacular smile. "When we are done, Sonora and your much-reviled freebooter, Outlaw Torn Slater, will grovel at your feet."

"Do you share El Presidente's intrepid optimism, Señorita?" Judith McKillian asked.

"Oh, I promise you," the Señorita said. "Today was nothing. When we are done, we will see Sonora's armies driven before us, hunted down, and exterminated— *soldado* by *soldado* by *soldado*, their women and children beaten, ravaged, and sold into our brothels, their babies bathed in blood, bawling in terror, helpless and trembling in our hands. For what Sonora did to us today, our hate will never end and our revenge never cease—not until the moon turns to blood, the sun dies blind, and the deathless stars, roaring in horror and screaming with pain . . . *expire*."

But more than her words, the look in the Señorita's eyes were what got to Sutherland, Judith McKillian, and Díaz—eyes vicious as crucifixion, vindictive as Satan scorned, and fathomless as hell's darkest pit.

"Well done, my dear," Judith McKillian said, genuinely touched. "You and I shall be *muy simpática amigas*, heartfelt allies in the much-deserved obliteration of these Sonoran *bastardos*. We will make them curse their mothers for giving them birth. I know it, feel it, so please count me in. In truth, I have never liked women—I have never liked anyone all that much—but, in you, I feel I have found a true sister.

Tell me how much you need. I'll write the check at once—any amount you can name, as high as you can count. *Por favor.* Whatever you need. I know about these things. Trust me. This will work out . . . *splendidly.*"

At that moment Sutherland shuddered with something that might have vaguely resembled pity—had he been capable of pity—for the people of Sonora.

But then the realization that the Señorita would also help him do these things to Slater brought him back to his senses. Yes, he would go through with his plans to back Díaz and the Señorita. Yes, he had made the right decision.

And Slater would suffer the tortures of the damned.

Turning to the Señorita, he gave her a long, slow, meticulously appraising look.

Damn, she was one fine-looking woman. Muy bonita, *as these damnable* mejicanos *would say.*

Chapter 44

Twilight in Sonora.

Richard stared out over the battlefield. Miraculously, there had been survivors. Men who were grotesquely wounded, but still alive. Screaming in agony, they begged:

"¡Agua! ¡Agua!" ["Water! Water!"]

Throughout the day they'd sweltered on that blood-ground in a hellish miasma of drifting smoke and dust, suffering in their pain and misery. All the while thousands of vultures wheeled above them.

The Sonoran forces had taken losses too. Men up and down their trenches were crying out for help or simply lying inert there, blown to pieces. A Gatling gunner named Cesar had mowed down line after line of the Señorita's men—until one of her crack snipers, armed with a scoped rifle, had sighted in on him, putting a fragmenting round through his chest, blowing a hole out his back a foot in diameter. Richard, impassive, inured now to so much slaughter, glanced at Cesar. The man lay less than thirty feet away from him in a pile of his own entrails and a coagulating pool of his own gore, his arms and legs spread-eagled, his sightless eyes fixed eerily on Richard, flies swarming above his face.

Averting his eyes from the dead man, Richard studied his own handiwork on the battlefield before him. Vultures rode the desert's dusk thermals, wheeling on massive wingspreads, studying the *fiesta de sangre*, the feast of blood below. Slowly, clusters of birds began their torturous descent toward the ravaged remains spread across the parched plain. They would feast through the night, their macabre, eternally patient vigil finally coming to an end.

To Richard's horror he suddenly felt a sick, crawling sense of pride at what he'd done. It was all there before him: The thousands upon thousands of dead and dying, washed in each other's blood, their sobbing cries and curses; the buzzing clouds of flies over them; the thousands of fallen horses; the funnel clouds of carrion birds; the shimmering pall of thick dust and creamy smoke drifting over the killing ground; the scores of thousands of forgotten rifles scattered everywhere on the ground.

Richard had studied the art of war—the theory, science, and practice of killing men en masse—at West Point for four years, and the education had clearly not been wasted on him. In fact, he'd shown a talent and aptitude for massacre, which he had never dreamed he possessed in such stunning abundance. He wondered what his professors at the Point would think if they could now see what their teachings had produced and what he, their student, had wrought.

Would they be proud of what he had done?

Was he proud of what he'd done?

Frankly, Richard did not know.

A few men were entering the killing-ground now. Some of them were carrying water bags for the wounded, but mostly they were there to scavenge weapons and ammunition. Sinaloa's crack cadre of snipers quickly picked off three of them.

A hundred Sonoran snipers returned the shots with a murderously accurate volley. All sniping ceased.

Mateo walked up to Richard, who asked him:

"The Sinaloan troops don't want us to help their comrades?"

"No, young Ricardo, they would rather see us dead. For Díaz and the Señorita Dolorosa will never let the battle end. They will never stop coming after us."

Richard nodded silently.

"Even worse, now that Sinaloa knows what we have, what we can do," Mateo said, "they will rebuild and resupply. They will match us gun for gun, round for round, and in terms of troop strength, they will overwhelmingly outman us."

"So it will only get worse."

"*Verdad.* There will be much bloodier conflicts to come, and, for us to prevail, we will need more cordite, more ordnance, more provisions, more pesos, more everything—and more men, if we can find them. That is why our men are already out there scavenging this field of blood, recovering arms and ammunition, anything of value. Our weakness is that we are and will always be but a few, a handful compared to their infinite, never-ending battalions."

"I don't think I'm going to like this story," Richard said.

Clapping Richard on the back, Mateo said: "Buck up, my friend. You did well. I am proud of you, and tonight we will drink deep—toast our victory and drink to friends living and friends dead. In fact, for the next week, we shall celebrate. You've earned it. But never delude yourself—I know you won't—that the battle is over. It has only just begun."

PART X

Chapter 45

It was past midnight when the tall gringo entered the hacienda of Ramon Guzman, one of Sinaloa's more successful bankers. They did not exchange pleasantries, and he walked Slater back into his personal office without a word.

The two men had done business for over a decade. Guzman had occasionally sold Slater financial information—word about the time and place of large-scale payroll shipments, major money transfers, and sizable bullion deposits. He had always been reliable and was responsible for Slater's biggest scores south of the border—and even a few scores in the American Southwest. The information was so good that Slater often went fifty-fifty with him, and each man had so much dirt on the other that Slater knew Guzman could never turn him in—not without going to prison himself. Now Guzman had gotten word to him that he had a deal so lucrative Slater had to hear about it in person, and frankly, Slater could not have been more pleased. He needed a big score.

Guzman wore a white linen suit, a cream-colored cotton shirt, and an expensive red tie of French silk. He had hard eyes, dark skin, and thinning gray hair. Seated behind a massive oak desk, he was surrounded by book-lined wall shelves and portraits of Mexico's greatest historical figures, including Benito Juárez and Porfirio Díaz. His spacious bay windows overlooked a lush, moonlit, tree-filled *plazuela* featuring sparkling fountains and flamboyant flower gardens.

The director of the Mexicano Minería y Banco Central, Guzman was responsible for the banking and shipping of most of the country's gold as well as minting its coined currency. In Méjico, paper money had never had much intrinsic value, and gold coins were the only currency that had ever been worth anything.

Guzman pointed toward a leather armchair, but Slater ignored it. He simply stood off in the corner and away from the windows. He studied Guzman in silence. Slater was wearing his usual black, flat-brimmed, flat-crowned Plainsman hat. His collarless shirt matched the hat, and his Levi's were faded and frayed. His boots were heeled with Chihuahua rowels. Guzman watched them clink on his polished hardwood floors, and it annoyed him to no end even though he tried hard not to let the outlaw see it. He also tried to avoid Slater's flat black eyes and his unwavering stare. Instead Guzman focused on Slater's crisscrossed leather bandoliers, filled with .44-40 pistol-rifle cartridges, as well as his bullet-studded belt, on which was holstered a heavy ivory-handled .44 Colt. Another .44 with a worn walnut grip was stuffed in his pants. Slater held a sawed-off, double-barreled, twelve-gauge shotgun in his right fist, the barrel resting casually on his shoulder. His left thumb was hooked under the belt near the Colt under his belt. That thumb was always near that Colt.

"That, compadre, is one big-bore gun you're carrying," Guzman observed, nodding toward the sawed-off.

Slater still said nothing, all the while gazing on Guzman with dark, bottomless, utterly inscrutable eyes.

"I have an opportunity for you," Guzman said. "Not your usual line of work but highly lucrative. A bandit gang, Los Lobos Duros y Locos, is about to put my bank out of business. You can hunt them down and retrieve our gold, ¿*es verdad*? [is it true?]"

Slater said nothing.

"You help me out, you will have not only money— much money—but a letter of transit, a letter authorizing you to represent the Bank of Méjico. You will be able to travel anywhere in Méjico from now on with impunity—without fear of the police, federales, or any other law enforcement group. For a man with so many enemies, such carte blanche would be desirable indeed, no?"

His guest said nothing, and Guzman looked away. He always had difficulty dealing with the man, but then Torn Slater made most people uncomfortable.

Slater had recently taken on a nickname—El Macho. Everyone called him "Macho" or "El Macho," which meant "stud mule" in *mejicano*. Many *mejicano* men admired his namesake for its meanness, intractability, fearlessness, and its propensity for brutalizing jennies and mares during sexual congress—acts of coition so violent that they sometimes cost the females their lives. Moreover, since all mules are sterile, these conjunctions produced no offspring.

Men who fucked women to death and produced no offspring were much admired by those men subscribing to the *mejicano* cult of machismo.

But while some in Mexico viewed Slater's nickname as a compliment, others, of course, despised the code that the mule represented. Many people—including most well-educated, highly civilized women—thought that the animal embodied nothing more than stark male barbarism and that machismo was a code of conduct that had never honored—or even sentimentalized—women and children.

Many who knew Slater claimed he was the incarnation of macho evil. Throughout Méjico that country's law enforcement officials circulated posters featuring his unflattering likeness, under which were printed in large type the words:

Outlaw Slater:
Se Busca
Muerto
[Wanted Dead]
REWARD: 80,000 PESOS.

The price on his head was always the same: Eighty thousand pesos or $20,000 in hard *americano* dollars. Not that Slater was in any way dismayed or deterred by the posters. Men had tried to kill him his whole life long. He cared nothing about the threat they posed, and he cared even less about what anyone thought of

him. He was only offended that Díaz did not offer
more.

And anyway the fact that he couldn't spend the
$150,000 that he'd made from his last bank heist—
which was still interred near the hell-mine that had
buried Moreno alive—had forced Slater to find new
sources of revenue. True, he'd taken $15,000 from
Moreno's gold mine cave-in, but he'd given that to
the man's family in Durango. In the old days, he'd
have just hit another bank or train. Recently, however,
Díaz had begun posting detachments of federales
around those institutions. He wouldn't do that forever, but for the time being, robbing those places
wasn't worth the risk.

In some ways, hunting banditos would be a come-
down from robbing banks and trains, but times were
hard. And anyway the banditos that he'd be killing
massacred villages, stole from the poor, and raped
women. Slater owed *hideputas* like that *nada*.

"How much you lose on this last year?" Slater asked.

Again, Guzman averted his eyes.

"Over four hundred thousand pesos—a hundred
thousand dollars in New Arizona currency."

"I take the first twenty-five thousand dollars. You
can have whatever's left."

"You get ten thousand dollars, and that is the most
we've ever paid out."

"Then it's *adiós—vaya con Dios y diablo* [good-bye
and go with God and the devil]."

Slater started to depart. He was halfway to the door,
when Guzman said:

"Espera." ["Wait."]

Slater gave him a silent, backward glance.

"We've tried several of your less expensive . . . colleagues, señor."

"And . . . ?"

"They're all *muerte* [dead]. These hombres robbing us are *muy duros*. Still I'm not authorized by our board to give you more than . . . twenty thousand dollars."

Slater let out a long, slow breath. "To get your gold back, I have to kill them—all of them—and then retrieve the gold. Afterward I got to transport it a long way—through more bandit country."

"That is your business, señor."

"How long has this gang been robbin' your gold trains?"

Guzman stared down at his desk. "As long as I've worked here—over ten years."

"What have they taken from you during that period? I'd guess five hundred thousand dollars in yanqui dinero."

"More. But that's why the Central Bank can't afford to pay your . . . rate."

"How much these boys gonna take from you over the next ten years?"

"A lot."

"Not if I kill 'em, so I'll be protecting all those future shipments. I'll also return to you some of that past money they stole. Write my expenses off against losses past, present, and future. It's what you bankers call *am-or-tizing*. It'll be worth that extra dinero."

"All I can offer is twenty thousand dollars."

"Since you're haggling, my cut is up to thirty-five thousand dollars. Tell them board directors the extra ten is for the heads of them *hideputas* [sons of whores] who been robbin' you blind. Tell them you can spread it out over all them future *mucho-dinero* gold shipments y'all be makin'. With impunity, to use your phrase."

"The board won't go for it."

"Then it's their funeral. 'Cause them *bastardos*, like you said, are fixin' to rob you out of business. Do that, they put your whole country out of business. The Señorita Dolorosa won't be pleased, least of all with your directors or . . . *you*. And I'll make sure she finds out you could have stopped those bandits and didn't."

Slater had no intention of doing any such thing, but he knew the effect that the Señorita's name had on people in Méjico, and it worked again. The banker shuddered at the name of the Lady Dolorosa.

"Where are you staying?"

"I'll be in the hotel one day—probably in the hotel bar. After that, I'm gone."

The banker cleared his throat nervously. "How would we know whether you . . . *eliminated* . . . our future problem?"

"Oh, I'll bring back proof of death, meaning their heads. You can count on it. I know you ain't payin' me squat without them."

Guzman shook violently, involuntarily—as if someone had stepped on his grave . . . his open grave.

As Slater left, his rowels clinked and scraped irritatingly on Guzman's hardwood floor all the way out.

Chapter 46

Stretched out on the operating table, Rachel was surrounded by a man and four women dressed in surgical gowns, masks, and sterile gloves. Dr. Frank had just bored a dime-size hole into her right temporal bone with a precision-made surgical hand drill.

"Nurse Murphy, please sterilize the area again." While the attractive blond-haired surgical assistant swabbed Rachel's temple with iodine, Frank said: "We have to get that clot out of there now. Since the fracture is compounded with some fragments protruding through the epidermis, other parts of the injury are depressed, putting pressure on the brain. Our only course in that case was to trephine the anterior cranium—which we've done—remove the bone fragments, and put them back together later. The large fragments we soaked in sodium chloride disinfectant solution and reassembled. The larger fragments we have already wired together. If the dura is ripped, we must repair it. The patient has most likely sustained at least one subdural hematoma, which may require postoperative treatment. Infections, seizures, and abscess formation also have to be watched out for in the postoperative phase."

"So what do we do next?" Katherine said.

"We have no choice," Frank said. "There's serious cranial pressure building up, and we have to vent it. I'm surprised she's survived this long."

The tall, blond-haired nurse handed Fran a trephining kit.

"Nurse Murphy," Frank said to her, "sterilize those instruments. Have your colleagues come back with Posey restraints and get the anesthesiologist. The best surgical anesthetic we have is chloroform. For post-op we'll use morphine."

A diminutive brunette in a white surgical gown entered.

"Nurse Roberts," Frank said, "get me some antiseptic, shampoo, some shaving soap, and a razor."

"I can shave her for you," Nurse Roberts said.

"I'm doing this one myself," Frank said. "I'm worried about those bone fragments and hate touching them. As I said before, sepsis and abscesses will still be critical problems, assuming we pull this surgery off."

"Frank, I once saw you take a jagged grenade fragment out of the middle of a soldier's brain," Katherine said, "and he lived. If you could do that for him, you can patch up our daughter's skull."

"I hope you're right," Frank said. "Let's get on this. If Rachel is to have a chance, we have to work fast."

Katherine had earlier swabbed the area surrounding the hole and the instruments with iodine. Rachel was already sedated and secured with poseys.

"The hooked-blade scalpel, please," Frank said.

With its sharp point and curved edge, he cut a question mark–shaped incision in front of Rachel's ear. Taking a deep breath, Frank then pulled the scalp away from the forehead. Beneath the skin a linear fracture clearly transited the skull. Blood seeped up through the crack.

"Stenographer," Frank said, "we will need the notes on this operation for future post-op procedures."

"I'm ready, Doctor."

"All right. I am now about to make a hole in the skull just above the zygomatic arch. In case anyone is curious, if you stick your finger in your ear, the zygomatic arch is the arch of bone immediately to the front of that. It then progresses forward to form your cheekbone. Once I make that hole, a burst of blood will come out. So this is the life-saving move. The blood now comes out of the hole and it will no longer push against the brain. Nurse Murphy, you will stick your suction cup in there and aspirate any remaining blood."

Frank made the hole, the blood came out, and Nurse Murphy suctioned out what was left.

"Now, blood is not all liquid," Frank said. "Some of the blood will be congealed and will still be pushing on the brain. It is a bright red, tough, gelatinous material that is very adherent. So our next move is to 'turn a bone flap'—make a circular window of bone with a bone saw. When I have enough room, I have to remove that gelatinous blood and then get the clot. I'll have to mobilize it away from the dura. I can use the blunt backside of the forceps for that maneuver."

After Frank was finished, he took a deep breath and announced:

"Now that the blood and the clot are all out and the pressure is off the brain, we need to cauterize the middle meningeal artery. So Nurse Murphy has heated the tweezer tips, they are red-hot, and I will close them around the artery stumps. In all likelihood, I will be performing this procedure several times."

Twenty minutes later, they were staring at the cauterized meningeal artery.

"We must now," Frank said wearily, "close the muscle—everything—with horsehair sutures. I hope and pray it'll all be good after sixty years from now."

Chapter 47

Mateo and Richard were sitting in the officers' mess. Empty tequila bottles and plates full of leftover *pollo*, beans, and tortillas were scattered around the hundred-odd tables. Forty or fifty drunken officers were still hanging around, laughing, offering toasts to war, sex, death, pesetas, cojones, and . . . *El Diablo*. But somehow Mateo and Richard, despite trying as valiantly as they knew how, could not get drunk.

"You told me out on the battlefield," Richard said, "that this victory meant nothing, that the real war has just begun."

"*Es verdad, amigo*. Díaz and the Señorita now know what we can do."

"I'm told *también* that the Señorita's slave-labor silver mine is a bottomless trove of infinite riches," Richard observed mordantly.

"That is true, my young friend, and if there is hell, it is not in the hereafter but in that Pit—in the Infierno de Plata [the Silver Inferno]."

"And so we will make more cordite powder," Richard said.

"But of course. You saw us strip the Díaziste dead of thousands of rifles and tens of thousands of rounds of ammunition," Mateo said, nodding, "and we have gathered up all our Gatling guns' brass shell casings. We can reuse them. Thanks to your munitions factories, we can reload those casings, and after we rehabilitate our confiscated weapons, we can load them as well."

"So we will have even more weapons and more ammunition," Richard said.

"Díaz and the Señorita will ransack Méjico, rounding up more *indios* and more mestizos, then pressing them into their military."

"Still, our men are motivated," Richard said, "and theirs aren't. Their *soldados* have almost no training. They barely know how to fire a gun. They died like dogs on our wire."

"Whatever the case, we have no choice," Mateo said. "We have to fight."

"But can we ultimately win?" Richard asked. "Against so many men, against so much money, against so much wickedness and power?"

"We can hope," Mateo said softly, giving Richard a clap on the shoulder.

Again, Richard was skeptical.

"What's wrong, amigo?" Mateo asked. "You do not believe in hope."

Richard allowed Mateo a small smile. "I believe there is infinite hope."

"But?" Mateo asked.

"But not for us."

"Come, amigo, all is not lost," Mateo said, suddenly laughing, attempting to jolly Richard out of his dark mood. "There is much to hope for. Don't the poets tell us that we live in hope?"

"Yes, and we die in despair," Richard said, repeating an old trope.

"But we will not die sober," Mateo said, laughing heartily and grinning irrepressibly.

The man next to Mateo passed out drunkenly and fell off his chair. Mateo grabbed his half-full tequila bottle and poured Richard and himself each a full glass.

"Come, compadre," Mateo said, laughing, "if I teach you nothing in our much-maligned land, I will teach you how to drink."

"I know how to drink."

"Like a gringo. I will teach you to drink like a *mejicano*."

"And that is a good thing?"

"In Méjico, it most assuredly is. For in Méjico, to drink like a *mejicano* is often the only hope any of us have."

Chapter 48

A tall man with wide shoulders on a big gray was leading a pack-mule strung by its mecate up a quiet mountain trail when a series of earsplitting yowls ripped the morning stillness apart.

Only jaguars scream like that, Slater thought, swinging down from his horse. Slater went forward to investigate.

Fifty or so yards up-trail, hidden behind a big boulder and a dozen or so trees, Slater could tell that the big cat was going insane. Slater doubted he could do much about the feline—except send it to an early grave. His gray and the pack animals, however, were a more immediate problem. Big cats scared horses and mules halfway to death, and Slater's stock was rearing up and attempting to bolt. Lashing their reins and pack line to thick, heavy tree limbs, Slater also tied the lead mule tightly to a tree trunk. He did the same with his mount. He didn't unhitch the mules' pack saddles. Their panniers held almost nothing. The man had been tracking the bandit gang all month and expected to load the mules' crossbucks with canvas sacks of gold coins and yanqui dollars.

After he secured his stock, he unbuttoned his tan duster, rolled it up, and stuffed it into one of the empty panniers. He had also expected it to be cool this high up, but so far it wasn't. The scenery was changing, however, with almost surreal rapidity. His base camp had been surrounded by cactus and yucca, maguey and mesquite. He was now riding into stands of spruce and, higher up, Slater could spot ponderosa pine. His dirty Levi's, dark shirt, black Plainsman hat, and even blacker boots now felt hot and humid.

All the while, the big cat's yowling continued unabated.

Unlimbering both his lever-action Henry and the sawed-off shotgun from their saddle sheaths, he gripped the scattergun in his right fist. Slinging the rifle under his left shoulder, he began circling the huge boulder, moving toward the sounds of the hysterical cat.

As he got closer to the battle, the animal's snarling screeches and guttural groans blended with the sounds of physical brawling. He eased back the sawed-off's double-clicking hammers and raised the barrel, his fingers tightening on the outside of the trigger guard. Reaching the other side of the boulder, he quickly took cover behind a nearby tree.

On the trail in front of the boulder a full-grown, jet-black jaguar, nearly eight feet from nose to rump and with a tail over six feet in length, writhed in the coils of a twenty-foot *Eunectes murinus*—a green, black-spotted anaconda.

Jesus God.

The big cat kicked and clawed, but the snake's death lock was iron tight. The only time the anaconda eased its hold for even a split second was so he could gather himself up and then crush the life out of the cat with even greater power. With each squeeze, Slater could hear the jaguar's ribs cracking. Toward the end, after one particularly agonizing vise turn, the big cat glanced at Slater. He could see her amber, vertically distended pupils pinning him with incomprehensible malice: Even in death, its eyes radiated a defiance of almost demonic dimensions.

No, Slater thought grimly but with no small admiration, *the big snake might kill you, even eat you whole, but nothing will intimidate or even humble you—not even death.*

Slater decided he liked the big jaguar.

Slowly, the anaconda's head circled around, and, levitating over its convoluted coils, it began its inexorable descent over the animal's upper extremities. The double-hinged, impossibly wide jaws opened like Hellgate, then closed over the big cat's yowling head and blazing eyes.

Suddenly, a black cub—no more than eighteen inches in length—exploded out of nowhere, jumped up and over his mother, over the spiraling coils, and leaped straight at the python's face. The snake's jaws were sunk into the mother's head, but now the cub—screaming and scratching crazily, its taloned paws windmilling over the snake's gaping jaws—was slashing the snake's eyes like a blizzard of straight razors, blood spurting out the sides of the snake's face and along the edges of its furious orbs. Dropping to his haunches, catching his breath, the cub prepared for another attack, while the snake peered at him through blood-filled eyes, insane with rage. Releasing the head of the dying jaguar, the anaconda suddenly seized, enveloped, and swallowed the mother's tiny offspring.

Now Slater could see—through a series of cascading neck bulges—the cub making a terror-racked odyssey through the anaconda's gullet. From his deranged thrashing and still-audible yowls, Slater could tell this was not a pilgrim's progress the animal wished to take.

He decided to deal himself in. Since the python was now fixated on the moribund jaguar and returning to its meal, Slater walked up behind the snake's head and aimed the right barrel of the twelve-gauge Greener at the back of his head. He was less than a foot away from it when he shot the python's cranium off its body and into bloody oblivion with a load of double-ought buck.

He did not have time to get his ax, not if he was going to save the cub. Finding its location—about a foot and a half from the missing head—he placed the left barrel a half a foot below the baby cat and blew the rest of the snake's neck free from its body. Hacking away sinew and skin with his thirteen-inch bowie, he unhesitatingly reached into the beast's belly and pulled the flailing feline out by the scruff of his neck.

Holding him up off the ground by his hind legs, he shook him hard, dislodging the snake's internal residue out of his throat. Sluicing the cub off with half a belt-canteen of water, he then wiped him clean with his black neck bandanna. Again lifting him up, Slater studied his face.

"Well, little buddy," he said, "you've been in the belly of the beast and returned to tell your story. What did you learn? How did you like the trip?"

But the cub said nothing; instead he grew strangely quiescent. Staring at Slater not with anger or fear but with the steadiest, calmest, most intensely curious eyes the man had ever seen, the cub began to purr. When Slater took him into his arms, his purrs swelled into a heavy, throbbing, almost motorlike hum, the cub's whole body vibrating violently against his chest.

"Now what am I going to do with you?" Slater asked his newfound friend with a feeling of genuine bemusement. "What in hell's name am I going to do with you?"

PART XI

*When I am done with young Ricardo, the earth will
bleed, the stars darken and die, and Satan,
trembling at my feet, will plead with me for . . . pity.*
—LA SEÑORITA DOLOROSA

Chapter 49

Katherine, Frank, Eléna, and Antonio sat on the
front porch. Frank and Katherine were in the big
swing, Eléna and Antonio in rocking chairs. A bloodred sun was sinking below the distant rimrock lining
the horizon.

Not only had Rachel's recovery been miraculous,
Frank's cancer seemed to be in remission. In fact, he
was decked out in white surgical garb, having just
finished performing an appendectomy on one of the
hired hands. The two women and Antonio, having
spent the day branding heifers, were attired in Levi's,
work shirts, and boots.

"You know I don't approve of your insane plan,"
Frank said.

"Look, Frank, you and Rachel are doing fine. To
the extent that you need help, hell, you can look after
each other."

"But you want to go to Mexico?" Frank said.
"Mexico?"

"Rachel believes that Richard was conscripted

against his will into the Sonoran rurales. Eléna and Antonio agree. They even say they can find the rurale officer who abducted him—a major named Mateo. I speak Spanish. We have money. The Sonoran military always needs money. Maybe we can get him out of there and bring him back. Eléna and Antonio know Sonora inside out and know lots of officers. I just can't stand here and do nothing."

"But Sonora is embroiled in a bloody war with Sinaloa and Chihuahua. They just had a battle down there in which thirty thousand men were killed and wounded. Díaz and the Lady Dolorosa are involved. They're some of the bloodiest people on earth. You'll be riding into hell."

"Which means Sonora is even more desperate for funding," Katherine said. "Which means they need weaponry—repeating rifles, Gatling gun cartridges, field pieces—like we need air to breathe. We can cut a deal and get Richard back. I know it in my bones."

Antonio nodded. "I served in the federales for ten years. Down there everything has a price. Also Richard has taught them everything he knows. They can get along without him."

"I know Mateo," Eléna said. "He always had a thing for me. He'll at least talk with us."

"I'll play on his greed," Katherine said.

Rachel came out to join them. Having just overheard them, she pulled up a bentwood armchair. "I know Mateo too. He fractured my cranium with his quirt's leaded stock. As far as I'm concerned, he owes me. He doesn't give us my brother back, I'll give him some of what he gave me. I'll crack *his skull* for him. So you aren't going down there without me."

Katherine stood. "Rachel, I'd consider bringing you along if this were six months from now and you could ride all day and night. But you can't, and your coming wouldn't be fair to Richard. The first time you got bucked off a horse and hit your head, our expedition would come to an abrupt end. Richard would be the one who'd suffer."

"You don't get it, Mother."

"Don't get what?" Katherine was growing angry with her daughter.

"I can make Mateo listen. You can't. Eléna, tell my mother how hardheaded that bastard is."

Eléna was forced to nod her assent. "He is *uno hombre duro* [a hard hombre]," she said.

"You can't ride," Katherine said.

"I've been riding Gunfire. I don't see you getting up on him."

That froze Katherine. "What?" she finally stammered.

"When you and Dad weren't around, I saddled him up and rode him all around the llano."

"How many times did he buck you off before you took off on your crazy trip to Mexico?" her father asked.

"Plenty of times. But that's why I've been riding him. I needed to prove to you two that I'm ready to go, that I can handle a horse as well as any of you."

"All you've proven is that you're mentally ill," Frank said, "that Mateo's buttstock destroyed your mind."

"And I'm not letting you three go down there without me."

"There's no way you're stopping us," Katherine said.

"We'll see."

"Try it," Katherine said, "and I swear before God I'll take a knotted plowline to you."

"You don't understand," Rachel said. "He's my brother. I talked him into going to Méjico, and *I* took him down there. *I* was responsible for him being there, and all *I* did was get him dragooned into the bloodiest war in Mexico's history."

"Getting your skull fractured again won't help anyone," Frank said.

"Maybe, but you three won't get him back without me."

"We'll try," Katherine said.

"Not without me you won't," Rachel said.

"How do you know?" Katherine said.

"Because Mateo owes me, and I can play him. I can get Richard back, and you three can't. Believe it or not, you need me."

Chapter 50

The Señorita, Díaz, Sutherland, and Judith sat on the veranda of the Señorita's palatial hacienda. Supported by tall, thick Corinthian columns, it was spacious enough to host the most lavish parties and receptions. This afternoon, however, the Señorita wanted privacy and a chance for her associates to enjoy the cool late-afternoon Sinaloan breeze. They were seated on thick leather cushions on narrow, high-backed, silk-upholstered chairs of the finest hand-carved hardwoods. On each side of the chairs was a small circular walnut table. An assortment of cheeses, chorizos, and peppers was spread out on the large oval cherrywood coffee table before them. The three bottles of champagne, chilling in ice buckets, were all Juglar Premier Cru Classé 1829. Alongside the 1829 were bottles of 1811 Year of the Comet Cognac—Díaz's perennial favorite, the one he continually proclaimed was the finest on earth.

For once Díaz wasn't wearing a military uniform. Instead he was dressed casually in a white shirt, open at the collar, black trousers, and boots. He smoked a Havana cigar and stared absently at the far-off Sierras lining the horizon, all the while sipping the champagne. The Señorita helped herself to a glass.

"A most excellent vintage, Señorita," Díaz said.

"It better be," the Señorita said. "It's the Juglar Premier Cru Classé 1829—the last year the shit was bottled."

"Something happened?" Sutherland asked.

"The vintner merged with the House of Jacquesson in Châlons-sur-Marne," she said, her voice reeking of boredom. "Their damn wines were never the same afterward."

"Then I pray we are not drinking your last bottle," Díaz said politely.

"I have countless cases of it," the Señorita muttered. "I bought up every available bottle in Méjico."

"How nouveau riche of you, my dear," Sutherland said with a condescending smirk.

Sutherland was also staring out over the desert at the black, distant mountains. He was still smoking his fruity-smelling tailor-made cigarettes, and he stuffed a new one into his ostentatiously hand-carved teak holder. One of the Señorita's livery-clad servants appeared apparition-like, as if out of nowhere, and lit it. Sutherland was attired in a summer suit of pale gray linen and matching shoes of soft, pristine doeskin. He wore a matching panama hat and dark, wire-rimmed glasses. His mouth was hooked in a supercilious sneer. It was always hooked in a supercilious sneer.

Standing beside him was his companion, the everradiant Judith McKillian. She was, once again, dressed in black—this time in tight, black silk breeches, hanging over black boots with three-inch heels and a matching ruffled silk blouse. Her honey-red tresses flowed loose and free down her back. Her emerald eyes glinted cheerfully with lewd, merry malevolence. She reflexively cracked a wicked-looking ebony riding whip against her boot top.

This afternoon the Señorita favored casual attire—tight ebony leather pants, a matching silk blouse, and gleaming, thigh-high riding boots, sporting sterling silver Chihuahua rowels. A black felt hat with a low flat crown and a narrow, circular brim was tilted on her head in a rakish angle. A rhinoceros-hide riding crop was tucked under her armpit She smoked a thin cigarillo. She was sneering, and unlike Sutherland's lopsided smile, which was insufferably arrogant, hers was evilly erotic, filled with libidinous mischief and sinful sensuosity. It unnerved and intimidated even the most intrepid of men.

Díaz cleared his throat, announcing that there was business to conduct. Someone had to explain the battlefield cataclysm that had transpired the day before.

"Bring the general back in," Díaz told the Señorita's crimson-clad head servant. He immediately went to fetch the officer, and suddenly the Señorita's sensual sneer turned into an angry scowl.

General Armando Lopez, Díaz's director of military intelligence, quickly reentered the veranda and approached their table. Ten minutes earlier, the Señorita had been dressing the general down in the most terrifying of terms. She read him a riot act so menacing that the general, who was unfailingly fearless under fire, had trembled under her withering verbal assault. He finally turned in his traces and fled the room.

Díaz had insisted on a break. He thought the Señorita might thrash the officer with her riding crop.

"*Mi General,*" the Señorita said angrily, immediately picking up where she'd left off, "I ask you how we can defeat Sonora but instead of presenting us with a winning strategy, you made stupid excuses for your recent disaster and even stupider reasons for what you believe will very likely be our next military defeat."

Red-faced, the Señorita suddenly stood up and whacked the table with her rhinoceros-hide crop so violently that the decanter, glasses, and food plates jumped and clattered.

"Please, Señorita," Díaz said, touching her forearm. "*Por favor.* Let the general finish." Díaz gave her his kindest, most placating, most insincere smile.

"Mi Presidente," the Señorita shouted, "you must understand I am not a graceful loser. Another such failure, and there will be consequences!"

"What kind of consequences?" Sutherland asked, leaning toward the Señorita and smiling amiably.

"*I'll flay that son-of-a-whore general whole and stretch his* puto *hide on a high rack!*" the Señorita roared, leaning toward General Lopez, her voice filled with demented rage.

"General," Díaz said soothingly, attempting to calm the terrified man, "I apologize for the Señorita's angry interruptions. Could you please explain again the problems which you foresee in our next assault on Sonora? Like yourself, I am a military man, and unlike the Señorita here, who demands nothing but good news, I only seek clarity, honesty, and objectivity—nothing else. If the news is bad, I insist on hearing it

immediately and in the clearest possible terms. So—
por favor—sugarcoat nothing."

"Of course, Mi Presidente. You know the results of
our last battle. Our army outnumbered the Sonora
military almost eight to one. Our last six assaults had
so radically reduced their ranks and so battered their
weaponry that their defeat seemed inevitable."

"So what went wrong?" Sutherland asked.

"The unpredictable—the arrival of a military genius,
a young americano named Lieutenant Ricardo. Our
spies tell us he is the youngest, most gifted, cadet ever
to graduate from that country's military academy,
West Point. An ordnance engineer and artillery officer, he not only instructed the Sonora military on
the use of the new ultrapowerful, smokeless cordite—
recently developed in Europe—he set up factories for
manufacturing it and also for reconditioning their
Gatlings, cannons, and rifles as well. He even taught
their artillery officers to recompute their artillery
trajectories in accordance with their new, far more
potent cordite powder. By using this new explosive
and by refining their artillery's trajectories, this young
man made their large guns infinitely more accurate
and powerful than they had been before. In fact,
their Gatlings killed thousands of our men without
one of them ever jamming. Thanks to this young man,
Sonora hammered us to pieces."

"Sounds like I'm backing the wrong horse," Sutherland said softly to no one in particular.

"No shit, amigo," Judith McKillian added. "Maybe
you and I should both cover our bets—lay some of
our investment off on the military genius."

"Which is precisely what we need," the Señorita

said, "more money. We need to upgrade our forces and at the same time hire mercenaries who can teach our artillery officers integral calculus. They can then show us how to compute trajectories with it. We bring in chemists and engineers who will teach us to create and manufacture cordite gunpowder. We will dragoon hundreds of thousands of peon-*soldados*, who, driven forward by our officer corps, will storm Sonora like banshees from hell and drive them into their justly deserved graves."

The general stared at her, incredulous.

"Come, my friend," Díaz said to the general, "you still anticipate problems? Speak frankly, ignore the Señorita. She will not hurt you. You have my word."

Díaz's smile was radiant.

"Mi Presidente," the general said, "an americano writer named Poe once wrote that 'wisdom must reckon on the unforeseen.' That is what bothers me— the unforeseen. Sonora is now unpredictable. Their army has become unpredictable."

"They're only men," the Señorita said. "They fight, they bleed, they die—just like us—and next time, since we will have better weaponry, they will bleed and die en masse. What then is so unpredictable?"

"The young lieutenant, Ricardo, has made Sonora unpredictable," General Lopez said. "He defeated us this last time. Why assume he cannot think up something new to use against us the next time? He knows we will learn from our mistakes and that we will come back at him stronger and better armed, so he will adjust."

"Coward!" the Señorita snarled.

"I fear . . . *the unforeseen.*"

"General Lopez has a point," Díaz said. "Who knows what the young man will hit us with next time?"

"What will be his Trojan horse," General Lopez said, "his Petersburg Crater? What will be his version of the sling that slew Goliath? I cannot guess his next moves, but I know in my soul he will come up with . . . *something*."

"So we must outthink the boy, *¿sí?*" Díaz said.

"That is the challenge, Mi Presidente," General Lopez said.

The Señorita nodded to a waiter, who refilled her snifter with more Year of the Comet 1811 Cognac.

"I have been reading a book on strategy—*The Art of War*—by a great Chinese general named Sun-tzu," the Señorita said. "This extraordinary thinker despised mass-casualty conflicts—the sort General Castrato here has been engaging in. He believed the most powerful of enemies could be defeated through clever, unorthodox, often nonviolent strategies."

"The man was clearly . . . *mad*," Sutherland said. "Battles are won through the application of overwhelming force—raw, naked, irresistible power."

"Not necessarily," the Señorita said. "I too believe every enemy has an Achilles' heel, a critical vulnerability, something that they cannot do without, and that if a commander can destroy or capture that indispensable asset, that commander could destroy a foe a thousand times his size with minimal losses and minimal violence."

"And you believe you have found our magic panacea?" Díaz asked.

"I do," the Señorita said.

"So what do you propose we do?" Díaz asked.

"To paraphrase the inimitable Sun-tzu," the Señorita said, "I shall take hostage what Sonora holds dear."

"And what shall we take hostage, what is that indispensable asset?" Sutherland asked, still mocking, still incredulous.

"I shall send my men to capture and abduct the boy genius," the Señorita said. "I shall debrief him personally—with painstaking meticulousness. I shall learn Sonora's every trick, every secret, and, most important, every new stratagem that the young man is planning to use against us. I shall then turn his tactics and strategies against Sonora."

"It sounds as if you will be very . . . *hard on him*," Sutherland said. He was sweating visibly, clearly excited at the prospect. "I don't suppose I could watch?"

"An arrangement could be worked out," Díaz said pleasantly, clapping Sutherland's shoulder.

"But be prepared, Señor Sutherland," the Señorita said. "You may get more than you bargained for."

"In what way?" Sutherland asked nervously.

"When I am done with young Ricardo, the earth will bleed, the stars darken and die, and Satan, trembling at my feet, will plead with me for . . . *pity*."

Chapter 51

In the half-light of predawn Katherine rousted Eléna and Antonio and served them eggs, ham, beans, bread, and coffee at the kitchen table. She wanted them to eat well. They would be on hard rations for some time to come.

As they ate, they watched three of the ranch hands cut eight horses out of the corral, saddle them, and round up three mules. The gray was feisty—feeling his oats. The vaquero known as Rogelio topped off the recalcitrant ponies. Giving the gray his head, Rogelio let him whinny and buck. Putting his head between his legs, the big horse sunfished, spun, snorted, and dragged Rogelio against the rails.

The gray was the toughest of the broncs but also had the most bottom. In her own way Katherine liked him the best. Still Katherine was starting to conclude he was too much trouble. She planned to swap him at the first relay station.

All the while, the mule packer was flattening the pads and placing the crossbucks onto the mule's back.

His was a highly prized, highly specialized skill. If the pad wasn't smooth and the pack perfectly aligned, if any of it chafed the mule in any way, crossbucks and pack would gall the animal's back, throw him off-stride, and even cripple him. A crippled mule would play havoc on their trip.

Katherine absently glanced at the packer through the kitchen window. He was near the corral and taking his time, working with almost exaggerated care. Their supplies were already loaded into the pack's panniers—its large broad pockets. The man and a wrangler then lifted the pack onto the smoothed-out pads and sawbucks. On top of them, he piled canvas bags filled with gear and lashed them to the sawbucks, careful to always balance the load. He then sedulously constructed the complicated diamondback hitch that would hold the pack tight. Taking a deep breath, he threw the hitch. As he pulled it tight, the towering load sagged, groaned, came together, then came to a rest. The packer heaved a sigh of relief.

The last items, which the packer hung from the mule's crossbucks, were eight two-gallon canvas water bags. In between the bags were strung eight more smaller canvas bags, each containing a quart of Jackson's Sour Mash, wrapped and padded with old grain sacks. When Eléna had spotted all that whiskey she asked Katherine, only half facetiously, if she had a drinking problem, Katherine answered:

"No, but I am afraid of a dysentery problem. You may be used to that mejicana *agua*—my family isn't. We'll use the sour mash to disinfect it. That's what Zack Taylor used when he stormed the gates of Monterey in the Mexican War thirty-five years ago. If it was good enough for old Zack and his soldiers, it should be good enough for us."

"It also cuts the dust," Eléna said with a wry smile.

"Es verdad, amiga," Katherine admitted. *"Es verdad."*

They got up from the breakfast table. Intending to travel incognito and attract as little attention as possible, they all wore standard *mejicano* trail attire, dark gray cotton pants, pale gray collarless broadcloth shirts, and coarsely woven, light-colored ponchos. They all wore the short-brimmed, flat-crowned straw sombreros that were ubiquitous to most of Méjico.

Under their ponchos, each of them wore leather cartridge belts and a brace of pistols in cross-draw leather holsters, .44 caliber Army Colts—all of them rechambered to take .44-40 cartridges, which also fit their .44 Winchester rifles, already in their saddle sheaths. Under their ponchos, canvas bandoliers, also filled with .44-40 cartridges, crisscrossed their chest. Their saddle sheaths boasted lever-action .44 Winchesters. In their saddlebags and in the mule pack's panniers they had extra .44-40s.

They were ready for business.

As Katherine and Eléna started up the trail, dawn was breaking. Antonio came up behind them, pulling jerkline, heeing and hawing over his shoulder at the pack animal. The snuffy mule was braying, stomping, blowing long, rolling snorts, and reluctantly following Antonio's lead.

Chapter 52

Major Mateo and Ricardo were wearing sombreros. Disguised as campesinos, they drank mezcal out of bottles and kept their *pistolas* under their ponchos. They quickly lost themselves in the mob enjoying Hermosillo's Fiesta del Muerte parade.

"Come, my young friend," Mateo said, teasing the young man. "You, above all, have earned a celebration. You saved Sonora. You saved us all from the Señorita's torture chambers and prison mines. I am determined to thank you personally—to give you a night on the town you'll never forget. In fact, I believe you've never slept with a woman. Correct me if I'm wrong. There's no shame in that. We were all innocent once. I was innocent too—but only upon leaving my mama's womb—a condition I remedied with lightning speed. Your innocence is a situation which I can and shall remedy *muy pronto*—in fact . . *tonight*. After all, what is the point of coming to Méjico if you do not enjoy our illustrious, *muchas bellas, muchas caliente putas* [very pretty, very hot whores]?"

Richard stared at Mateo in silence.

"I have been hard on you," Mateo said. "I admit it, but now that you have saved Sonora, all of Sonora is in your debt. I am in your debt, and I am a man who always pays his bills." Mateo slapped his chest hard with an open hand. "And tonight our debt to you will be paid . . . *in full*!"

"I'd settle for a couple of *tortillas de carne y queso.*"

"You'll will find no beef in this fiesta tonight, only goat meat. But well-seasoned goat meat with *muchas* chilis and onions."

"And *muchas* music," Richard said, smiling.

He was pointing at the mariachi band, serenading the crowd. Consisting of two trumpets, a drum, a guitar, a mandolin, and two women singers, the group was flamboyantly dressed in colorful shirts and blouses, the two women enticingly attired in tight-fitting low-cut gowns. During their faster songs they danced flamenco-style and snapped castanets. Mateo motioned them over. He held a ten-peso note in front of the men, and gave each a swig of mezcal.

"Hey, muchacho," he said to Richard, "you got any favorite *mejicano* music?"

"'La Golondrina,' 'La Paloma,' 'Los Sierras de Chiapas.'"

"But, *mi bueno amigo,* those are songs of sadness and farewell, and you are in Madre Méjico, at the Fiesta del Muerte. You are with your great compadre, the legendary warrior and lover, Major Mateo Cardozo." The last sentence he whispered into Richard's ear, wanting to keep their identities as rurales a secret. "You have great, great food, great music. Why do you want Madre Méjico's songs of sorrow?"

"Méjico is not my *madre*," Richard said softly to his friend.

"Ah, you miss America. I unnerstand. But America, she is not so popular down here. I would not bring it up, not at this fiesta."

"*Es verdad*, and you are my amigo. We have fought together. We have been through hell together. I would not be surprised if, in the battles to come, we died together. Still my home is far to the north. My parents are there, and God knows where my sister, Rachel, is."

Mateo gave his amigo the *abrazo*. He did not want to think about what he'd done to Ricardo's sister.

"But you are right!" Richard shouted. "And the night is young. We are in Méjico, and, yes, we saved Sonora. Why not celebrate?"

The mariachi band was wailing out "La Golondrina," the men and women harmonizing the lyrics, until Richard thought his heart would break. But instead he took the bottle from Mateo and drank a full three fingers.

"Is it true what you said about fine *mejicanas muchachas*?"

"The finest!"

"But I do not want *putas*, and I do not want any of your *enfermedades mejicanas* [Mexican diseases]."

"Of course. In fact, I am thinking not of *putas* but of *una señorita muy espléndida*, who lost her husband a year ago. She is only nineteen and has only known that one man. She is pure as the Madonna, and I think she needs some comforting—and perhaps a few pesos."

"I don't know what to say."

"She also has a sister who is also pure as sierra snow. These are not *putas* and have no diseases."

"Mateo, you are a joy forever. Their names are?"

Mateo shot him a wicked grin. "I refer to these *santas mujeres* [sainted women] as the Sin Sisters."

Shaking his head in dismay, Richard took a long swig from the mezcal bottle.

"Ey, Ricardo, I am your amigo. What are amigos for? You will spend the weekend in heaven—a weekend you will never forget. None of us forget our first *mujer*, no?"

Chapter 53

The black jaguar cub awoke to the smell of roasted meat.

Before he'd fallen asleep he remembered his rescuer methodically dressing out the anaconda, pulling off its skin and filleting the densely muscled meat. Slater had even started to dig a firebed with his knife, placed a large flat stone in its center, and had gotten a fire going around it. When the cub woke up, Slater had encircled the firebed with heavy rocks and had a stack of raw python steaks piled up on a strip of python hide. Slater had a metal pot filled with water on the flat rock and was roasting the snake meat on green sticks over the blazingly hot flames.

Now the cub was wide awake. Although the smell of the broiling meat was appealing, he knew he couldn't eat meat. Still his stomach grumbled with an unimaginably painful hunger. He feared he was starving to death. Without soft, liquefied food, he would die.

He then noticed the man was also throwing raw snake fillets into the cook pot and stirring the soup inside. Every so often, his rescuer also raised a large clear bottle to his lips and poured some kind of foul-smelling liquid down his throat. When the bottle had only an inch or so left, the man upended it and didn't stop till he was sucking air. His rescuer, at that point, was starting to sway and seemed a little . . . wobbly.

Sticking a metal mess cup into the pot, Slater ladled out a large portion of the broth. He poured it into the empty bottle. Cooled it down with some canteen water. He wrapped a piece of rawhide over the bottle's neck, which he held in place with his fist. He then poked a hole in the top of the rawhide with a sharply whittled stick.

The cub waddled up to his rescuer, curious. The man eased him onto his lap. He lifted up his chin and poured some of the warm fluid down the small feline's throat. Once the cub got past the bottle's foul smell and the broth's heat, the cub found he liked its taste. It also placated the fiery hunger in his belly. The jaguar cub realized the stranger had saved his life twice—first from the python's belly, and second, he'd saved him from the agony of starvation. Thanks to the stranger, he was going to live.

Then it hit him that he was eating the snake. How was that possible? The anaconda was the strongest beast he had ever seen. The monster had crushed his mother—the most powerful creature he'd known up to that point—as if it were snapping a twig. But the man—who was obviously stronger than the snake and his mother put together—killed the anaconda with his fire-stick, as if the python were nothing, and now they were both consuming its flesh. The man devouring its meat, the cub drinking it. His weakness subsided as the python's strength entered his body, and he could feel himself growing stronger. All the while, the man continued pouring the anaconda's essence down the cub's throat.

Slowly, inexorably, the cub began to feel the python's power coursing through his veins and the beast's strength infusing his body.

Chapter 54

"Another man struck out in your bed?" Roberta asked, shocking the Señorita Dolorosa.

"That man," Maria said, "deserves every inch of the Via Dolorosa."

"And I shall see he gets it—all the fires of hell," her Lady screamed. She had some of her old rage back and was feeling better now. "I gave him my harangue on the Spanish Inquisition, and he turned mountain oyster on me."

"Mountain oyster?" Catalina asked, not recognizing the colloquialism.

"It's *americano* vernacular for fried *cojones del toros* [bull testicles]," her Lady explained.

"I'll begin his lessons by teaching him what the Inquisition did to those poor ladies," their Lady said, chortling melodically, "while he's stretched out on the rack. I'll teach it on his bones and his blood."

"You'll explain the Spanish Inquisition to him," Catalina asked, "even as you torture him with all of its instruments? That is so . . . *amazing.*"

"Of course I will," the Señorita said, her smile scintillatingly bright, her eyes glinting happily. "I've done it before. I love leaning over them then till we're nose to nose and saying: 'Maybe then you'll find out what those Spanish widows felt when they were burned, broken, and beaten, begging hopelessly for mercy, where there was none!'

"All my former lovers inevitably break down at that point, sobbing and pleading: 'Don't hurt me anymore, please! I can't take it! I can't take it!' Oh, I love nothing more than torturing and mortifying these morons until they actually scream: 'Please! I haven't done anything wrong. I have a wife, children, parents. They haven't done anything wrong either, and my parents are old. They need me for financial support. I'm all they have.' Catalina, these imbeciles are truly shameless in their . . . *begging*."

"How disgusting!" Catalina said.

"His behavior, however, was the most despicable example of self-abasement I have ever seen. And he wouldn't quit his hideous sniveling. Then he screamed: 'I know what those Spanish widows felt. I really do. I'm feeling it right now. Please! Mercy! Don't make me prove it to you! Make the Inquisitor stop, My Lady. Don't send me to the stone. I do! Please, I'll do anything!'"

Her court ladies erupted in a rousing chorus of hilarious giggles.

Their Lady's smile, however, suddenly fell from her face, and she was no longer laughing. At which point her ladies' laughter instantly ceased. In truth, the Señorita hated it when her men whined and moaned. She was still pissed off that this last one had lost it so fast and so furiously. Her Spanish Inquisition bullshit had completely unhinged him. He'd apparently believed that the Señorita actually gave a shit about the plight of some deranged old biddies five hundred years ago.

She'd had high hopes for him too, until he'd become so unmanned, so utterly unnerved . . . so quickly.

Oh well, there'll be others, she thought wistfully.

"What happened to that last one?" Isabella asked.

"I did with him what I often do when they break down. I released him from the rack, then had him returned to my boudoir. I waved him up to the head of the bed, then held him in my arms, his head on my breast, and rocked him gently.

"'There, there,' I said softly. 'There, there.' All the while, I cooed like a dove. 'You'll be all right. No one will hurt you. I truly love you. In fact, think of me not only as your lover and protector but as the mother—yes, the mother—you never had. I will send you wine, flowers, and chocolates every day for the rest of your life. You'll never have to work again. You'll always be safe. I promise.'

"I sat him up on the bed next to me, and I smiled lovingly. Chucking him under the chin, I looked pathetically into his eyes and then kissed his tears away. 'See?' I said. 'Mama made it all better. Now Mama is going to sleep and you will go back to your quarters and not worry about a thing.' When he pulled himself away, I gave him a playful smack on the behind, then rolled over and pretended to go to sleep.

"When he was gone, I rang for my head servant. When he came in, I said: 'Give that sniveling imbecile who was just in here the usual—chocolates, wine, and flowers at his quarters plus a day off from the army. Tell him he's getting the same tomorrow. But then tomorrow at midnight, send some guards in black hoods and robes to yank him out of bed, unannounced, in the dead of night. Kick his sorry ass all the way to the Grand Inquisitor's quarters. Tell that demented joke of a priest to give the blubbering fool who was just in here . . . *everything*! Tell him I'll be in his chambers in a day or so to inspect his handiwork. If I don't like what I see, I'll stretch that black-robed bastard on his rack myself!'"

Her ladies burst into peals of frightened guffaws. Then an almost beatific smile spread across the Lady Dolorosa's wide, generous mouth, revealing two gleaming rows of perfect, ivory white teeth.

"God, I feel good!" she moaned happily. "I feel like I could actually . . . *sleep*!"

Since she was an obsessive insomniac, sleep came hard, slowly, and begrudgingly to their Lady.

But not tonight.

Rolling over, she sank instantly into the arms of Morpheus.

She passed the night without wakefulness or dreams, utterly at peace.

PART XII

"You will never understand Méjico," Isabella DeVargas said to Richard, "not if you lived with us ten thousand years. You will always be norteamericano in your soul."

Chapter 55

At the first relay station, Katherine discussed trading the gray with Eléna and Antonio.

"I hate giving him up," Katherine said. "He's the toughest mount we've got. Get into trouble, he's the one you want under you."

"So he's the one we keep," Eléna said.

"But he's too much goddamn bother," Katherine said.

"Ey, Señora Katherine," Antonio said with surprising affection, "you want him, don't worry. I'll top him off when we get up, leave him gentle as a kitten for you."

Katherine stared at him a long appraising minute.

"You're all right, Antonio," she said. "Goddamn it, you'll . . ." Then Katherine said softly: "You'll qualify."

To tell a man he'd do or that he qualified were the preeminent ranch hand compliments.

After examining the remounts and the mules, Antonio and Eléna recommended a paint, a big buckskin, and a small but energetic sorrel. Antonio recommended *mejicano* mules because they could live off the land. The americanos couldn't.

"You're right," Katherine said, agreeing with his analysis of *mejicano* versus americano mules. "We've got nothing but desert from here to that train station, real heartbreak country. There won't be enough grain for the horses and the pack animal. We need to save what we have for our mounts. *Mejicano* mules'll live off trail-graze."

They'd unsaddled and unpacked their stock. Eléna and Katherine began helping Antonio straighten the pads on the new mule. They would saddle their mounts last.

They were just about to lift the crossbucks onto them when Katherine spotted a familiar-looking figure in a roiling cloud of dust, heading up the trail toward them, at least a quarter mile distant. The desert country this close to the Rio was flat, dry as an old sun-bleached bone, and hellishly hot. Consequently, Katherine could see for miles in any direction. Even though this traveler was still a quarter mile away, she noticed something familiar in the rider and the mount.

Walking over to the gray, Katherine took a small sniper scope out of one of the saddlebags. Leaning her elbows on the saddle, she raised the scope to her eye and studied their newfound guest for a good minute.

"Goddamn it to hell," she finally whispered.

"Rachel," Eléna predicted.

"The same," Katherine said, returning the scope to the saddlebag.

"She's in no shape to travel," Antonio said.

"She couldn't bear to stay behind," Eléna pointed out.

"I should have tied her up," Katherine said, "and had Frank hand-feed her until we were on that train and steaming into Sinaloa."

"She blames herself," Eléna said, "for her brother's troubles. How could she stay behind?"

"She missed Madre Méjico's joyful fiestas, bountiful deserts, and soaring sierras—all her *belleza natural* [natural beauty]," Antonio said with mocking cynicism.

"Anyone who'd come to Mexico for fun and natural beauty," Katherine said, shaking her head in disgust, "would go to hell for the nightlife."

"In that case, Katherine," Eléna said, "welcome to hell."

"Rachel," Katherine said softly to herself, "what am I going to do with you? And what about Richard? Richard?"

Chapter 56

Mateo had told Richard that the two of them had earned a blowout and that Richard in particular deserved a celebration. Richard had to admit that Hermosillo was one gigantic party. The harvest was over, and the people were out in force. He and Mateo were swept up among the thousands of drunk, loud, flamboyantly attired people thronging the streets. Many of them had spent the previous year designing and hand-sewing these multicolored costumes—the three-day festival meant that much to them. More widely and enthusiastically celebrated in Méjico than Christmas, Thanksgiving, and Easter combined, this fiesta was Méjico's biggest event, nationwide, and most of the country's businesses were closed. In fact, Richard had never seen so many people in one area— to say nothing of so many hysterical, out-of-control people, Mateo and himself included. All over the country *mejicanos* were turning out to honor their Día de Muertos—the Day of the Dead.

Mejicanos were turning out all over the country to

commemorate death, and tonight—the final night—
was the biggest event of all. Mateo and Richard were
joining the raucous parade to the cemetery, where
the partiers would cavort with the spirits of their dear
departed and present them with gifts of food and
drink in an attempt to assist their journey through the
afterlife.

Unlike Christians, who viewed their afterlife in
binary terms—eternal bliss versus eternal pain—the
Mayas and the Aztecas believed that the dead went
through eight nightmarish worlds before reaching
their final destination, the Ninth Level. That journey's end presented its worshippers with their last,
best postmortem hope for eternal life, a state that was
neither happy nor hellish: *utter oblivion.*

Since the fiesta was more Maya/Azteca than
Christian, the Catholic Church had suppressed it for
centuries, but the last decades in Méjico had been
so violent and trouble-filled that Porfirio Díaz had
brought back Día de Muertos as a release for his
people, a catharsis, a chance to blow off stream.

Richard was new to the extravaganza and ignorant
of its background, but its purpose was immediately
apparent to him. Everywhere he looked, he saw visual
reminders of the medieval exhortation of memento
mori:

Remember death.

Remember that you shall die.

It was impossible to ignore the injunction. Death
was all around him: Men in black garb illumined with
dazzlingly white skeletons and skulls. Women had
likewise costumed themselves as skeletons with alabaster facial makeup as well as eyes colored black as

a raccoon's and mouths painted broad and black as obsidian. Skull masks and devil masks, called *calacas*, adorned people's faces as well. People up and down the street dangled papier-mâché skeletons like macabre marionettes.

"Why so many skulls and skeletons?" Richard asked.

"Believe it or not," Mateo said, "many of the women believe them to be aphrodisiacs, and many of our hombres agree."

One woman in a dark, tight-fitting skeleton-decorated dress approached him, her face made up like a death's head, a ebony skullcap covering her hair. Death's-head tattoos were snaking up and down her arms, and she shook a poster in Richard's face, illustrating a wealthy woman gaudily attired in an expensive, erotically suggestive, low-cut dress but instead of shapely legs and voluptuous cleavage all she had were leg bones, breast bones, and an evil snarling sneer twisting her luridly licentious skull-mouth.

Ghoulish posters were everywhere, depicting skeletons on skeletal horses, charging into battle with other skeletons, brandishing lances and sabers, piercing and slashing at other deceased, bone-racked soldiers. Skeletal mothers nursing skeletal infants. The skeletal dead digging their way out of cemetery graves and rising up en masse by the thousands

"*¡Todos somos calaveras!*" she shouted in Richard's face. ["We are all skeletons."]

"We are all food for worms," Mateo interpreted, "nothing more, nothing less."

She then bolted from them, laughing hysterically.

"Speaking of food," Mateo said, "all this mezcal and *muerto* are giving me an appetite."

"I could eat sticks and rocks *como un perro rabioso* [like a hydrophobic dog]," Richard said.

"*También*, Mateo," a young woman, Richard's age, said, running up to them. "Did you offer us dinner?"

"I could eat something too!" her companion yelled excitedly, following behind her.

The two girls appeared to be highly attractive sisters, perhaps even twins.

"My young friend," Mateo said to Richard, "meet Rozanna and Isabella DeVargas—the two beauties I told you about. I refer to them as the Sin Sisters—they take the appellation as an honor—and, *sí*, we'd be honored to treat such *señoritas muy bellas* to dinner."

Richard was pleased to note that the two women weren't dressed like the dead. In fact, they may have been the only two señoritas present who didn't look like bone racks. Instead Rozanna wore a long red skirt and a white blouse. Her lush ebony hair hung loose all the way down her back. Isabella was decked out in a black skirt and a turquoise blouse, and her thick, lustrous, black-as-night hair was flung provocatively over her left shoulder.

Immediately, three mariachi bands surrounded the four friends, competing for pesos. Mateo paid all three and asked them to play and sing the great *meji-cano* Día de Muertos love-death ballad—"Solo Los Muertos Saben Amor" ["Only the Dead Know Love"]. The two girls clapped and swayed to the melancholic music while a small mob of drunken *mejicanos* crowded around to listen to the ever-popular, ever-poignant refrain of *amor y muerte*. The singers harmonized:

Tu belleza cava mi tumba.
¿Por qué es tu amor mi agonía?

Even though Richard spoke Spanish fluently, Mateo translated the first two lyrics into English, making sure his young friend absorbed their meaning and impact.

Your beauty digs my grave.
Why is your love my agony?

"Why, indeed, young friend?" Mateo roared with joyful laughter. "Why indeed?"

"Why indeed?" Richard muttered under his breath.

Food venders were all around them and they bought paper-wrapped *queso y chorizo tortillas*, the fiesta's eponymous *pan de muerto* [bread of the dead]. A *pan dulce* [sweet egg bread], the baker had molded the pan into the shape of skulls and crisscrossed arm bones. Filled with anise seeds, it was stamped with impressions of skeletons and skulls. Sugar and candy skulls were sold everywhere. Some women and children wore them on strings around their necks when they weren't eating them.

"But enough fun and gaiety," Mateo said. "We're approaching the pièce de résistance, the cemetery, where we will commune and converse with the dear deceased, then hurry them along on their journey."

"Is it true that, once again, we will crucify our Savior at the graveyard?" Richard asked.

"But of course," Mateo roared. "After all, His was the holiest death of all. Should we not reenact it yearly?"

"I want to see it," Rozanna said.

"También," Isabella concurred.

To his surprise Richard wanted to see it too.

"Absolutemente!" the drunken Mateo thundered. "We will drink mezcal, fill our bellies, and do many other things as well."

Rozanna and Isabella shouted their encouragement and hugged and kissed Richard. He found their laughter marvelously melodic.

"I don't know which of you is the more beautiful," Richard said.

"Don't worry about it, amigo," Mateo said. "The night is young. You will have all night to decide."

Richard wasn't sure what his friend meant, but now the mezcal was hitting him. Also Mateo was hurrying Richard and the two women up to the front of the parade, while they upended mezcal bottles and wolfed down the festival food with their free hands. Dancing to mariachi bands, ducking in and out, around and about the skeletally clad and the death's-head revelers, the four friends hurried to the front of the procession.

Chapter 57

From atop a high, rock-strewn hill, Slater sat cross-legged behind a trunk-size boulder. He had been tracking and hunting Los Lobos Duros y Locos, the bandit gang, for over two months. He petted the jet-black jaguar cub asleep beside him. The cub was now as big as a good-size dog. He was hunting on his own and was no longer dependent on his friend for food, for which Slater was grateful. The cat's appetite was now prodigious. He could eat quantities of meat that would destroy a grown man. Just two hours ago, he'd killed and eaten most of a five-pound Gila monster and was now sleeping off the feast. The man knew from past experience that the young jaguar would be out for hours.

Several years ago, Slater had known a black French-speaking Haitian bandit. He never knew his real name, but he was the toughest human being Slater had ever heard of, let alone known. Slater knew only the man's French nickname: Monsieur Mort

[Mr. Death]. So now the young obsidian-black jaguar was Monsieur Mort. Or Mort, for short.

Meanwhile Slater studied the two dozen banditos down below. His sniper scope brought them into close, clear focus. They were attired in old, discarded rurales uniforms, some with bloodstained bullet holes and sombreros, with canvas cartridge belts strapped across their waists and chests. Rifles of every make and model were slung from their shoulders. They were preparing to rob a payroll train. He observed a bandit climb one of the telegraph poles lining the far side of the track and cut the wire with a machete, while the rest of them took turns rolling and levering a surprisingly massive boulder onto the tracks. They then backed it up with dozens of smaller boulders. Slater estimated the big rock to be at least six feet in diameter—more than enough mass to stop a train all by itself.

He next saw them scramble behind clusters of wagon-size boulders and wait for the Banco Central's gold train. Its money car would be filled with bags of gold coins and gringo hundred-dollar bills.

For the next hour he drank canteen water and gnawed at jerked beef. When the train approached, he could see through his sniper scope that the locomotive was a black Jupiter #60 with a Mogul engine, a funnel-shaped, spark-arresting crownpiece, and a tender piled high with kindling. When the engineer spotted the big obstruction, he slowed to a stop. He had nowhere else to go.

The banditos made no attempt to negotiate the surrender of the money, passengers, and crew. Instead four of them approached the locomotive with a white truce flag, then emptied their pistols into the engine compartment, killing the engineer and the fireman. Then the rest of the bandits opened up on the troop-filled boxcar, where the safe was kept, with every weapon they had, killing everyone inside. The bandits then went from car to car, shooting people randomly, willy-nilly.

One of the men was barking orders at the rest of the bandits, so Slater took him to be the leader. Among other things, he dressed differently. He wore a Chihuahua generalissimo's uniform and smoked a large black cigar.

He ordered his men to drag off the train the dozen or so passengers who had escaped the massacre. Lining them up in front of the train, he then made the prisoners kneel down on the rock-filled trackbed. Walking behind them, one of the banditos began shooting the men in the backs of their heads.

After he shot the third man, one of the bandits shouted:

"Estás perdeno balas." ["You're wasting bullets."]

He considered the statement a moment, then yelled back at his men:

"Colgar los hombres!" ["Hang the men!"]

Tying noose-knots around the men's necks, they then threw the ropes over the telegraph poles' crossbeams. Hitching the lines to their horses, they hauled the men up off the ground and hung them two to a pole. All the while, the men gripped the ropes and pulled themselves up, kicking and screaming, fighting to hold on to their lives. Eventually their grips weakened, and they all died. When a young woman in a red traveling dress and waist-length auburn hair couldn't stand it anymore, she leaped up, screaming:

"*¡Mi marido! ¡Mi marido!*" ["My husband! My husband!"]

She ran to her husband before they could stop her. She leaped up, grabbed his knees, and hoisted herself off the ground. Her additional weight broke his neck, and she ended his misery.

"Bravo! Bravo!" the bandit leader shouted. "*¡Ahora les daré su recompensa por esa valentía!*" ["I now give you your reward for such bravery!"]

He shot her in her right eye.

The leader did not have to tell his men what to do next. They staked the women prisoners out alongside the tracks, stripped off their clothes, and then began systematically raping the women. Slater averted his gaze.

When it was over, the leader shouted at the screaming, sobbing women:

"*¡Cortar la raqueta!*" ["Cut the racket!"]

When Slater heard gunshots, he returned his gaze. The bandits were shooting the screaming, battered, bleeding women in the heads and chests.

The bandits then set up ramps and walked their horses up into several of the boxcars. They were going to steal the train and take it most of the way to their camp. Why not? There was a lot of valuable stuff aboard, more than they could pack back on their horses.

Slater knew what he would do next. He saddled his broad-backed, broad-chested gray and tightened the cinch. Dallying the mules' mecate around the horse's pommel, he placed the still-sleeping cub over the animal's wide, muscular withers. Swinging onto his mount, he eased himself into his saddle. Seated right behind the slumbering cat, he led his mule string on up the mountain trail.

Chapter 58

Katherine and her crew were camped on a hill outside the railroad junction, where the next day they would catch the train south into Sinaloa. After getting off, they would ride toward the Señorita's infamous hacienda on horseback.

From the hilltop they could look down on the station. A small brown adobe-block building, it had an even smaller house, where the stationmaster lived. A barn-stable, constructed of the same adobe, was near the house as was a corral with a dozen horses in it. The mounts were for those passengers who got off and needed transportation. An unhitched buckboard sat near the station for the same purpose. On both sides of the station and house looked to be fifty or sixty of acres of *mejicano* maize. Chili peppers and maguey were planted in alternating rows.

Sitting around the fire, they were just finishing their beans and salt pork. Katherine was pouring Jackson's Sour Mash into her coffee. Katherine was clearly upset that her injured daughter had forced herself on the group. Her abducted son obviously worried her as well. Eléna decided she might want some company, so she poured some sour mash into her own tin mess cup. Antonio followed suit. When Rachel tried to help herself to the sour mash, Katherine shook her head.

"Not with your brain injury." Her voice was not unkind.

Taking the bottle anyway, Rachel poured herself a healthy slug anyway. Katherine looked away.

"Ey, Mama," Eléna said, hoping to get Katherine's mind onto other things. "Frank told me that when you were young, you lived three years with the Chiricahua Apache down along the border. You ever talk about it?"

"Not really. A raiding party killed my family and abducted me. They didn't beat or rape me, but it was a time I'd just as soon forget."

"Same thing happened to me," Eléna said. "They was Yaquis though, not Apache."

Katherine stared at her a long minute. "I heard the Yaquis were even worse than the Apache."

"They were tough. The Spanish and French couldn't defeat them."

"But Díaz is doing it."

"He just hunts them down and kills them," Eléna said, shaking her head. "He enslaves those he doesn't kill. The men he sometimes castrates. If the women rebel in any way, he sells them into *puta dura* slavery."

"Díaz's admirers call him a military genius," Katherine said. "I heard he calls his strategy the Doctrine of Sufficient Force."

"I call him a monster," Eléna said.

"He's doing things the Mongol khans did six hundred years ago," Katherine said, nodding in agreement. "He's committing acts of barbarism that should have disappeared long before the ancient Greeks."

"Welcome to Madre Méjico, Mama," Eléna said. "Welcome to the land of my birth."

They were quiet a long minute.

"So how did you get free?" Katherine asked, breaking the silence.

"Díaz was killing the Yaquis so systematically that he eventually caught up with my abductors. He killed them all, including my Yaqui friends—the ones who'd looked after me. A sergeant finally found me crouched in a ravine, hiding in the brush and mesquite. They were about to scalp me—Díaz had put a bounty on Yaqui scalps—when the sergeant saw I was *mejicano*, not Yaqui. He took a liking to me. He kept me and used me sexually. He told me the whole time my hair was black as any *india*'s and he could scalp me for the bounty anytime he tired of me. He wasn't joking. No one knew the difference between *india* and mejicana scalps. Finally, however, we got near Sonora, and I figured out where we were. One night, when he got drunk and passed out, I escaped. I made it back to my village and got on with my life. I eventually married, and my husband and I bought a cantina. Then Rodrigo died, and you know the rest."

Katherine looked away.

"Ey, Mama," Eléna said. "You want to tell me about the Chiricahuas?"

Chapter 59

Richard couldn't believe his eyes. The mob was entering the cemetery, and there at the front of the parade was a young *mejicano* man, naked, save for a loincloth. Blood streaming from a jagged crown of thorns impaling his forehead, temples, pate, and nape. His hair was wet, stringy, and caked with gore. He was stumbling under a huge, impossibly heavy cross. Several men were dressed in centurion gear—*lorica plumata*, tunics, balteus belts, and caligae sandals. With hooked whips they flogged the foundering man toward the graveyard. Blood flowed promiscuously from those raw slashes. The man had the most dismal, pain-racked eyes Richard had ever seen.

"They certainly strive for authenticity," Rozanna noted.

"They've been teaching him the Stations of the Cross," Mateo said, "all fourteen of them."

"They even had Pilate judge him first," Isabella noted.

"And scourged him afterward," Rozanna said.

"Did you see the man's eyes?" Richard asked Mateo. "I've never seen such despair. He seems to really feel Christ's suffering."

"Oh, this is much more than a Christian ceremony," Isabella pointed out.

"This country is still Aztec in some ways," Rozanna said.

"That man carrying the cross," Mateo said, "he has the anguished eyes of the Aztec death god, Mictlante-cuhtli, and Coatlicue, his death goddess."

"They are often portrayed as festooned with skulls, human hearts, and dripping blood, eyes blank as the abyss and black as obsidian," Isabella said. "Theirs are the eyes of all our *indios*—eyes dark as death, empty as void, eyes that know now and forever they have nothing left to lose and nothing left to love."

"But this is not supposed to be an Aztec ceremony," Richard said. "They're supposed to be honoring Christ's death and resurrection."

His three friends broke into laughter.

"Will you never understand, young friend?" Mateo said. "You are no longer in Norteamérica, where life is gentle and people kind. You are in Méjico, the land the Aztecs never left, a world where life is hard and our people unforgiving."

Rozanna leaned forward, till they were almost nose to nose. Her voice, however, was compassionate, and her eyes were not unkind.

"You will never understand our ways, gringo."

"And you will never understand Méjico," Isabella DeVargas said, "not if you lived with us ten thousand years. You will always be norteamericano in your soul."

Richard looked away from the martyred man and surveyed the cemetery in its entirety—and its individual gravesites. He'd seen stone crosses before, but tonight the deceased's relatives had turned them into shrines and altars, on and around which were spread candies, chocolates, tortillas, sausages, *pan de muerto*, sugar skulls, glasses of tequila and pulque. The air was thick with the smoke and the smell of copal incense.

"The altars are called *ofrendas*," Mateo explained. "Their friends and relatives leave food and drink in order to nourish the dead on their trip through the underworld, a pilgrimage which can take years. Before their loved ones leave, they spread pillows and blankets around the graves, so the departed can pause and rest on their journey through hell. Do you see the orange marigolds?" Mateo asked Richard, pointing to the gorgeous flowers strewn around the multitudinous graves. "They are the Aztecs' 'flowers of death,' called *cempasúchil* in the Nahuatl tongue. They are spread around the altars in order to comfort the deceased on their odyssey through afterlife."

"And that odyssey is difficult?" Richard asked.

"*Muy* terrible," Rozanna interjected, crossing herself. "The departed must make their way through eight violent hellworlds, including an abyss of obsidian knives, a hideous hell, where the deceased are flayed whole; through a black pit of freezing winds, through a nightmare world of cannibalized hearts; through another of eternal darkness. The ninth world is Mictlan. It is bad but still the gentlest of all our hellworlds."

"Who gets to go there?" Richard asked.

"Infants, women who died giving birth the first time, those killed by water, great warriors, and suicides," Isabella said.

"Why suicides?" Richard asked. "Why are they rated as highly as noble warriors who sacrificed themselves to Madre Méjico, who died for their friends and loved ones in battle?"

"Good Ricardo, our people honor death first and foremost," Mateo explained. "It does not matter whether one inflicts it on another for a great cause or one inflicts it on his- or herself. What counts is . . . *death.* So the suicides consecrate and immolate themselves *también* to Mictlantecuhtli and his mate, Coatlicue, the god and goddess of the dead. Both of them are depicted on shrine walls and in our sacred codices as wandering the afterlife with death's-head faces, their bodies festooned with our skulls, their fists brandishing our beating hearts."

"The suicides, more than anyone else, comprehend the truth of Madre Méjico, your so-called Méjico Lindo," Rozanna said.

"They alone," Isabella said, "understand what our world is all about—that this life is a living hell and that the afterlife is worse."

"I don't get it," Richard said.

"And you never will," Mateo said.

"How many times must we tell you, amigo?" Isabella said. "You are not *mejicano.* You do not know our country from the inside."

"Then help me," Richard said. "What is it you understand that I don't?"

Isabella leaned toward Richard, fixing him with a hard, intense stare.

"We get the joke," Isabella said.

Chapter 60

The big man in dirty Levi's, a black Plainsman hat, a dark broadcloth shirt, and boots crouched behind a boulder. He was studying a large railroad trestle spanning a deep desert gorge. It was almost a three hundred feet across.

Slater had been waiting for this moment for days—ever since the bandits had robbed the train and he'd heard the bandit leader order his men to walk their horses up the improvised ramps and into the boxcars. The man was taking the gold train up to their fortresslike mountain redoubt a hundred miles away.

Slater knew about these bandits. The intelligence had cost El Mexicano Minería and Banco Central a small fortune, but Slater had finally found out the location of their hideout, and he knew they always returned to it after a big score. This time they were taking the train back most of the way, and Slater knew that he'd beat them to the trestle by a full day on horseback. His route would be faster and more direct, and

*the only way anyone could reach their Sierra Madre bastion
was over that trestle.*

*From Slater's vantage point, the trestle looked solid. Its
matrix of crisscrossing, X-shaped beams and boards—which
was approximately three hundred feet across and a hundred
feet down—shored up the train tracks above. The structure
was substantial enough to support heavy trains and with-
stand the barranca's occasional flash floods.*

*Still Slater saw the bridge as the bandit's choke point,
and he planned to stop them there—train and all. Now,
after levering and rolling a dozen big rocks onto the train
track on the trestle's far end, he waited for the train to arrive
and come to a halt. They would have to. The boulders were
small enough for him to move, but big enough to derail a train.*

Slater saw the Jupiter #60 approach the vertiginous
crossing. The eight-wheeler slowed, then carefully
inched its way out over the canyon. The big black be-
hemoth was coughing smoke and sparks out of its
funnel-shaped stack. Steam floated up and out of the
Jupiter's undercarriage, merging with the smoke in a
thick miasma. Even so, the locomotive's brass fittings
caught the afternoon sunlight and glittered brilliantly
through the hot, humid haze. The bandits sat on the
boxcar roofs, but when the train reached the rocky
barricade blocking their passage, they swung down
onto the tracks.

Slater stood and stepped out from behind the boulder. He was level with the train tracks but approximately two hundred yards to the side. He had to shout
at the top of his lungs to make himself heard.

"Ey, amigos. You need some help movin' them rocks?" he roared in Spanish.

"We need some help *chingo*-ing your *puta* mama, gringo!" the leader thundered back at him.

His men roared with laughter.

Slater joined them in their hilarity.

"I saw what you did to those people that were on the train," Slater yelled back at them. "But you aren't massacring innocent people anymore and you aren't *chingo*-ing any more *mamacitas* ever again—not after I'm done with you."

"You think you gonna kill us all?" their leader asked, grinning.

"Every damn one of you *madre*-pimpin' *hideputas*!"

They all laughed uproariously, Slater laughing the hardest of all.

Of course he had not laughed when, a month before, he had walked into the main office in one of the Mexicano Minería and Banco Central mining towns and placed his order for black powder. There was nothing funny about Ramon Guzman's letter of credit either, which he'd personally signed on the managing director's stationery. The mine's majordomo had not laughed either when he took Slater's supply order, which included two dozen canvas bags of black powder and two hundred blasting caps.

Nor had Slater laughed when two days before he'd swung down from the track-bridge and clambered through the labyrinth of boards and shoring timbers. Negotiating that jungle of intersecting beams and planks, he had not found funny. The laborious planting of those two dozen powder-packed canvas sacks into the crisscrossing wooden X's, then

*charging them with fulminate-of-mercury caps, he'd also
viewed without humor. He'd placed them so strategically that
when one blew, it would set off a chain reaction of sympathetic detonations, which he believed would blow the trestle's
top to kingdom come and send the train plummeting into
hell, bringing down most of the trestle's underpinnings with
it—that deed he also considered no laughing matter.*

Bracing the Big Fifty Sharps rifle against his shoulder, Slater studied a huge canvas bag filled with black
powder affixed to the trestle. The bag was jammed
inside a large steel bucket, all of which was tightly
lashed to the trestle. The bucket's opening faced
Slater, and in it on the sack was drawn a thick, black,
foot-in-diameter circle, densely filled with demolition
caps, each one shoved into the powder bag. Slater
had actually taped a black *X* across the circle of blasting caps. Slater had deployed it in the middle of a
meticulously placed system of mines. Since the mines
were close together, when one went off, it would trigger those nearest it sympathetically. Also since the
trestle was narrow—its width less than twenty feet
across—when the mines blew, they would demolish
the top tiers of support beams. The weight of that
collapsing upper structure combined with that of the
plummeting train would increase the force on the
underpinnings below incrementally, shattering them
with accelerating force and power. The entire trestle,
top to bottom—Slater reasoned—would vanish into
the void.

At last, Slater squeezed the trigger. Two dozen
blasts went off in a sequence so rapid that they seemed

to be a single, gut-shaking, earth-cracking, earsplitting roar. A burgeoning ball of fire and whitish smoke rose up, converged with a dozen similar balls, creating a single massive, upwardly ascending mushroom cloud, propelled by the spectacularly huge fireball underneath it.

The explosions blew the train in two, lifting both sections, the locomotive included, a full fifty feet above the track-bridge. The blasts then began taking the boxcars and the trestle apart—one board, one wheel, one decoupler, one rail, one rail tie, one rail spike, one beam, one crossbeam, one nail at a time. Hunks of shoring timbers, ties, and rails were now levitating above the gorge and the track-bridge, breaking up into thousands of fiery remnants.

The piece-by-piece, section-by-section obliteration of the train and the bridge was, from Slater's vantage point of two hundred yards away, occurring with surreal, almost hallucinatory lassitude. The trestle's wreckage rose and rose and rose and rose until the whirling maelstrom of smashed wood and steel was a hundred yards across and a hundred yards above the canyon. Reaching its apex, the vast fiery vortex of smoking rubble hung abeyant, suspended above the chasm for at least a dozen heartbeats of eternity, appearing to temporarily defy all the laws of gravity and motion.

Then the debris began to drop with incomprehensible indolence—not a chunk at a time but all at once, bits and scraps of the locomotive and its cars, the shards of the tracks included, in a single blazing, smoking mass—plummeting into the gorge with the trestle fragments. The trestle's destruction and descent did not stop until the blazing, shattered remains crashed with one enormous, resounding thundercrack of annihilation on the canyon floor. For a while the trestle's demise was obscured by the incendiary smoke cloud. But when the obfuscating flames and dissipating haze finally cleared, Slater could see what he had done.

The trestle was no more—just charred fuming junk on the arroyo's bottom.

Guzman's isn't gonna like losing that trestle, Slater said to himself with a small half smile. *Or that train. You best take your money straight off the top.*

As he headed down the steep trail toward the canyon floor, M. Mort fell in behind his leader.

Chapter 61

Katherine felt that after Eléna's story about her captivity among the Yaquis, she had to say something. Also maybe it was time Rachel knew something about her mother's childhood.

"My family had a small spread outside of Tucson. It was beautiful country, high enough up not to be too arid and hot. There was a market in town for everything we grew. We were doing well and expanding.

"But then some Apaches went on a raiding spree. The U.S. Cavalry eventually caught up with them, but not before they'd killed my parents and taken me. Red-haired *pindah* women were prized, so they hid me away, and I wasn't rescued."

"Pindah?" Rachel asked.

"Pindah-lickoyee," Katherine said. "White-eyes."

"It must have been horrible," Rachel said.

"It could have been worse," Katherine said. "The Apache made some effort to protect young girls from sexual predators. Our hair was tied up in the back in a kind of bun with a *nahleen*, a hair bow. In fact, we were called *nahleens*—hair bow virgins. To have sex with a *nahleen* was a capital offense. So as long as I was underaged, I was safe from rape. I was worked like a slave though."

"Doing what?" Rachel asked.

"Anything and everything."

"I spent a lot of time with the Yaquis sewing moccasins," Eléna said.

"Same here. We went through a lot of moccasins."

"How were you called?" Eléna asked.

"Alchine Gah," Katherine said. "Little Rabbit."

"I was called Kuu Gujei, or Fire Heart," Eléna said, "because I was so rebellious. But maybe that rebelliousness helped me to escape."

"Your anger probably kept you alive," Katherine observed.

"Perhaps, but what gave you the will to live?" Eléna asked. "How did you get free?"

"There was another *pindah* in the camp. He was a few years older than I and a precocious warrior. The warrior named Go-Yath-Khla, he-who-yawns—whom you know as Geronimo—was his chief rival. Both vied for the attention and approval of our great chief of chiefs, Cochise. In fact, when the *pindah* was first captured, Go-Yath-Khla immediately saw him as a threat and attempted to torture him to death. He staked the *pindah* between two anthills and started an ant war over the young man's spread-eagled body. When no one was looking, I rubbed some sweet, sticky maguey juice on one of the wrist thongs, and the ants swarmed the thong and devoured it. The young *pindah* untied his other wrist and got up. Go-Yath-Khla was so furious, he ordered his friends to hold the boy down and he started to pour hot coals on his hand.

"Just then Cochise showed up. He'd just heard that the ants had eaten through the boy's thong, freeing him. The great Cochise declared it to be a divine act, what we would call a miracle. He said he was adopting the *pindah* as his son-through-choice, and that he was declaring the *pindah* to be Go-Yath-Khla's *hunka* brother, his spirit brother. He named the young *pindah* Blood Ant.

"A few years later, I was old enough to marry and conceive, and Go-Yath-Khla wanted me for his bride. I hated him with a passion and told the *pindah*. He told me he'd heard the white-eyes had a struggle to the northeast that they called their Civil War or the War Between the States. He recognized that he would never be an Apache full-blood and confided to me that he planned to leave. If I wanted to leave, he said he'd take me with him and that he'd find a home for me to the north with a *pindah* family.

"He came to my wickiup one night. He'd staked our horses a few miles outside our *ranchería* in the desert. We sneaked out of the village, mounted up, and never looked back. Go-Yath-Khla led a party after us, but the *pindah* was too smart, too trail-wise. They never caught up to us.

"The *pindah* asked around and located a ranching family in the Arizona Territory who'd lost a daughter to cholera. He asked them if they wanted to adopt me. They took me in and raised me as one of their own. They immediately introduced me to Frank. We instantly fell in love and married young. Richard was our firstborn. When the couple died, they left their ranch to Frank and me. We expanded it many times over and that ranch is now El Rancho del Cielo.

"I owe them much, but in truth everything I have, everything I ever will have, I owe to one man. I owe him a debt I can never repay."

"The *pindah-lickoyee*?" Eléna asked softly.

"*Enju,*" Katherine said. "Yes," in the Apache tongue.

"Did you ever find out what happened to him?" Rachel asked.

"I know everything about him. He's internationally famous. His face has appeared in newspapers and rotogravures all across this country—all over the world—and reporters write about his life continually. So, yes, I have followed his life, and he's never been out of my mind, not ever, not once. It's as if part of me is still with him, has always been with him—escaping from that Apache village all these years—instead of being with you, Richard, and Frank."

"You owe him a debt you can never repay," Rachel said. "We all do."

"He sounds like a very great man," Eléna said.

"If robbing banks and trains makes a man great," Katherine said, "he is."

"He's not . . . ?" Eléna started to ask, intuiting who the man might be.

"Outlaw Torn Slater," Katherine said. "He's the worst desperado any of us has ever heard of and the best man I've ever known."

"Did you ever see him again?" Rachel asked.

"No, but remember that last time Slater was captured? It was in all the papers. The judge sentenced him to the Yuma Territorial Prison, where he would work in the stone quarries until they hanged him by the neck until dead."

"So you visited Slater in prison?" Rachel asked.

"No."

Rachel stared at her mother, silent. "But I know you, Mom. You didn't just do nothing."

Katherine nodded her head slowly. "*Enju.* I did something. I broke Outlaw Torn Slater out of Yuma."

Chapter 62

"But enough talk," Mateo interjected. "We have something far more exciting for our young friend."

Grabbing Richard by the arm, he led him and the two women up a nearby hill, at the top of which was a stand of trees.

"What's this?" Richard asked.

"You'll see," Isabella said. "Go up there and take a look."

Richard headed the rest of the way up the hill to the stand of trees, and Mateo whispered to the two women: "Do not tell him about the ceremony below— what's really happening."

"I hear this time it won't be a ritual," Isabella said. "Those people down there are going to actually crucify that man."

"I heard that too," Rozanna said.

She hurried up the hill and joined Richard en route toward the trees and away from the horrifying spectacle below.

Mateo stood on the hillside with Isabella and studied the goings-on below.

Sure enough, the crucifixion was beginning. They had indeed resurrected Golgotha, the Hill of Skulls—on an adjacent hill. In fact, it was surrounded by piles of skulls. The cross was flat on the hilltop, and they now lashed their sobbing victim's neck, belly, and extremities to its crossbeams. A wadded-up rag had been shoved into the man's gasping mouth, and they tightened it with a gag made of braided maguey. With heavy wooden mallets, they hammered iron spikes into the man's hands, wrists, and feet while he bucked and convulsed violently on the big beams and groaned into his gag.

At the base of the cross Mateo noted was a pre-dug pit, and when the centurions finished with the nails, they lifted the cross up and slid its bottom beam into the deep hole. They shoved stones and dirt into it to shore up and steady the vertical beam.

"Los indios ahí abajo es muy loco," Isabella said. ["Those Indians down there are very crazy."]

Mateo crossed himself. Isabella studied the mob scene below, then looked at Mateo.

"You like our young friend very much. I can tell, and you no like nobody."

Mateo shrugged.

"Because he helped you defeat Sinaloa?"

Mateo looked away. "Among other things."

"What other things do you like about him?"

"In some ways he does understand us."

"¿Verdad?"

"For a gringo he is *simpático*. I've never known one like him."

"But he will never be *us*."

Mateo was silent.

"I don't know, Mateo," Isabella said. "You liking a gringo? It makes no sense."

"I owe him. *También*."

There. Mateo said it.

"Really? You believe you owe . . . *¿uno gringo?*"

"Mucho."

"Why?"

"His sister."

"So you screwed his sister. You screw me too. You screw my sister. I never hear you say you owe us."

"I didn't screw her."

"What?"

"I brained her with the leaded buttstock of my quirt. She attacked me when I tried to abduct her brother. I was mad and didn't realize how hard I hit her. I think I killed her."

Isabella stared at Mateo, stunned.

"So when my sister and I make love to the boy, that will make it up to him? Make up for you killing his sister?"

Her face was filled with derision.

"No, but it's something."

"So you sacrifice my sister and me to him? In that stand of trees?"

"I couldn't find an Aztec altar."

"You are *más loco que los muchos locos indios ahí abajo* [more crazy than the crazy Indians down there]."

Now Mateo looked at her a long hard minute.

"You better help your sister attend to Ricardo," Mateo said, "before he gets curious and comes out to look."

"When we are done with him he will be too weak to look. You will have to carry him out of here."

Mateo allowed her a small smile.

Isabella smiled back at him. "*Es verdad*. We will give Ricardo a rite of passage he will never forget."

PART XIII

My sister and I will teach you much.
—ROZANNA DEVARGAS

Chapter 63

Jaguars are incredible climbers, and he followed his friend down the mountain switchbacks with no effort. He still couldn't get over the scene up by the trestle, however.

There was a lot the cat did not understand. He'd watched confused when his friend had lowered himself over the edge of the trestle, swung out over that vertiginous abyss, and then climbed into the forest of underpinning, packing the criss-crossing joists with bags full of God knows what.

Afterward, he and the jaguar had climbed down-trail to the boulder, where they had waited for the train. The big cat had come out from behind the boulder only when he saw his friend expose himself to the men on the train. He'd heard the verbal exchanges between his friend and the train people. Then his friend lifted the rifle to his shoulder.

He knew the man was tough, but he'd never dreamed he

*could disintegrate a bridge, a train, and the two dozen men
standing on the tracks with one rifle shot.*

*This was, indeed, a man worth traveling with. He'd chosen
his companion well.*

Finally they reached the bottom of the gorge. The
man had staked, hobbled, and tethered his horse and
the mules a quarter mile or so down-canyon. They
rounded the stock up, then returned to the smoking
ruins that had been the train.

There, the man began poking through the rubble,
and rubble it was—the shattered remains of dozens
of boxcars, the iron wreckage of the still-smoking, still
scorchingly hot locomotive engine parts, the busted-
up tender, and the piles of kindling that had fueled
the engine. Big steel wheels and greasy axles were scattered all over the place. M. Mort paused to sniff and
study a diamond-shaped smokestack, black with soot
and grime.

Then there were the remains of men who had
fallen a dozen stories to their deaths. Their bodies
were everywhere—scores of them, many more buried
and crushed beneath the junk that had been a bridge
and a long train of boxcars. Those men, parts of
whom Mort could see, lay smashed and flattened from
the force of their fall. They had been taken unawares,
their faces suddenly transmogrified by stark terror
and the shock of suddenly hurtling through space
toward their inevitable death. So their faces were not
at peace but terrified beyond all reason. They had
not gone gentle. Arms and legs had been broken by
the fall and were skewed at grotesque angles. Most of

them were attired in the gray military uniforms of
their trade. They had been dead less than an hour,
but already plagues of flies were buzzing above their
faces, and high overhead legions of vultures and
hawks circled, keeping their patient vigil, their eternal
deathwatch.

One at a time Slater located and picked up the
shiny gold bars and the canvas bags filled with green
paper—the loot that Mort's master had clearly come
for. Why on earth he wanted the metal and the canvas
bags, the jaguar could not understand. They couldn't
eat metal and paper. What use were they?

Well, it was not his to reason why. His friend knew
things he could not comprehend. After all, he had
not known his friend could blow up the bridge, a
train, and all the men in it either.

And he had saved him from the anaconda.

Lowering himself onto his haunches, Mort watched
his friend sift through the wreckage, searching out
the glittering pieces of metal and the banded stacks
of green paper.

Chapter 64

The next morning Katherine and her people were up at first light. Katherine did not know when they'd have another real meal, so she insisted on a cookfire—with more beans, salt pork, tortillas, and coffee. After Antonio had packed the mule, they mounted up and headed down the hill.

They were by the station when the train pulled in. A Cooke-Danforth eight-wheeler, it was topped by a soot-blackened funnel-shaped crownpiece and spark-expender. Black smoke and flaming embers spewed out of it. In front of it was mounted a massive cowcatcher. Behind the locomotive was a firewood tender, which was almost completely depleted and in serious need of refueling.

After a half hour of haggling with the stationmaster, Katherine purchased an entire stockcar. They not only took their mounts and their pack animals on board with them, they shared their car with a half-dozen federales, whom she viewed as bodyguards.

The car was actually a ventilated boxcar with every

other slat ripped out. If banditos or rurales attacked them, Katherine figured that they could aim at them through the missing slats and the desperadoes would have a harder time spotting and shooting at them.

The trip was to take sixteen hours. Eléna, however, warned them that this was Méjico and nothing ran on time. It would take a full day, minimum. They would spend half their time on sidings, while the trains in front of them loaded and off-loaded their people and goods. A good part of the time would be spent negotiating their right-of-transit *mordidas* [bribes] as well as their refueling and rewatering bribes, a tradition bequeathed to Méjico long ago by the Spanish conquistadors.

The trip took closer to a day and a half.

On and on, the desert rolled. It was some of the harshest terrain Katherine had ever seen, and she'd lived her life in hot, harsh deserts. They rolled past every variety of cactus, except the saguaro—barrel cactus, organ-pipe, cholla, agave, peyote, hedgehog and bird's-nest cactus, and ocotillo. Every variety of rattlesnake, Gila monster, tarantula, and scorpion was out in force. It seemed to Katherine she'd never seen so much cactus, mesquite, and wind-bent sage in her life.

This was hard land, Katherine thought grimly. No wonder the people it produced were so tough. This was a land where nothing and nobody was safe, ever.

Only the dead.

Was her son dead? That was a possibility she could not allow herself to contemplate. *But don't worry about it until you have to.* As the Bible said: "Sufficient unto the day is the evil thereof." Today's evil is enough. Deal with tomorrow's tomorrow.

All that counted was getting her son back. To make that happen, she would do anything and everything. His freedom was all that counted, and no means or methods were off the table—money, subterfuge, even violence, anything.

Not even putting weight on friendship—particularly on that of an old-time, longtime amigo—someone who now owed her. If the Señorita and Díaz were as bad as everyone said they were—and it was only prudent to assume those stories were true—then Katherine and her friends would need someone wielding some serious firepower before this was over.

But how, where, and when could she find that person?

And why would that person want to help them?

Chapter 65

Isabella joined Richard inside the stand of trees. Rozanna had spread blankets out on the ground.

"But we're missing the ceremony below," Richard said.

"We have a ceremony here that will be *más placentero* [more pleasurable]," Rozanna said.

Isabella joined them inside the cluster of trees. *"Muy más placentero,"* Isabella said. ["Way more pleasurable."]

"It will be the greatest *placer* of your life," Rozanna said.

"It will be a night you will remember forever," Isabella said.

"What will we celebrate?" Richard asked.

"Your baptism of fire," Rozanna said.

"Your rite of passage," Isabella said.

"It sounds . . . *intimidating.*"

"Come, compadre," Rozanna said. "Mateo told us you have never been with a woman before. Well, my sister and I are here for you—pure as the heavenly choir. Mateo will vouch for us."

"He knows?" Richard asked, dubious.

"He has tested us himself," Rozanna said.

"Many times," Isabella said.

"But we're in a cemetery," Richard pointed out.

"Mateo will stand outside," Rozanna said, "so we will not be disturbed."

"I will stand nearby," Mateo said, sticking his head into the trees, "and see that no one bothers you. And I promise not to look myself." He then smiled at them. "Not too much."

Mateo stepped away, and Rozanna sat Richard down on the spread-out ponchos, seated herself beside him, facing him.

All the while, Isabella was pulling off his boots, and Rozanna was laying him out on his back, staring into his eyes. Then Rozanna was joining them both.

Suddenly to his undying surprise a mariachi band surrounded the trees and began tuning up. Among the instruments Richard could discern trumpets, guitars, violins, even a viola.

"They will play for you all the great *mejicano* classics, young friend," Mateo said, "and I shall serenade you personally."

"Mateo has a great voice," Isabella said.

"The best," Rozanna enthused.

Richard did not even know his friend could sing. The band began to play. The first song was the heartrending ballad, "¿Por Qué Es Amor Muerte?" ["Why Is Love Death?"] Mateo began to sing:

¿Por qué me matas con besos?
¿Por qué me debes crucificar con ganas?

¿Por qué tu toque es mi tortura?
¿Por qué es tu amor uno bandido?
¿Por qué es tu amor mi . . . muerte?

Just to make sure Richard fully understood the poignant lines, Mateo sang them for him in English, his deep tenor voice trembling with emotion:

Why do you kill me with kisses?
Why do you crucify me with desire?
Why is your touch my torture?
Why is your love an outlaw?
Why is your love my . . . *death*?

"Never fear, amigo," Rozanna whispered in Richard's ear. "The night is young, and we will have all the time in the world."

"And it will be a very, very long night," Isabella said.

"And if you do not do everything we tell you," Isabella said, her voice scolding him, as she shook a finger in his face, "a very stern night."

"For my sister and I will teach you much."

"We will not be easy on you."

"You will receive *mucha educación*," Isabella said.

"*Una educación* you will remember always," Rozanna said.

Richard's attitude was one of utter trepidation. He genuinely feared that he was not up to everything these young women had planned for him. What if he failed them?

His last conscious, lucid, semicoherent thought—before he began his descent into a bottomless maelstrom of sensuosity—was that he dreaded the good times to come.

Chapter 66

Slater rode down the main street of Corala with a black jaguar walking beside him. He had the mecate for the string of six heavily laden mules behind him dallied loosely around his pommel. He had ridden a long way, dodging and fighting banditos throughout much of the trip, and at dawn he had deducted his piece of the bank's money, which he'd taken off the bandits, and he had buried it in a wooded hilltop outside of town.

At the same time, he had stashed nearly $20,000 in large American bills in the two money belts under his shirt, crisscrossing his chest.

He still had the $100,000 plus in large bills and gold bullion packed on his mules, which he'd taken off the Los Lobos Locos y Duros Bandidos, to deposit in the Mexicano Minería y Banco Central—Méjico's biggest and most heavily secured bank.

He pulled up in front of the bank and tied his stock up to the hitchrack. He then entered the establishment. Telling the security guard to watch his mules, he walked straight into the manager's office and told the man that he had over $100,000 for him. That got the man's attention.

Slater then brought the man outside. While the manager's staff unpacked the mules, Slater and the banker watched—watched them haul the bags of cash money and gold bullion into the man's office. Slater and the manager followed them back inside, Slater dragging two large grain sacks filled with what appeared to be gold bullion behind him.

After the staff had left the manager's office, the banker had closed the door. He then riffled through the stacks of money and examined the bullion. Slater showed him the letter specifying the terms of his employment with Guzman. Even so he had not been confident the banker here would honor it, which was why he'd taken his piece off the top and buried it outside of town under a pile of rocks the night before.

He'd been right to be wary of the manager. He said he was Augustin Sanchez, and he was dressed in a spotlessly white suit, a boiled white shirt with a celluloid collar, and a matching tie. The man's forehead was furrowed, and crow's-feet etched the corners of his deeply wrinkled eyes. Anxiety wrinkles. He was obviously a man who worried a lot. Like Guzman, he had a big dark wood desk. Slater stood opposite him, refusing to accept a chair, Mort lying comfortably by his side. The banker kept glancing nervously at the animal. The man almost acted like he was reluctant to accept the deposit. He wanted to question everything. Finally, Sanchez got to the point:

"How do we know you didn't find more than a hundred thousand dollars on that gold train? Also many of these coins you brought us were melted and fused together. I don't even know what they're worth."

"They're worth what I say they're worth."

"I cannot tell Señor Guzman that the terms of your agreement have been satisfied in full. Among many other things, there is a train and a very expensive trestle which the bank must make good on. Señor Slater, you destroyed a lot of very valuable company property, and the company will insist on deducting those bills, which you incurred when you wreaked so much destruction, from your stipend. In short, you owe us money, not the other way around."

In truth, Slater had kept quite a bit more of the split than he'd agreed on. He had kept $40,000 in pesos and greenbacks—enough money that he would not have to worry about living expenses for a long time to come.

Goddamn it, he did need to relax and have some fun.

Slater fixed the banker with a close, tight stare. Reaching down, he patted Mort on the side of the neck and hissed softly, almost inaudibly. The cat stood instantly, his neck fur horripilating. Baring his teeth, spitting and hissing, he treated the banker to a feral snarl as horrifying as the jaguar's dark jungle heart. Mort then reared back as if he were about to vault the desk and eviscerate the seated man.

Sanchez turned white as a winding sheet—hyperventilating so violently that he almost went into convulsions. Slater then dumped out the contents of each of the big grain bags. Seventeen desiccated, badly banged-up bandito heads slammed, bounced, and rolled across the man's desk, half of them hitting the floor.

"Guzman wanted proof that these *bastardos* wouldn't

be hitting future banks and trains," Slater said to the trembling, slack-jawed businessman. "Here it is as I promised: Proof of death. Business concluded."

He rubbed Mort's ruffled neck, whispered sooth-ingly to him, rose, and picked his double-barrel twelve-gauge up by its breech. Grabbing two more bags filled with hundred-dollar notes, Slater and the big tom headed out the door.

Pausing halfway, Slater said to Sanchez, pointing to the two bags:

"These are for the aggravation your bullshit has caused me."

He closed the door behind him and Mort and he headed out of the bank. He paused for a moment on the plank sidewalk, contemplating how he'd spend the rest of the day and the evening. First he planned to sell his mule string. Then he'd find a hotel that would accommodate both himself and his compan-ion, M. Mort. He'd have a bath, a few drinks, a big meal, a hand or two of cards, then purchase the most expensive woman in the town. He was trail-weary—rode hard and put up wet. But he also had *muchos pesetas* in his money belts, saddlebags, wallet, and even more buried outside of town. Furthermore, he hadn't enjoyed a good meal, a good saloon, a hand of cards, and a pretty woman since he could remember.

At times such as these, it seemed as if his entire life had been work and worry—spent robbing banks and trains, in prison or on the run.

But not tonight.

Tonight, Torn Slater would have some fun.

Chapter 67

For Richard the night was unreal. He'd slipped into a whole other realm, a demented, otherworldly abyss of demented delirium—exciting, to be sure, but also twisted and terrifying. Not only were Rozanna and Isabella transporting him to places he'd never heard of, never imagined, and had truly never wanted to explore, but at times he felt they had unmoored his mind and stripped him of his soul.

At times, the sensations were so extreme he could not control himself, and he'd start to scream. At that point, one of them would grab his mouth hard and hold it until he'd lose his breath and almost pass out.

Once when he'd experienced one of their more amorous machinations—and the two women had barely gotten their hands over his mouth in time to contain his howl—another protracted, mind-shattering scream erupted out of the Aztec ceremony below. Since it was precisely the kind of scream Richard would have made had the two women not silenced it, he assumed that some *indios muchos locos* down there were doing something similar.

Well, good for them. Richard hoped it was as good for that guy as it was for him.

From the sound of the guy's scream, it was.

Still he was not coherent long enough for serious speculations. It was not for nothing that Mateo had once called the two women taking him on this long, dark night of the soul, the "Sin Sisters."

Even worse, Mateo's singing and the mariachi band's endless groaning-moaning repertoire *amor-como-muerte* [love-as-death] ballads were merging with the myriad manipulations of Rozanna and Isabella until Richard, in his unhinged state, actually believed that love and death were one, that he was truly coming to understand Madre Méjico, Méjico Lindo—Méjico *muerte*.

Mateo sang to him:

> *¿Por qué tu amor es tan escalofriante?*
> *¿Por qué tu amor me hace llorar?*

And again came Mateo's rhapsodic translation:

> Why is your love so blood-chilling?
> Why does your love make me sob?

"Mateo," Richard wanted to scream in the throes of both ecstasy and trepidation, "you're wrong. I'm as *mejicano* as you, as any *mejicano*. I'm *mejicano* in my blood, in my bones, in my soul."

But deep down inside, Richard knew that he was only *muy grande loco* and indeed had lost his mind.

Es verdad.

Isabella and Rozanna had now blurred into one single beautiful *mujer* [woman], in part because they seemed to be omnipresent, everywhere at once, turning his entire corpus into one single conflagration of furious feelings, his mind-and-body passing in and out of focus, yet his whole being, deep down inside, focused and transfixed by impulses and thoughts he would never understand.

And still the music went on.

Mateo in his throbbing tenor enthused about the unanimity of lust and violence, of love and death. He sang to him all the great old *mejicano* ballads, intoning such immortal lines as:

> *¿Por qué es mi amante mi asesino?*
> *¿Por qué es tu amor mi matadero?*

As usual Mateo sang the soulful sentences in English for his unfocused friend:

> Why is my lover my assassin?
> Why is your love my house of death?

And, yes, here in Méjico, Richard had come to understand the meaning of those hard truths.

He'd engineered the killing of scores of thousands of men en masse, in a single day, and he was lauded for it by tens of thousands. And now he'd gotten drunk, watched a man be crucified, and experienced pleasure that transcended comprehension. If that didn't make him *uno mejicano verdad,* what did?

Well, he and his sister had come here to find the real Madre Méjico.

Rachel, I don't know about you, but I've found the real Méjico now. I've learned more about it than I ever wanted to know.

And still Mateo's voice rang in his ears.

> *¿Por qué es mi deseo si depravado?*
> *¿Por qué amas hacerme sangrar?*
> *¿Por qué amas me cruz de muerte?*

And again Mateo warbled the translation to his friend:

> Why is my desire so depraved?
> Why does your love make me bleed?
> Why is your love my cross of death?

Chapter 68

Major Pedro Morales and his men were following the Fiesta de Muerta celebrants, helping themselves to tamales and tequila along the way. Still, at all times, he kept his eyes on Richard, Mateo, and the two women, who had finally departed the cemetery and were heading on up the street.

He was with four other handpicked, hard-bitten cavalry *soldados*. Fifty feet behind them, six more federales led their string of a dozen horses. A spy named Luciano Riaz, dressed in loose-fitting white peasant garb, stood next to Morales.

"You say you are certain that man up there is Lieutenant Ricardo?"

"*Sí*, Major Morales."

"But if he is so important to the Sonoran cause, why would they allow him to wander the town, guarded only by drunks and *putas*?"

"It is the fiesta," Luciano said. "The officer in charge wanted to celebrate, let go, have fun. The gringo had helped them so much he wanted him to have fun too."

"That wasn't very smart," Morales said.

"*Sí*, but flesh is weak."

Morales stared at the man a brief moment.

"It was ever thus."

"But so much the better for us," Luciano said. "This way Ricardo will be much easier to capture."

"Why?"

"You will catch him in a most vulnerable position."

"In what way?"

"I am told that his commander, Major Mateo, has been supervising the loss of his innocence. He has been bedding down two of the most desirable women in Hermosillo this very night and is now going to a house of assignation for even more dalliances with even more desirable *putas*. They are and will be drinking even more tequila and mezcal tonight, and they look forward to consuming more liquor and more *mujeres muchas bellas* in bed tomorrow. With so much excitement on their minds, their guard will be down. We will apprehend the notorious Ricardo as easily as taking fiesta candies from a sick *bebé*."

"I wish I was drinking tequila and bedding down *mujeres muchas bellas* instead of hunting and abducting men for Díaz and the Señorita," Morales grumbled softly to himself, staring up the street, keeping his eyes fixed on Ricardo and his three friends.

"I hear one of the women Mateo is fixing Ricardo up with is the most desirable widow in all of Hermosillo, and she is of only twenty years. I wish someone would fix me up with someone like her. Believe me, she is so *mucha bella* he will be completely preoccupied and present no opposition at all."

"What floor will they be on?"

"The second floor."

"The mode of entry?"

"I would enter the back door—the one reserved for women that work there and the help. You will be less obvious, less noticeable."

"*Bueno.*"

Morales abruptly stopped and motioned to his men to halt as well. Two of his men signaled the six men down the street walking their mounts.

"We'll give them twenty minutes to get settled, maybe get into bed with their señoritas, and then we will storm their room and grab the invaluable, much-sought-after Ricardo."

"Maybe we should lay a gun butt up alongside his invaluable head and let him know just how invaluable we think he is," Sergeant Enrico Gonzolez said.

"You kill him or even seriously injure him," Morales said, "Díaz and the Señorita will have your hide on her Inquisitor's rack and your heart in her High Priest's hands. Your head will bang down her pyramid's steps."

The sergeant quickly, silently crossed himself.

"Where do we find *mujeres* [women] like the Señorita?" the sergeant asked.

"In Díaz's Méjico, that is where. Where do you think we are? Paradise? God's Peaceable Kingdom?"

The sergeant crossed himself again.

"Let us get that *hideputa,*" Morales said.

They started up an alley, motioned the men and horses behind them to follow, and headed toward the back of the brothel.

Chapter 69

All the way back to their hotel, Mateo sang, but soon it was clear that he, not Richard, needed help. While Richard had been otherwise occupied, Mateo had been drinking mezcal in order, he said, "to inspire his singing and lubricate his vocal cords." Rozanna and Richard flung one of Mateo's arms over each of their shoulders and half walked, half dragged him through the streets. From time to time, Isabella spelled one of them. All four of them continued to slug mezcal out of the bottle's neck. Mateo's drunken singing never ceased, and occasionally his three friends joined him. Mateo's favorite, the one he sang over and over, was the achingly sorrowful *mejicano* love-as-death ballad, "Por Qué Es Amor Muerte?" ["Why Is Love Death?"]

> *¿Por qué me matas con besos?*
> *¿Por qué me debes crucificar con ganas?*
> *¿Por qué tu toque es mi tortura?*

¿Por qué es tu amor uno bandido?
¿Por qué es tu amor mi . . . muerte?

Just to be sure his young friend understood not only the song but Méjico herself, Mateo, once again, sang the lyrics for him in English, his tenor voice vibrating, almost cracking with passion, heartbreak, and pain:

Why do you kill me with kisses?
Why do you crucify me with desire?
Why is your touch my torture?
Why is your love an outlaw?
Why is your love my . . . *death*?

At last, they reached their hotel. Actually, it was a hotel brothel, but Mateo knew the owners and had gotten them a good rate on a room with two beds.

"I can get us a good rate on the *putas* too, amigo," he had said to Richard after they checked in. "Finest *putas* in all of Méjico!" He then laughed uproariously.

The three of them needed every ounce of their strength and stamina to half drag, half carry the singing, mezcal-drinking major up two long flights of steps. As soon as they reached the top of the second flight, however, Mateo lost his balance, broke free from his friends' grip, fell backward, and tumbled head over heels back down the stairs. When he attempted to get back up, he slipped and somersaulted back down the next flight.

"Where is the *letrina* [latrine]?" he shouted up the steps at his friends. "I don't feel so good."

Actually, Richard was now starting to wobble as well, so the two sisters pushed him into their room.

"You wait here," Isabella said. "Get some sleep. We'll join you after we help Mateo to the latrine and back."

The two sisters bounced down the stairs, laughing. The Sin Sisters, indeed. In truth, Richard thought they were the two finest women he'd ever known— his sister and mother notwithstanding. He stared down the stairwell and watched as they each flung one of Mateo's arms over their shoulders and hauled him out back to the can. He was utterly unable to walk, his feet dragging across the floor.

Still he continued to sing—drunkenly, incorrigibly, incoherently:

> *¿Por qué tu amor es tan hermoso?*
> *¿Por qué tu amor me hace llorar?*

And again Mateo's hoarse, rasping, stammering translation:

> Why is your love so beautiful?
> Why does your love make me sob?

PART XIV

"And, anyway, who cares if he's dead?" the countess said with an annoyed shrug. "The man was lowborn, disgustingly common. The world—at least, my world, the places myself and Lord Oliver frequent—is better off without him."

Chapter 70

Corala was a gold mining town, which only exacerbated its general decadence. When Slater and M. Mort headed down the dusty streets, on each side they observed an endless assortment of cantina/brothels, which catered round the clock to the drunken miners' wants, needs, and desires. Their names denoted their offerings: La Puta del Diablo [the Whore from Hell], El Hoyo Negro [the Black Pit], and El Fuego del Azufre [Fire and Brimstone].

Slater finally found a hotel that said he could take a cat into his room. He naturally did not tell them *el gato* was a full-grown jaguar—eight feet long from tip of nose to end of rump plus a six-foot tail. So he had to sneak the black jaguar into his room by the stratagem of quietly walking him up the side stairs. His room had an outside balcony, and Slater assumed that Mort—not being a fan of the great indoors—would choose to sleep on it.

Slater was restless, though. He wanted a drink and maybe some cards, not a bed. They had slept and eaten on the trail. For lunch he and M. Mort had split a twenty-pound *jabalí* [wild pig] and a pot of beans just outside of town. Mort had eaten most of the pig and was still digesting it. The animal could barely keep his eyes open and needed a good five hours of uninter-rupted slumber. Slater doubted, however, that even Corala's most violently dangerous watering hole/saloon—la Cantina del Malo, where Slater planned to play cards that night—would allow jaguars on its premises, which was okay with both him and Mort.

Since Slater was looking for a high-stakes poker game, he didn't want to look like a flat-broke cowboy. After treating himself to a long bath, he'd trimmed his beard, then brushed and put on his black frock coat, black pants, and a matching shirt. He carefully cleaned off his boots.

When Slater entered la Cantina del Malo, the cat slunk under the cantina's raised wooden porch and lay down for his nap. Once inside Slater felt right at home. Cantina del Malo was luxurious by the stan-dards of impoverished, war-torn Méjico. It featured high ceilings, big cut-glass, candlelit chandeliers, and over twenty tables, half of which ran games of chance. A *puta muy bella* in a tight red dress was banging out a fair rendition of "Amour Es Muerte" ["Love Is Death"] on the piano. Slater could hear the whisk and snap of the cards as they slid across the green baize, the dealer's nonstop chatter: "*cuatro damas* [four ladies]," "*nueve de los diez* [nine on the ten]," and "*ante veinte* [ante's twenty]." He counted three blackjack tables, where men in white shirts with black elbow garters dealt the pasteboards out of boxy-looking shoes, one roulette wheel, and a half-dozen serious poker games.

The one in the far corner—where the dealer had just shouted *"Ante viente"* looked to be the most promising game. The table looked to be full but he thought that after they saw his money, they'd make room for him.

He turned his back on the cantina long enough to order a bottle of mezcal and a glass, when he heard a half-dozen pistol shots. He turned and the dealer at the big-money corner table was flipping backward, taking the upended straight-backed, bentwood chair with him. One of the six cardplayers was standing, his guns drawn and smoking, as the man toppled backward. Six charred, bloody bullet holes were erupting in the late dealer's chest and stomach.

Slater could tell from the high stacks of blues, reds, and whites in front of his toppled chair and the minuscule stacks of chips in front of the other six players that the murdered man had been the table's top, undisputed winner. Slater also noted that the table now had one very empty seat and that if he wanted serious high-stakes poker, that table was the one.

If he didn't mind a little risk along with his reward.

Which, for Slater, was no problemo.

Chapter 71

Richard was just starting to pull off his boots when the door burst open. Four men in military uniforms jumped him. Two grabbed his arms, another his legs, and the fourth hammered his left temple with the butt of a heavy, large-caliber pistol. Instantly, Richard's vision was swimming, and his knees were also turning to *sopa pollo* [chicken soup].

Suddenly the hallway and the room were also filling with hysterical *putas* in nightgowns. Beating the men with anything and everything they could find—chamber pots, stools, fists, shoes, water pitchers—they were also screaming frantically for Mateo. Even in his drunken, terrified, pain-racked state, Richard could not help but notice that Mateo was friends with a lot of *putas*.

Apparently, the commotion even reached Mateo and the two sisters in the *letrina*. As the four men dragged Richard out the room's door and toward the steps, Mateo and the women were reentering the establishment. Mateo had drawn his .44 Army Colt and was clambering up the steps, firing rounds in the general direction of his and Richard's room. He was so drunk he was as great a threat to Richard and the *putas* coming to Richard's aid as he was to the young man's abductors.

Rozanna and Isabella were also coming to his rescue. Somehow they'd commandeered pistols, and they too were shooting at Richard's kidnappers. Their aim was far better than Mateo's, and they actually winged one of the intruders.

Now Richard was getting his legs and his coordination back. A big man who had fought in the ring, he was throwing hard, even lethal, punches at the four men, dropping one of them. When a *soldado* tried to throw an arm about his throat, Richard got his teeth into the arm and bit it so hard the man howled.

Now Rozanna and Isabella had reached the hallway. They threw themselves on the disguised *soldados*, hammering them with empty pistol butts, biting and clawing them, kicking at their groins and shins. But suddenly five more of Morales's men—who had been among the six *soldados* watching the horses—were entering from the street, bounding up the steps and wading into the mayhem. Flailing at the two women and Richard with pistols and weighted saps, they quickly subdued them.

Again a hombre with a heavy revolver pounded one of Richard's temporal lobes with the pistol's butt. This time Richard's legs collapsed, his arms dropped, as if they were pure lead, and his vision twitched uncontrollably. Nonetheless, he could hear the drunken Mateo, roaring like a grizzly bear brought to bay, firing his pistols and shouting obscenities. A big *soldado* quickly grabbed Mateo and beat him into bloody oblivion with a weighted sap.

The room and hallway were now packed cheek by jowl with screeching *putas*. The disguised federales tried to fight their way through the mob of outraged whores, but quickly gave up. That left only one way out. The street was only one story below, so the drop was not deadly. Since Richard was barely conscious and incapable of resisting, four of his captors simply picked him up under his back and legs and hauled him to the window. Hoisting him up over the sill, they dropped him feetfirst into the alley below.

All the while, *putas* threw anything and everything at Richard's captors—boots, empty guns, tequila bottles, coal-oil lamps, broken furniture—pelting them with whatever they could get their hands on.

Then each of the men—amid the torrential barrage of *puta*-hurled rubble—crawled over the sill and leaped into the alley below, trying not to land on Richard and each other.

One of them threw Richard over his shoulder, and they jogged up the alley and toward the street, where the rest of their men waited for them with horses. Lashing the unconscious Richard belly-down over the saddle of a big bay, they mounted up and headed out of town at a hard gallop.

They had a long, hard, hellishly hot ride ahead of them.

They were taking Richard to the Señorita's hacienda from hell.

Chapter 72

Slater studied the cantina in the bar mirror. After receiving his bottle of mezcal and a glass, he paid the barkeep. Grabbing the bottle, he placed the glass over its corked neck.

Glancing in the mirror, he accidentally caught his reflection. As usual, everything he had on was black: His flat-brimmed Plainsman hat, his thigh-length frock coat, shirt, and knee-high boots. Even his brace of Navy Colts in their cross-draw, tied-down holsters was ebony-handled. His gun belt also matched the hue of those handles although it glinted brightly with brass cartridges. Slater was aware that some people disparaged his attire as unduly sepulchral. In truth, he cared nothing for clothes, less about his appearance, and he favored black simply because he spent most of his life on the trail and on the run, and dark clothing was easier for him to keep clean.

So he turned toward the big room and closely studied the large octagonal card table where the cantina's high-dollar game had been in progress. For the moment, the game was on hold. One of the players had unceremoniously emptied his Colt .45 into the dealer, and the shots had knocked the man over onto his back. He was still in his chair, still on the floor, his arms, legs, and head jerking convulsively, six charred, smoking, blood-spurting holes still decorating his stomach and chest.

The surviving players were already dividing up his massive stacks of chips, the shooter, who had had the next-best hand, raking in the lion's share of the pot. He then rooted through the man's pockets for the rest of the game's spoils. Placing the dealer's wallet, pistols, rings, stickpin, and pocket watch on the table, he divided them up with the rest of the players.

Slater hoped the vultures, now starting to drag the man outdoors, would have the grace to get him out of the cantina before stealing his boots. As if on cue, however, two of the men, who were dragging the dealer out, began stripping off his boots well before they made it to the batwings.

Well, that didn't take long, Slater thought ruefully.

Grabbing a rag off the bar, Slater crossed the room and placed his glass and bottle on the poker table. Wiping the blood off the late dealer's chair and off his part of the table, Slater sat down in the dead man's chair.

"Guess I found me the *mucho dinero* table, the hot game, no?" Slater asked. "And an empty chair, no less."

The six other players stared blankly at him, their eyes empty of any empathy or concern for the recently deceased player.

"Hot as the hinges of hell," a player said. Slater turned to the speaker. He was a large-framed, dark-haired, goateed gentleman, decked out in a white planter's suit, a matching ruffled shirt, and a panama hat. His smile glittered extravagantly. His gaze glittered as well, but more maniacally. He never blinked, and his stare never left Slater's eyes.

He was the one who'd just killed the dealer, and the big .44 nickel-plated Colt was still smoking in his fist.

Chapter 73

Twilight in the canyonlands.

Mateo did not know what to do. General Ortega had entrusted Ricardo to Mateo's care, and then Díaz and the Señorita had abducted him. Now there was no way Mateo could get him back. Nor had he had time to ride to the fort and round up a company of proper *soldados*. Instead, he'd had to hastily conscript six vaqueros, whom he'd dragged out of a cantina at the point of a gun and forced into these infernal criss-crossing canyonlands. Mateo had hoped to pick up the abductors' trail, but the canyon floor was hard as brick and almost impervious to hoof prints. And now that the sun was up, these desert arroyos were hot as Hades with the doors blown off.

Their water bags would not last Mateo and his men another day. Unfortunately, water would not be a problem for the men he was pursuing. Every twenty miles or so, Mateo found evidence that those men were being resupplied—water, grain, ration bags, and fresh horses. Clearly, they had cached provisions for themselves going all the way back to Sinaloa. They even had men with remudas waiting for them. When they wore out their mounts, they exchanged them for the new ones waiting for them, cut the old horses loose, and continued on. Meanwhile Richard and his men struggled to force extra miles out of their dehydrated, hard-used, worn-out stock.

There was no way Mateo and his crew of untrained, nonmilitary cowhands could track, catch, and kill a team of professional *soldados*, no doubt handpicked for this special, well-planned assignment.

But what could Mateo do then? Returning with a band of *soldados* and picking up the trail all over again was fruitless. By the time Mateo and his men reached Sinaloa, Richard would be in the Sinaloan army or in the Señorita's torture chambers or in her infamous slave-labor prison mine—or, if he was lucky . . . *dead.*

Mateo shuddered at the thought.

Nor did his own prospects look much brighter. He'd wanted to reward Ricardo for his hard work, for his stunning victory over the armies of Díaz and the Señorita, so he'd sneaked the young man away from the post without permission. Damn it, Ricardo had deserved a real victory celebration. He'd deserved a chance to experience the real Méjico—Madre Méjico, Méjico Lindo!

Y las mujeres muy bellas de Méjico. [And the very beautiful women of Mexico.]

But Mateo hadn't counted on a rurale informant turning him in to the Señorita's federales.

Well, that experience had cost Ricardo his freedom and probably his life.

No, going back to the fort and his men was, for

Mateo, not a viable option. He had single-handedly cost Sonora its last, best hope for defeating Sinaloa. That, General Ortega would never forgive. Ortega's justice would now be harsh, swift, painful, and . . . *lethal*.

Nor could Mateo blame the general. Mateo's atrocious judgment had cost Sonora . . . *everything*, and now Mateo was a man without a country.

Luckily, he'd wanted to show Ricardo such a spectacular time that he'd taken all of his savings with him for this Fiesta of the Dead. He still had most of it in a money belt. But where would he go? He would soon be a wanted man in Sonora, which was a shame. He'd loved the Sonoran army. He'd believed in its cause, and he'd also hated Sinaloa, Díaz, and the Señorita for what they'd done to his own family.

And what they would now be doing to Ricardo.

No, what *he* had done to Ricardo.

Well, whatever he'd done, that bell could not be unrung. No, it was cracked—perhaps even shattered—forever. Nor could he fix what he'd done to Ricardo's sister. Instead he would tell his vaqueros to head on back to Hermosillo by themselves. He was riding off in another direction—toward Sinaloa—and what he would find when he got there, what he would do, and how it would end, hell only knew.

Chapter 74

"Permit me to introduce myself: Señor Juan Del Gaizo at your service, *mi buen hombre* [my good man]." Please let me welcome you to our table."

Señor Del Gaizo was the big, dark-haired, goateed man in the white planter's suit, ruffled shirt, and panama hat. He was the man who had just emptied his pistol into the dealer.

"*Muchas gracias,*" Slater said with a terse smile.

"If you have the dinero, amigo, you got the chair," the federale general sitting across from him pointed out.

"And the price of admission is?" Slater asked.

"Two thousand pesos, or five hundred New Arizona paper dollars."

Slater reached under the table and inside his pants. He had plenty of money in his pants, and the criss-crossed oiled silk money belts under his shirt and coat, which the players could not see, were heavily lined with hundred-dollar bills, its coin pockets packed with hundred-dollar gold pieces. The rest of his take was interred outside of town. Slater had loot buried all over Méjico and the U.S. He couldn't remember where half of the caches were anymore.

Slater pulled out a small rawhide pouch filled with Liberty Head double eagle gold pieces and emptied it out onto the table. He stacked the double eagles in front of him, then pushed $1,000 worth of coins toward Señor Del Gaizo, who also served as the banker. He exchanged them for stacks of white, red, and blue chips.

"Ante's twenty dollars."

Slater pushed a double eagle into the pile in front of him.

"About the last dealer," Slater asked. "What was the problem?"

"With duty comes responsibility," Del Gaizo said, shrugging, "and the man failed miserably in both areas."

"Still, it's a high price to pay."

"So?" Del Gaizo said, smiling. "Who wants to live forever?"

"Look at it this way: The man's sins had finally found him out."

The woman who spoke was an English countess tastefully attired in high-quality riding gear. Sitting on Del Gaizo's right, she was exquisitely featured and alarmingly attractive—almost disconcertingly beautiful—but her smile, while dazzlingly brilliant, was utterly unreadable. Slater had no idea what, if anything, was going on in her head. He did not take that as a good sign.

"And anyway, who cares if he's dead?" the countess said with an annoyed shrug. "The man was lowborn, disgustingly common. The world—at least, my world, the places myself and Lord Oliver frequent—is better off without him."

"My dear," Lord Oliver, the dissolute Englishman sitting on her other side, said in a gratingly upper-class English accent, "we can't all be to the manor born."

"THANK GOD!" the countess roared.

Lord Oliver wore an expensive, dark brown Savile Row, H. Huntsman & Sons silk suit and tie. He favored gold-rimmed eyeglasses and was hatless, his thin bleached-out hair neck-length. His eyes were habitually mocking, elaborately insincere.

Del Gaizo was obviously dangerous. The countess and Lord Oliver were both demented and dangerous.

Slater wasn't sure which of the three he disliked the most.

Chapter 75

Richard and his captors could now see the Señorita's hacienda off in the distance. It had been a long hard journey but finally it was coming to an end.

The trek through the canyonlands had been horrendous—hot, dry, interminable, riding sunup to sundown—and his head still throbbed from the beating he'd taken in the brothel. The soldados *had kept his hands and wrists lashed to the pommel the entire trip. His head and every bone in his body hurt.*

Nor had escape been an option. The soldados *paid close attention to him every second of the trip. Nor did they attempt to conceal from him their destination. These men were taking him to meet Porfirio Díaz and the Señorita. They were taking him to hell, and Richard could not imagine the horrors that awaited him.*

Still the men tried to cheer him up.

"Listen, muchacho, you aren't in bad shape," Capitán Pedro Ramirez had told him that first night. "Believe it or

not, we are here to protect you. People way high up want you in Sinaloa. If they'd wanted you maimed or dead, we'd have done that to you back in your whorehouse room. They want you well and alive, so we want you well and alive. Here, amigo, have some tequila. Maybe we risk a fire and cook you some chili, frijoles, and tortillas. Try to relax. Look on the bright side: The Señorita, we are told, is muy bella!*"*

The joke brought peals of derision from the men.

Try to relax, *Richard thought.* Yeah. Right.

He first spotted the Señorita's palace as they were coming up over a rise. Even at a distance of several miles, it was the biggest, most imposing structure he'd ever seen. It was flanked on both sides by a dozen or more smaller buildings. Since she ruled much of Sinaloa and Chihuahua from that palace, the ancillary buildings also served as housing and office buildings for countless government officials. Since the Señorita's personal safety required a praetorian guard of nearly five thousand *soldados*, several large barracks were also part of her hacienda.

Behind and around her palace were ten million acres of cotton and sisal, from which the Señorita's mills fabricated cloth, rope, and twine. She also raised blue agave out of which she distilled tequila for export. In the wetter regions of her empire, her peons cultivated sugar, and in the highlands, coffee. Everything the Señorita grew she sold abroad for hard currency; nothing she raised went to the *mejicano* people, but then that was true of virtually all Méjico's *hacendados*. The real money was in foreign sales. The *mejicano* people had to rely on imported corn and grain from the United State for their meager subsistence.

Beyond the Señorita's endless acreage loomed the *sierras*. The most infamous of these mountains was El Infierno de Plata [the Silver Inferno]. Richard recognized it immediately. Surrounded at its base by countless smoking smelters, ore-stamping mills, and amalgamating operations. The end purpose of these operations was to remove the carbon and the oxides from the ore, leaving only the elemental metal, which was eventually melted and poured into ingot molds. Richard could see the vast gray-white pall of toxic smoke the industry generated, which shrouded that infernal mountain in a truly hellish haze.

When they were five miles out, sentries and scouts began stopping them, checking the Sinaloan *capitán*'s papers. As the men passed them through, Richard noted the fear on their faces. He had heard many stories of the Señorita's bloodstained windowless torture chambers, where those who failed to follow her commands with unfailing, excruciating exactitude howled like rabid dogs. Now looking at the terror that these men evinced—men who worked within eyeshot of her horrific hacienda—Richard knew that all those horrific stories were true.

"Looking forward to meeting the Señorita?" the captain of the guard, Pedro Ramirez, asked with a mirthless smile.

"Like a turkey looks forward to the ax."

"Ah *sí*, if she only killed as quickly as an ax," his lieutenant, Bernardo Rodriguez, said.

"I hear she's also quite beautiful," Richard said, trying to make conversation.

"*Sí, amigo,* but remember *también* that all great beauty is invariably bloodthirsty."

"Hers certainly is," Rodriguez said, nodding. "Definitely toward her lovers."

"You are suggesting I should avoid her bedroom?"

"Like hell itself," Ramirez said.

"Sounds like the kind of woman I want to take home to Mother."

"If you mother is the Medusa," Rodriguez said.

"Or some other fiend from hell," Ramirez added.

"She must want something from me. I'm not dead yet."

"And you think that's a good sign?" Alvarez asked.

"Maybe not," Richard had to admit.

"*Es verdad,*" Ramirez said. "You might soon wish you were."

"You might beg *tu Dios* for that gift," Alvarez said.

"*Por el presente de muerte,*" Ramirez said. ["For the gift of death."]

On they rode. Richard could now see that on the corners of the Señorita's high white adobe-block walls were deployed one-hundred-caliber Gatling guns, ringed by sandbags. In front of the walls were batteries of Napoleon cannons, probably left over from the American Civil War, and also the Señorita's infamous disciplinary handiwork—men bucked and gagged, stripped naked, and spread out on huge caisson wheels, left hanging on flogging posts, their backs bloody, swarming with plagues of flies.

"The Señorita also has billeted over three hundred battle-hardened cuirassiers behind her palace," Ramirez said. "Well mounted, every one of them is armed with multiple pistols, sabers, and repeating rifles. Paying them each a small fortune, she has purchased their loyalty as well as their murderous skill and utter ruthlessness."

"They will do anything for her," Alvarez said. "Their livelihoods and good personal fortune depend on her survival. Those who threaten her suffer hideously at their hands."

Low rows of fire trenches protected the hacienda and the cannon batteries. The *capitán* led them over a wooden bridge laid across the first of the firing pits. Each cadre of white-clad conscripted peon soldiers was commanded by a sergeant, corporal, and private, each of whom was attired in sweat-stained uniforms and field caps.

And, of course, backing these federale noncoms were the Señorita's army of hard-core killers, her cuirassiers, the cutting edge, the killing edge of her bloodiest blade.

"*Mi capitán,*" Richard asked Ramirez, "before we part, do you have any words of advice for me in dealing with the Señorita?"

"You will not only meet her, you will meet El Presidente Porfirio Díaz, who is her frequent guest. Just remember those two—in fact, all *mejicanos*—respect one thing and one thing only: cojones. You must never show the feather, never cringe or cower. Always talk back to them and under no circumstances whimper."

"Apologizing for our victory over your troops is not recommended?"

"Oh, young Ricardo," Alvarez said, "this is not a joke. Any sniveling will only drive Díaz and the Señorita into paroxysms of hate and rage. At all costs, no matter how frightened you are inside, no matter how much you suffer, you can never crawl, never back down."

On they rode, trundling and rattling across the makeshift plank bridges, traversing the Señorita's fire trenches, their saddles creaking, their bits and rowels jingling, their horses heaving. Finally they crossed the last traverse of the last breastwork and were heading toward the entrance of the hacienda. Not a gate, but a deep, high, wide tunnel, it ran under the ten-foot-thick adobe wall. Blocked at both ends by thick oak doors, belted by heavy iron bands, each a half-foot wide. Secured by massive oak crossbars, reinforced by steel rods, the hacienda tunnel was pretty near impregnable.

El Capitán shouted a password—*"Abandonar toda esperanza todos los que entran aquí"* ["Abandon all hope all who enter here"]—to the sergeant standing atop the wall above the tunnel and he ordered the men below to open the big doors.

Part XV

"Oh, I am a marvelous host," Díaz said, "for in truth I am *muy simpático.* Our Señorita, however, is of a different disposition. Under her angelic beauty, incomparable smile, and incandescent it, she has the heart of a hard-trade *puta*, the soul of a *serpiente de cascabel* [a rattlesnake], and the compassion of an exploding, lava-erupting, metropolis-obliterating volcano. So, in truth, you do not understand me, you do not understand our people, you do not understand Méjico, and— most of all—you do not understand our Señorita Dolorosa, whom in your mother tongue you call 'Lady Pain.' How could you understand . . . *her?* You've never known anyone like her in your life. I've never known anyone like her in my life. No one's ever known anyone like her. So your pretensions and protestations notwithstanding, you will never know the country or the people that created the Señorita and . . . *myself.*"

Chapter 76

An attractive *puta* in a tight red chemise with hair and eyes black as onyx walked up to Slater. Putting her hands around his head, she eased herself down onto his lap.

"I love you, gringo, no shit," she said.

Slater eased her off his lap.

"Maybe later, darlin'," he said with surprising gentleness.

"Ah, was that true love," the countess asked the

table with an elaborately cynical smile, "or the pesos in his pocket?"

"I would not rule out the former," Lord Oliver said to the countess with mock sincerity. "The young woman seemed quite smitten with our sinister-looking stranger."

"Really?" the countess asked, her face a condescending mask of malicious mockery. "Perhaps you think she's also not really a *puta* at all. Maybe she's a slumming angel . . . down on her luck?"

"Who's to say?" Lord Oliver said with a wry smile. "To quote the Bard: 'The course of true love never did run smooth.'"

"Speaking of the Bard," Del Gaizo asked, "you two are clearly English—and of considerable breeding."

"Rather," the countess said with a superior smirk.

"So what are you doing in our unfortunate land? Aren't you slumming yourselves, *solo un poco* [just a little]?"

"Poco un mucho," Lord Oliver mumbled unhappily. ["Rather a lot."]

"Then why are you here?" Del Gaizo asked pleasantly.

"Why, we came for the intellectual stimulation," the countess said, "for your scintillating wit, for your country's classical theater, for its internationally famous ballet."

"And for the erudite discourse at this table," Lord Oliver said.

"I understand completely," Del Gaizo said, still smiling. "You are no longer welcome in 'this earth, this realm, this England.'"

"Oh, we're welcome all right, ducks," the countess hissed, her upper lip curling disdainfully. "The magistrates there would welcome us straight into Newgate Prison if they caught even the briefest, tiniest glimpse of us."

"I don't think they've forgotten our last few indiscretions," Lord Oliver said, laughing merrily. "You see, at one of our last little parties, the countess and I got . . . *carried away*."

"We were experimenting with something called *erotic asphyxiation*," the countess explained. "Have you heard of it? It's the latest thing, you know."

"Perhaps you could enlighten us?" Señor Del Gaizo asked.

"You engage in several rather ingeniously complex acts," Lord Oliver explained, "with your arms and legs trussed up behind your back, while your partner hoists you up above the bed by your neck from a noose. It increases one's ardor quite dramatically."

"And quite perilously, if memory serves," the countess said. Now she was chuckling with eyes shut as if at some secret sardonic joke.

Lord Oliver was giggling so uncontrollably he lost his breath, choked, and could not continue.

"It seems that Oliver and I were the only two participants who survived our last little lovefest," the countess was finally able to explain.

"Two of the more aristocratic guests, who had so unceremoniously expired, were members of the royal family," Lord Oliver said when his own laughter had subsided sufficiently for him to talk. "After their demise, the British constabulary did not view our little games with either understanding or amusement."

"They were quite put out with us," the countess said, nodding her head in suddenly somber agreement.

"So our families passed the hat, so to speak," Lord Oliver said, "and sent us on our way. We have rather generous stipends to live off of as long as we stay away from jolly old England."

"Four or five thousand miles away," the countess said.

"So you are remittance people," Del Gaizo said.

"An unfortunately vulgar turn of phrase," Lord Oliver said. "I view it as fair remuneration for services rendered."

"For a hard job . . . *well done!*" the countess shouted, slamming her open palm on the table so hard the chips and cards jumped.

"Tell that to our late dealer," Slater muttered.

Chapter 77

Richard entered the grand sala of the Señorita's palace, and its grandeur was indeed overwhelming. The hall was at least 150 feet by 75 feet and was easily one of the largest and most expensively decorated he'd ever seen. Its walls were densely filled with original oil paintings by Velázquez, El Greco, and Goya, as well as Rembrandt, Rubens, and a scattering of the great High Renaissance artists, including and most prominently Tintoretto. The walls looked like they belonged in the Louvre, not in Sinaloa. A great forty-foot mahogany banquet table with matching chairs was off to his right. Scores of circular mahogany tables surrounded by quartets of Méjico's ubiquitous narrow, straight-back, leather-upholstered chairs were everywhere. Multicolored sunlight filtered in through the room's massive stained glass windows along the western and southern walls.

What the hell had he gotten himself into?

* * *

An hour earlier he'd been a lot dirtier. After his long desert journey, his Día de Muertos garb was little more than dirty rags. If anything, Richard was even filthier underneath the soiled clothes, so Capitán Ramirez had immediately taken him into a barracks laundry room, stripped off his clothes, and put him into a tub of water. He'd then had the orderlies scrub his body and head with a rough laundry brush and lye soap, taking off the travel dust and half of Richard's hide at the same time. They'd then shaved him with a razor and more lye soap. Dressing him in a new, freshly pressed uniform, Ramirez explained:

"The Señorita likes her gentlemen visitors well scrubbed, neatly dressed in military attire, and close-shaven."

They ordered Richard to dress himself in a federale officer's uniform, and el capitán *escorted him to the palace's main sala.*

Díaz sat on one of the high, narrow mahogany chairs. He was wearing a dress generalissimo's uniform, his chest arrayed with a plethora of ostentatious medals. The Señorita sat on a leather and mahogany couch. She was decked out in a long, close-fitting dress of crimson silk, revealing a disconcerting amount of highly provocative cleavage—too much for a lady of her high station.

Nor, judging from the conceited sneer upwardly twisting the corner of her mouth and the cynical flash of her feral eyes, did she seem to care.

Still, despite the wicked sneer, the violent eyes, the shockingly sensual cleavage, and the almost incomprehensible danger everything about her represented,

Richard couldn't stop looking at her. She was the most blindingly, breathtakingly, heart-stoppingly, hair-raisingly, singularly beautiful woman he'd ever seen.

And clearly the most malevolent.

In front of them were laid out the most expensive wines he'd ever heard of. A 1787 Château Lafite. A 1775 Massandra sherry. A Château d'Yquem 1784. Also cheeses, chorizos, and *pan de campagne*. While he'd never tasted or seen caviar, he believed he even saw two dishes of it. Blacker than pitch, one was for Díaz, the other for the Señorita.

"So how do you like our *Méjico muy bello*, our *santo Méjico* [our very beautiful Mexico, our holy Mexico] so far, compadre?" El Presidente Díaz asked.

To call a man *compadre* was an ultimate compliment in Méjico. Meaning "co-father" in English, implying that Díaz felt as close to Richard as if he were a blood relative, his father-by-choice. But his exaggerated smile and mockingly insincere eyes meant that he was merely ridiculing the young man.

Richard quickly remembered what el capitán *had told him:*

"Just remember, young Ricardo, those two—in fact, all mejicanos—*respect one thing and one thing only: cojones. You must be all balls. You must never show the feather, never cringe or cower. Always talk back to them and under no circumstances whimper or snivel."*

"So I should not apologize for massacring their army and I should not beg them for their forgiveness?"

"Ah, Ricardo," el capitán *said, ignoring the sarcasm,*

"such sniveling will only drive them into paroxysms of rage. At all costs, no matter how frightened you are inside, no matter how much you suffer in agony, never crawl, never back up, and never back down."

"So how do you like our Méjico *amoroso* [our loving Mexico] so far?" El Presidente Díaz asked Richard.

"Your whole country ought to be cemented over," Richard said.

"You have a very poor attitude toward us, no? You talk as if Méjico were a sort of hell on earth."

"It isn't?"

"Ah, you jest, no?" the *mejicano* strongman said.

"Not at all. If I owned hell and this miserable land, I'd rent out Méjico and live in hell."

Throwing his head back, Díaz treated Richard to a long, loud, up-from-the-gut belly laugh.

"I cannot tell you how much I am starting to enjoy your company. You are *precisamente* why I love norte-americanos so much."

"And why is that?" Richard asked.

"You yanquis are so hilariously ignorant and so endearingly naive," El Presidente Porfirio Díaz said. "When you come down here, all of you are filled with such shining dreams, noble visions, and glimmering hopes. You see Méjico as *mucho* barbaric and *muy estúpido*, sorely in need of your clever minds and your yanqui know-how. You believe you can fix us, redeem us for your democratic ideals, convert us to your paths of justice, truth, and right—and, of course, you plan to grow rich in the process. But you discover in the end your hero's journey was all *por nada*—nothing more than a fool's errand, a tournament of windmills. To your dismay, you learn that you've never known anything like our intransigent peons with their infinite idiocy, their hateful hearts, their violent Aztec souls, their grave faces, and their cold, dead, black-as-hell-itself eyes."

"To say nothing of your murderously avaricious aristocrats," Richard said. "People such as yourself and the Señorita."

Suddenly, Díaz was no longer smiling.

"Were it not for the Señorita's whips and shackles," the tyrant said, "and were it not for my stern hand, our peons would instantly return to their old ways."

"Which were?" Richard asked.

"Blood for blood's sake, gorging on each other's entrails, sacrificing their sons by the hundreds of thousands to their demented Aztec gods."

"All of which justifies your own brand of slaughter, slavery, and pandemic penury?" Richard asked.

Wild anger flashed across Díaz's face, but only for an instant. With stunning suddenness a truly transcendent smile replaced his rage, and El Presidente was clapping Richard on the shoulder.

"Come, amigo, I have known you yanquis for decades, and I know more about you than you might realize. You always come down here from Norteamérica, where women are worshipped, children are spoiled, and all men are divinely blessed. In your land all problems are peacefully, easily resolved and all lives have happy endings. Here, however, life is solitary, poor, nasty, wicked, vile, vicious, and short. So you do not understand us—our wisdom, our ways. You become disillusioned. You come to see Méjico as doomed, and you turn your head and walk away in the end, cursing Méjico, cursing men like Díaz, cursing women like our beautiful Señorita, cursing those of us who remain and who must deal with the *Ding an sich* of Méjico, the 'thing in itself,' life in Méjico as it really is, a world devoid of your foolish fantasies and your fraudulent illusions. You eventually, inevitably, go away, all of you, muttering: *The horror, the horror,* denouncing Méjico as a hopeless, helpless, hideous hell. You abandon her, take French leave of your *puta*-lover, Méjico, and you return to your home, your golden land, your Edenic garden, sadder but no wiser, derogating Méjico as a monstrous nightmare from which you one day hope to awaken and never remember, never think of again. But the Señorita and I, we *are* Méjico—in our bones and blood, in ways you can never understand. We have no gringo Garden of Eden to return to, no Land of Nod, no sacred sanctuary of the Lord. Every day, every second of our lives, we must deal with the hatred that is at our country's heart, the barbarism that is in her soul—that *is* her soul—and the despair that is in every fiber of her being. We continue the *revolución* you lacked the cojones to stay and fight for, that scared you off, that you abandoned but that, for us, never ends, and for the sin of your cowardice you can never forgive us and will blame people like Díaz and the Señorita, the ones who stayed and fought and fought and fought . . . *who fought forever.* Instead of thanking us, you will condemn us forever."

"I am not naive about Méjico," Richard said simply.

"Perhaps," Díaz said, his smile still boldly unwavering, "but forgive me if I point out that I have seen your kind before, that I have known other men from other lands who came here long before you. Perhaps I confuse you with them. In my mind after all these years, you all blur into one callow, cruel, composite . . . *gringo*. For I've seen many other foreigners come to our much-abused land—Spaniards, French, *tejicanos*, and, most of all, americanos-gringos— you bring your armies. Each of you takes your turn, has your way with Méjico, plundering her silver, ravishing her women, killing her people, ravaging and ransacking the land. Even you, Ricardo. Especially you, Ricardo—you who think you are so singularly different. What did you just do on your first trip to Méjico? You used your fabulous weapons and scientific skill to kill thirty thousand of our people. And for what? What did you accomplish? How did you make Méjico better when the smoke cleared and the dead were stripped of their possessions?"

"I kept you and the Señorita from taking over Sonora."

Without missing a beat, Díaz and the Señorita stood, clapping long, hard, and loudly.

"Bravo! Bravo!" the Señorita shouted, giving him the merriest, most malignant smile he'd ever seen, a smile so malign he almost winced.

"A compliment on your machismo!" Díaz roared at the top of his lungs.

They then burst into hellishly hilarious laughter.

At last, still smiling, the Señorita leaned forward toward Richard.

"Ah, my young friend," she said, caressing his cheek, "we shall have such times together, you and I."

"Sounds . . . *delightful*."

"For me, most assuredly."

"And for me?"

"I fear not."

"I'm not going to enjoy my stay here?"

"Oh, when I am done with you," the Señorita said, "the rocks themselves shall scream and our desert sands will sob in horror at the wonders I have wrought."

"Ummm," Richard said, "sounds . . . *exciting*."

"Beyond all imaginings. For I intend to teach you much: things that only the dying know and those forever damned in hell can even remotely imagine—things that will be burned into your brain, seared into your soul, and engraved on the very hallowed halls of hell . . . *eternally*."

"Or, at least, for the rest of your mortal life," Díaz said pleasantly.

"However brief a span that may be," the Señorita said.

"But on the other hand," Richard said without inflection or expression, "no one lives forever."

"Always remember that, my young gringo friend," the Señorita said. "It will make your stay in Méjico even more meaningful, more poignant, more . . . *beautiful*."

"Why's that?" Richard asked.

"Because death is the mother of beauty," the Señorita said.

"You think so?"

"I know so," the Señorita said, "and in your case I will teach the immortal truism to you . . . *personally*."

"Should I thank you now?" Richard asked.

"Perhaps you should," Díaz said. "I'm not sure you will feel like thanking her afterward."

"But you've been such great hosts so far," Richard said.

"Oh, I am a marvelous host," Díaz said, nodding in agreement, "for in truth I am *muy simpático*. Our Señorita, however, is of a different disposition. Under her angelic beauty, incomparable smile, and incandescent wit, she has the heart of a hard-trade *puta*, the soul of a *serpiente de cascabel* [a rattlesnake], and the compassion of an exploding, lava-erupting, metropolis-obliterating volcano. So, in truth, you do not understand me, you do not understand our people, you do not understand Méjico, and—most of all—you do not understand our Señorita Dolorosa, whom in your mother tongue, you call, 'Lady Pain.' How could you understand . . . *her*? You've never known anyone like her in your life. I've never known anyone like her in my life. No one's ever known anyone like her. So your pretensions and protestations notwithstanding, you will never know the country or the people that created the Señorita and . . . *myself*."

"You think I might have a problem with the Señorita?"

"Oh, you'll come to grief with her," Díaz said.

The Señorita stepped directly in front of him. Her smile was . . . *unnerving*.

Richard kept remembering the capitán's words: *Show them nothing. Never cringe. Never cower. All they respect is cojones.*

"I find that hard to believe," Richard said with a studied nonchalance.

"Ah, my young friend," Díaz said, his voice almost kind, almost compassionate, "I sincerely wish that were otherwise. I do. I, as you may have inferred, have an amiable disposition. Unfortunately, our Señorita is not as lovingly generous and infinitely gentle as your *bueno gentil presidente* most assuredly is."

"Are you saying I should be afraid?"

"Am I ever, young friend. I have seen Our Lady do things to those who disappoint her that would make the earth shudder, the gods sob, and the heavens roar."

"That doesn't sound very promising."

"It isn't. So do not disappoint Our Lady. Ever. Never. That is my final advice to you, for, as much as I enjoy your company, I must leave now, and you are hers and hers alone. Duty calls."

"Then *vaya con Dios* [go with God]," Richard said.

"*Y diablo,*" the Señorita added.

"Whom you will get to know quite well," Díaz said to Richard, his eyes suddenly somber, expressionless, absent of emotion. "In case you didn't know it, El Diablo and our Señorita are on most excellent terms. She will introduce you to him personally. By the way, Señorita, how is Our Lordship, El Diablo, doing these days?"

"He's been preoccupied, away on other business, but he complains continually that he misses me. 'Without my Señorita,' he says, "life in hell is relentlessly dull, terminally tedious.' He cries out in his misery for his Señorita to return—to smile, beguile, seduce, and . . . *amuse him.* 'Without my Señorita,' he screams, 'my life is a truly hellish . . . *bore!*'"

Díaz turned his gaze to Richard. He studied him for a long, pensive moment. His eyes were still understanding, in fact, almost sympathetic. But not quite.

"It was ever thus, my young friend," Díaz said. "Now, before, always, world without end."

Díaz rose, bowed to Richard and the Señorita. Smiling, chuckling softly to himself, he walked out of the grand sala without looking back.

When Richard turned to the Señorita, she was smiling again, her eyes twinkling with macabre merriment.

"Well, young Ricardo, I finally have you all to myself. You are all mine, you know, and I can't wait to get my tingling talons into you. In fact, I think I've been waiting for *uno hombre* like yourself my whole life long, for all eternity, it now seems, and guess what? Here you are. So let me show you around. Let me introduce you to my ladies. Let me welcome you to my Kingdom of Darkness, to Méjico *verdad*—and to our much-feared and much-reviled Hacienda from Hell."

Chapter 78

"Do not worry about the loss of our former card-player," Señor Del Gaizo said affably to Torn Slater. "We have a far more beautiful dealer coming up."

Even before the men, who'd dragged the dead dealer into the street by the feet, had returned, Slater spotted the new dealer. The woman at the piano was getting up and walking toward their table. Swinging her hips belligerently, her posture was ramrod straight and her long cascading jet-black tresses cascaded down her back. Her red, low-cut, long-sleeved dress superbly showed off her superlative figure. Her black net stockings and high-heeled shoes showed off her legs. With her fine bones and exquisite nose, she had the face of an angel—and the body of a thousand-dollar-a-night puta. But her eyes were what got to Slater. Dark and impenetrable as india ink, they glinted wickedly, and her lips were painted a scintillating scarlet—as bright red as new-spilled blood. When she smiled, her teeth looked white, large, and sharp. Almost as sharp as the folded razor in her shoe.

Slater also noticed she kept an over-and-under .38 derringer up her right sleeve.

"Welcome, amigas and amigos," she said.

She was standing next to Del Gaizo, and Slater wondered if she was with him.

"Sorry about the previous dealer," she said, finding an empty chair and sitting down, "but in this town, a man can get killed for anything—for slights real or imagined, for the boots on his feet. Hell, for the . . . *soles*."

"Sounds like a great place to raise kids," Slater said.

"If your kids are diamondbacks," Señor Del Gaizo said.

"If they're Genghis Khan and Attila the Hun," Lord Oliver offered.

"Or Porfirio Díaz and the Señorita," the attractive dealer added. Then she studied the pile of gold coins and blue chips in front of him and gave Slater a sly, insidiously insincere grin. Turning to Del Gaizo, she pointed at Slater and said: "I like him."

"What she likes is all those yanqui dollars in front of him," a federale generalissimo sitting across the table announced.

"You got a name?" Lord Oliver asked the new dealer.

"My friends call me La Escorpion [the Scorpion]."

"What do other people call you?"

"El Beso de la Muerte [the Kiss of Death]. But you, my wealthy Anglo friend, can call me Muerte for short."

"Do you also deal cards, ducks," the countess asked, "or do you prefer boring us to death with all your tedious . . . *talk*?"

"I do both—as well as a few other things, which you may get to know, if you aren't more polite."

"Are they as amusing as your discourse?" Lord Oliver asked.

"Far more."

La Escorpion began shuffling the cards in three-foot-high cascades, the dazzling pasteboards flowing and flickering like flamboyant flowers in her deviously dexterous hands. During the second of La Scorpion's high-arching shuffles, Slater spotted a second double-barreled derringer—this one up her left sleeve.

Slamming the deck down on the table, she turned to Slater and said:

"Ey, amigo, you want to cut?"

Chapter 79

The Señorita had just introduced her ladies to Richard and was now reclining on her couch, a small, knowing smile playing on her lips.

"How do you like my *mujeres*?" she asked him.

He'd never seen so many spectacularly gorgeous women ever—and certainly not in a single room. And their smiles, incorrigibly coy and cute, almost as if they were afraid to relax their mouth and cheek muscles for even one second and let the slightest hint of an honest look shine through.

All but one.

In a corner a young woman stood facing the wall, whimpering softly.

"Something wrong with the young señorita?" Richard asked, pointing at the woman.

"Renata," the Señorita said sternly, "come over here."

Turning, eyes downcast, the young woman joined them.

"What happened?" Richard asked.

"As everyone knows, I am most kind and generous with my ladies," the Señorita said. "However, I sleep poorly and am easily, agonizingly bored, especially at night. So I require that we all strive to cheer each other up, that we don't sink into ennui, tedium, and melancholia. Renata is new here and has behaved, quite frankly, like a spoiled little bitch. She's sulked, refused to join in the fun, and turned up her nose at our little games. She's acted as if she were better than us—and most insulting of all, better than her Señorita."

"I was wrong," Renata gasped, clearly frightened out of her wits, "and I'm so sorry, Señorita."

"So what happened?" Richard asked, confused.

"Ricardo, Porfirio's harsh critique of me notwithstanding, I only want what's best for all of us, and despite much rumor and false report, underneath this sometimes stern exterior, I am the sweetest of señoritas. Only when I am provoked—as Renata so sorely provoked me earlier—does my darker side emerge, but I am sure that you and I will get along fabulously and that you will never experience that part of me."

"And I avoid your anger how?" Richard asked.

"By giving me everything I want and doing everything I tell you to do."

"And can you give me a hint as to what some of those things might be?"

"You will teach us how to make the superpowerful, smoke-free cordite powder, which we will then use in our rifles, Gatlings, and howitzers. You will teach us the in-te-gral cal-cu-lus, which allowed you to calculate Sonora's cannon trajectories with such murderous precision. You will then set up factories in which to manufacture that explosive in industrial quantities, and you will likewise train our artillery officers and Gatling gunners. In short, you will do for us what you did for Sonora. You will then help us strategize our merciless massacre of Sonora, which most assuredly must and will come. For with your guidance and tutelage, young friend, I intend to scourge all of my enemies' shadows from the face of the earth . . . *forever*. In sum, I intend to burn Sonora down to bedrock and sow its fields with salt. After Porfirio and I finish our conquest of all of Méjico, then we shall turn our attention to your homeland, to your Norteamérica. We shall take back all the land your yanqui friends so unjustly stole from us almost forty years ago."

"Arizona included?" Richard asked, thinking of his own home, his mother, his father, his friends.

"Arizona first of all," the Señorita said.

Remember what el capitán *said. You have to be all cojones with Díaz and the Señorita. Never whimper. Show them nothing but machismo. Never let her see you sweat.*

"You're asking me to betray my home, my country," Richard said. "That's asking a lot."

"*Es verdad,* but then the night is young. Let us talk in private. I have a pleasant side—indeed, a most pleasurable side. I personally believe we will get along fabulously—most lov-ing-ly." She stretched the word into three long, drawn-out syllables. "Don't you agree, ladies?"

Her court ladies shouted excitedly.

"*¡Sí, Señorita!*"

"Bravo!"

"*¡Naturalmente!*"

"But you say you want to destroy the land I was born in," Richard said, "the land of my family."

"Which you stole from us, but, for you, this will be an infinitely generous bargain, from which you will benefit immeasurably."

"In what way?"

"In exchange for your help in the conquest of Sonora and Arizona, I shall give you a far better land, a far better present, a far better future, vastly more money"—here, she stood and gave him the most penetrating stare he'd ever known—"infinitely more power and pleasure than you could ever imagine for the rest of your days."

"And my alternative is?"

"Oh, young amigo, that is an option you do not want to contemplate."

"Why not?"

"Because that road is darker than our people's hard obsidian eyes, darker than our souls, darker than the darkest pit in the darkest abyss of hell, darker even than your Señorita's black, bottomless, infinitely vindictive . . . *heart.*"

"Sounds pretty . . . *dark.*"

"Ah, but my Ricardo, you need never know about such things."

"Really? Why am I so blessed?"

"Because, *verdad,*" the Señorita said, leaning toward him, seeming to give him all of her myriad smiles at once, brighter than ten thousand blinding suns, "young Ricardo, I have been searching for *uno hombre* as smart and strong and ballsy as you. Someone I could work with and partner with. You'll never know how long I've looked for you."

"Still you're asking me to engineer the total destruction of everything I hold dear," Richard said, keeping his face expressionless, without emotion.

"But in exchange, I shall give you something infinitely precious. I shall give you something far more wonderful than anything you have ever known—all of which, in any event, will soon be lost, barren, dreadful, and dead—that world known to you as . . . *Arizona*. In fact, future generations, when they wish to describe ultimate, eternal, irrevocable, irredeemable demise will say *dead as Arizona*. In short, when I am done with that godforsaken piece of turf, it will cease to exist. You will have nothing left to go home to. So all such qualms and considerations will be moot. And in any event, you'll no longer want that blighted place."

"And that is good for me, how?"

"I will give you something of infinitely greater worth."

"Which is?"

". . . *Myself*."

Richard stared at her, silent, his face void of affect or connotation.

Again the gorgeous grin. Again the merry laugh.

"Of course, Ricardo, you can also consider the alternative."

Richard still said nothing.

"Renata, show young Ricardo some of my personal handiwork, namely your much abused bottom . . . *por favor.* And remember, young amigo, if you cross me, Renata's fate is the very best you can hope for."

Renata walked up to Richard, turned around, bent slightly, and pulled up the back of her nightgown. Her behind was garishly scarlet and luridly livid. Richard immediately felt ill.

"Fetch me the instrument of your . . . *enlightenment.*"

Renata hurried over to the wall to Richard's right. He hadn't noticed it before, but a dark piece of wood was hung amid some Aztec artworks and Mayan hieroglyphs. When Renata brought it back, Richard saw it was an oblong mahogany paddle, a full foot long. The words *Via Dolorosa* were burned into one side, *¡Señorita de Infierno!* on the other. The Señorita laughed as she took it by the handle and lovingly fondled it. She then returned the paddle to Renata.

"The gringo is new to our ways, but still I think there is hope for him—and great potential. Of course, if he reacts with ingratitude, I will be forced to educate him—personally—just as I educated dear Renata. Yes, I could turn him over to my Inquisitors, but I do not choose to break him into a thousand little pieces— after which he would be no good to anyone, not even me. So for the time being, I choose to handle his edification personally. Assuming such instruction is even necessary. I promise you, my ladies, if that time comes, I shall invite all of you to watch. Your laughter will add to young Ricardo's humiliation."

"You're still asking me to murder everything that I hold dear," Richard said quietly.

For a second he saw violence blaze in her eyes, but smiling, she quickly mastered it.

"Perhaps, but then you haven't seen me at my best. You will find much about me to like, perhaps even love. So come with me, Ricardo, welcome to my boudoir. And, Renata, please join us—and bring along the instrument of your . . . *tutelage*. If Ricardo proves recalcitrant, I shall see to it that he finds your paddle equally . . . *pedagogical*."

Richard found the Señorita's sneer stunning in its malevolence.

Part XVI

"Fairness?" Señor Del Gaizo repeated, almost sobbing at the sheer hilarity of the idea. "Fairness? You expect to find fairness here in Sinaloa? Here in Méjico?"

Chapter 80

All night Slater studied his opponents. Almost every one of them struck him as dangerous and disreputable. One man in particular warranted watching. Dark complected, dressed in a military uniform, he had a broad nose and piercing, probing eyes. His black hair was shoulder length. His holstered .45 revolver hung from a Sam Browne belt. He had introduced himself as General Alejandro Alano de Vargas, but if he was an army general, Slater was Montezuma. His pants' wide, deep pockets clanged and jangled with gold coins—hardly soldier's pay. Slater took him for a train-robbing bandit, like himself, who was using a military uniform as a cover. He also struck Slater as more than a fair hand. If the night turned violent, Slater planned to kill him first.

First there was William James Oliver—or Lord Oliver, as he fancied himself—and his consort, the countess. He talked to himself in low tones, burst into inexplicable laughter on occasion, but he also kept a Mauser in a shoulder holster, and the countess maintained a pepperbox in her left sleeve. In the other sleeve she'd stashed a double-bladed throwing knife. Lord Oliver was stark staring mad, but his obvious derangement in no way made him less dangerous. He was the kind of crazy that did not have to have a reason for killing a man. An insane hallucination or angry impulse would do just as well.

Then there was the woman sitting next to Slater. She had reddish-blond hair and wide, flaring cheekbones. Modestly dressed, she wore a pearl gray Stetson and a matching blouse. She drank black coffee, and when she looked at Slater, her eyes were both gentle and familiar.

She had not given her name, but Slater swore he knew her from somewhere.

Who the hell are you? Slater wondered. *And what the hell are you doing here?*

Five players facing him—six, including the dealer. Slater made it seven in all.

La Escorpion began dealing. Her patter was standard, much of it in English, in deference to the four gringos sitting at the table.

"Ace on a king . . . No help to the straight . . . Flush a bust . . . Jack on a lady . . ."

Within the hour, it was clear that the Señorita Fortuna was smiling on Slater. He was riding the tiger, raking in pot after pot, to the entire table's obvious dismay and disbelief. The stacks of blues, reds, whites, and double eagles piled higher and higher, even as the stacks of his opponents sunk lower and lower, and their tempers seethed.

And he'd also seen what had happened to the last

man who had enjoyed the blessings of blind luck, the tiger's ride—six bullets in the chest and stomach.

Doesn't seem fair, Slater thought idly. *What's the point of winning, if you can't live to enjoy the spoils?*

At which point a big man—a *soldado* in a faded gray rurale uniform and two of the darkest, flattest eyes Slater'd ever seen—shouldered his way through the batwings. He stopped at the bar for a bottle of tequila and a glass, then headed straight toward Slater's table. He looked angry enough to murder a rock. Lord only knew what kind of fury was bubbling up inside of him.

"Damn, I'm getting tense," the federale general with the hard eyes said.

"A few minutes with one of these daughters of joy might untense you," Lord Oliver suggested.

"I suppose you're an expert in soiled doves," the countess said to Slater. "Perhaps you could give El General some advice."

Slater studied his hand, silent.

"You look like a man who's had more than a few," Lord Oliver said to Slater.

"And left them far more soiled than when he found them," the countess offered.

"Who are you anyway?" Lord Oliver asked Slater. "Your attire is black as any undertaker's. Is that a profession you aspire to?"

"I expect he's arranged for his share of funerals," Del Gaizo said.

"Cheap funerals," Lord Oliver said.

"I say," the countess asked Slater with another brilliant grin, "before the night is over, do you suppose you might arrange for . . . *your own?*"

But Del Gaizo was less interested in the repartee

than he was in Slater's considerable winnings. Staring at the piles of Slater's chips, Del Gaizo shook his heads skeptically.

"Amigo," he said to Slater, "I have seen runs of luck many times, but none so extravagant as yours. Your streak defies all logic. To what do you attribute your extraordinary success?"

"Prayer."

"You do not strike me as a particularly devout man."

"Depends."

"On what?"

"The cards."

"I hope that is all your run of luck is."

"Are you suggesting it's something else?"

"No, I am not omniscient. I do believe, however, that what one does in the dark will come to light. I believe, as the countess said earlier, our sins will find us out. The previous dealer is a case in point."

Slater put down his cards, met Del Gaizo's stare, and said nothing. Slater's stare was hard enough to hurt.

"Ah, stoic silence," Lord Oliver said.

"The Grand Inquisitor meets the Silent Christ," said the countess with her usual enrapturing smile.

She threw a booted foot up on the card table, driving its rowel deep into the wood.

"Still, amigo," the countess said to Slater, "in my opinion this lucky streak of yours has earned a good hard spanking, and Mama's going to give it to you. In fact, before the night's over Mama's going to spank . . . *Mama's going to spank very hard.*"

Chapter 81

Richard was in the Señorita's boudoir, and it was far and away the biggest, most ostentatious bedroom he'd ever seen. Its walls were filled with Aztec and Mayan artifacts. A long purple satin couch with huge cushions stood against the far wall, an assortment of immense, matching overstuffed chairs faced it. A rectangular coffee table of hand-carved walnut stood in the middle. The pièce de résistance, however, resided in the center of the room: a spectacularly massive bed. Perfectly square, it was almost twenty feet on edge.

On the elaborately carved walnut table sat buckets of extortionately expensive Henriot Brut Souverain champagne, more wheels of cheese, more platters of chorizos, mountainous piles of flamingly hot chiles—which the Señorita ate by the handful—more caviar, more pâté de foie gras, more *pan de campagne*.

Grabbing a handful of the incendiary chilis, the Señorita began wolfing them down as quickly, easily, and greedily as if they were sweet chocolates, then washed them down with a large crystal goblet of

Henriot Brut Souverain. Then, throwing back the satin spread, she placed herself on the red silk sheets and reclined against the voluminous pillows with almost sensual indolence.

"Here, young friend, rest yourself next to your Señorita." She patted on the left side of the bed. "Never fear. I intend to show you my *muy simpático* side."

"The one that whaled on Renata's ass like it was a government mule?"

Her eyes flashed furiously, but quickly calmed.

Again, her alluring smile.

"I think of it as elucidation, exegesis, explication, teaching her the way of the world, the ways of God to womankind, imparting to her critical social skills, in the case of my hacienda, indispensably critical skills— in fact, survival skills. Is that not so, Renata?"

"Most assuredly, my blessed Señorita."

"See, young Ricardo, my ladies appreciate my basic goodness, my eternally caring nature. Why do you treat me with such insolence and distrust?"

It burst out of him unbidden, reflexively, without thinking. "Do the words Infierno de Plata [Silver Hell] mean anything to you?"

Her eyes skewered him, blazing like daggers, and her mouth trembled with scarcely contained fury.

"Renata," she said in a deeper, almost contralto voice, "young Ricardo needs a lesson, an object lesson. Let us show him what awaits him if he continues to rebel. Let us renew your education. Let him see what happens to mean young boys who provoke my wrath. Now get me the mahogany and get into position."

Renata burst into terrified tears, but nonetheless fetched the instrument and placed herself over the

Señorita's knee, sobbing softly, gritting her teeth. Hefting the paddle meditatively, the Señorita said to Richard:

"Now let me show you how it's done—the fate that awaits you if you anger me again in any way."

She pulled up Renata's nightgown, exposing her darkly crimson, shockingly swollen rump. Renata began to shake hysterically.

Treating Richard to a sweet yet savage smile, the Señorita raised the mahogany high over her head.

Chapter 82

"Are you sure the secret to your success at cards is prayer?" the countess asked Slater. "If so, you're going to need a lot more of it before the night's over."

Her booted foot was still up on the card table, its rowel sunk deep into the wood.

"Maybe our friend thinks he's tough," Lord Oliver suggested.

"Perhaps," Del Gaizo said, "but I am a rancher by profession, and I know much about 'tough.' I have raised *muchos toros duros* [many tough bulls]. You must know I have seen many tough *toros* in my life, no?" Del Gaizo said to Slater.

Slater stared at him, saying nothing.

The countess pulled a silver dagger out of her boot and drove the blade through Slater's highest faceup card—an ace of spades—and into the table a full three inches. After she released it, her dagger thrummed both visibly and audibly, like an arrow.

"No tough steers, I bet," she rasped, leaning toward Slater and pinning him with her wickedly insolent eyes.

"The hard truth is that our compadre here is winning way too much," Lord Oliver said, "and I don't like it one bit."

"Nor do I," the countess said. "We play by certain rules here, and the rules are immutable. You win, we lose, you . . . die. You. Die. Anything about that statement," she said, staring straight at Slater, "you don't understand?"

"Hardly seems fair," Slater said with a faint hint of a smile.

The table exploded with laughter.

"Fairness?" Señor Del Gaizo repeated, almost sobbing at the sheer hilarity of the idea. "Fairness? You expect to find fairness here in Sinaloa? Here in Méjico?"

But Lord Oliver saw nothing funny in Slater's statement. He pointed at Slater, outraged. "You know, I find everything about you offensive—not only your tedious tripe about 'fairness' but your face, your voice, your manner, your clothes. What do you think of that?"

Slater stared at him, silent. Finally he said softly with only the tiniest hint of a small, secret smile:

"Just talk."

"Ey, amigo, *uno momento*," the rurale said again. "You're getting way too stressed. We came here for poker, *¿verdad?* Let me buy a couple of bottles for the table."

He ordered two liters of the cantina's best tequila.

La Escorpion continued to deal, and Slater raised
$400.

The attractive redhead on Slater's left folded, but
the rest of the table called, pushing stacks of blue
across the table.

*No way everyone had cards worth $400 at the table, yet
they were all in—except for the woman on his left, the only
honest player in the cantina. So this was the hand during
which they planned to kill him—and after which they
planned to accuse him and possibly the* soldado *of cheat-
ing. He had been winning some of the hands ever since he
sat down.*

*To Slater's surprise, he found himself hoping that the
woman beside him survived the night in one piece. This was
unusual. He seldom concerned himself with the welfare of
others—not in hellhole cantinas, not at poker tables like this
one—but there was something about her. Again, he found
himself wondering if they'd met before.*

Whatever was going to happen, Slater was ready.
All his pistol butts were turned in for cross-drawing—
especially when sitting down; in a chair or on horseback, he still could draw them quickly and effortlessly,
pulling them across his body instead of straight up
along his side. Still he needed to improve the odds.
Holding his cards one-handed down along the edge
of the table, he eased the .44 Colt out from under his
belt and laid it on his left leg. The sear was filed down,
the trigger wired back, so he could slip-hammer—that
is, thumb—rounds as fast as he could ear back the
hammer. That way he did not have to pull the trigger.
He eased his other slip-hammered .44 out of its cross-
draw holster and placed it on his right leg. He had an
Arkansas toothpick in a back sheath, which he could

throw overhand—with either hand—at the players around him in a second or less.

He could work pistols and throw knives with either hand, a surprisingly rare skill. He could shoot men with his wrists crossed or uncrossed, together or separately, two shots at once or one at a time, it didn't matter. So when the deal was done, and if any of these assholes threw down on him, he'd grab both guns, dive to one side, and start shooting at them under the table. If they wanted to carve Slater's scallop, they'd have to circle around behind him and shoot him in the back of the head the way Jack McCall had gunned down Hickok. But so far Slater hadn't seen anyone working their way behind him.

And if they came at him face-to-face, they'd win nothing but an early grave.

He wondered idly if they had any idea who or what they were up against.

Chapter 83

Later than night, the Señorita crept back into her bed. Laying herself down next to the snoring Ricardo, she studied him with fascination, with no small amount of fear, and something almost resembling . . . *awe*.

She had never known anyone like him.

She could not believe what he'd done to her.

Five hours before, just as she was preparing to give poor Renata the most pugnacious paddling of her life, Richard had sprung across the bed in a blind rage. Relieving her of the mahogany board, he threw the Señorita over his own lap, threw his right leg over the backs of her knees, and proceeded to beat her behind with all his might. The Señorita had never known such agony existed!

Biting her lips, she'd sworn not to give him the satisfaction of hearing her cry or scream, let alone beg for mercy. After all, she was the Señorita Dolorosa, Lady Pain, and he had to realize at some point the enormous folly of his suicidal actions.

And when he came to his senses, he would be the one begging for forgiveness.

But he did not stop.

If anything, he paddled her bottom even more relentlessly.

Still she held out, gritted her teeth, refused to give in to him. She held out with every ounce and inch of her iron will, until the pain was beyond bearing and her resolve broke all at once. She didn't merely cry but howled like a dying animal gone mad with feral suffering. Sobbing hysterically, she pleaded.

"Stop, Ricardo, stop! Please! I'm so sorry! I'll never hit my ladies again!"

Like hell, she wouldn't. She'd give each of them a thrashing like they'd never imagined, her servants too, just as soon as she finished beating the gringo's ass like it was all the spikes on America's first transcontinental railroad rolled up into one and she was the legendary rail driver, John Henry, who once outhammered a steam drill. Just as soon as she'd—

Slowly, however, she realized that was no longer an option. She was changing against her will, slowly, insidiously. Instead of staring up over her shoulder at the gringo with her usual insuperable arrogance, she gazed on him with something resembling . . . respect—a feeling she'd never experienced in her entire life. Who was this young man who not only refused to bend to her unbending will but forced her bend to . . . his.

And afterward he'd then had the temerity to lay her out on her bed and do things to her she'd never known existed. Ah, caramba, the things he'd shown her. There was the usual stuff, of course, and that was muy magnifico, the best she'd ever had, but then he'd done these other things to her, little things she might have thought beneath the dignity of uno caballero verdaderamente fuerte [*a truly strong man*], *but he'd done them anyway.*

Oh, how he'd done them!

Now every inch of her body burned, not only her brutally engorged, bloodred rear end but every part of her with a . . . lewdly libidinous tingling.

She needed the young man as she'd never needed anything in her life. He was more than muy hombre, more than mucho macho, he was more hombre than any hombre she'd heard of.

Possibly more macho than any hombre who'd ever lived.

She longed to touch him, longed to hold him, longed to enfold herself in his arms. With great fear, she moved closer to him, pulled herself up against his back, and took him fearfully into her arms. Instead of driving her off, he gripped her wrist and pulled her even more tightly up against him.

A feeling came over the Señorita Dolorosa that she'd never before known—something akin to relaxation, contentment, peace, even, even . . . Could it be true? Was she really feeling that thing she'd never ever believed existed? What her people called *amor* and the gringos called . . . *love*?

Whatever it was, the Señorita never wanted it to go away. She held the gringo close and shut her eyes and prayed for the night to never end.

Chapter 84

They were now playing five-card stud, Oklahoma style: Three cards down, two up. The high-dollar courtesan-dealer was now handing out card number four—faceup. Del Gaizo got a jack of clubs, the countess a diamond queen. Slater a faceup seven of hearts. The remaining players got nothing higher than deuces, treys, and fours, yet they seemed unperturbed.

Slater peeked, once more, at his first three cards, which were still facedown. Four, five, six of hearts in the hole and a seven of hearts faceup. He needed a three or an eight to fill a straight. If he wired the hand with a heart, he was looking at a straight flush.

Slater had one of those once-in-a-lifetime revelations, in which he knew with utter, inviolable certitude—as sure as death and sunrise—that he was filling that straight flush and that guns would blaze the second his fifth card turned over.

Slater glanced absently around the bar. He felt time slow down, then stop. But his mind was starting to wander.

* * *

How many times had he gone through this before—the moment of death, that final instant of violent truth—in how many banks and trains, brothels and bars, prisons and battlefields? The blaze of guns, the women's screams, and a surprised new face or two in hell? Was that all there was to his life? Was that all it amounted to in the end? "Cards and guns ain't no life for a grown man," Calamity Jane had once told him, and she was right, of course. That point was indisputable. But what could he do about it? She had him nailed. It was who he was, what he did. It was the only life he'd ever known—his backtrail strewn with the banks he'd hit, the trains he'd robbed, the women he'd abandoned, and the men he'd killed. His was a life of hot guns, cold graves, and sobbing widows.

Not a life spent but misspent.

He remembered a señorita in Sonora, named Dolores, who took him in after he'd escaped from a particularly hellish Sonoran prison mine. He was all busted up, inside and out, starving and dehydrated with a breathtakingly high price on his head, with federales all over Sonora searching for him. Still at great risk to herself, she'd hid him out, nursed him back to health, never asking for a centavo, all the while showing him a kindness, an inner grace, and a peace of soul he'd never dreamed possible.

But he'd finally healed up, and it was time to move on. She asked as he was leaving what he'd planned to do.

"Same as always," he'd said, eager to get free and be on his way.

"And that is?"

"Fuck every woman, rip off every bank and train . . . then kill every lawin' sonofabitch that gets in my way."

She'd looked away with tears in her eyes. She asked him if it was true—about "fucking every woman."

He'd said "no" and that he was just kidding. He then promised when he had a stake he'd come back for her, but of course it was a lie and he never had. In fact, he found out later that Díaz's men were on his trail and had traced him to Dolores. They'd tortured her hideously, trying to find out where he'd gone. She'd never given him up, not even on pain of death.

He remembered—after he'd learned what she had sacrificed for him—that he'd felt something inexplicable, unprecedented, something resembling real feelings, something he had never dreamed possible. He'd wondered at the time if that was what love was like.

But that was then. It was only a vague memory, little more than a dream, and this card game was . . . *now.* This cantina was the real thing, something he'd gone through countless times before, and he knew in his soul how it would go down. It was always the same: cards turned, guns drawn, women screaming, and men dead.

So be it.

It was Slater's life, and he did not apologize for it.

The dealer flipped him the pasteboard, and Slater dived to his right even as the last card was still spinning in midair, even before anyone could see it, yet knowing in his bones and blood that it would fill the straight flush, both his hands already raising his pistols, other guns already blazing, but hitting the back of his empty chair, himself cutting loose with the loudest, shrillest, screech of a whistle anyone in the bar had ever heard.

Now even before he hit the floor six more pistols were shooting at where the back of his chair had been, some of the rounds fired by banditos whom someone had hired, who'd been stationed at the bar.

The gunshots were instantly followed by the most nerve-fraying, hair-frying, soul-shattering yowl anyone had ever heard, an unearthly wail rising up out of the hottest furnaces in the bottommost pit of hell. M. Mort, awakened from his nap, was bolting out from under the wood front porch and rocketing through the batwings, a full five feet off the ground. Eight feet of evil feline—from end-of-rump to tip-of-nose, his half-foot talons arched and fangs bared—he was blacker than pitch and streaking straight at Slater's gun-drawn enemies.

Sitting up on the floor, Slater was already slip-hammering rounds into cardplayers with both hands. The bullshit general, he gunned first, a heartbeat later Señor Del Gaizo, who'd assassinated the last dealer without warning or preamble and who, sure enough, was reverting to form. He had been the first to fire his pistol, this time into Slater's bullet-riddled chairback, which was now no longer there but crashing over backward under a withering hailstorm of many other bullets.

After Del Gaizo, however, Slater hesitated to fire—for fear of hitting M. Mort. The big cat was everywhere at once, a whirling dervish of bloody, ebony death, his long curved claws windmilling so rapidly Slater could not even see them, perceiving only dark but blindingly crimson blurs, where the big tom had disemboweled someone's body, his throat-slashes almost decapitating another of Slater's would-be killers, his vertically distended, flame-yellow pupils blazing amid the hurricane of blood like hellfire itself.

Bolting away from the table, Mort next attacked the *soldados* whom the general had hired and who were charging the table from the bar, their pistols out. Dispatching them—in what seemed to Slater little more than a blinding carmine flash—he turned on Slater's fellow cardplayers. His jaws now open a full foot, he hit Lord Oliver head-on. The man was madly and awkwardly brandishing his Mauser, but it was too little, too late. Seizing the man's neck, Mort broke it like a fox biting a rooster's in two. Twisting in midair toward the countess—who was just pulling the pepperbox from her sleeve—Mort's jaws opened even wider, clamping down on her entire now-howling head, cracking it like Slater might crack a walnut in his fist, drenching her inconceivably costly riding gear with gore.

A big brawny bandito in a red felt sombrero, a long ponytail, and bandoliers was slower in abandoning the bar but he was coming up behind the cat and drawing his gun. Whipping an Arkansas toothpick out of his back sheath, Slater threw it so hard the thirteen-inch blade caught the man just under the chin and exited his nape a full five inches.

Mort glanced at Slater's handiwork with brazen indifference.

Two more banditos circled the edge of the room. Slater had been so fixated on the maelstrom of violence in front of him, he hadn't seen them approaching him on his flank.

Red, however, had been more alert. She'd seemed modest and decorous earlier—utterly out of place in this cantina from hell—but now she was standing up, pulling a pair of over-and-under Remington derringers out of each of her sleeves, and killing the two gun thugs who had been slipping up behind Slater, at point-blank range, shooting one in the sternum, the other in his left eye.

When the dealer, La Escorpion, stood, drew her own sleeve gun, and angled the pepperbox up behind his head, Red shot her, left-handed, just above the right eye.

Slater decided he liked the woman he thought of as "Red."

More than ever, he was now positive he knew her from someplace, sometime, some other world.

Chapter 85

The weeks passed like a dream before the Señorita's eyes. The feelings of peace, tranquillity, and happiness that she'd originally felt after that first night with the young gringo never really left her.

He was uniquely fearless around her, seemed to think she was worthy of only the most derisive of jokes, and deep down inside she was genuinely intimidated by him. She would never—never!—forget what he'd done to her that very first night. She trembled with excitement every time she thought about it. More than merely attracted to him, she was obsessed with him. One sideways condescending glance from the gringo, and she was delirious with desire.

She also found him uproariously funny. He made her laugh out loud—even when he mocked the Señorita in the most humiliating of terms. It was as if he'd given her a sense of humor about . . . *herself*.

She was so supremely narcissistic that she'd never dreamed this was even remotely possible. In truth, the only object she'd ever believed worthy of reverence and genuflection had been . . . *herself*.

Not anymore.

The young man, whom, had she chosen, she could have tortured to death in a heartbeat, insulted her outrageously at every opportunity and then made her . . . *like it*. Very simply, he had become the most important, most indispensable being in her life. Were he to disappear, she doubted she could go on living.

Nor was her astonishing transformation lost on those around her. She caught her ladies giving her strangely oblique glances, as if to say: *What happened to you, Señorita?* They were, of course, delighted with the changes in her. She was less vindictive toward them, less gratuitously cruel, more patient with everyone— and patience had never been her strong suit. Previously, patience had always been anathema to her. Instant gratification of her most trivial whims had always seemed to her eternally, agonizingly slow.

Díaz had always been her ubiquitous houseguest, and he was still appearing on her doorstep with his ingratiating grins and his thunderous laughter. As always, he was seeking emoluments and/or investments from his Señorita—who was, at once, the wealthiest person in all of Méjico and his most financially generous supporter. But even Díaz was mystified by the change in her attitude. Among other things, she was now patient and understanding with Díaz, no longer making him cadge like a mendicant for her handouts. She satisfied his requests before he could get them out of his mouth.

"What can I do for you, my dear Porfirio? Anything

you want? You only have to ask. *¡Por favor!* Just let me know. What are friends for?"

She observed the cruel tyrant sneaking incredulous glances at her with a quizzical look in his eyes, as if questioning her . . . *sanity*. She would have questioned it too, except she'd once read that all poets referred to love as *sublime madness*, and if that was true, the Señorita had fallen for the young gringo like a ton of iron-cast cannons dropped into a fathomless sea, and she was now "sublimely mad" about him. She hung on every word of ridicule and doted on his every look of derision.

Then there were her nights. If before the gringo, they had been a living hell of boredom and melancholia, with him they were an eternity of wildly explosive bliss. She could not believe how endlessly inventive he was. Where had he learned such mind-shattering, body-shuddering wonderment? Once after a long night of interminable delight, she'd asked him, trembling with trepidation, how he'd come to learn such devious techniques and so many mad but masterful manipulations?

He'd rolled over and was falling deeply asleep, yet still she'd heard the words softly, almost inaudibly escape his lips:

"*The . . . Sin . . . Sisters . . .*"

Who were these wicked witches?

On the one hand, she owed them a debt of unimaginable gratitude for instructing Ricardo so rigorously in all those arcane arts of prurient passion. On the other hand, she could not help but be furious with them for having spent so much time with Ricardo, locked in the throes of *amor*. The thought of sharing him with anyone—past, present, or future—she found maddeningly, impossibly . . . *unbearable.*

Surely, they had to die.

Nonetheless, the Señorita owed them an undeniable debt. When she caught up with them—and most assuredly she would, one day, somehow, somewhere—she would not make their *muerte* [death] one of unendurable agony. She would make it a good, quick, clean kill. She would have their throats cut or perhaps have them garroted.

All of which she found confusing. The old Señorita would have had the two sisters tortured maniacally. She no longer wanted such things. The gringo had imparted to her some of that americano softness that she had always so angrily and arrogantly despised. Even so, letting them live was not a possibility. The world was not big enough for the three of them to inhabit. The two sisters had to go.

But staring at the sleeping gringo and remembering the little, dirty, secret things he'd done to her earlier in the evening, she wondered if she'd dare wake him and suggest another go-round.

No.

Reticence would be the better part of valor. She would simply hug and observe. Perhaps he would wake suddenly from a dream, and she could commence enticing him into another demonically delectable dance of desire.

So the Señorita watched, waited, and held him as tightly as she dared.

PART XVII

"Since I'm a guest and since I am investing so much money in your godforsaken hell-mines, may I have a go at young Ricardo first? Or do you think I carry this horsewhip everyplace I go, every hour of the day and night, because I think it looks . . . pretty?" Judith McKillian began boisterously cracking her boot-top with her riding crop.

Chapter 86

Red and her three friends—her daughter, Rachel, an attractive señorita named Eléna, and an ex-military hombre named Antonio—took Slater to their camp on a hill outside of town. It wasn't far from where he'd buried his take from the last job, and so after retrieving it, he joined them by their fire. They were roasting a venison haunch and boiling a pot of beans, onions, and corn, flavored with cane sugar. Eléna had just baked the lightest, fluffiest biscuits he'd ever eaten, and instead of the rotgut tequila he was used to, they had a supply of real gringo whiskey—sour mash, no less. It was the best liquor he'd had in years . . . and he was drinking it in Méjico, of all places.

What the hell? Slater thought. You got attractive women to look at, and Eléna, it turned out, could sing. In fact, she sang all his favorite ballads, including "Solo Los Muertos Saben Amor" ["Only the Dead Know Love"] and "¿Por Qué Es Tu Amante Mi Asesino?" ["Why Is Your Love My Assassin?"] Even M. Mort was happy. He lay between Eléna and Katherine and let them pet his neck and scratch his chin. Rolling on his back, he let them rub his belly—things he'd never let anybody do to him. He never let anyone even get close to him. The two women then cut chunks of rare venison off the rotating haunch. After feeding them to Mort, the cat even purred.

And Mort purred for nobody.

What was going on?

Aw, the hell with it, Slater thought. You don't need guards or sentries. You got M. Mort lying here, and he can hear and smell intruders a quarter mile off. You have beautiful *mujeres*, good food, great whiskey, and one of the *mujeres bellas* is singing your favorite songs. For maybe the first time in your life, you're relaxing. For the first time in anyone's life even M. Mort is happy.

And he isn't happy 'less he's killing something.

Picking up a liter bottle of Jackson's Sour Mash, Slater put it to his mouth, leaned back his head, and took a long, luxurious pull.

The night passed pleasantly. Red—her name turned out to be Katherine Ryan—walked him away from the fire at one point, so they could talk privately. It turned out she was a well-to-do rancher from the Arizona territory, and the two of them were old friends. She reminded Slater of their shared childhood with the Chiricahuas, and Katherine told him how much she owed him.

He responded saying that he'd heard from one of his former men that a woman named Katherine Ryan had sprung him from Yuma.

"Maybe," Katherine said. "Still, you freed me from the Chiricahuas."

"Yeah, but a lot of it was I never cared that much for old He-Who-Yawns, now known as Geronimo. The idea of him takin' you as his bride just didn't sit well. A lot of what I did was because I didn't like him. Question is, why were you lookin' for me? And how'd you know to look for me in that cantina?"

"Belle," Katherine said simply. "She said you'd just made a big score and would be looking for a big card game. That was the place in Hermosillo."

"Goddamn you to hell. You wired Belle Starr."

"In Younger's Bend back in the Nations. Your friend told me I could always reach you through her and gave me her address."

"And you need me. Why?"

"The Señorita Dolorosa's abducted my son."

"The story's all over Sonora and Sinaloa," Slater said, nodding his head.

"So we're going to pay the Señorita a visit," Katherine said, "and ask her to give Richard back to us."

"And when she says no, you want me to break him out of her hacienda," Slater said, "the most heavily fortified structure in all of Méjico."

"*Es verdad,*" Katherine said.

"That won't be easy," Slater said, "and I'm wanted all over Méjico. Katherine, I like you—maybe I even owe you—and I'm not afraid of a little risk. But I don't see that there's anything I can do. Not this time."

"Then do it for Richard."

Slater stared at her a long minute, his face unreadable, expressionless. "Why?" he finally asked.

"Remember that last night on the trail? Before you dropped me off at the rancho?"

Slater stared at her, silent.

"We made love? You remember that, don't you? I do."

Slater still said nothing.

"I remember," Slater finally said.

"Richard's your son."

Chapter 87

It was a hard, arduous trek Katherine, Slater, and their crew had of it—a horseback journey from hell straight across the Sinaloan desert. Riding through the parched chaparral, it seemed to Katherine an eternity of cactuses—prickly pear, ocotillo, organ-pipe cactuses, as well as the dagger-leaved Spanish bayonet, agave, stunted wind-bent sage, and the indomitable, irrepressible mesquite, some of the bushes sprouting up as high and massive as trees. Then there was the fauna: Gila monsters, interminable diamondbacks, tarantulas eight inches long, the wary scorpion. And always the scorching heat by day and the shockingly frigid nights, the eternally barren, never-ending waterless wastes, stretching from horizon to horizon, from sunup to sundown, not a breath of breeze stirring, not a hint of smoke rising up in any direction, only the sun blazing down on them like a white-hot branding iron, like a forge-heated hammer blow to the neck.

At last, they spotted the distant specter of the Señorita's infamous hacienda. The sight of her magnificent palaces, vast agricultural holdings, and legendary mining empire, however, did not inspire in Katherine and her friends anything resembling hope. They all knew what they were getting into. They had no illusions. Their odyssey was not war's end but an abominable beginning to something truly terrible. However it turned out, it would not make for an edifying story, and where it would end, no one knew. Even worse, the Señorita was central to this narrative, and it was not for nothing that the her hacienda was known throughout Méjico as La Casa Que El Dolor Construyó.

The House That Pain Built.

Not only were La Casa del Dolorosa and La Señorita Dolorosa notorious for their torture chambers, their Grand Inquisitors, and their sacrificial Aztec pyramid already visible, looming behind the hacienda from hell and behind that, less than fifty miles away, was the mountain named El Infierno de Plata—the Señorita's dreaded Silver Hell.

Wreathed in an almost satanic smoke—rising up from smelters, stamping mills, and amalgamating plants surrounding the mountain's perimeter—were scores upon scores of hell furnaces, drop forges, and acid immersion tanks. Even this far away, across the endless expanse of Sinaloa's arid wilderness, Katherine believed she could hear the din of those monstrous machines and fuming refineries.

What are we getting into? Katherine asked herself. *What has Richard gotten himself into? How did he get involved with Díaz and that pernicious woman? Why on earth did he and Rachel come to Méjico? Why were any of them in Méjico? In Méjico.*

Méjico.

All Katherine knew was that she was not leaving her son to the untender mercies of people like Díaz and the Señorita. She was not leaving here without him. Her son would not die in Méjico.

Driving her rowels into the gray's flanks, she was anxious to reach the hacienda. It was time to settle up with Díaz and that wicked woman and bring her son back home.

Chapter 88

The Señorita would never forget the day that changed her life forever—and ruined everything: Ricardo's mother, Katherine Ryan, came to call. Her daughter, Rachel, and a young woman named Eléna were with her. The Señorita wisely told her major-domo not to let anyone tell Ricardo the three women were visiting, and she met them in private.

The four women sat in an anteroom of her *grande sala* on high, dark, narrow-backed chairs upholstered with dark brown leather. Before them was a long, large, dark wood table on which the servants had set bottles of Laurent-Perrier Grand Siècle champagne chilling in ice buckets as well as chorizos, chiles, bread, and cheese. The Señorita decided to make a fulsome display of hospitality and find out what they wanted before showing them the gate and sending them back north of the border. Or, if their presence in any way threatened her relationship with Ricardo, she would have them tortured and killed.

The women had come a long way and were attired

in trail garb—Levi's, shirts, riding boots whose rowels were hung from their belts out of respect for her hardwood floors. They'd also left their weapons strapped to their mounts, which were tied up to hitchracks by the front door.

Katherine and the two women thanked the Señorita graciously for the champagne and the food. They said, yes, they had come a long way to meet her, and it had been an exhausting journey.

"We come here, however, because we have learned that my son, Richard, is staying here at your palace."

The Señorita stared at them, feigning a pleasant look. "Is that why you've made such a long, difficult trip? To visit him?"

"In part," the sister, Rachel, said, "but also because our father is very sick. His abdominal cancer has returned, and he does not have long to live. He would like to see his son before he dies. It is important to him."

The Señorita nodded, pretending to care about their feelings and the condition of the sick man.

"I hold no one here against their will. Regardless of what you have heard about Méjico, or its esteemed president, Porfirio Díaz, or even about your Señorita, we are not barbarians. If your son wishes to return to Norteamérica with you, I will not stand in his way. In fact, I shall put pesos in his pocket, give him provisions, and all of you can share a private car on one of our express trains. Your Ricardo is a good man, and I only want what's best for him."

"Señorita," Katherine said, "I do not know how to express my gratitude."

"A simple *gracias* will suffice, but let me speak to Ricardo first."

The Señorita rose, bowed, and headed for Ricardo's room. She found him in his quarters, where he sat at a table eating a lunch of *carne, arroz y frijoles*. He was dressed in dark trousers, a dark shirt, a dark bandanna tied around his neck.

"My good Ricardo," the Señorita said, "I have some most exciting news. I have just visited with your mother and sister."

She watched his reaction, her face friendly and caring. His face was expressionless, devoid of any feeling or reaction at all. She could tell, however, that he was suppressing his true feelings with ruthless discipline.

Madre de Dios, how he must love those two . . . putas—his puta *mamacita and* puta *sister.*

The realization made her secretly tremble with rage.

"They wished for you to return with them to your Rancho to visit your dying father," the Señorita said in her sweetest voice. "They fear he does not have long to live and hope that you can spend time with him before he succumbs."

"He's had problems, that's for sure. Still I thought he'd make it a few more years. He must have taken a turn for the worse."

"I am sure he has. They have come a long way to track you down. It must be serious. I'm surprised they found you at all."

His face remained blank, unreadable. Except to her. The Señorita saw and understood everything.

"What do you want me to do?" Ricardo asked carefully.

Ah, the boy is clever. Now he was studying her, drawing

her out, trying to gauge her feelings, perhaps hoping to react
to her response.

"Oh, my dear Ricardo. Your beloved father is ailing. In times such as these, the question always is, what do you want? What do you think you should do?"

She gazed on him with empathetic eyes.

"Yes, I would like to see him," Richard said, "but I don't want to leave you. We've grown so close these last few weeks. I've never known anyone like you. I've never dreamed I could be with anyone like you. I've never imagined anyone like you even existed. I want to spend the rest of my life with you."

God, he was laying it on thick. He was obviously out of his mind with love for his family, but he knew the Señorita and he didn't want her to know his true feelings. Clearly, his desire to be with his loved ones had robbed him of his reason, of any survival instincts he might have had. Had he been of sound mind, he'd have known that she'd see through his lies. Did he really think she would agree to play second fiddle to two *putas* and some pathetic, moribund old man for even one second, let alone the time it would take to make the trip both ways and to nursemaid the old fool?

She knew what he was about to say next—that he would return to her as soon as his *hideputa* old man was at rest and that he would be hers forever, till the stars themselves fell from the sky and all the rivers ran dry. Was he so deranged by love and grief that he thought she would believe that shit?

As if by clockwork, Ricardo began to lie.

"Perhaps you are right. He is my father, and he is dying. Perhaps I should go back home one last time and see him. I will stay no more than a week even if he is at death's door. I cannot bear to leave you longer than that. I can take yours and Díaz's express train both ways—to ensure we aren't apart for long. Does that sound all right to you?"

"Of course, dear Ricardo. I am pleased to see that you are such a dutiful son. It indicates to me that you will always show me the same kind of love and loyalty."

"Siempre." ["Always."]

"I do however have one more request."

"Anything."

"Your mother and sister have ridden back to their camp, to inform their friends of your journey to come. They will return for breakfast and you will go with them to the train station. So I want you for dinner now, for the rest of the evening, and then I want you to show me the greatest night of my life. I want something to remember you by during your long journey to and during your sojourn in America. I want something to look forward to on your return."

"It will be my pleasure," he said, getting up from the table.

"Perhaps we can even indulge ourselves in a small . . . *aperitivo* . . . in my room before dinner."

"I would love nothing more."

Richard followed the Señorita out of his bedroom and down the hall.

Chapter 89

When Richard came to the next morning, a bucket-ful of ice-cold water was slamming into his face, drenching his head, neck, and naked body. He was strung up by the elbows from a rope hanging from an overhead beam in a black-walled room, his wrists lashed across his stomach. His joints hurt horrifically, as if they were being wrenched out of their sockets, which essentially they were.

He immediately knew where he was. He'd heard over the years that the Señorita had darkened the walls, floor, and ceiling so they would conceal the vast amount of gore that was continually splashed across the room.

Suddenly, the Señorita appeared in front of him, smiling and chortling merrily.

"Welcome to the land of the living, Señor Ricardo," she said pleasantly. "We lost you for a while after that last titillating tête-à-tête."

He wished he could have stayed unconscious awhile longer. He noticed that a wrist-quirt was hanging casu-ally from the Señorita's fist and looped to her wrist.

Standing next to her was a woman with white flawless skin and flame-red hair hanging all the way down to her waist. Both women were dressed entirely in black. Black clothing also camouflaged bloodstains. The other woman also had a black riding crop, hers tucked under her arm.

He studied the two women more closely. His first thought was that they must have been out riding, because they were attired in horse gear—tight ebony jodhpurs; matching high-heeled riding boots, fitted with sterling silver rowels, footwear and spurs both as glitteringly bright as well-burnished mirrors; matching, close-fitting blouses, the first three buttons undone, revealing prurient plentitudes of cleavage.

"I thought we had a thing," Ricardo said amiably to the Señorita. "I felt a connection. Didn't you?"

"What I felt was you taking me over your knee and paddling my bottom so hard and so long that I couldn't sit down for a week. That's what I felt. Did you think that little *projet d'amor* would go unrequited?"

"I did fuck you to heaven, hell, and back again afterward," Richard said with an affable smile.

"You most assuredly did," the Señorita said wistfully, staring off over his shoulder into space, enjoying the reverie, a wistfully wicked smile playing on her lips. "Which is the only reason I did not have you cut into a thousand pieces and killed that very night."

"We could still have other nights like that, as many as you wish."

"*Es verdad,* but the skills you learned from those two *puta*-harpies, what did you call them?"

"Mateo called them the Sin Sisters."

"Those skills are portable. I can instruct other

lovers, *hombre y mujer ambos*, to employ them. I shall not go . . . *unfulfilled.*"

"But you won't have me."

"But I will have the memory of our last dalliance together—the most important of our dalliances—the one here in our little *chambre d'amor*, the one that will be etched eternally on the hallowed halls of hell, the one I shall personally engrave . . . *myself.*"

Never let them see you sweat, Mateo had told him. When they get out the whips, hot coals, and knives, don't whine and snivel. Whimpering acts on them like catnip on cats.

She was fondling and contemplating her quirt with unalloyed excitement, when Díaz and the foppish limey, Sutherland, pulled open the door and entered the room.

"Sorry we're late for the festivities, old sport." Sutherland's voice was full of good cheer and boomed ebulliently throughout the chamber.

The Englishman was dressed in silk trousers, calf-skin boots, a satin shirt and coat, even a broad-brimmed hat, the entire ensemble immaculately white. He clearly wasn't afraid of the soon-to-be splattering blood. He was smoking a black, weird-smelling cigarillo stuffed into an ivory holder. The lewd lopsided leer was still locked onto his face. He was dressed like an antebellum, old-time, slave-driving, bloodthirsty plantation owner.

Díaz wore an immaculately cleaned and pressed, perfectly tailored dress uniform. A dark, thick, downward-sweeping mustache surmounted his scintillating grin, which dazzled like polished ivory against his nut-brown skin and closely cut beard. He was slowly circling Richard, meditating on the young man's elbow-suspended corpus.

"*Mucho bueno, Señorita,*" the dictator said. "I'd feared that your naive, misplaced—may I say moronic?—affection for the young man had dulled your truer instincts, but you are still in touch with your feelings . . . as viciously violent as they may be. Bravo, *mi amiga.*"

"Coming from you, *mi presidente*, that is indeed *muy complimento.*"

"*Siempre verdad,*" ["Eternally true"] Díaz whispered almost to himself, nodding emphatically, his eyes still focused on Richard's body, his grin upwardly hooking the left corner of his mouth. Slaver was also forming on his chin.

"Now that's the way I like my ruddy yanks," Sutherland shouted enthusiastically, "trussed up like a Christmas goose, waiting for the downward swing of the old hatchet. God bless you, one and all, Tiny Tim!" he roared happily at the top of his lungs.

"Tiny Tim?" Díaz asked, not getting the allusion.

"It's literature, ducks," Judith McKillian grumbled under her breath to the dictator. Then she muttered half to herself. "You wouldn't understand, you ignorant piece of dried-up Aztec goat shit."

"I'm not sure I like your attitude," the mejicano strongman said to Miss McKillian, having heard her aspirations.

"Oh, you'll like it as long and as much as you like my money," McKillian shouted at the tyrant.

"Indeed, *mi amiga*," Sutherland said, a vile smile now blazing across his face. "For our *muchos dineros* you will learn to . . . *love it.*"

"And, *mi presidente*," the Señorita said, "Señor

Sutherland and Señorita McKillian have already agreed to invest a small fortune in my little silver enterprise, which you profit from as well, backing we need most urgently. Is that not so, señor?" she said, staring at Sutherland, her own smile shimmering as brilliantly as El Presidente's.

"And a sound investment it is," Sutherland said. "I've never seen such an efficiently run mining operation. Usually the extraction and refining of ore is constantly interrupted by costly safety procedures and the coddling of indolent employees."

"What kind of safety procedures?" Richard asked, looking down on them from his makeshift strappado.

"The shoring up of the shafts," the Señorita recited numbly, automatically, by rote, "which includes the endless replacement of cracked and damaged timbers, which could have served as fuel for our smelters; the eternal pumping out of gas, dust, and floodwater, again to save and protect the lives of our laborers; the nursing and nurturing of injured, starving, decrepit miners; the squandering of much-needed investment capital on their care and feeding. All those boring inessentials that you gringos and Señor Sutherland's Anglo mine owners waste their time and resources on. We ignore them totally. We focus on the only thing that counts, nothing else."

"Which is?" Richard asked quizzically.

"Making money, you stupid cluck!" the Señorita shouted. *"Lining our fucking coffers with mountains of filthy lucre! Get the picture, you goddamn moron!"*

All the while Sutherland and McKillian laughed like ululating hyenas.

Richard turned his head and looked away.

"Oh dear," Díaz said to the Señorita, "I think you've hurt his feelings."

"Quite so," the Señorita said, feigning contrition. "And to think just last night, locked in the throes of *amor*, he was bringing me to the heights of deliriously demented desire and we were swearing eternal love to each other, and now, here I am, bringing him downward to darkness, into the depths of depraved despair and the slough of despond. I must seem to you, the Bitch of Babylon, no? It does not seem fair, does it, young Ricardo?"

Richard continued to avert his eyes.

"Tell you what, *bebé*," the Señorita said, "suppose I chucked you under the chin and looked pathetic? Would that make you feel better?"

She leaned forward till their noses touched, then she gently touched the bottom of his chin with a closed fist. She then gave him the saddest mock-sad stare he'd ever seen in his life, and rearing back she drove the clenched fist into his solar plexus as hard and as deeply as she knew how. Gasping, Richard choked for air. His stomach muscles spasmed and his body convulsed, while the Señorita and her two friends howled with hellish laughter.

"Ey, compadre," Díaz said to Richard, "why you look so unhappy? Just 'cause you had *mucho bueno* ecstasy with Our Lady, you think she is yours forever?"

"Maybe he expected compassion from our Señorita?" Sutherland asked with faux sympathy.

"Oh, that item's long out of stock," the Señorita said, still nose to nose with Richard, still smiling giddily at him.

"Assuming it ever existed at all," Díaz said.

"In any of us," McKillian added.

"In case you still believe in things like pity, love, and compassion," the Señorita said evenly, "let me disabuse you of those delusions. This is Madre Méjico, young Ricardo. You are in the Señorita's oubliette. These things don't exist. Not here. Not now. Not ever."

Never let them see you sweat, the federale had told him. Never whimper, snivel, or whine. You have to have cojones of iron, of case-hardened steel.

"Are you suggesting I may not enjoy our little *projet d'amor*?" Richard asked.

"Oh, you are in the Ninth Circle of Dante's *Inferno*— the hell of betrayers," the Señorita whispered conspiratorially in Richard's ear. "Satan, who turned on God, is in its nethermost pit, and next to him is Judas Iscariot. Your attempt to abandon me and return to your family has landed you right down there in between those two devils."

"Ah, young Ricardo," Sutherland said, "you know I make jokes, but in all seriousness, I wouldn't want to be you."

"Es verdad," Díaz said, nodding his head. "You are about to soar on the wings of night."

"Speaking of which," Judith McKillian said, "since I'm a guest and since I am investing so much money in your godforsaken hell-mines, may I have a go at young Ricardo first? Or do you think I carry this horsewhip everyplace I go, every hour of the day and night, because I think it looks . . . *pretty*?" Judith McKillian began boisterously cracking her boot-top with her riding crop.

"But, of course, my dear," the Señorita said brightly. "Do you want to borrow my *cuarta*-quirt?"

"No, my crop will do quite nicely."

Circling around Richard, she bent her whip in a 180-degree arc. Letting it go, she watched with amusement as it whistled, hummed, vibrated, thrummed, and finally came to a stop. Bowing histrionically in front of her friends, McKillian turned and began flogging Richard's backside with everything she had, her cheerful chirps and melodious giggles soon merging with the raucous guffaws of her friends. Eventually Richard broke down and howled in pain, his screams harmonizing discordantly with the horrendous laughter of his tormentors. Reverberating through the Señorita's Casa Que El Dolor Construyó, the House That Pain Built, their combined wails echoed into the everlasting night.

Chapter 90

Richard sat on the floor of the mule-drawn prison wagon. His leg irons and wrist manacles were coffle-chained through the big wagon bed's rows of eyebolts lining its edges and running across the wagon bed's center. Since multiple mule teams were hauling three wagons each, Richard was technically on a prison train—one drawn by mules.

Richard leaned onto his side, his back and behind in hideous pain. Still he was acutely aware that the men around him were in far worse shape—starved, flogged with bullwhips and knotted, salted cat-o'-nines. Some of them had even been scourged with hooked cat-o'-nines, not merely beaten with crops. While Richard suffered weals, his fellow *prisioneros* had been whipped to the bone. While Richard still had on decent clothes, even boots, those around him wore filthy frayed prison rags and decrepit rope sandals or they went half-naked or barefoot.

Then there was their backs. Like most slave-labor

prisons, the guards were ordered to bullwhip only the hardest of the hard-core inmates, since the bone-deep slashes the bullwhip left radically reduced the slaves' usefulness. Consequently, while most of the men had been horrendously flogged—most of them sentenced to hundreds of lashes—they'd been whipped with thick heavily braided and salted cat-o'-nines. But the men too were in such dire agony that most of them held their shirts on their laps. Their bare backs—too sore to endure clothing—were lined with the red stripes. Nor were most of the *prisioneros* in the train true criminals but illiterate mestizos and *indios puros*. Guilty at the most of petty thefts and penury, most of them had simply been in the wrong place at the wrong time. Many were only guilty of running into a bounty hunter's downward-swinging truncheon when the man was struggling at the last moment to meet his quota and collect his bonus.

Richard supposed he'd been lucky. Even the Señorita had made that clear:

"I'm not having you flogged with a hooked-whip cat-o'-nine, young Ricardo, let alone bullwhipped, as I have done to so many countless other *prisioneros* I have sent to my mines. Not out of mercy. I want you to enter my Silver Hell in the peak of health. I want you to dwell there a long, long time—as long as humanly possible—for as long as you survive in that place you will suffer hideously, suffer the tortures of the damned, writhing and screaming in that Infierno de la Señorita . . . in hellfire everlasting."

Curiously enough, the Señorita had declined to whip him herself in the oubliette. Richard wasn't sure why. Judith McKillian had enjoyed the exclusive rights to that privilege—rights she exercised with extravagant exuberance.

God, the McKillian woman had enjoyed herself that night.

Richard hoped in his soul to one day return the favor.

The Señorita, nonetheless, had sentenced him to life in the mine, which was gratuitously excessive. Almost no one lasted more than a year in El Infierno de Plata, so a single year, for most, was a death sentence, and those few who had miraculously survived a one-year sentence routinely had another year tacked on, and if they survived that year, another and another and another until they died in those pits.

Almost no one walked out of Silver Hell alive.

Almost no one lived to tell their tale.

All the men on Richard's prison train, Richard included, were going there to die.

A grizzled, ragged-looking *prisionero* with a dark beard and hard eyes sat next to Richard. His shirt was on his lap, his back a maze of clotted slashes.

"What's your name?" Richard asked him.

"Sergio."

"What's El Infierno like?" Richard asked the man "Any idea?"

"Yeah, I was a federale and got into trouble. They punished me by making me work in El Infierno as a guard. When I couldn't take it anymore and ran away, they caught me, then convicted me. I'll never get out alive. Neither will you."

"That's a cheerful thought," Richard said. "What's the mine like?"

"The first thing you'll notice is the absolute darkness. Except for a few candles and torches, we work in a world devoid of light."

"Dray beasts can't work down there it's so dark," an inmate named Diego said. "They bring the mine donkeys down there when they're newborn, so they grow up in the dark. Living there from birth, they don't know any other condition. When they can't work any longer, they are slaughtered nearby. Blind as bats, they navigate the tunnels by touch, feel, and smell."

"Then there's the noise—the din is incessant," the first *prisionero*, Sergio, said. "The mines are never quiet: the banging of deadfall, the groaning of the shoring timbers, the endless rain of debris dropping down from the hanging rock itself."

"Hanging rock?" Richard asked.

"The tunnels' ceiling rock," Sergio said. "We call it *hanging rock* to remind ourselves that there's very little holding it up. It hangs overhead with only a few pieces of wood bracing it—very few pieces of wood. Our jailers use most of our shoring timbers to fuel our smelting plants."

"They use most of our shoring timbers," Richard asked, "which are supposed to protect us from cave-ins, for smelter fuel? Why?"

"Our lives are worth nothing to them. The ore—everything!" Diego said.

"*Es verdad,*" Sergio said.

"The noise," Diego said, "will drive you nuts."

"The shoring timbers creak and moan nonstop," Sergio continued. "Then there's the banging of picks against the mine faces, the groaning of the *prisioneros*, the *dripdripdripdripdripdrip* of leaking water, the squealing and scurrying of goddamn rats."

"Rats?" Richard asked.

"The mine is filled with rats," Sergio said.

"What do they live off of?"

"The dead and the dying," Diego said. "Sometimes even the living if the men are stuck in cave-ins."

"Sometimes you hear the roar of the firestorms," Sergio said.

"If you hear that, it'll be the last thing you ever hear," Diego said.

"What burns in a mountain?" Richard asked. "Rock?"

"Mountains and mines are filled with all kinds of minerals and debris," Sergio said, "thrown up by the subterranean fires that spawned them—shale, shale oil, coal seams, methane. This mine is sitting atop a gigantic methane sump, which constantly floods the tunnels with the gas. That stuff can blow at a moment's notice."

"Then there are the shoring timbers," Diego said. "They keep the tunnels from collapsing on us but they're tinder for fires."

"And the candles set them on fire?" Richard asked.

"*Sí, amigo,*" Sergio said, "and when you've found a new big silver vein or drift and it's encased in too much hard rock to get to with hammer and pick, they tell us to blast it open with black powder."

"That's also part of the noise," Diego said.

"Explosions too," Richard muttered under his breath.

"We left out floods," Sergio said.

"Floods," Richard muttered to himself.

"Underground rivers are everywhere," Diego said. "We have to pump out the tunnels continuously just to keep them from flooding, and sometimes the waters just overwhelm us."

"Actually I'd prefer drowning to being burned alive," Sergio said.

"As if the Señorita gives us a choice," Diego said.

"We're looking at hellfire everlasting," Sergio said.

"Funny," Richard said, "that's what a woman said to me not all that long ago."

"She had the gift of prophecy," Diego said.

"She should. She was the Señorita."

"You've met her?" Sergio asked, impressed.

"She sentenced me personally to this mine."

"She must have hated you," Diego said.

Or loved me, Richard said silently to himself.

"I hear she calls it the most beautiful hill on earth," another inmate said.

"Díaz too," Richard said quietly.

"You know them both?" Sergio asked.

"For my sins."

"They must be *imperdonable* [unforgivable]," Diego said, crossing himself and mouthing a mute "Hail Mary."

Granite-gray, Infierno de Plata was now looming over them like Death itself. Richard couldn't vouch for the hill's beauty, but at this range, it was the biggest thing he'd ever seen, almost touching the clouds, as if threatening to usurp God's very throne.

At its base, on the other hand, was the antithesis of the mountain's Olympian grandeur. Surrounding Richard was an earthly inferno—a complex of booming, crashing, smoke-shrouded stamping mills;

soot-belching smelters; and a myriad of fuming, stinking amalgamating plants, in which the pure silver was chemically extracted from the muddy, ground-up, sandy ore. The plants—in fact, the mountain's entire base—were wreathed in a sickening corrosive haze.

"I don't think I'm going to like it here," Richard said.

"They don't mean for you to like it," Sergio said. "Your wants, needs, and desires are none of their concern."

"They want us to hate it," Diego said.

"They don't call it Silver Hell for nothing," Sergio agreed.

"It is hell on earth for *mejicanos*," Diego said.

"And gringos!" Sergio said, laughing and pointing at Richard.

"And gringos indeed," Richard mumbled inaudibly to himself.

Chapter 91

Katherine and her friends were back at their camp several miles outside of the hacienda and just getting up. They'd spent the night with Slater and Antonio, celebrating the good news that Richard was being released. Now, however, as the sun was coming up, Katherine saw in the distance a roiling cloud of dust and a lone rider approaching them at a high, hard lope.

"Wonder what he wants?" Eléna asked.

"I'm always suspicious about anyone who's in that much of a hurry," Katherine said, clearly displeased.

"The Señorita does not inspire confidence," Antonio said. "That's someone's trouble coming to meet us."

"Maybe he's not looking for us," Rachel said.

But he was. In under a dozen minutes he'd caught up with them, halted abruptly, and swung off his lathered, panting sorrel. He had hard eyes, looked even harder used, and was wearing a federale uniform.

"Is one of you Katherine Ryan?" he asked.

"The same," Katherine said.

"My name is Garcia Guttierez. Mateo Cardozo sent me. When the Señorita abducted your son, Mateo had been responsible for him. He was forced out of the Sonoran rurales and barely escaped Sonora with his life. So he took a job with the Señorita."

"He's working for the Señorita?" Eléna said. "I didn't think he was like that."

"It's not what you think," Garcia said. "He's running her security detail, but he's working for the resistance. When Mateo heard you were looking for Ricardo, he sent me. He's trying to help your son. He's even fomenting a revolt in El Infierno de Plata, where Ricardo is headed, even as we speak. If Mateo is successful, Ricardo could escape."

"The Señorita's sent Ricardo to Silver Hell?" Katherine asked in shock.

"The Señorita arranged to send him there yesterday. He made the mistake of telling the Señorita he wanted to return and visit his dying father."

"I told the Señorita I wanted him to do it," Katherine said.

"Señora, you did not think that if he asked the Señorita for permission to leave her, even for a week, she would view his request as a betrayal?"

"It was a reasonable request," Rachel insisted.

Garcia burst into sardonic laughter.

"What's so funny?" Katherine asked.

"You just suggested that the Señorita was reasonable."

"She cannot understand how a son might want to be with a dying parent?"

"Instead of her? Of course she can't."

"Why not?" Rachel asked, indignant.

"Because your request has nothing to do with the Señorita," Garcia said simply. "In fact, it runs counter to anything and everything she desires."

"In what way?" Rachel asked.

"You're asking her to do something for . . . *someone else.*"

"Oh my God," Rachel said. "Mother, he's right. And when Richard told the Señorita he had to leave her for a month or two, she had to assume he was choosing us over her and that he would never return."

"And that all he wanted to do was escape her, Díaz, and their entire world," Katherine said, nodding, suddenly understanding. "The Señorita must have immediately realized it."

"Oh, Mom, when Richard asked her to let him leave, he signed his death warrant."

"And now the Señorita's signing yours too," Garcia said. "She's ordered a contingent of her security forces to track you down and drag you back to her hacienda. They'll be leaving the barracks any minute now. If they take you alive, you will become vividly intimate with her dungeons and with torture implements."

"What about you?" Katherine asked.

"I'm absent without leave. They'll assume I informed on them. I signed my own death warrant coming here."

"Which means?"

"You're all about to ride the hocks off your horses, cut every telegraph wire along the way, and lose those federales on your tail. I'll ride with you for a while, but when I get the chance, I'm going to disappear into southern Méjico—somewhere in Chiapas, where I'll attempt to become just another peon."

They could now see a distant cloud of dust and a

cadre of riders leaving the hacienda. They were heading toward them.

"It's time to adios," Eléna said.

"Rachel, I want you on a train back to the U.S. Anyone else who wants to go can go with you. I'll pay their fare—no hard feelings. I'm grateful you all came this far. But I screwed up by talking to the Señorita, and I'm sticking around in hopes of getting Richard out of that hell-mine. I'm not going back without Richard."

"We can discuss it later, Mama," Eléna said. "First we got to get clear of Díaz and that infernal harpy."

"*Es verdad,*" Antonio agreed.

"Torn," Katherine said, "you know more about escaping federales than anyone I've ever heard of. You're in charge."

Slater nodded.

"*Verdad,*" Katherine muttered quietly to herself.

Slater then leaned over to Katherine and whispered in her ear. "We have to talk later. I might have an idea or two about getting Richard out of that mine."

"You did escape from Monte de Riqueza," Katherine said.

"I'm thinking about pulling off something similar," Slater said, his face and voice impassive.

They swung back up onto their mounts, roweled, quirted, and rode them like all the hounds of hell were at their back.

Because, in fact, they were.

PART XVIII

Díaz stared in shock at the obviously demented but prodigiously rich and powerful woman whom he now had to placate. Madre de Dios, how he despised himself—and Méjico!—for needing her money so desperately. He'd hated sucking up to so many of the world's worst, most brutally plutocratic potentates, but this lunatic lady was truly beyond the pale, indisputably the most violently insane financial mogul he'd ever had to kowtow to.

Chapter 92

Richard awoke in a cavernlike room called a sleeping stope. Encased in hard rock, it was relatively stable. He was surrounded by sleeping *prisioneros*. Since no candles were lit at night, the stope was blacker than black, without vision or light. Staring sightlessly around him, Richard pondered his last time in hell.

He thought of it as a month, but he quickly realized that in Infierno de Plata no one gauged time in days or weeks or months, let alone years. A measurement that impossibly long had no discernable meaning here. Their stay was measured in terms of events.

"That was the day pumps blew and three-shaft flooded," a *prisionero* would say, "killing twenty-two *prisioneros*."

"That was the day," another would say, "when eight-shaft caught fire and incinerated a dozen souls."

Or: "Six-shaft collapsed and buried eighteen of us alive."

Or: "A methane leak asphyxiated twenty-seven."

"Hondo killed himself," Richard told his friends when he learned the news.

"The *hideputa* couldn't take it anymore," Emilio confirmed the news. "He cut his fucking throat."

"He took the easy way out," Jose said cynically.

If a candle flickered, Richard had to shut his eyes. The tiniest ray of light could be agonizing.

Some *prisioneros* slept topside in barracks. The mine's skilled workers—the explosives experts, the timbermen, the foremen, the trustees—slept there. Also the highly skilled topside workers who labored in the mills and refineries—the millwrights, smelters, stampers, and the amalgamators.

As a common convict, however, Richard slept inside the mine. He and his amigos were nothing more than mine fodder, wretches the Señorita threw at the hard-rock ore like peons charging Gatlings, and they almost never saw the light. As the Señorita used to brag, it cost her one male slave for every kilo of silver.

"Why not?" she enthused. "Men are worth nothing in Chihuahua and less in Sinaloa."

"Without silver," Díaz said, "Méjico is worth nothing."

"And in this blighted land," the Señorita had said, nodding her agreement, "silver is worth everything."

Men in the mine were now rising from their dirty worn blankets and frayed ponchos—most of which were made of woven maguey—and lining up to relieve themselves in slop barrels. Soon a mess slave would bring them buckets of *desayuno* [breakfast]. It was usually pinole—a thin gruel of ground corn, pulverized mesquite beans, and water. Occasionally there were some goat guts mixed in it. The best and the strongest workers got first crack at it. The weak and the sick got the dregs.

Richard, who was still relatively new, was healthy enough to make his daily ore quota. He was up at the head of the *desayuno* line with Sanchez, a tall, smart—even literate—*prisionero* who had a talent for surviving the mines. He'd already made it through an unprecedented three years in the Infierno de Plata.

"Madre de Dios, what will we have to endure today?" Emilio asked.

"How about death?" Richard asked.

"You fear death?" Sanchez asked.

"Doesn't everyone?" Richard said.

"Topside perhaps but not down here."

Richard stared at him, saying nothing.

"Down here," Sanchez continued, "death is not the termination of life but a deliverance from hell, a passage into another dispensation, which cannot possibly be worse than this *infierno.*"

"Sounds like shit to me," Emilio said.

"In what way?" Sanchez asked.

"Every hell has a hell of hells."

"Perhaps," Sanchez said, "but down here we should not fear death. It is our friend, our wisest advisor. Only the hope of death keeps us sane. Down here, death is a gift."

"Are you saying we should love death?" Richard asked.

"Not at all," Sanchez said. "Only understand that we are dead already, that what we believe to be life down here is an illusion, that the worst has come and gone and that we have nothing more to fear and nothing more to love."

"You're saying that for us, hope is dead," Richard said.

"Or that death is our sole hope?" Emilio asked.

"No, I only say that hope, like death, is an illusion and that down here in hell we have transcended hope."

"So I must see myself as dead already—as beyond fear, beyond love, beyond hope, even beyond dying?" Richard asked.

"Something better—something that will bring you peace. Know that your body might suffer a little longer but that nothing can touch your soul. Your soul is free."

"What is death . . . in the end?" Richard asked.

"Death is one thing and one thing only," Sanchez said. "A new beginning."

"And here I thought death was the end," Richard said.

"It is, but to make an end is also to make a beginning. Now. Then. Always."

Chapter 93

"My dear Miss McKillian," Díaz said, "I'm sorry to see you in such dark attire. I understand you lost a loved one lately."

He and the Señorita were entertaining James P. Sutherland and his friend and fellow magnate Judith McKillian in the Señorita's grand sala. Sitting at a large teak table, they were enjoying iced Laurent-Perrier Grand Siècle champagne, a truly exquisite Persian osetra caviar, and endless snifters of Year of the Comet, Le Premier Cru Classé Cognac. The Señorita's terrified waiters refilled their champagne flutes and brandy snifters with a truly unnerving alacrity.

"A very dear friend passed away only this last month."

"You must have loved him very much."

"*Es verdad,*" she said simply.

Judith McKillian was dressed in all black—from her buckskin trousers to her ruffled blouse of sheerest shantung silk to her thigh-high, high-heeled riding boots, polished to a scintillating sheen—yet nothing in her inky-hued couture suggested, to Díaz, grieving widowhood. Her waist-length vermillion tresses were casually flung over her right shoulder. Her lips and nails were painted a garish crimson, and she deigned to offer her friends a smile, which featured large, feral teeth, all of them horridly sharp and spotlessly white. Her eyes reminded Díaz of her hard, sharp teeth—snake's eyes. The first three buttons of her blouse were unbuttoned, revealing amazing amounts of stunning décolletage, and when she rose from the table to nervously walk around the room—all the while fiercely cracking her boot-tops with her riding crop—her eyes darted back and forth, as if she were looking for something more animate to whip. Díaz quickly discerned that her black buckskin breeches were stretched far too tight—skintight, voluptuously tight—around her outrageously protuberant rear end.

"Miss McKillian's late inamorato, the international mining magnate, T. Charles Carmony," Sutherland explained, "had been spending a great deal of time with Judith. But she hated the long sea voyages to Chile that she had to accompany him on when he visited his mines down there. She insisted he liquidate them and put them into something more conveniently located. He sold them to a consortium of Russian aristocrats for four hundred million dollars in gold bullion—cash on the old barrelhead, so to speak—which is now safely ensconced in a federal bank vault in Philadelphia, all of it under Miss McKillian's name. Since Judith had advised Carmony to do so, he concluded the gold should be hers when he expired."

"An inheritance the lovely Miss McKillian most

admirably earned and deserved," the Señorita said, smiling with admiration.

"I feel so badly about his passing," Miss McKillian said to Díaz, "and I hate having all that damnable lucre on my hands. I must get rid of it. I was hoping, Presidente Porfirio, you could help me invest it in something lucrative—in T.C.'s honor—in the very near future."

"But of course," Díaz said, rubbing his hands together. "Whatever I can do. The gentleman clearly loved you very much."

"He loved me to . . . *death*," Miss McKillian said softly, almost to herself.

"I can understand why you hated that long ocean voyage," the Señorita said.

"I also despised visiting the mines. You know what kind of mining he had most of his money in?"

"I'm afraid not," Díaz said.

"Guano mining," she said.

El Presidente looked confused.

"Explain guano mining to El Presidente," Sutherland said.

"In Chile, the Andes mountains," Miss McKillian explained, "are honeycombed with countless tunnels and caverns—many of them vertiginously deep bat caves. Billions of bats hang from the overhead stalactites as well as from the crags and escarpments at the tops of these shafts. At the bottom are unimaginably deep pits, filled to overflowing with oceans of . . . *bat shit*."

Díaz's eyes were blinking rapidly. "I don't understand," he finally said.

"You fucking moron!" Suddenly exploding, McKillian was now shouting at Díaz at the top of her lungs and pointing at him. "You don't understand anything, do you? Well, try to understand this, bucko! That guano was worth a fortune—hundreds of fortunes. Bat shit makes the greatest fertilizer and the most powerful explosives in the world!"

"And Miss McKillian's late lover owned half the world's supply," the Señorita said, smiling soothingly.

"Still I understand completely why you wanted him to sell it," Díaz said soothingly to McKillian, hoping to calm her down. "I can see how that ocean voyage must have been stressful."

"You want to know why I really had him sell it?" McKillian asked the room.

"As a matter of fact, yes," Sutherland said.

"I made him sell it because . . . I HATE BAT SHIT!" she thundered, beating her boot-tops incessantly with her riding crop, then shaking the whip in Díaz's face. "The stuff pours like black lava out of the asses of those bats, hanging from the ceilings and stalactites up above those shafts, day and night, night and day, a nonstop torrential downpour of thick, filthy black noxious crap. It's not only packed with nitrates for fertilizer and explosives, it's loaded with pure protein. Subsequently, those oceans of excrement underneath teem with vermin and vipers which grow to insane proportions—rats with asses like cocker spaniels, two-foot spiders and centipedes, ordinary snakes the size of anacondas. I HATE BAT CAVES! I HATE BAT SHIT! I HATE VIPERS AND VERMIN! I HATE CHILE! I HATE MEXICO!"

Díaz stared in shock at the obviously demented but prodigiously rich and powerful woman whom he now had to placate. Madre de Dios, how he despised himself—and Méjico!—for needing her money so desperately. He'd hated sucking up to so many of the world's worst, most brutally plutocratic potentates, but this lunatic lady was truly beyond the pale, indisputably the most violently insane financial mogul he'd ever had to kowtow to.

Moreover, despite the paranoid violence and macabre madness of her tirade, try as he might, Díaz still could not take his eyes off her jaw-droppingly spectacular . . . *backside*. She had the most stunningly awesome ass he'd ever seen in his entire life.

And he also had to get into her bank account. She could be a monetary mother lode for Madre Méjico—and himself.

Chapter 94

At the mine face, Richard and Sanchez were hammering drill holes into an unusually large vein of silver ore. After driving in a half-dozen holes, they began breaking the ore out of the veins deeply embedded in the rock. Richard worked his vein, and Sanchez worked another a dozen feet downshaft from him.

So far, Richard wasn't having much luck. Sanchez had told him to aim his hammer-swing just above the holes but with a slight downward slant. All Richard got when he hit the rock was a loud clang and a sharp, stinging pain in his fists.

Finally, Sanchez walked up to him.

"Back up," he said.

Rearing back, Sanchez nailed the rock just above the vein with a single blow. The mine face all around the drill holes exploded into a hundred pieces. Shattering like bone china, half the hard-rock wall burst into pieces and tumbled down onto the tunnel's bottom.

Richard had to jump back to keep his feet from being smashed.

"How did you do that?" he asked Sanchez.

"It's not how hard you hit," Sanchez said, "but where."

Richard resumed his hammering but with mixed results. He feared he wasn't cut out for mining El Infierno de Plata.

After a half hour or so a new man approached them. A grizzly of a man, he had a short beard, black curly hair, and was massively muscled—shoulders like anvils, biceps like cannonballs, thighs like tree stumps. His eyes were dark, emotionless, and incomprehensible, eyes that stared right through you—graveyard eyes. He was clearly a man you did not mess with.

"You're the one they call Ricardo," the man said.

"And you are?"

"People call me Hernando."

Richard said nothing.

"Mateo said we should talk."

Richard nodded. "I know Mateo. I've heard of you. You're the powderman, no?"

"*Sí.*"

Everyone knew the powderman. He had the most dangerous job in the mine. His assistant carried a canvas knapsack of black powder and at his waist hung a bag of rags, among which were scattered fulminate-of-mercury blasting caps. The powderman packed the holes around the ore veins with the black powder, then inserted the charges and later set them off. Sometimes they opened up new veins of ore, sometimes whole new shafts.

Richard noticed Hernando's assistant, Bardo, a young beardless boy of perhaps seventeen, wasn't with him. He'd heard the boy was blown up in an accident. He was starting to think it was true. Hernando carried his own powder, and the fulminate-of-mercy cap bags hung precariously from each hip.

"You just got a promotion," Hernando said. "You're my new assistant."

"Señor," Richard said with a small but slightly mocking bow, "I respectfully decline your very great honor, but I'd rather die a common miner. I'll end up just as dead, but it will take a little longer."

Richard returned to prizing chunks of ore out of the silver vein with his pick. Hernando gripped his shoulder and led him into a quiet, secluded part of the tunnel, so they could speak privately.

"Hombre, you got no choice in the matter. You're doing it. Mateo and I say you're doing it."

"And here I thought Mateo was my amigo."

"Best amigo either of us ever had."

"*¿Verdad?* What happened to your last blaster?"

"He is *muy muerte* [very dead]."

"Then why should I want to take his place?"

"You will be more careful."

"How do you know?"

"You couldn't be more clumsy."

"What happened to him?"

"He dropped the cap bag on the way back to the explosives depot. The caps blew up him and five of his muchachos to kingdom come."

"So why should I want to take his place?"

"Fear will make you cautious. Fear clears the blood and the mind, is it not so?"

"Clears the blood?" Richard asked, incredulous.

"Tell you what: You walk with me awhile, and I'll fill you in on your new job. You won't have it for long, and it will be even more dangerous than even you imagine." He treated Richard to a small cruel smile. "But it might get both of us out of this hell-mine."

Shrugging out of his knapsack, he eased it onto Richard's back and slipped the straps under his arms. He handed Richard a thick, new, unfrayed rope belt, and untying the two leather cap bags from his own belt, gave them to Richard. He studied Richard, as he tightened the heavy rope and knotted it twice. He then assiduously lashed the bags to it, tight enough so that they did not bang against his legs and hips, one atop each upper hip.

"Come with me," Hernando said. "We'll walk and talk. I'll teach you the finer arts of mine demolition and also explain Mateo's plan for us."

"Why do I assume I'll hate Mateo's plan?"

"Why assume the worst?" Hernando said.

"Because thinking was never Mateo's strong suit," Richard said.

"*Sí*, he is doer, not a planner."

"*Imbecil* is the word we're looking for."

"*¿De verdad?* [Really?]"

"If you put Mateo's brains in a hummingbird," Richard said, "it wouldn't know a mule's ass from a morning glory."

Hernando treated Richard to a series of long hard guffaws. "*Gracias, amigo*, there is so little that is amusing in these mines, but you have given Hernando something to laugh at. Still you are right. It's taken a truly devious imbecile to devise a plan as *muy loco* as this one. Only a *hombre muy maníaco* could come up with one like this."

"I hate Mateo. I hate his plan."

"Don't hate it until you've heard it. Let's walk and talk. Then you'll come to despise it *también más* [even more]. I promise."

Chapter 95

It took a few minutes, but Díaz and the Señorita had finally managed to calm Judith McKillian down. Talking about her late lover, his fortune in bat guano, and how much he'd sold it for seemed to have psychically unhinged her. Throughout her whole deranged diatribe against bat caves, bat shit, the vipers and vermin that resided in all that excrement at the caves' bottoms, and the infernal idiocy of her late lover, McKillian had been horsewhipping her boot-tops with an almost preternatural passion, her eyes glaring hatefully at Díaz the entire time. The one time she stopped beating her boots, she paused only to bend her crop in a perfect 180-degree parabola. When she released the tip, it thrummed and vibrated violently. Shaking it only inches from the dictator's hysterically frightened face, she shouted:

"*I'd also love to give you—you butt-kissing, money-grubbing, brain-dead retard—some of what I gave my bat shit–crazy, couldn't-die-soon-enough-from-my-point-of-view pervert of a lover: an apocalyptically painful ass-whipping!*

*And if you don't stop staring at my ass, you're going to get
some of that . . . RIGHT NOW!"*

If he hadn't needed her money so badly, he'd have
walked out of the room and never spoken to her
again. But he and his country were desperate. He had
to get that eight-figure check.

Also he had to admit, she had a point. In truth, the
McKillian woman's trousers were almost terrifyingly
tight, and Díaz could not take his eyes off her prepos-
terously pugnacious bottom, try as hard as he might.
So Díaz tried desperately to propitiate her.

"Still," he said "your late lover must have cared for
you very much to have given you the proceeds from
the sale of those mines."

"Quid pro quo," McKillian snarled. Beating the servants to the bottle, she poured herself another prodigious snifter of Napoleon brandy. Taking a long
pull, she said: "I promised that asswipe Carmony five
full days and nights of excruciating pleasure—the op-
erative word in this instance is *excruciating*—in the
penthouse suite of the Excelsior Hotel in Philadelphia if he sold off all that shit and gave me half of the
proceeds!"

"And he did it?" Díaz asked, still in shock.

"You bet your sweet ass, he did it. Locked in the
throes of the most hellishly hot fornication you ever
heard of, he eventually promised me the proceeds
from his whole damn bat shit mine sale if I gave him
two more nights."

"And he was true to his word?" Sutherland asked,
grinning wickedly.

"He had to be," McKillian said. "I instantly summoned a notary, took out the will I had in my purse,

and made both of them sign it just as fast as they knew how."

"He did all this for . . . *sex*?" Díaz asked, still mystified.

"To be precise, he did it in exchange for certain rather indelicate amorous acts, which, by contract, I'm not at liberty to discuss."

"I find it hard to believe that a woman of your breeding and refinement would do such a thing," Díaz said.

"Oh, I did it, El Morono, and made it all legal first— t's crossed in blood, the i's dotted with dollar signs."

"But then the poor man also died, loving you, no?" Díaz asked sadly.

"He sure did, though he never actually made it through the first week. That seventh night we were still at it, but he was wearing down. To extend his stamina and ardor, he had me inject him with homeopathic doses of strychnine. I don't know, maybe I got a little carried away with that needle, but during that final, fatal act, his shockingly savage passion and truly deplorable desires—combined with those interminable strychnine injections—did him in. The old geezer suddenly straightened up, screamed like a banshee, then rolled over on his side and . . . *croaked*."

"Such a tragedy!" Díaz said. "But he died happy. He died for you. He died for love."

"Which is a polite way of saying I fucked him to death," McKillian said.

"You aren't alone," the Señorita said. "Porfirio did the same thing to his first wife, and it was far more gross than anything you can imagine, let alone do."

"It even disgusted me," Sutherland said, shaking his head, staring at the floor but with a small, half-to-himself smile on his mouth.

"This, I have to hear," McKillian said, a sly smile of her own forming on her lips.

Chapter 96

Richard and Hernando walked, semi–bent over, trying not to bang their heads on the overhead cross-beams and the upright timbers holding them up. They not only wanted to protect their heads, the two men didn't want to knock the crosspieces loose and bring the mountain down on them.

Now that Richard carried the black powder and blasting caps, he no longer clutched a candle but relied on Hernando, who walked in front of him, to light the way. All of which made him more aware of his surroundings—of the miners' interminable clanging, droning, and groaning; the *dripdripdripdripdrip-drip* of leaking water; the moaning of the shoring timbers, sagging and bending under a billion tons of mountain; the banging of deadfall on the tunnel floor, as pieces of rock and wood hammered it; and often the cries of the men—their shouts, their sobbing, their whispers, and their dying prayers.

"I don't see we got any choice," Hernando said. "Mateo and I been working on this plan for a month.

You're perfect for it. Mateo said you were a nationally acclaimed high-platform diver at West Point. You were also their top heavyweight boxer and wrestler. Your last year you were the undefeated Northeast U.S. Army boxing champion. You don't even have to beat El Toro. Keep away from him and stay on your feet—long enough for Mateo's plan to take effect. But you have to fight him so you and I can get into the courtyard the night of the fight, and to get us there you have to get into the cage with Toro."

Richard stared at him in skeptical silence.

"Ey, come on, amigo," Hernando said. "You're six-four, two hundred thirty pounds, and a bona fide boxing champ. El Toro's an over-the-hill, *chingo-tu-madre hideputa* pimp. You can do this. We can escape from this place."

"We'll be trapped like rats in that courtyard in the gunsights of the guards. They have a Gatling in one of the gun towers."

"Mateo says they'll be too busy to worry about us. Stuff's going to go down you and I don't know about."

"And that is?"

"I can't tell you till you commit. No one can know unless they're committed."

"Excremento de toro. [Bullshit.]"

"Ricardo. You have to help us. We are your amigos. You cannot make it in this mine without amigos."

"Amigos don't ask their compadres to commit suicide for them."

"No, suicide's staying here. In the hacienda's courtyard we will have a shot at freedom."

"And you're asking me to commit to all this on faith?"

"Mateo wants you to do it."

Richard burst into laughter. "Mateo got me into all this." Richard gestured to the mine surrounding them.

"But now he needs you."

Richard stared at him, silent.

"We all need you there. I need you there."

Richard was about to say: "Fuck the mine. Fuck Mateo. Fuck the men. And fuck you."

But then Hernando cut him off:

"You have to do this, amigo. *Es verdad.*"

Suddenly, Richard got a good look at Hernando's face. His lips were trembling, his chin quivering. Richard caught himself.

Shit, Hernando was serious. Something was going down. Maybe they had a chance of pulling it off after all.

He stared at Hernando a long hard moment, then slapped him on his shoulder.

"Why the hell not? We're amigos, no? In for a centavo, in for a fucking peso. Let's do it. Let's rock this mountain. Let's bring this hellhole, the entire Infierno de Plata, down around the Señorita's ears and down around Díaz's cojones!"

"You won't regret this, my friend."

"No, I regret it already, but you have a point. Why shouldn't we give it a shot? Why the hell not?"

"Okay, here's the plan."

"Mateo's plan?"

"And that of the infamous gringo outlaw, the man who, when he was imprisoned in Díaz's Monte de Riqueza, blew that mine to hell and gone. So he knows what he's doing. His name is Slater. Torn Slater. Perhaps you've heard of him?"

"Outlaw Torn Slater's working with Mateo?" Suddenly, Richard was impressed. "I know who he is. I always suspected he and my mother were friends once.

She cuts out articles about him and keeps them in a drawer, but she won't say why. I'm not sure my father even knows."

"Slater worked out the plan and an intermediary fed it to Mateo."

"Something tells me I'm still not going to like it."

"But it's brilliant. See, you and I mostly work the drift tunnels. These shafts are the ones that had the richest veins of ore. They don't go in any particular order but follow the veins wherever they drift and wind. Hell, sometimes the drift veins even corkscrew. They're dangerous and difficult to work, but they're fantastically lucrative. Our job is to blow them open, so the other miners can break the pure silver loose."

"So?"

"Because we work the drifts, we enter parts of the mine that no one else works, and no one supervises us. The foremen won't go where we go. Too many tunnels collapse. Where we go it's too dangerous."

Richard stared at him, silent.

"You know all those abandoned tunnels along the mine's periphery? The ones near the outside of the mountain?"

"Yeah? They're lethal as hell. Some of them have been empty for centuries."

"You're going to love them."

"Bullshit. No one's replaced the rotten shoring timbers or cleaned out the deadfall since God knows when. Those half-collapsed crosscuts are choking with dust—much of it coal dust—flammable methane, even oil. Those abandoned shafts are mine explosions waiting to happen. Even the Señorita knows that. She's ordered us not to go into them. Entering these half-collapsed crosscuts is a flogging offense—for good reason."

"Our rats like them," Hernando said, grinning.

"*Sí,*" Richard agreed, "the rats love them. They flock there en masse. They eat all the shit in them, the rotten shoring timbers, the refuse we throw in them. They also eat anyone who goes into them and gets trapped. The rats own those damn tunnels. The rats are another reason no one goes into those tunnels."

"You're going in. You're going to pack those abandoned tunnels—filled with methane, oil, and combustible dust, with rats and rotting wood—and all their adjacent tunnels with explosives, set the charges and fuses, and then the day of the fight, we're going to blow this hell-mine, the entire mountain, to kingdom come."

Richard's face stared at him in dumbstruck disbelief. "How do you plan on setting the charges off?"

"When the time for our great escape comes, I have compadres who will sneak into the abandoned crosscuts, light the fuses, and then run like hell for the exits. We're going to bring this whole mine down. We're going to bring the mountain down."

"They'd have to light hundreds of fuses simultaneously," Richard said. "The men who lit them would all die."

"Not at all. Since the abandoned shafts will be filled with capped-off explosives, the nearby demolition will create a chain reaction. Sympathetic detonation will set off explosion after explosion after explosion, destroying these shafts and collapsing all the other shafts. Forever. All we need is a few men desperate enough to trigger the first few blasts."

"Pandemonium will reign," Richard said softly, suddenly appreciating the almost incomprehensible magnitude of Slater's plan and nodding his head.

"Slater's done this before at Monte de Riqueza," Hernando said. "He knows what he's doing."

Richard stared at Hernando, speechless.

"And in the chaos we will escape," Hernando added.

"Or die?"

Hernando treated Richard to another wide, unabashed smile. "You want to live forever?"

"So how do we make our grand escape?"

"Oh, young Ricardo, does Mateo have a plan for you?"

At the mention of Mateo's name, Richard froze—as if he'd just stared into the eyes of a grinning ghoulish Gorgon.

"You no like our *muy bueno amigo* Mateo?"

"Everything he touches turns to *excremento*."

"And I tell you his plan is *muy brillante*. It will work!"

"Is Slater involved in this plan?"

"Only Mateo."

"You just said his name again."

"Mateo's plan is *muy brillante*!"

Richard stared at him with hard-bone, hard-eyed skepticism. "That'll be the day."

Chapter 97

Still seated at the big table in the Señorita's grand sala, Judith McKillian said in her most infuriatingly conceited voice:

"Dear Generalissimo Porfirio, you were about to tell us about your illicit relations with your own niece? The Señorita said they caused the poor young girl's . . . *demise*. Please, I must hear everything about it."

Díaz averted his eyes, clearly furious.

"Oh, let me tell the story," the Señorita said, grinning maniacally. "Porfirio's mother's birth name was Mori, which means literally: 'I die.' It's your name too, dear Porfirio—your full name being José de la Cruz Porfirio Díaz . . . *Mori*. No wonder you're such a depraved degenerate. Who walks around with the name . . . *I Die*?"

The Señorita's high burbling chortles rang through her hacienda.

"And who, but a hopeless idiot, marries his niece?" Sutherland asked, shaking his head in feigned disappointment.

"Why, El Dimwit Díaz, here," the Señorita said.

"You married your sister's daughter, the delectable Delfina Díaz 'I Die' Mori. It doesn't get much dumber than that. Don't you agree?"

"Aren't you being a little too . . . judgmental?" Díaz asked, his feelings strangely hurt.

"Not at all," the Señorita said. "You married blood of your blood and had seven children by the poor child. During her seventh childbirth the young woman couldn't take it anymore and gave up the ghost. The seventh kid killed her. Would it hurt your feelings if I assert that you not only married your niece-by-blood, you . . . *fucked her to death!*

"Hey, it could be worse," Sutherland said. "He could have fucked his sister to death."

"Or his mother, the late Petrona 'I Die!' Mori," the Señorita said. "Tell me, Don Porfirio, you had children with your sister's daughter. Do the words *incest, inbreeding,* and *congenital idiocy* mean anything to you?"

"My children aren't very . . . *bright,*" the generalissimo had to admit. "I've sometimes wondered why."

"Maybe we ought to call you El-Shit-for-Brains-O instead of El Presidente," Judith McKillian said.

Suddenly, Díaz was incensed. "I don't have to take your ridicule."

"WANNA BET?" Judith McKillian thundered.

She then laid her riding crop across Díaz's ass as hard as she could. The dictator leaped up and down, frantically rubbing his backside.

"You'll take it and like it, bucko," McKillian said. "As long as you need our pesos. As long as you need the money of our financier friends, who frankly think you have tamales in your head instead of a brain and avocados instead of testicles."

The Señorita howled with laughter.

"What's so funny?" Sutherland asked.

"In Nahuatl," the Señorita explained, "the Aztec tongue, *avocado* means 'testicle.'"

"You don't say?" Sutherland said. "How droll."

Díaz glared at Judith McKillian. Even as he rubbed his rear end in pain, however, even as he trembled in fury at the whipcrack she'd given him, he could not stop staring at her . . . *behind.*

Whirling around like a deranged dervish, McKillian, again, laid a singing, stinging, whiplash across Díaz's ass. Again, leaping up and down, yelping like a dog and rubbing his rump, Díaz glared at her, enraged.

"That's for your dead niece-wife, Señor Estúpido," McKillian said.

"Do the words *honor* and *loyalty* mean anything to you?" Sutherland asked.

"I've always stood up for my friends," Díaz said.

Their howls of derision echoed through the hacienda.

"My peons elect me year after year by overwhelming majorities."

"You're elected because of your ballot stuffing, gerrymandering, kidnapping and jailing of opponents, your political oppression, your terror and intimidation, your murder-most-foul. Because of your subjugation of the legislature, your corruption of your court system, and because you jailed or killed every honest reporter in Méjico."

"All of which I prefer to call *aggressive campaigning.*"

"You view murder, torture, and the incarceration of political rivals as acceptable campaign practices?" McKillian asked.

"If my opponents can't stand the heat, they should stay out of my kitchen."

"Speaking of which," Judith McKillian said, "I've heard you're an incorrigible crook, a devious degenerate, and that you'd steal a red-hot stove."

"No, but I might order my federales to requisition the oven as a national security threat."

"With no probable cause, I suppose," McKillian said.

"Requisition first, probable cause second," Díaz said with a gloating grin.

"May I remind you that you came to power through a coup d'état?" the Señorita pointed out.

"After which I've been duly reelected three times in a row."

"But you pledged to run only one time and never again," Sutherland said.

"You wouldn't mind if I called you a despicable liar, would you?" McKillian asked.

"Consistency is the hobgoblin of little minds."

"Do you have any idea who said that?" Sutherland said.

"I just did."

"You really are an idiot, you know," the Señorita said.

"A retarded reactionary idiot," Sutherland said.

"But a reactionary idiot who's radical in his approach to our economy. I've radically increased the railroad system, strung telegraph wires nationwide, reorganized agriculture and mining."

"All of it through slave labor!" Judith McKillian shouted.

"So?" Díaz said pleasantly with a shrug.

"So you've thrown millions of your peons off scores

of millions of arable acres and sold their birthright to foreign plutocrats," McKillian said heatedly, "while forcing those former landowners into slavery on their land that they previously owned."

"You have sold off ninety percent of your nation's wealth—your country's railroads, your agriculture, land included, your oil and mining industries—to a handful of foreign devils, mostly gringos," Sutherland said. "Your agricultural barons sell almost everything they produce to foreign countries—mostly to America. They grow sisal for cloth, rope, and twine; coffee; sugar; fruit and blue agave for hard spirits—all of it for foreign consumption. They produce almost no corn or beans for your peons. What little sustenance your people ingest, they must import from . . . *America*!"

"To escape the debt-peonage slavery into which you have so hideously bound your people," McKillian said, "they must flee north, their only hope lying in escape to . . . *America*!"

"Can you imagine anything more shockingly sadistic?" the Señorita thundered.

"I view it as shockingly lucrative."

"Lucrative for a handful of foreign investors— most of them gringos—but not for your own people, who live in grinding, abject poverty," the Señorita said.

"All of which you profit off of personally, obscenely, and prodigiously," Sutherland observed.

"I view it as strict, classic, Adam Smith capitalism," Díaz said, "with a labor-management philosophy, untrammeled by the bleeding-heart do-gooderism of people who only wish to ruin our country's good old bottom line."

"You mean America's 'good old bottom line,'" Judith

McKillian said. "The *mejicano* people gain nothing from your economic policies, while the United States gains . . . *everything.*"

"Then more's the pity," Díaz said.

"I hope you don't expect us to pity . . . *you?*" McKillian asked, spitting the last word in Díaz's face.

"Not at all," Díaz said. "But you should, at least, pity poor Méjico."

"Why in God's good name should we do that?" Sutherland thundered at him.

"Because we are so far from God and so close to the . . . *United States.*"

Chapter 98

The abandoned tunnels, which lined the outside of the mountain, were vital to Mateo and Hernando's plan. They had been mined out for decades, even centuries, their silver long depleted. No one went into them anymore. No one replaced the cracked, rotten shoring timbers. Filled with deadfall, choking with dust, reeking of methane and leaking shale oil, these half-collapsed crosscuts were a haven only to the hundreds of thousands of rats who seemed to live off anything and everything, particularly dead and dying miners. If a miner expired—or even worse was seriously injured and lay helpless in a shaft—the rats swarmed and devoured him.

So into these hell-tunnels Hernando was sending Richard. Packing any and all crevices, cracks, and old drill holes with black powder and blasting caps, Richard was finishing the work that Bardo, Hernando's previous assistant, had so assiduously begun.

The last day he would hide fused, capped-off bags

of black powder in the last of the abandoned shafts. When the time came, their amigos would light them up, then race for the shaft head and . . . *freedom.*

All the while, he and Hernando would be in the hacienda courtyard—Richard in the cage for however long the fight lasted . . . not that anyone had ever lasted more than a single round with El Toro Malo. Finally, when the miners poured out of the shaft head and the mine blew, during the chaos that followed, Mateo swore Richard and Hernando would attempt to escape El Infierno de Plata . . . *forever.*

Unfortunately, Richard did not trust Mateo. True, he'd fought alongside him, and they had saved each other's lives more than once. Mateo and the amazing Sin Sisters had also given Richard the most thrilling night of his life, but Mateo had dragooned him into the Sonoran army, and had it not been for Mateo, the Señorita never would have abducted him, forced him to have sex with her, and now enslaved him in her Silver Hell.

On the other hand, Hernando had said Richard's mother, sister, and Torn Slater were involved in the plot, which meant everything in the world to Richard. If they were in on it, he and Hernando might just have a chance. And anyway, what choices did Richard have?

So he followed Hernando on his daily trek through Infierno de Plata—which now included packing the abandoned tunnels with capped-off charges, which would transmogrify sympathetically into a chain reaction of ear-cracking, tunnel-shattering explosions. The two *prisioneros* then moved from drift lode to drift lode, from ancient abandoned tunnel to ancient abandoned tunnel, all the time packing the long-forgotten shafts with more and more explosive charges.

He hoped that he and Hernando could pull it off. And that they could blow this mine to holy hell.

PART XIX

"El Toro looks like El Steer-O," Judith McKillian said, genuinely impressed.

Chapter 99

Two weeks had passed, and the Señorita had invited Díaz, Sutherland, and Judith McKillian to watch the cage fight from the top balcony of her smaller hacienda. It overlooked not only the hacienda courtyard but the main entrance to El Infierno de Plata as well as the Fuerte River.

"El Presidente, you positively eat betrayal," Judith McKillian shouted, her words echoing across the courtyard. "You deceived and rebelled against your sainted mentor—Méjico's savior, its Jesucristo—Benito Juárez."

"Who soundly defeated your treasonous ass at the battle of La Bufa in Zacatecas," the Señorita said.

"Lerdo took over after Juárez died," Sutherland said. "He generously granted you amnesty and forgave your unpardonable wrongs."

"Instead of hanging you from the nearest saguaro or sending you *in perpeturio* to the *penitenciario*," Judith McKillian added, "which you so richly deserved."

"After which you promptly double-crossed him,"

the Señorita said, "campaigning against him on the slogan 'one term only'—a pernicious lie that you've broken during every campaign since."

"I view it as a truthful hyperbole."

"Are there no depths to which you will not sink?" Sutherland asked, shaking a finger at Díaz. "Is there no limit to your deviousness and deceit?"

"If your peons had any brains and balls," McKillian said, "they'd have flayed you whole the first time you ran for office."

"Done you up the day your mamacita dropped you," the Señorita howled.

"Perhaps," Díaz shouted angrily, "but you three, and your entourage of foreign investors, have profited quite handsomely off my peons, bond laborers, and my admittedly aggressive labor-management practices. You oppress Méjico's wretched of the earth just as ruthlessly as I do."

"He has a point," Sutherland conceded. "His mines have flooded my coffers with tsunamis of filthy lucre, filling them to the bursting point."

"And I have to admit he does it all on such low overhead," Judith McKillian said, scratching her head meditatively.

"We do run them on slave labor, you know?" the Señorita cheerfully admitted.

"And rightly so," Sutherland said. "I've always complained that in England we coddle our workers—particularly our miners—as if they were small, spoiled children and grossly overpay them. Well, Porfirio here has found a way to pay his deserving poor . . . *nothing at all.*"

"How splendid," McKillian said. "Bravo!"

"El Presidente," Sutherland said, "once again you are so right. I hope your employees don't bother you, the way ours do their masters in jolly old England. Our workers pester us nonstop with their endless complaints—harangues about no food, no overtime, seven-day work weeks, lack of shelter, medical care, clothing, and unsafe working conditions."

"My dear Mr. Sutherland," the Señorita said with faux scorn, playing the game they so often played, pretending to be outraged at Sutherland's heartlessness, "your problem is you have no sympathy or compassion for anyone at all. You don't even comprehend the meaning of the word, do you?"

"Of course I do, dear," Sutherland said with mock sincerity. "I just looked those two words up in our *Oxford English Dictionary.* Know what I learned? In that book, sympathy falls squarely between . . . *shit* and *syphilis.* You know where compassion's located? Right between . . . *come* and *cunt.* So why on earth would anyone use such foul terms?"

"He does have a point," Díaz said.

"I SHOULD HOPE SO!" Sutherland howled with all the upper-class indignation he could muster.

"In fact," McKillian said, "two foreign plutocrats—plus the illustrious Señorita Dolorosa—stand before you now."

"And we are expressing our heartfelt appreciation," Sutherland said.

"And we can't thank you enough for all your emoluments and remuneration and for your infinitely gracious hospitality," the Señorita said.

"And those fantastic fifty-year tax waivers," Judith McKillian said in a low hiss.

"Outstanding!" Sutherland enthused.

"How can we express our gratitude?" the Señorita asked.

Again, Díaz's eyes drifted toward McKillian's voluptuous bottom.

"Did I just catch you, once again, gawking gapejawed at Miss McKillian's deliciously delectable derriere?" Sutherland raged.

"YOU LIKE THAT *GRINGA GATITA*, NO?" the Señorita shouted.

"I am an unapologetic admirer of the feminine gender in general and of Miss McKillian in particular," Díaz snorted hoarsely.

Suddenly, Sutherland was standing in front of him. Grabbing Díaz's wrists, he squeezed them hard, grinning dementedly the whole time.

Jesus, Díaz thought, *that pretentious limey has hands like power-vises.*

It was true, and he was squeezing El Presidente's lower arms so tight Díaz couldn't even move. But McKillian could. She came up behind Díaz and shouted:

"All you do is stare at my ass, and I can't take it anymore. Do you hear me? *I CAN'T TAKE IT ANYMORE!!!!*"

Wheeling off a pivot, Judith McKillian began beating Díaz's behind with one whistling whiplash after another. Locked in place by Sutherland's iron grip, Díaz was helpless. He couldn't move, even as Judith McKillian flogged him with all her might. Soon his howls filled the room.

"I can't help it!" Díaz sobbed. "It's so . . . *amazing.*"

"Judith, I have to agree with Porfirio," Sutherland said, pretending to placate her but still refusing to let Díaz loose. "You have the most impudent posterior I've ever observed. I'm sure all of your dead husbands would agree."

Still McKillian continued whacking the dictator's ass and shouting in between whipcracks:

"I hate everything about this detestable despot . . . I hate his idiotic uniforms . . . I hate his moronic medals . . . I hate the way he fucked his sister's daughter to death . . . I hate the way he steals from people . . . He has no moral compass . . . He stole an entire nation and sold it to a bunch of oligarchic hideputas *and—"*

"But, dear Judith, he sold it to . . . *us,*" Sutherland said. "We have benefited prodigiously from El Presidente's thievery."

"Oh," McKillian said. "Perhaps you have a point. I'm so sorry, Mr. Sutherland."

She suddenly stopped beating Díaz's backside, but it was too late. By now Díaz was a shaking, shuddering, sobbing wreck. Sutherland finally released him.

"Oh, what are you upset about?" the Señorita asked Díaz. "Judith apologized to you—sort of."

"But you don't understand," Díaz sniffled and snorted. "All I want is for you three to invest money in my country. You'll grow rich, and we'll bring Méjico into the modern age. It's not too much to ask. Yet you accuse me of the vilest things, then beat me with a riding crop and call me . . . *muy idiota.* It's not right. It's uncalled for."

"Porfirio," the Señorita said, "Judith understands all that now. She just got carried away. Can't we just forget about this little episode and write it all off as blood under the bridge?"

"You said I enslaved my entire nation," Díaz muttered, his feelings actually . . . *hurt.*

"But, as I pointed out to Miss McKillian," Sutherland said, "you made us all filthy rich in the process."

"And therefore we cannot thank you enough," the Señorita said.

"So we stand before you, three of the most grateful beneficiaries of your magnanimity," Judith McKillian said.

"You've been philanthropically generous to us, old sport," Sutherland said, slapping Díaz on the back.

"After sixty-five years of discord and unrest, I brought peace," Díaz said, still sniffling.

"Meaning, you brought Méjico . . . *us,*" the Señorita said with a merciless grin.

"Speaking of which, if I cut you a check, would that make everything all right?" Judith McKillian asked.

She clapped her hands and the liveried servants quickly refilled their glasses with eighty-five-year-old Napoleon brandy.

Chapter 100

Richard followed Hernando through the hacienda's huge courtyard. The massive steel death cage was mounted on a high platform so everyone would have a decent view of the battle to come. It was made of thick steel bars and was surprisingly large: twenty feet by twenty feet and a dozen feet high. Only the most highly skilled workers in the mine and in the stamping mills and smelters surrounding the mine were invited. Still they were there, seemingly by the thousands, and they packed the courtyard and surrounded the big cage.

Hernando escorted Richard past the front row. El Toro Loco was also threading his way through the crowd, graciously accepting handshakes and slaps on the back. He obviously had an enthusiastic following.

"Ey, amigos," El Toro shouted, shaking hands with both of them but shaking Richard's with extra force.

"Ah, my young friend," El Toro said in a loud voice, "Hernando has told me so much about you—four-time national boxing champion in America's armed forces, a national wrestling champion to boot, and an acclaimed high diver. I am honored to make your acquaintance—both here and in the . . . *death cage*!!!"

"El Toro," Hernando said, "I promise you, you shall be most pleased with this young man's pugilistic prowess."

"It sounds like I should be very much afraid," El Toro said in a squeaky falsetto, pretending to wince and cower.

The *prisioneros* around them convulsed with mocking laughter, pointing at Richard and howling with derision.

Oh fuck. He was in for it now.

Now El Toro was nose to nose with him. "In truth, this shall be a very good fight, a very bloody fight, for I intend to take my time with you—to take you apart piece by piece in that cage. You know why?"

"Why?" Richard asked.

"Because I hate . . . *gringos*!" Roaring like the *toro* he was, the big man threw his head back and thundered an earsplitting chorus of horselaughs in Richard's shocked face.

"I will obliterate you *también* for the Señorita and El Presidente Porfirio Díaz, who have honored us with their presence. They are up in the balcony behind you. They asked me to give you an especially violent and painful beating and have promised to reward me royally if I do. So, Ricardo, I am taking you down slow and hard."

El Toro pointed to the top-floor balcony, so Richard turned and looked. Sure enough, there, seated high overhead were Díaz, the Señorita, James P. Sutherland, and the woman who had whipped him so maniacally with the riding crop when he was strung up by the elbows, Judith McKillian.

Shit, the four of them came all the way to El Infierno de Plata, crossing fifty miles of desert, just to watch you get stomped into a thousand pieces by this moronic madman, Richard thought grimly.

But El Toro loved what was happening to Richard. His booming laughter reverberated across the prison yard like a rolling artillery barrage.

"I also plan on kicking to you to death with my pointed, steel-toed boots."

Oh my God, he was *wearing pointed, steel-toed boots.*

Richard stared hopelessly at his own filthy, frayed pathetic-looking footwear—a pair of ancient brogans with holes in the toes and no heels. He then turned to Hernando and moved him a dozen feet away from El Toro.

"How bad is this guy? *¿Verdad?*"

But before Hernando could speak, an inmate interrupted him:

"Ey, gringo, I seen El Toro hammer fence posts into hard ground with his closed fists."

Richard stared at Hernando, saying nothing.

"I seen El Toro straighten cold horseshoes with his bare hands," another *prisionero* said.

"You know where El Toro got that cage you're fighting in?" a third *prisionero* asked.

Richard stared at the heavens, mouthing mute prayers.

"It's a bear cage. The owner took a grizzly round the country and challenged all comers to fight Victorio, El Oso Grizzly Asesino [Victorio, the Killer Grizzly Bear].

Richard turned his eyes toward the ground and shook his head, still silent.

"You ain't seen that grizzly around no more, ey,

amigo?" the man said, doubled over with coughing, choking laughter. "Victorio made the mistake of sticking his face up to the bars and growling at El Toro. He hit Victorio with a single punch between the bars and right between the eyes."

"And?" Richard asked, not really wanting to know the answer.

"He killed that *hideputa* grizzly deader'n Montezuma!"

"Lots of luck," the first *prisionero* shouted, "fighting El Toro the Oso Grizzly Asesino [the Grizzly Bear Killer]!

The *prisioneros* gathered around Richard and slapped him on the back and shoulders while exploding into sadistically contemptuous guffaws.

Chapter 101

Díaz could not believe it was happening to him once more, but this time it was worse. Sutherland had escorted Díaz back into the sala for a private talk. When they were alone, however, the man had again seized Díaz's wrists without warning. Locking them in his viselike grip, he was now pushing Díaz's lower forearms down, doubling the dictator over at the waist, at which point Judith McKillian and the Señorita joined them. McKillian began beating Díaz's backside with her riding crop, but even more barbarically. It was as if she'd lost her mind, which she clearly had. Nor were Sutherland or the Señorita of any help to the dictator. When Díaz looked up at Sutherland, the ludicrous limey just stared back at him through that idiotic monocle, still stuck up against his right eye, the ivory cigarette holder clenched in his teeth and bouncing up and down when he talked, which he did incessantly:

"Sorry about Miss McKillian, old chap. Just can't take her anywhere anymore. Acts out all the time, just like she's doing now. Nothing to be done about it, really. She's just not right in the head. All you can do is let these rages wear themselves out. She's almost normal afterward—well, sort of. Still it can't be very pleasant for you, getting horsewhipped by a madwoman. Sorry about that. Ouch! That riding crop must really smart! Hope you aren't going to be too put out with her. She is quite rich, you know. Maybe she'll cut you a big fat check afterward."

Then there was the Señorita. Glancing up to his right, Díaz watched her throw her head back and chortle giddily. She was clearly having the time of her life, as merry as he'd ever seen her. In fact, it might have been the only time Díaz had ever seen the Señorita genuinely, sincerely . . . *happy*.

"I must say, Porfirio," the Señorita said when she caught Díaz's upward, teary-eyed stare, "Judith handles that riding crop really well—like she was born to it. No wonder she carries one with her everywhere she goes. I wish you could see her form, from my vantage point, that is. Smooth, even, level strokes, every one of them perfectly placed. There's something almost mystical about it: the absolute unity of work and purpose, creator and creation, of means and ends. In this case, the dancer has definitively become the dance. Judith McKillian has found the still point, the immovable spot . . the jewel in the lotus heart. She is Gautama, forsaking India and nirvana—bringing the bodhisattva into China, she has become the Buddha. In this matchless moment, Beauty has indeed become Truth, and Truth, Beauty. Oh, dear Porfirio, if you could only see her as I do! She is now a natural, an original, one of a kind—but suddenly transcending herself. I thought I was pretty good with a riding crop, but she's . . . *a genius with it.* Of course, I'm sure it's less pleasant for you—being on the receiving end—but from my point of view, this whole thing is really quite splendid. I just love watching a pro in action, doing what they do best, and I'm telling you, Miss McKillian has turned this little pastime of hers into high art. No longer a mere master of her craft, Judith has transformed herself into an incomparable . . . *artiste.*"

"Less pleasant for you," the Señorita had said to Díaz. It sure was "less pleasant" for him. Díaz's ass felt like it was on fire, and tears now flooded his face. Even worse, glancing over his shoulder, through his tears, he could see McKillian in action. Her eyes were hooded with paranoid rage as she focused monomaniacally on the task before her, which was flagellating his behind with a fury that surpassed all understanding. He had to admit she was putting everything into it. She was commitment incarnate. Nothing interfered with her concentration. From time to time, he could hear her mumbling inaudible curses under her breath—in fact, the ones he could make out were among the most unnerving obscenities he'd ever heard. Díaz had spent his life in the military, had seen men wounded in battle, and had heard some truly shocking outbursts in moments of extremity, but even those foulmouthed utterances could not rival Judith McKillian's. They didn't even come close. Her execrations were far and away the most disgustingly depraved Díaz had ever heard.

Sickened and in unbearable agony, he tried to look away from the three fiends, particularly Judith McKillian, who were tormenting him so wretchedly—only to find himself staring into a wall mirror off to the side. He could see them all, himself included, and it wasn't a pretty picture: Sutherland had him bent over in his utterly unbreakable wristlock; the Señorita, her head thrown back, was laughing like a loon, and Judith McKillian also bent over in order to get more leverage behind her horsewhip.

Then suddenly in that side-mirror he caught a shocking glimpse of her incredibly beautiful . . . *butt.* Since she too was bent at the waist, the small of her back was arched. Her black buckskin riding breeches were, consequently, pulled up taut as a drumhead, delineating every delicious micrometer of Miss McKillian's always resplendent . . . *rump.* He found his fascination with it horribly humiliating. Here he was, getting his own backside scourged by a true harpy from hell with a blind passion that defied all comprehension or belief, and yet the only thing Díaz could see and think about was . . . *her rear in that goddamned mirror.* He couldn't take his eyes off it. The damn thing charmed him like a snake, as if it were some sort of holy grail or philosopher's stone, a sacred totem that held the secrets to all mysteries everywhere . . . to life itself. Each perfectly round globe seemed, to Díaz, a work of genuine art—at once arrogantly insolent but at the same time impossibly impertinent. The sheer imperiousness of her extraordinary bottom held him transfixed.

Díaz attempted to shut his eyes, but still he couldn't stop staring at it.

Then it hit him all at once. He felt it, but couldn't believe it: The sick, sneaking sensation of despicable delight. Despite the shame of being mercilessly flogged by Judith McKillian—while his friends and colleagues watched and scoffed, aided and abetted, laughed and mocked—despite the conflagration burning up his own much-abused backside, Porfirio Díaz was getting . . . *aroused*.

These foreign devils really were the incarnation of evil. In the short time they'd been around him, Sutherland and McKillian had turned Porfirio Díaz, the strongest, most capable man in all of Méjico into . . . *a pervert*.

What had they done to him?

Porfirio Díaz began to sob.

At last, Judith McKillian's insanity ran its course, and she stopped beating the dictator. When Sutherland released his wrists, Díaz found himself immobilized by the sheer horror of what had happened, still bent at the waist and unable to move. Finally looking up, he saw Sutherland and the Señorita putting their arms around McKillian and attempting to console her.

"There, there, you poor thing," the Señorita was saying. "It's all right now. It's all over. Porfirio won't bother you anymore."

"I understand your feelings entirely, my dear," Sutherland was saying. "Díaz can be quite unbearable at times."

"He's such an idiot!" the Señorita said.

"You absolutely did the right thing!" Sutherland said emphatically.

"I've wanted to give him a good thrashing on countless occasions," the Señorita said, "on occasions too numerous to mention."

"And a superlative job you did of it too!" Sutherland enthused.

"Really first-rate!" the Señorita shouted.

"You were poetry in motion!" Sutherland exclaimed.

"I thought I was good with a horsewhip," the Señorita said, "but you, dear Judith, are nonpareil, ne plus ultra."

"Still, while I wholeheartedly agree, Judith," Sutherland said, "you might have been just a little . . . *hard on him.*"

"You think so?" McKillian asked, looking genuinely confused at the possibility.

"I think so," Sutherland said softly.

"And you know those slave-labor silver mines of ours really are a very good investment," the Señorita said.

"I'm thinking of putting all my money into them," Sutherland said. "No wages at all! Imagine such a thing! Díaz and the Señorita are labor-management geniuses. Think of it! They've figured out how to pay their drudges absolutely . . . *nothing!*"

"They could teach our businessmen back home a thing or two," McKillian admitted.

"In jolly old England as well," Sutherland said.

"No union problems here!" the Señorita shouted.

"Maybe I should put some of my money into one of these mines, after all," Judith McKillian said, suddenly quite serious. "After all, I have to do something with all that dreary cash."

"The one you're looking at right there," the Señorita said, leading Judith back out onto the balcony and pointing at El Infierno de Plata, standing directly in front of them, "would make for an excellent investment. Porfirio supplies me with all my workers free and gratis at no cost, and it's already making a fortune."

"Splendid," McKillian said. "All I need is a check and a pen."

When Díaz heard the word *check*, he immediately began to perk up. Maybe this day wasn't a dead loss after all. Perhaps things were already starting to improve, even if his ass felt like it was on fire and he was incapable of sitting down.

But after all, money always made everything better.

He quietly asked his majordomo to get him a blank check, a pen, and an inkwell.

It was looking to be a good day after all.

He could think of many other investments he wanted the ever-delightful Judith McKillian to make on behalf of El Presidente.

Chapter 102

Hernando turned Richard around and said in his ear: "Just keep away from him. You're in great shape. These are only three-minute rounds. If you stay on your feet for three rounds, we have a chance at freedom when the charges go off. If they don't, what the hell. We still get *mucho* tequila, *muchos tortillas carnes*, and a night in the hacienda. For one night you don't have to sleep in the mine shaft. Maybe they let you move into the barracks permanently. So either way, you win, no?"

"Was this any part of Slater's plan?" Richard asked.

"No. Mateo thought it up all by himself. How do you like it? *Muy brillante*, no?"

"Muy estúpido," Richard muttered under his breath.

"Ey, it's better than *nada*, which is what we got otherwise. At least, this way we have hope, and anyway we all need hope to live. We all live in hope, no?"

"*Sí*, and die in despair," Richard said, repeating the old trope.

Taking Richard by the arm, Hernando walked him

to the cage door. El Toro was already inside, dressed in a silk robe of shiny, shimmering, purest vermillion. He was feigning mock punches and dancing and prancing back and forth and side to side in an elaborate parody of pugilistic footwork.

Jesus, his opponent was six feet nine inches, if he was an inch, and three hundred pounds. This was the biggest man he'd ever seen in his life. The black patch over Toro's right eye made him look even more frightening. It was as if Richard was David, El Toro, Goliath, but David had no sling. Richard had never been more depressed in his entire life.

Fuck it, he finally said to himself. *What do you have to lose? Your life? Get over it. You're in El Infierno de Plata. What is your life? A trifle. And anyway maybe you'll get lucky. So focus, bob and weave, duck and dodge. Keep away from him. Maybe you can last the three rounds. Just remember: Don't get knocked down. There are no refs, and that big asshole will kick you to death if he has the chance—with steel-pointed toes.*

Richard entered the cage door. Glancing around him, he saw that the *prisioneros* were now grabbing the bars on its sides, shaking it insanely, making the cage bounce up and down, their faces deranged by bloodlust, desperate to see someone—who would almost undoubtedly be Richard—maimed, mauled, and murdered, ululating like crazed apes, their eyes huge as saucers, their lips curled taut above their teeth. They didn't even look human but like *lobos locos* [mad wolves].

"*¡Muerte! ¡Sangre! ¡Cojones!*" they screamed en masse. ["Death! Blood! Balls!"]

But Hernando was shouting at Richard too:

"You're going to do this, Ricardo. You're going to whip his ass like he *chingo*ed your mamacita *and* your sister. You'll do this."

Richard stared at him, saying nothing.

"Do it for your mamacita! Do it for your *hermana* [sister]. Do it for me!"

Richard still stared at him, speechless.

But now El Toro was on the move. Beating his chest like a gorilla, he roared as if he were all the fiends in hell, storming the gates, hammering on it, howling to break free. Slipping out of the red robe, he crossed to the cage door and handed it to his manservant, who was also dressed in red livery.

Standing stock-still, Richard stared at him quizzically.

El Toro put his hands up in a boxing pose and gestured to Richard to approach. He was ready to fight him. The contest was about to begin.

"We really don't have to do this," Richard said to him.

"The hell we don't."

"Are you as mean as they say?" Richard asked.

"Mean enough to kill Jesucristo."

"That's pretty mean."

"You ain't seen nothing, gringo. I'm going to kick your ass till you puke up my boots and choke on your colon."

The captain of the guard hammered a bell, and El Toro went into the serious boxing crouch. Richard instinctively went into his own routine, circling the big brute. Jesus, the guy was huge. He had a chest like a yearling steer and legs like full-grown oaks, biceps like howitzer shells, and shoulders like concrete blocks.

He was now moving in on Richard, not even attempting to defend himself. He stalked the young man like a tiger, devoid of fear or hesitation, relentless as a juggernaut.

Richard concentrated on evasion and on running out the clock.

He desperately wanted to be standing when the mine blew . . . and not be dead.

Punches were coming now, flurries of them, then full-blown blizzards. The man was so big and his arms so long that Richard could see them coming and duck them at will, the big hamlike fists rocketing over his head, each one with a terrifying whoosh!

Avoid the corners, Richard said to himself. *If he traps you there, you'll never get out. You'll die there.*

Still Richard could feel the cage growing smaller and smaller, El Toro closing in on him, walling him in, shrinking the space, whooshing closer and closer and closer, now grazing the top of his skull, occasionally hitting his forehead, and when he did, driving his head back with a resounding *crack!*

Backpedaling wasn't enough. To elude the man-monster, Richard had to teach him respect. Snapping lefts, he periodically followed through with rights—instantly raising his other fist up under his chin to defend against an uppercut—all the time hammering El Toro's nose. Richard focused exclusively on the big proboscis, ignoring every other square inch of his opponent's body. El Toro was big but he was slow, so Richard could hit it at will, over and over again, no one punch terminal but the accumulated effect lethal, hammering Toro's big ugly snout repeatedly.

After maybe the twentieth blow, Richard heard it crack. Madre de Dios, *he'd broken El Toro Loco's nose.*

Blood was hemorrhaging out of it as out of a ruptured fire hose.

El Toro, unhinged by rage, was wading into Richard, swinging wildly, dangerously, any one of his round-house swings capable of taking Richard's head off. But Richard could also see them coming, could duck them if he kept his head up and his eyes open.

And the rage and the punches were wearing Toro out.

Bob and weave, duck and dodge, run out the clock.

Slipping under a long looping right, Richard got directly underneath Toro and, reaching down as low as he could, came up under him with a right-handed uppercut, forged in the bottommost bowels of hell. He caught El Toro on the point of the chin, hitting him so hard Richard's fist, elbow, and shoulder absorbed the jolt, blazing as if they were on fire.

Richard knew physics, knew Newton's laws of motion, the third law being that for every action there is a counteraction, driving the first action backward. It was true in billiards and with almost all punches. A really good uppercut was the exception. That punch was not backed by the fighter's body weight but by the entire mass of planet Earth. And Richard had gotten every ounce of his 230 pounds under it as well, hammering El Toro's head back and rocking him on his heels. His eyes went out of focus.

Driving a straight right into Toro's defenseless Adam's apple, Richard then spun his body a full 360 degrees in a violently spiraling pirouette, hitting Toro in the temple with the hardest left he'd ever thrown, every bit of his body weight compounded by the centrifugal force of the death spin behind it. El Toro's head snapped sideways so hard Richard thought he'd broken his neck, but then Toro righted himself. Still the light was fading in his one good eye. As he rocked backward on his heels, his eye rolled into the back of his head until only the white showed, at which point Richard wheeled off a pivot in the opposite direction of the pirouette and hit Toro with a straight right to the solar plexus as hard as he knew how.

When the big man bent at the waist, gravity accentuated the next punch's power, and blood hemorrhaged from El Toro's nose so convulsively that Richard wondered if the man might bleed out, and then his wind was exploding out of him as it might out of a collapsing dirigible.

Toro was doubled over, so Richard hammered his pain-racked nose again with uppercut after uppercut—punches so forceful that he thought they might demolish his knuckles. When Toro finally pulled himself up and covered his nose with his big fists, he sobbed in agony:

"*¡No más, no más!*"

Believing Toro's words were bullshit and wanting Díaz and the Señorita to see their champion destroyed, Richard responded by speed-bagging Toro's brows, opening them up, until blood was deluging his eyes, blinding him like Samson. All Toro could do was paw at his unseeing face.

"This one's for Victorio!" Richard thundered, reminding El Toro of the bear he'd killed.

Rearing back, Richard kicked him in the cojones so hard pain shot through his foot and knee, as he drove El Toro's cojones straight up into his crotch, shattering the man's pelvis and driving fragments of it deep into his prostate.

El Toro toppled over onto his back, his knees yanked reflexively upward, locked immobile in a violent travesty of divine-supine genuflection.

Chapter 103

Oddly enough, Díaz and his friends were so absorbed with their own altercations that they'd missed the fight in the cage.

"El Presidente," Sutherland said sternly, "as profitable as your undertakings have been for us, I do have a personal bone to pick with you."

"*¿Es verdad?*" Díaz asked, astonished.

"That Sonoran silver mine I invested in some years ago, Monte de Riqueza?"

"*¿Sí?*" Díaz asked.

"One reason I invested so many hundreds of millions of dollars in it was that my spies told me you had a certain reprobate, Outlaw Torn Slater, laboring in the bottom of that godforsaken pit. I told you that in exchange for my investment, I wanted Torn Slater delivered to me in person, alive, well, with a ribbon wrapped around his neck."

"And you wanted the gentleman for?" the Señorita asked.

Sutherland removed his ubiquitous bowler hat.

"You know the reason I wear these bowler hats everywhere?" he asked.

"Why?" the Señorita asked.

"Some years ago I had it in my mind to hunt down that legendary outlaw and impale him with my trusty longbow and tri-bladed, steel broadheads. I planned to decapitate him, stick his head in a drum full of alcohol, and travel the world with my own Wild West troupe, reenacting how I'd killed the nefarious brigand. I'd have been bigger than God! I'd have made a fortune. I'd have been even richer than I am now."

"What a splendid idea!" the Señorita said. "*Muy magnifico*, Señor Sutherland! If only I could have been there! If only I could have invested in your undertaking! But what went wrong?"

"The man killed my posse one by one in the most hideous and most unsportsmanlike ways imaginable. He killed them with cougars and diamondbacks. He shot them from twelve hundred yards with his damnable Sharps rifle. Three he captured, scalped, skinned alive, and hung upside down from pole tripods over long-lived, low-flame fires. Miss McKillian was with me. She witnessed the whole bloody spectacle."

"The man's a monster!" Judith McKillian said, confirming Sutherland's assessment.

"You don't say?" the Señorita said.

"But I do say," Sutherland said, "because after he'd killed my whole crew, the rapscallion scalped the right half of my pate and hung me from the hocks over another of his slow-burning fires. Only after the intervention of my ramrod—an old grizzled trail hand named John Henry Deacon—did he relent. He and Deacon were old friends. They'd ridden with some freebooter named Quantrill during the American War of Northern Aggression. After Slater rode off, Deacon was allowed to cut me down."

"Outlaw Torn Slater is a fiend from hell!" Judith McKillian roared.

"Indeed," Díaz said, nodding his agreement.

"So that is how I come to receive this disgusting abomination of alabaster keloid covering my right pate. Slater not only lifted part of my scalp, he later . . . BLEW UP EL MONTE DE RIQUEZA! That was the prison mine I'd invested three hundred million dollars in. I never got Slater—because Díaz here was trying to persuade him to rob norteamericano banks and trains for Díaz and for Madre Méjico—and consequently . . . SLATER BLEW UP THE MINE, THE WHOLE FUCKING MOUNTAIN AND COST ME THREE HUNDRED MILLION DOLLARS. I LOST ALL THAT MONEY AND HALF MY SCALP TO OUTLAW TORN SLATER, BECAUSE OF YOU, YOU GODDAMN *HIDEPUTA* GREASER. YOU RENEGED ON OUR DEAL, KEPT SLATER FOR YOUR OWN NEFARIOUS ENDS, FUCKING ME OVER IN THE PROCESS, AND JAMES P. SUTHERLAND IS . . . *NOT A GRACEFUL LOSER!*"

"For which I am most aggrieved," Díaz said, his voice painfully contrite. "The fault is mine, all mine, and I assure you any further investments will be inviolably, impregnably, unimpeachably . . . *safe.* You have my word on that."

"And what will you do about Slater?" Sutherland asked.

"You will have Outlaw Torn Slater, Mr. Sutherland, to do with as you please," Díaz said. "On that you also have my personal guarantee. You shall have the outlaw before the year is out."

"I don't know," Judith McKillian said. She was just about to write a blank check on the First National Bank of Philadelphia and was waving it at Díaz. "I was planning to make this out to Porfirio personally, but after hearing Mr. Sutherland's story, how can I be sure my investment in El Infierno de Plata will be secure? Maybe your Outlaw Torn Slater will blow that mine up just like he obliterated Monte de Riqueza and Mr. Sutherland's three hundred million dollars along with it."

Díaz gave them his most gorgeous grin.

"Because, my dear," Díaz said, "your investment will be backed by my full faith and credit."

"Really?" Judith McKillian said. "And you will bring Outlaw Torn Slater to Mr. Sutherland and myself, alive, trussed up, and with a ribbon wrapped around him, so Mr. Sutherland and I can have him for our personal use and delectation?"

"For our little fun and games?" Sutherland asked.

"Señor Slater is yours," Díaz said. "He just doesn't know it yet."

"Then the money is yours," Judith McKillian said, lifting the pen from its inkwell and sitting at the table. Placing the check on it, she commenced filling it out.

"Look outside!" the Señorita suddenly howled. *"The fight! We're missing the fight! Ricardo is supposed to be getting a royal, unbelievable, very-much-deserved ass-whipping, but you won't guess what happened!"*

"Madre de Dios," Díaz groaned, amazed at what

had transpired, "it looks like young Ricardo killed . . . *El Toro*."

"No," Sutherland said, "Toro's still moving. He's writhing on the ground and clutching his gonads."

"Look at the way his knees are locked upward, as if in prayer," Díaz said. "It looks as if—"

"As if . . . young Ricardo gelded *the bull!*" the Señorita thundered.

"Young Ricardo is *muy hombre*," Díaz said appreciatively.

Judith McKillian had been writing down the bank, Díaz's name, the amount—$300 million—and was just starting to sign her name when the Señorita's howls distracted her. Putting down the pen, she stood up and joined them at the railing."

"El Toro looks like El Steer-O," Judith McKillian said, genuinely impressed.

The first mine explosion suddenly knocked all four of them to their knees and brutally shook their balcony. At the same time, the main shaft head—and a thousand other mine entrances and exits all over the mountain, many of them ancient long-forgotten apertures—were billowing black smoke and burgeoning fireballs. El Infierno de Plata was rapidly turning into one massive conflagration, a single ball of fire.

"SLA-*TERRRR*!!!!" Sutherland thundered.

Díaz gaped at the blazing mountain and at the unsigned check.

"This time," he shouted to no one in particular, "Slater's *hideputa* hide is mine."

Chapter 104

As Richard stood over the sobbing El Toro, the ground shook beneath his feet. A series of rapid *whump-whump-whump-whump-whump-whumps!!!* were convulsing the entire courtyard. El Infierno's innumerable, labyrinthine shafts, many of them long-lost and heretofore hidden, were blowing up in an apocalyptic symphony, an *1812 Overture* of interminable, heart-wrenching, gut-rumbling eruptions, black smoke roiling out of the myriad shaft holes covering the sides of the mountain as well as out of the main shaft head itself, which was belching out of its massive maw an infernally black thunderhead of hellishly noxious smoke.

Díaz and the Señorita were in the top-floor balcony. Looking up at them, Richard met their furious gaze unflinchingly, thumped to his chest, and shouted in a paraphrase of the great, warrior-wanderer Odysseus:

"Tell them it was Ricardo did this to you!"

Charging out of the cage, he joined Hernando, who dragged him through the mobbed courtyard to the hacienda wall that abutted the raging white-water river, roaring far, far below. Snow- and ice-melt from the icy glaciers atop the nearby mountains fed the waterway, engorging it into a crashing cataract, which later metamorphosed into a series of vertiginous water-falls downstream.

But from this vantage point—150 feet above—it looked like a slender, delicate thread winding through an endless array of steep cliffs.

"Are you ready, young amigo? You can do it. You were a high-platform diver."

"My highest dive was fifty feet."

"So this is just a little higher—nothing but a hop, a skip, and a jump."

"This is your plan?" Richard stared at him in stunned incredulity.

"*Sí, amigo.* Any suggestions? You're the expert."

"You want to maximize your air resistance in order to slow your fall," Richard said. "If you can, stay hori-zontal on the way down. Flap your arms and legs, if you start to tumble or spin. That ought to help stabi-lize your fall, but remember at the last minute to turn vertical, point your toes down, flatten your hands and arms against your sides."

Hernando unwound a length of knotted rope from his waist and tied if off on one of the wall's turrets.

"Climb this down to the end and it will get you fifty feet closer to the river. Push off against the wall as hard as you can, three or four times, then let go and pray."

Richard stared at him, silent.

Again, Hernando's grin was perversely optimistic. But then gunshots were hammering the wall on both sides of them. Looking up, Richard saw armed guards were forcing their way through the mob of *prisioneros*, making a beeline for the two amigos, revolvers raised, banging away at the two men.

"So much for the rope," Richard said.

Hernando watched the young man mount a parapet and kick off, diving hard and flat out over the river. Seeming to float forever above the cataract, he only gradually began to fall. To stay horizontally aligned, he began waving his arms and legs up and down for almost the entire 150-foot drop. Only at the last second did he lower his legs. Clutching his sides, toes angling downward, he entered the water at an astonishingly straight, perfectly perpendicular angle and disappeared into a colossal mushroom cloud of foamy water and spray.

Richard surfaced in time to see Hernando leap wildly off a parapet and fall spinning toward the river, pancaking the white water like a thunderball from outer space. Richard was still struggling for air, and the water was stunningly, agonizingly cold. It was moving fast, bouncing him along like a cork, bobbing him up and down, half drowning him. Still he managed to spot Hernando. The man had been knocked unconscious, was half-submerged and facedown. He looked about to drown. Swimming toward him, Richard looped an arm under Hernando's chin and struggled to keep his face up and out of the water.

The river's snowmelt was freezing, and Richard suddenly realized his arms and legs were going numb. He was in danger of passing out and drowning.

All at once a large tree trunk over ten feet long

and a foot in diameter, covered with a dozen thick branches, banged into him. It almost knocked Richard out, but still he was able to grab hold with his free arm and drag Hernando in between its protective tree limbs. If he could hold on to Hernando and still keep a grip on this miserable excuse for a raft, they might have a chance.

Now, however, Richard had more to worry about than the unconscious Hernando and the rapids. Big boulders were lining the cliff walls and were emerging all around him. If they crashed into one of them, they'd be goners. Somehow Richard had to elude the large rocks.

Moreover, the river was approaching a right-angle turn. Careening off a cliff face and bloodying his nose, he fought to hold on to Hernando and the gnarled hunk of tree trunk. He was barely maintaining his grip.

Then they hit another bend, then another, then another. They were bouncing off more cliffs. Twice he lost his grip on the tree fragment, but still hung on to Hernando. Swimming frantically, with one arm toward his tree trunk of a raft, he grabbed a scraggly limb and worked his way back to the trunk. Hanging on for dear life, he was now seizing up with shock and hypothermia. Beyond agony, slipping in and out of consciousness, he was delusional with fatigue and freezing from the cold.

A drowning man in an ice-cold nether sea, clinging to a sinking spar.

He hit a boulder, than another, then another. He was now too weak and beaten down to even attempt to avoid them. He just gritted his teeth, tightened his grip on the tree and on Hernando, and took hit after hit. It was like he was new to the ring back at West Point, just learning to box, when the coach had told him how you survived punch after punch from a better, stronger, faster fighter.

"You swallow your blood," the coach told him, "eat your pain, and look for an opening."

But this was the river of no return, and there were no openings.

Even worse, he began to hear a distant roar and not the roar of rapids. No, this was something deeper, more terrifying, more portentous. The roar had taken on a gut-rumbling, body-shaking quality. It grew louder, louder, louder, till it was unbearably ominous, ear-shatteringly powerful, an undifferentiated din, dimensionless in its omnipresence, beyond deafening, almost preternatural in its violence, like the thunder of Armageddon, like the end of the universe, like the obliteration of time itself.

The death of gods and all that came before and since.

Then he saw it. The river abruptly disappeared, replaced by a vast, devastating emptiness. He, Hernando, and the tree trunk were rocketing toward the falls, closer, closer, until they reached its edge, until they were sailing over it and tumbling head over heels into a hideously deep abyss. Looking down, he saw he was falling well over a hundred feet.

Richard quickly remembered to pull and push himself free from the tree and from Hernando. The water beneath them would be hard enough to kill him and his friend. Richard did not want the two men to have to crash into solid wood and into each other.

And then it hit Richard all at once: to his eternal surprise, he felt suddenly, strangely liberated. For the first time in months he was free—free of the army, free of war, free of the Señorita's captivity, free of her sexual slavery, free of her torture chambers, free of the pain and the suffering of her prison mine, free of Díaz, and most of all, free of . . . *Méjico.*

It seemed to him in that brief moment that he was even free of time itself—hanging there abeyant, suspended between all the abysses of Dios and El Diablo. For the first time in his life Richard seemed to have achieved a state of spiritual solace and peace of soul. He was at one with his demons within as well as those without. He had escaped the surly bonds of earth. He was at one with—

Then he made the mistake of looking down, and he saw an inferno of boiling foam and thunderous water exploding up above the crashing bottom of the fall, lethal as the Pit, mind-cracking as Götterdämmerung and terminal as Eternity's Close.

He then realized with nauseating dread that he was about to hit that water like an earth-bent death star from the farthest reaches of the Outer Dark—except this killer star was fragile as crystal, frail as flesh itself. This killer star was a mortal man.

Well, he thought, *I guess this is what hell looks like.*

Nonetheless, he was still half-conscious when he again surfaced, again caught his breath, when he found somehow he was again hanging on to Hernando, when they crashed into the naturally, accidentally formed breakwater of rocks, a tree trunk, branches, dirt, and deadfall. Situated inside a small cove, it was protected by the canyon's sharp, right-angle riverbend. Richard struggled frantically to grab a branch, a rock—anything, everything—and pull himself up out of the roaring, freezing water.

Out of the blue a strong hand grabbed his biceps and pulled him and Hernando up out of the rapids. The next thing he knew the man was throwing each of them up over a shoulder. Climbing from boulder to boulder, their savior carried the two of them to the riverbank. All the while, Richard and Hernando were vomiting up river water.

From the bank, the man carried them up a series of switchback trails up to the canyon rim. Richard's vision still was not good, but he did see that the man was taking them to a small group of people, standing beside a half-dozen horses and a pack mule. They were obviously waiting for them and thei rescuer.

The man lowered them onto the ground. Richard sat there awhile. Puking up river water and catching his breath, he was getting his bearings. When his vision cleared and he finally looked up, he found himself staring at his mother and sister.

"How's Dad?" were the first words out of his mouth.

"As good as to be expected," his mother said.

"His cancer's in remission," Rachel said.

"You're alive," Richard said to his sister, "and you made it back to the ranch?"

"No, I'm an apparition."

"So what are you doing here?"

"We came to bring you back," his mother said.

Richard didn't know what to say.

"Which wouldn't have been necessary," Katherine said, "if you two ever did what I told you to do in the first place."

"You were right, Mom," Richard said.

"Richard and I never should have gone down to Méjico," Rachel said.

"It was nothing like we thought it would be," Richard said.

Katherine let out a long, slow sigh. "What the hell ever is?"

"The Señorita and Díaz are sure as hell everything they're supposed to be," Torn Slater said, "and they have a small army of federales on our trail."

The man was studying their backtrail through what looked to be a 15X telescope.

"We have to mount up and head 'em on out," Katherine said to Richard and Hernando.

Richard stared at Slater a brief moment. "We haven't been introduced."

"Richard," his mother said, "I want you to meet an old, much-valued friend of mine, Torn Slater—a man to whom, quite frankly, I owe everything. We all owe him everything."

"You don't owe me shit," Slater said, "but it is time to slope on out of here."

"Can we outrun them?" Rachel asked.

"If I can shut our back door."

Slater started up a small hill with his Big Fifty Sharps slung over his right shoulder, a saddlebag over his left. His saddle and horse blanket were in his right hand.

"You people move on up the trail," Katherine said. "Torn and I will catch up with you later."

"I can handle this, Katherine," Torn Slater said.

"You may need a spotter."

Slater shrugged and continued upslope, Katherine following him.

At the top of the hill, Slater placed his saddle on the high ground, folded his blanket over it, and hacked a groove in its center. While he studied the approaching riders through his 15X sniperscope, M. Mort spread his large bulk out beside him.

Katherine swore to God she heard the big tom . . . *purr.*

Slater was already unpacking his folding, vernier-scale peep scope to calculate distance and rifle elevation. He used the 15X achromatic, refracting scope for identifying his targets.

Sitting cross-legged alongside Slater, Katherine braced her elbows on her knees and studied the approaching dust cloud through her telescope. She could discern the phalanx of four dozen cavalry officers within a dust cloud. They were over a thousand yards away and no doubt saw themselves as invulnerable.

But now Kate was studying Slater, watching him work the trigger guard. Pulling the hammer to half cock, he chambered a round and adjusted the rear trigger, which loosened the trigger pull. When he was ready to shoot, she quickly returned to her telescope.

She heard the shot and sensed the big Sharps's mule-kick to Slater's shoulder—she would one day learn he'd double-loaded the cartridges. Through the corner of her left eye she'd also sensed the impossibly all-engulfing cloud of whitish black-powder smoke, shrouding his head, shoulders, and rifle, was blinding him to the shot's impact.

Slater didn't seem to care.

He was already pulling back the hammer to half cock, slamming the trigger guard forward, extracting the spent shell casing, and inserting a new .50 caliber round into the chamber. He then shoved the trigger guard back into place. Setting the double-triggers to the light touch, he pulled the hammer back to full cock.

Dispersing the smoke with a quick efficient wave of his hand, he was again studying the vernier peep sight, staring into his scope, calculating distance, rifle elevation, and windage, then sighting in on the chest of his next federale.

Katherine finally stopped thinking about Slater, sensing his actions instead, just watching stunned, as he blew hole after hole through their chests and stomachs, lifting the men high above their saddles and dropping them a full four feet behind their horses. And when those who were still mounted turned to flee, Slater put round after round through their backs, leaving, it seemed to Katherine, apertures, big, broad, bloody, and deep enough to march tigers, lions, and elephants through. One, two, three, four, five, six, seven, eight, nine riders were blown up and out of their saddles.

At last, a dozen or more men stopped, dismounted, and left their horses rein-standing. Seeking protection from Slater's Sharps, they threw themselves into barrancas or behind mounds of red clay desert. Slater then killed their mounts with headshots. As soon as the last pony fell, Slater picked up his saddle and returned to his roan. M. Mort reluctantly rose. Shaking himself, he yawned, growled, and followed Slater.

"Will more men come after us?" Katherine asked, eyeing the jaguar with amazed dismay.

No one had left. Their friends were still waiting for them.

"Eventually," Slater said. "Díaz and Sutherland won't quit."

"And no one wants to face the wrath of the Señorita," Eléna observed.

"She must be *muy malo*," Katherine observed with wry understatement.

"You have no idea," Richard said.

As they headed toward their mounts, Katherine sidled up against Slater.

"Torn, I hate to ask, but I'm really curious," she said softly. "What did you feel when you killed those men?"

Slater was silent a long moment while he considered her question. When they reached their horses, he finally said:

"Recoil."

Slater then loosened his cinch, put a boot in the roan's belly, and pulled the latigo tight enough that the horse whinnied and reared up.

"Them saddles will turn," Slater said to no one in particular.

He swung on and they started toward Campeseta—out of Sinaloa and into Sonora, where General Ortega's rurales held sway and where they would hopefully be safe from Díaz and the Señorita's federales. But who knew? The best they could hope for was to get on that Mexican-Pacific rail line and highball it north all the ways to Nogales and the *mejicano*-American border, then straight on through.

Even Díaz and the Señorita would be hard-pressed to follow them into Arizona.

PART XX

The dead never lie.
—EL PRESIDENTE PORFIRIO DÍAZ

Chapter 105

Major Mateo Cardozo was in charge of Díaz's security detail. He and the Señorita were comfortably ensconced in his El Presidente Tren Expreso Personal [his Personal Express Train]. Its eight-wheel Rogers locomotive pulled a tender and a double club car in which Díaz, the Señorita, Sutherland, and Judith McKillian could relax. They sat on floor-bolted, leather-padded, black cherry armchairs, and brass fittings gleamed everywhere. Alongside them were bolted-down matching end tables, which were brass-ridged along the edges so glassware could not slide off. On the tables were also silver ice buckets, in which bottles of Henriot Brut Souverain and Laurent-Perrier Grand Siècle chilled. Furthermore, the tables contained hand-carved circular holes into which the patrons could place their champagne flutes. Dishes of beluga caviar, Camembert, pâté de foie gras, Dijon mustard, chorizos, chili peppers, and sliced *pan de campagna* were spread out for them as well.

Behind the club car were four sleeping cars, in which each guest had a luxurious sleeping compartment. After the sleeping cars came two dozen ventilated stockcars. These were the quarters for their contingent of two hundred heavily armed federales, who traveled with full gear, including bandoliers of cartridges crisscrossing their chests. Their mounts, also loaded into stockcars, were saddled and ready for action.

Mateo had joined up with the Señorita and Díaz in hopes of sabotaging their operations, including Infierno de Plata. When Slater's plan enabled him to blow it up, he had succeeded beyond his wildest dreams. El Infierno de Plata was no more.

His hope now was to sabotage their current mission, which was to capture young Ricardo all over again and to kill his mother, sister, and any other companions traveling with them.

Mateo was determined not to let that happen.

The Señorita had surprised him on the trip though. In fact, she'd impressed him. She rode as easily and capably as any vaquero and was curiously indifferent to the difficulties of life on the trail. In fact, she seemed to like roughing it. She even seemed to like trail rations—the beans and dried beef, the tortillas and black coffee that were all they'd had time to pack.

Mateo wondered if she'd grown up on a ranchería. *Of course, he did not dare ask her. He was not shy around women, but her case was special. No one wanted to attract her attention or make her acquaintance. He even avoided eye contact. Everyone knew the fate that awaited those men and women whom she . . . befriended.*

Her racks and strappados, her iron maidens and sacrificial altars, her Grand Inquisitors and high Azteca priests were hated and feared throughout all of Sinaloa and Chihuahua, where she held sway.

But while the Señorita has seemed strangely comfortable, strangely at ease on horseback and on the trail, she was restless in this lap of express train luxury.

"*Mi muy bueno amigo,* Porfirio, I still do not see how we can catch up with Ricardo's mother and her friends. That man with the big Sharps rifle—Señor Sutherland's notorious brigand, Outlaw Torn Slater— delayed us beyond all measure. Our informants say they boarded their train a full day ahead of us, and the only place we could catch a train was in Mazalan, which was far south of Campeseta, where the stationmaster says they got on theirs."

"*Es verdad,*" Díaz said, agreeing, nodding his head. "But they are taking a common freight train, no doubt traveling by box- or stockcar. They will lose a full day of travel en route to Nogales, sweating on sidings, while the other cars are loaded and off-loaded. Not us. We are on the El Presidente Express. We have the ultimate right-of-way. We take precedence over everything and everyone. The mother and her group will wait for everything and everyone."

"I keep forgetting, Porfirio," the Señorita said.

"You're so humble, my dear," Díaz said. "You just have to get used to it. You are with El Presidente now.

We in this car are born to rule, and others are born to serve."

"Rank does have its privileges, I suppose," the Señorita said pleasantly, patting El Presidente on his knee and treating him to her most ingratiating smile.

Chapter 106

In Agua Verde, Katherine and her crew had booked passage in a ventilated stockcar. Ordinarily, they'd have kept their horses and mule with them, but nobody, stock included, wanted to be anyplace near their jaguar, whom Eléna called "El Gato Negro." To keep their distance from him, all others on the train, human or equine, chose different cars. So their horses and mule rode in a car full of other passengers' live-stock, while Katherine, M. Mort, and her friends had the stockcar all to themselves.

They had a good jump on Díaz, the Señorita, and her friends, but Slater was not optimistic.

"Since the Sonoran rurales fight under General Ortega and are in open rebellion against Díaz and the Señorita, Díaz can't order them to stop our train. They'll be traveling in El Presidente's car though. They'll have right-of-way over everything on the rails. We're going to spend a lot of time on sidings, while they're rocketing straight at us. So Díaz will catch up with us at some point."

"Do we have a plan?" Rachel asked.

"Luckily, there aren't any federales or any other law enforcement on this train," Slater said, "so at some point we can commandeer it."

"The federales fight for Díaz and the Señorita," Eléna pointed out.

"But Díaz will have a troop train full of federales with him," Antonio pointed out.

"So how can we fight off all those Díazistes?" Rachel asked.

"We can't, so at some point, we may have to find a way to hijack our train, then derail Díaz. After that we can highball our train straight through to the border and crash on through. If we commandeer this train too early and try to do all that, the Sonoran rurales might spot us, realize we've stolen a train, and decide to stop us."

"So what do we do while we decide when to hijack this thing?" Rachel asked.

"I'm heading back toward the caboose. I can rest on top and study our backtrail through this scope. If and when I see them gaining on us, we'll have to take charge of the locomotive."

Slater started toward the rear of the car, where a ladder, leading up to the car's top, was nailed into the stockcar's end.

"I'm going with you," Katherine said.

Slater stared at her a long minute. "All right. I may need your help when Díaz and the Señorita finally catch up with us."

Katherine followed Slater to the rear of the car and then up the ladder.

To her horror, M. Mort clambered up the rungs like he was climbing a tree.

What the hell have you gotten yourself into? she found herself wondering.

Chapter 107

"You know the trouble with this miserable land?" Sutherland asked Díaz.

The four friends were lavishly ensconced in his double club car.

"You can't mean our Madre Méjico," Díaz said, indignant, "our Méjico Lindo!"

Sutherland's sneer scintillated. "Exactly so."

"Besides Méjico's utter absence of couth?" Judith McKillian asked. "Besides Méjico having no class, no culture, no ladies and gentlemen of true discernment?"

"You mean no running of the hounds on Sundays?" Sutherland asked. "No cards at Claridge's? The lack of such august activities is truly appalling, but no, Méjico's problem is much worse, much deeper than any of that."

"What is our problem then?" Díaz asked.

"Enlighten me," the Señorita said, giving McKillian and Sutherland her sweetest smile.

"I can sum it up in a single word," Sutherland

said simply. "You have way too many goddamn . . . *Mexicans*!"

"That's it!" McKillian shouted enthusiastically. "Don't you understand? That's all of Méjico's problems rolled up into one simple explanation."

"I have to agree," the Señorita admitted sheepishly, "and I'm *una mejicana.*"

"I see your point," Díaz said, "but we do have other problems."

"Really?" McKillian asked.

"What really bothers me," Díaz said, "is that no one tells the truth anymore. I can't even *torture* the truth out of people."

"I agree completely," the Señorita said. "People are critical of my interrogation methods—my Inquisitors, my racks, my thumbscrews, my flogging posts, my iron maidens. But even I cannot elicit the truth from my *prisionaros*. The more I torture them, the more they . . . *lie*. They will lie just to make me stop hurting them. Can you imagine anything more . . . *dishonest*?"

"I can't, my dear," Sutherland said.

"Nor I," Judith McKillian said, nodding sympathetically.

"My dear Señorita," Díaz said. "I have always viewed your interrogation techniques as an 'aggressive search for truth.' That is all."

"But in plain fact," the Señorita said, "my methods do no good. Even when I apply the most extreme measures—hot coals, gelding knives, asphyxiation, joint dislocation—people still lie to me."

"How duplicitous!" Judith McKillian said, her voice rising. "To lie under torture!"

"Even on pain of death," Díaz said, "people lie to you. I've seen and heard it with my own eyes and ears."

"The hypocrites!" Sutherland roared, genuinely outraged.

"People really don't understand me," Díaz said. "Because, like the Señorita, the 'truth-acquisition' techniques I employ are admittedly aggressive. Consequently, weak-kneed liberal critics dismiss me as a depraved sadist, when all I'm looking for are simple, honest, truthful answers to simple, honest questions. When you get right down to it, I am at heart a philosopher. Part of me has always been with Socrates, telling his judges that he would rather drink the bitter hemlock than give us his quest for truth. I am joined with Aristotle in his pursuit of the primum mobile, the first cause of . . . *everything*. I will always stand forever with Christ before Pilate, while He denounces his accusers, saying that the truth is not in them, that they would not know the truth if they tripped over it, and with Christ, I suffer Pilate's horrifying answer: 'What is truth?' I've always sympathized with the immortal Immanuel Kant in his painstaking struggle to ascertain the ever-elusive noumenon, the ultimate, irreducible essence of all being, and with the Russian author Dostoyevsky, who wrote in his magnum opus, *The Brothers Karamazov*, that truth is so impossibly, so painfully, difficult to apprehend that only God alone can fathom it."

"And if there is no God?" the Señorita asked, suddenly serious, staring intently at the dictator.

"Dostoyevsky believes that if there is no God, my

dear Señorita, then . . . *nothing is true and everything is permitted.*"

"Oh," the Señorita said, "I do like . . . *that.*"

"None of which makes my work any easier," Díaz said. "My dogged search for honesty and accuracy rivals that of the great Greek stoic-turned-cynic Diogenes, who spent his life in search of a single honest man, and who died an abject failure, agonizingly unfulfilled. The older I get, the more I identify with that tragic man. Like him, all I have ever asked for in this life is honesty, yet all my efforts—no matter how excruciatingly extreme they might at times have been—have come to naught."

"Perhaps there is no such thing as truth," the Señorita said to Díaz.

"Oh no, it does exist," Díaz stated emphatically. "I know that in my heart and soul, in my bones and blood."

"Then where is it?" the Señorita asked, genuinely curious. "Like yourself, I've never found it."

"In death, there is truth," Díaz said softly.

Judith McKillian burst into laughter. "You're saying that only the dead speak the truth? That's preposterous. The dead have no voice at all. The dead can't even talk."

"True," Díaz said, "but the dead have other virtues. There's one in particular that is inimitable, indisputable, and nonpareil."

"What virtues could the dead, moldering in their loathsome graves, possibly . . . *possess*?" Sutherland asked, shaking his head in derisive disbelief.

"I thought you knew," Díaz said. "The dead may be still as death itself, silent as the malodorous graves in which they are interred. But there is one virtue at which the dead preeminently excel."

"And what is that?" Judith McKillian asked, her eyes also disparagingly cynical.

"The dead never lie."

Chapter 108

They were fifty miles from the norteamericano border and at the top of a high rise when Slater spotted the big locomotive pulling Díaz's El Presidente troop train. A half-dozen miles behind them, it was coming up fast and gaining on them.

"Time to take over this train," Slater said to Katherine.

He rose and started toward the front. Katherine took his arm.

"I gather this isn't the first train you've hijacked."

Slater shrugged, said nothing, and continued on over the tops of the cars. M. Mort fell in behind him, and Katherine followed them both. Richard, Rachel, Eléna, Hernando, and Antonio joined them along the way. When they reached the tender, which Slater was pleased to see was piled high with firewood, he had his people stop.

"Time to check your loads."

They took out their pistols and swung open the loading gates.

"Put a round under the hammer if you don't have one there," Slater said.

Reaching the tender, Slater swung down first and worked his way over and around the piled-up kindling.

The fireman was an older, white-haired gentleman in soiled blue bib overalls, dirty canvas gloves, and an engineer's hat. He looked long past his retirement age, and Katherine was sure if the man survived the last leg of this trip, he'd put in his papers. He had his back to them and was carrying chopped wood to the firebox, where he piled it up for future use. When he turned to get more wood and saw Slater and his gang approaching, he went for his sawed-off shotgun resting in a lidded box at the front of the tender.

Slater, however, already had his Colt on him.

"*Lento*, old timer. There's no reason *por tu muerte* [for your death]."

"I'm no hero," the old man conceded.

"*Mucho bueno*," Slater said, slapping him on the back. "Now, let's go take over this train."

Slater had hijacked many a train in his life, but never when he had a jaguar for a partner nor was the big cat in a good mood. Mort clearly didn't like the shaking, ear-shattering, abysmally smoking, grinding, coughing hellish engine or the filthy, angry men running it, and Mort was making his displeasure known to one and all. His throat rumbled and reverberated in a single, nonstop, horripilating growl, the raven-hued fur on his back bristling and coruscating in wave after wave after wave, his yellowish vertically distended pupils blazing like Luciferian fire. The engineer and the fireman looked at Slater's guns, at the massive ebony tom, and then turned back to Slater.

"Amigo, I've been robbed and hijacked by the best of them—by banditos, rurales, federales, by anyone and everyone. But I never had a *hideputa* jaguar *and* a bandit gang take over my train. You got anything and everything you want!"

"All we want is to outrun that train roaring up our backtrail long enough to get safe into the Arizona Territory," Slater said. "We only want to make it to the U.S. of A. in one piece."

The engineer nodded frantically, never taking his eyes off the massive, snarling, bare-fanged feline.

"I'll get you there if I have to feed that lazy-ass assistant of mine into the firebox. Just let me get to work."

Slater started back down the train, over the tops of the cars. Katherine, Hernando, M. Mort, and Richard followed him. Antonio and Eléna stayed to watch over the engineer and fireman.

What the hell, Slater thought. *You're attempting to fight off a troop train filled with maybe a couple of hundred federales and the president of Méjico as well as that harpy from hell, La Señorita Dolorosa, Lady Pain, why not drag along Katherine and her kids?*

But when Slater got on top of the caboose and got out the telescope, he quickly realized that outrunning their enemy was not an option. Instead of a half-dozen miles back, the troop train was less than a mile away and gaining fast.

And Slater saw why. A wood-burning locomotive wasn't pulling it but a coal-burner was. Coal-burners ran hotter and faster than their own wood-fueled engine. The big train was gaining on them by the minute, by the second. Staring at the big black locomotive, Slater felt like he was staring at his grave.

But then M. Mort was suddenly at his side. He'd probably sensed that Slater would need his help. *Oh well*, Slater thought, maybe Mort could jump ship at the last second, take off across country, and survive. No reason for the big tom to go down with his friend's sinking ship.

"You have a plan, right?" Katherine asked.

Slater said nothing. His plan had been to beat them to the border. He'd fire a few rounds at them if necessary, but he'd assumed he could beat them to the U.S. in the end. The coal-fired speed demon had changed all that. Now the locomotive was fifty feet away, forty, thirty, twenty. Then the cowcatcher was banging into the caboose's platform. Once, twice, three times.

Soon hundreds of federales would be climbing over and around the locomotive, shooting anyone and everything in their path.

When suddenly, four cars down, just behind the locomotive, the tender, and Díaz's presidential double club car, the troop train separated and dramatically slowed down. Someone had decoupled the troop train from Díaz and his cronies, who were up front. Slater and his friend had an ally on that train. Katherine and Richard instantly understood the implications.

"Let's go hijack the front half of that train," Katherine said.

Slater stared at her in shock.

Damn, he liked that woman. He'd always liked her—even back with the Chiricahuas.

"Hell, yes," Richard said.

"Why not?" Rachel asked.

The four of them leaped onto the cowcatcher at the front of the Presidente Express, M. Mort close behind. Just as they drew their guns and started around and over the locomotive, they saw the fireman and engineer cringe in horror at the big, yowling-howling-eyes-blazing jaguar, their faces contorted with screaming terror. The two men promptly jumped out of the locomotive and onto the passing ground beneath.

Once in the engine compartment, Slater showed Hernando how to operate the locomotive's throttle and brake. He then told him how and where he wanted him to stop it.

He, Katherine, Richard, and Mort reached the presidential club car at exactly the same time that Mateo entered it. Slater had a Colt in each fist. Mateo was holding the decoupler in front of him in both hands, his guns still in their flap holsters.

"Mateo's a friend," Richard said simply—something Slater had figured out as soon as he'd seen the decoupler and the holstered revolvers.

Slater's main focus was the four other people in the club car. Díaz was the only one with a sidearm, and Slater quickly relieved him of it. Still he didn't trust any of them anymore than he could throw the Rogers locomotive, pulling the train, at them. He knew Díaz, Sutherland, and McKillian from past encounters, and knew that their violence and avarice knew no bounds. He knew of the Señorita by way of friends who'd pulled time in her prison mines. In fact, he hated everything about every one of them.

Slater even hated their clothes. They always dressed outrageously: Díaz was in a generalissimo's uniform festooned with a small galaxy of medals, many of which were French. Since France had been Mexico's most recent conqueror and archenemy, any sane Mexican would have regarded those medals as inherently treasonous. Apparently, Díaz was too stupid to understand the difference between heroic patriotism and collaborating with the enemy.

For the time being, however, Díaz was trying to ingratiate himself with Slater, which was impossible under the best of circumstances. Even worse, Díaz now had to contend with the massive black jaguar that was standing between him and Slater. The beast's fur bristled up and down his body. His fangs bared, he menaced Díaz with low-throated growls. Díaz did his best to give Slater ingratiating smiles and ass-kissing grins but he could not contain the stark terror *el gato negro* instilled in him.

Then there was the McKillian woman. He'd known her for years as well, and Slater had read in the papers that she'd met the man of her dreams. Less than a week after they'd consummated their affair, however, the man died—but only after he'd rewritten his will and left her the bulk of his estate, which amounted to well over $500 million. Slater assumed she'd poisoned the imbecile. Slater personally thought it served the idiot right for leaving so much filthy lucre to someone as transparently homicidal as the woman standing before him. True, she was dressed in all black, as if to honor her late husband, but her perpetually sardonic sneer made a mockery of any and all grief. Then there was the manner in which she wore her so-called widow's weeds. Black, butt-tight buckskin pants, a matching silk blouse with the three top buttons missing, revealing a mother lode of concupiscent décolletage, high-heeled riding boots of the same shade reaching halfway up her thighs—nothing in her couture suggested sorrow at her lover's passing. The idiot was indisputably out of her sight and out of her mind. Judith McKillian was already trolling for another mindless, lust-mad, millionaire moron, whom she could quickly debauch, despoil, and then ruthlessly . . . *dispatch*. For the time being, however, she was also intent on avoiding the fang-bared tom—now snarling at her—even as she attempted to give Slater an almost lecherous leer.

Next Slater turned to his old nemesis, J. P. Sutherland. He was decked out in his usual jodhpurs and riding boots. He smoked a malodorous cigarillo stuffed in an ivory holder and wore a gold monocle over his right eye. Cocked on the right side of his head was a red bowler. The hat's angle was meant to appear rakish, but, in truth, it was a foolishly futile attempt to conceal the big, bone-white patch of keloid scar tissue, which Slater had bestowed upon him in Sonora several years past, when he'd excised that part of his scalp with a well-honed Arkansas toothpick. Sutherland clearly hadn't forgotten or forgiven Slater his crude attempt at cosmetic surgery. Neither Slater's jet-black, frighteningly flat eyes nor the blazing, amber orbs of his truly horrifying jaguar friend could distract Sutherland from his hatred of the outlaw. Sutherland stared at Slater, his eyes burning madly, maniacally.

Sutherland reviled Slater with a vindictiveness that outstripped all imagining. Slater wasn't sure why. The day he scalped the man, he did try to mitigate the damage. He'd hung Sutherland inverted over a bonfire and cauterized his bloody pate. He'd probably saved the man from bleeding out or from contracting gangrene or worse. He had to admit though that Sutherland's screams that night—while the fire scorched, crackled, and blistered the top of his head—had been transcendently terrifying . . . a true wonder to behold.

Then there was Madre Méjico's one and only Señorita Dolorosa—Lady Pain. According to the press, she was one of the wealthiest women in the world. Not that you could tell it today from her attire. She was clad in soft blue Levi's, a simple white blouse, and dark brown boots. Her long inky-hued tresses, which flowed freely down past the small of her back, were unribboned, unpinned, and uncoiffed. Her face was devoid of makeup. Her high forehead, slanted cheekbones, and disarmingly wide smile framed lively expressive eyes, which were dark and shiny as two Apache tears, those obsidian pebbles erupted up and strewn throughout so much of the land by Méjico's long-ago, long-forgotten volcanos.

Even without artifice, coiffure, or couture, she was easily the most beautiful woman Slater had ever seen—as well as the most wicked. For not only did she own some of the most prodigiously profitable plantations and mines in the western hemisphere, she ran these operations almost overhead-free. Méjico's legendary strongman, Porfirio Díaz, provided her, at no charge, a vast army of bond-laborers. That slave horde, over a hundred thousand strong, had wrung for her—from Méjico's mountains and croplands—an incalculable fortune. Toiling, day and night, in chains and shackles, suffering under the overseer's lash and terrifyingly taut tumplines, they staggered and eventually died under their burden-basket's stupendously crushing loads.

She was the only one of Díaz's crew who was not cowed by Slater's feline friend. As soon as he approached her and gave her his first, soft, low-throated growl, she bent down, looked him straight in the eye, and stroked the back of his head. When he lifted his head, she scratched him under the chin.

My God, Slater thought, *M. Mort has met Mlle. Morte. The world must be coming to an end.*

But now Hernando was stopping the train as per Slater's instructions. He had blown his steam whistle three times, signaling Eléna and Antonio in the first locomotive to do the same. Both trains were now coming to a halt on a trestle, spanning a large waterway, which flowed through a steep desert canyon over 150 feet beneath them. It was time to deal with Díaz and his cronies.

"Let's go outside," Slater said, "and stretch our legs. M. Mort gets nervous when he's cramped up too long."

Climbing down from the double club car, Slater walked them over to the trestle's railing. It was four feet high and ran the full two-hundred-foot length of the railroad bridge. The heavy plank bridge had two walkways, one on each side of the railroad tracks. Slater escorted them all over to the rail.

"Katherine," Slater said, "these four, in combination, have tortured, imprisoned, and killed people by the millions. They tried to kill Richard in a slave-labor prison mine. You rode a long, hard way to get him out and to settle up with these people. You got your son back, but now these people want to kill you, your loved ones—all of us. They're rich and powerful enough that given time, they will do it, so we aren't leaving them alive. You've earned the right to kill them."

He handed her one of his Colts, the butt out.

Katherine shook her head. "Everything you say is correct, but I can't shoot a man or woman down in cold blood. It's just not in me. I don't know how."

Slater leaned toward her and to Katherine's undying surprise whispered in her ear:

"There's no shame in that, Kate." Slater turned to Richard. "What do you say? You want to do it? You have more reason than anyone else here."

"Shooting's too good," Richard said. "Since a high dive and a long swim was good enough for Hernando and me, it ought to be good enough for these people." Turning to Sutherland, Richard said: "You first."

Sutherland stared defiantly at Richard, his monocle still locked in place over his right eye, the ivory cigarette holder clenched firmly between his teeth. Without averting his gaze, he shouted at Díaz:

"You're El Presidente. You aren't going to let him do this, are you?" He shook a finger in Richard's face. "You ruddy Yanks are rude, you know? You deserve a nasty lesson in humility, and I'm just the man to give it to you." The cigarette holder bounced up and down in his mouth as he talked.

Richard snapped Sutherland's head back with a short left. He then grabbed the dapper limey with both hands by the front of his belt and his shirt. Lifting him off his feet, he flung the man over the rail. Sutherland plummeted backward, the monocle still firmly fixed over his left eye, his arms flapping as if in a frantic simulation of winged flight. All the while, Sutherland screamed dementedly, and the cigarette holder, clenched in his mouth, never stopped bouncing up and down. Bits and pieces of his fragmented tirade echoed up and down the river canyon, bouncing off the cliff walls, over and over again, in endless, reverberant replication:

"Ruddy Yanks! . . . Rude, I tell you . . . Nasty lesson in humility . . . That's what's coming to you . . . Deserve everything you get, and I'm here to give it to you . . . no class . . . *No bloody class at all . . .*"

He hit the river like a hod of lead bricks, and his screams were heard no more.

Richard then turned to McKillian.

"When I was strung up by the wrists, you really enjoyed whaling me with that horsewhip, didn't you?"

"That was rather amusing, wasn't it?" Judith McKillian said, smiling brightly, clearly enjoying the memory. "But was it as good for you as it was for me? How did *you* like our little tête-à-tête . . . *ducks*? Did my riding crop . . . *smart*?"

She held it in front of Richard's face. Staring him straight in the eye, she leaned forward until they were nose to nose. She shook the riding crop menacingly and laughed.

Ripping the horsewhip out from her fist, Richard forced Judith McKillian belly-down over the rail. It was a good four feet high and her booted feet dangled a full half a foot above the bridge's plank walkway.

For a brief second, Richard stared down at her. She was, as usual, tantalizingly attired in black, shockingly tight, buckskin breeches.

"Yes, it did hurt," Richard shouted at her. "In fact, *this* is exactly what it felt like."

Hammerlocking her arms with his left hand, Richard angrily gave her a ferocious taste of her own medicine, beating her notoriously curvaceous bottom as if he were possessed. Roaring like a pain-crazed panther, she simultaneously thundered curses at Richard so bloodcurdlingly foul they horrified even Slater. Eventually, even Katherine couldn't take it any longer.

"Stop," she said simply to Richard, grabbing his arm.

Standing McKillian up, he gave her a last, disgusted look.

"How did you like that?" he asked. "Finding out what it's like?"

Glaring hatefully at him, McKillian's chin trembled in and out and her breath came in sharp spurts and rattling gasps. She was so winded she couldn't talk. Brimming with tears, her eyes were swollen and red with rage. Yet at the same time, those crazed orbs glittered maniacally at Richard—luridly furious yet also blazing with demonically depraved . . . *desire*.

Breaking the whip over his knee, he tossed it over the rail into the distant depths below, hurling McKillian over the side after it only a second later. All the way down, she flailed her arms and legs like a madwoman, ululating loathsome obscenities horrific enough to sicken Sodom and bring Gomorrah's famously unregenerate wretches weeping to their knees. Her astonishingly odious oaths, like Sutherland's taunts, boomed throughout the barrancas, arroyos, and mountain passes, continuing on and on and on even after McKillian crashed into the water and all her physical screams ceased.

Richard turned to Díaz. The dictator was standing up to him, fists clenched.

"I am *uno soldado*," Díaz said, "and I've personally killed hundreds of men better than you, *muy duro* than you. You are *nada, por nada*, and now I'm going to kill you too—right here where you stand."

Richard turned, as if to walk away, then off a pivot hit Díaz in his solar plexus three inches above his belt buckle. All the wind exploded out of the tyrant in one sudden whoosh, and he doubled over, sobbing for air.

Richard grabbed the upper half of Díaz's bent body, hoisted him above the railing, and dropped him into the vertiginous void. Still the tyrant managed to get his breath back, treating them, as he fell, to a single, ear-shattering execration, a five-second, four-syllable wail of:

"HI-DE-PUT-A!!!"

A street abbreviation of the ancient but still infamous insult *"Hijo de la vieja puta, Muerte,"* he was calling Richard in English: "Son of the old whore, Death."

Díaz's denunciation also resounded up and down the canyonlands, even after Díaz hit the river like a monstrous boulder out of the blue.

Turning to the Señorita, Richard was astonished to see her already standing on top of the railing, perfectly balanced, staring down on him with an amused, condescending but not entirely unfriendly grin.

"Young Ricardo," she said, "you never cease to amaze

me. Really. You are indeed *muy hombre, mi muy favorito hombre.*"

"That's a joke, right?" Richard asked, his expression dubious.

"Not at all, young amigo. You know, in my own way, I almost, nearly, actually, kind of . . . *like you.*"

Flinging her arms outward, the Señorita then fell backward, with interminably indolent grace, her smile as singularly brilliant as he'd ever seen it, her back arched in an exquisite reverse swan dive. All the while her eyes remained locked on his—lascivious as sin, lewd as Lucifer, indifferent as death itself, unfathomable as the undying blackness between the uncomprehending stars.

God, she was beautiful. Satan—Richard had once been told—was an angel of light, the most spectacularly gorgeous seraph in the firmament. If so, the Señorita was satanic in her almost unimaginable radiance. As she floated angelically downward into that bottomless abyss, she seemed to Richard the most ravishingly feminine, spectacularly sensual, and yet unimaginably evil creature he'd ever seen.

Let alone made love to.

Richard could not take his eyes off her. She was dropping, dropping, dropping, yet facing him all the time, her chest and head upthrust, her arms outstretched, her unblinking eyes pinning his inexorably. Then at the last second, her arms clenched her chest. Righting herself, her legs pressed tightly against each other, she pointed her toes, like a prima ballerina, straight down toward the river. She was no longer staring at Richard but looking directly ahead, peering off into sheer nothingness—into the farthest of all the illimitable horizons, into that inconceivable emptiness beyond time, place, and space. Her form was now superlatively vertical, and she hit the river like a hell-bent thunderbolt, disappearing into the drink, leaving in her wake an effervescent explosion of the purest, frothiest, most spotlessly alabaster foam Richard had ever seen.

With excruciating lassitude, the eruption settled, dimmed, and disappeared.

And the Señorita was no more.

EPILOGUE

Robbing banks and trains, it's all I ever done.
I stopped doing that, I wouldn't know who I was.
When I looked in a mirror in the morning,
I wouldn't recognize myself.
—OUTLAW TORN SLATER

Slater, Katherine, and their friends quickly crossed the border into Arizona without problem or delay. They then headed north toward Katherine's rancho. Slater stayed with them all the way to the ranch to make sure they got home in one piece. He planned on cutting out early the next morning, but Katherine talked him out of it, saying he deserved a blowout, time off, some really good whiskey, really good food—instead of hard rations, which is what he would be eating on the trail—a warm soft bed, and anything else hers and Frank's considerable wealth could buy for him.

"My way of saying thanks," she'd said.

Truth is, Slater wasn't as young as he once was and he decided he could use a few days off. Also he genuinely liked Katherine—always had, going back to their childhood days with the Chiricahuas. He even found himself liking Richard, Frank, Rachel, Hernando, Mateo, Eléna, and Antonio, all of them . . . which was weird. Torn Slater liked almost nobody.

So they spent several days sleeping, drinking, and telling stories. Eléna and Mateo could sing, Rachel could play the guitar, Katherine the piano, so they even listened to music. One day led to another, and eventually he knew it was time to go. Katherine anticipated his mood and told him she didn't want him taking off quite yet.

"You're safe here, you know? Frank and I own half the state, and no one will mess with you in Arizona. If you need to be by yourself, we have a hunter's shack with a good stone fireplace up that big mountain there just above the tree line. It's near a great trout stream. There's mule deer, antelope, wild turkey—everything. An old silver mine is nearby if you get bored and want to look for the mother lode. Anything you find is all yours."

"Sounds good, Katherine. Even that damn mine."

"Really? You don't strike me as the mining type."

"I'm not, but a while back I lost an amigo in a mine. Always figured I should have been with him. Maybe I could have gotten him out."

"Or gotten killed with him."

"Maybe."

"Also I've had a few ideas about you and your run-ins with the law. I want to photograph you."

"What?"

"But first I want to cut your hair and shave off your beard."

Slater's stare was wary, but still he went along with it. Afterward he headed up the mountain and spent the better part of the month in the shack, hunting and fishing. He even tried his hand at mining. He kept thinking how Moreno kept telling him they had a fortune in gold in that old Mexican mine, but how the man had died looking for it. In fact, he seemed to have found it—just before he died.

So Slater went into the mine and started hammering at the ore face in the east stope, and to his eternal surprise found a vein of ore two feet thick that seemed to go on forever. Katherine and Frank had a mountain of pure silver right on their rancho just a few miles from their house.

However, Slater had made his amazing discovery by himself. M. Mort, for the first time since he was a cub, was no longer at Slater's side.

Something strange had happened to M. Mort up on that trestle. He'd been studying Richard for some time back on the train with a fixity of expression and a rapt fascination that everyone had commented on. Finally, when the young man threw Díaz and his friends off the bridge, something in Mort had seemed to snap. He walked Richard back onto the train and began following him everywhere he went, and Richard had responded to the big feline with genuine kindness, something that was missing from Slater's character. Mort even slept next to Richard's bed at night. M. Mort still treated Slater with respect and deference, but it was clear the big tom had found a new leader.

Katherine was afraid that Slater's feelings would be hurt by the cat's change of allegiance.

"Hell, no," Slater said. "I'm glad to get rid of the bastard."

"You aren't big on pets?" she asked.

"Not hardly."

"You ever had a dog?"

"Yeah, one time I had one. Half-wolf, half-mastiff, he

was black as sin and looked more like a bear than a mutt. Everyone called him Bear Dog."

"How did you end up with him?"

"Some Comancheros had pitted him against a grizzly bear, and he actually tore out the bear's throat and killed him. Bear Dog was half-dead and underneath the griz—in fact, choking on his throat blood—when I found him. I got the bear off of him and hung him upside down to get the blood out of him. I gave him to a Mexican family, and they nursed him back to life. Then I forgot about him. The dog never forgot it though. He tracked me down and followed me everywhere I went."

"What happened to Bear Dog?" Katherine asked.

"He and I ran into another grizzly. The thing was mauling me and Bear Dog intervened. He killed it, but it got him too."

"He was one tough dog," Katherine said in amazement.

"I saw him kill a cougar once."

"He killed bears and mountain lions?"

"He sure did," Slater said. "I never wished him dead, but I was glad to get rid of him in the end. Same with Mort. You have to understand. People and animals don't have much luck around me. They don't seem to last. My kind of life isn't conducive to long relationships."

Katherine stared at him, silent, her eyes empty of expression or meaning.

"It's worth remembering, Kate—in case you and Frank ever think about befriending me."

Finally, rested up, Slater came down from the mountain and back to the ranch. The first thing he did was tell them about the fortune in silver that he'd found in their old mine. Slater had exposed the ore vein, and he was now afraid someone might stumble on it and try to jump their claim. Frank assured Slater that their deed to the mine was still good and that no one could steal the silver from them.

Then it was Katherine and Frank's turn to surprise Slater. That night they spread his new identification papers out on the dining room table. He had a birth certificate from Michigan City, Indiana, dated June 1, 1844, and separation papers from General John Bell Hood's Confederate Army of Tennessee, dated July 21, 1864, Battle of Atlanta, Atlanta, Georgia.

"The Michigan City hospital was obliterated by a tornado," Katherine explained to him, "and the Sixth Army headquarters was destroyed in a fire, during the so-called Burning of Atlanta. No one can prove you aren't what the papers say you are."

Slater stared at Katherine, saying nothing.

"Get it?" Richard asked the outlaw. "Keep your face shaved and your hair cut, and you'll look nothing like your wanted poster. Plus you have a new name and legal papers, proving you're John C. Calhoun, not Outlaw Torn Slater."

"Katherine and I are also giving you a letter," Frank said, "naming you as our personal representative and authorizing you to transact business on our behalf. And believe me, Torn, Katherine and I cast a long shadow around these parts. No one around here hassles us."

"You're a free man, Torn," Rachel said.

"If you want it," Katherine said softly.

Slater was silent.

They had a great evening—good food, good drink,

a few people, there was music, and everyone, except Slater, danced. Eventually, however, Katherine got out a week-old newspaper—the *Tucson Tribune*. There was an article on how Porfirio Díaz had vanished from sight but had now resurfaced.

"Here's another good reason why you want to change your identity," Frank said. "You have too many rich, powerful enemies dogging your trail."

"My attempt at murder didn't work," Richard said, shaking his head in disbelief. "They all survived the impossible—a hundred-fifty-foot fall."

"The mystery of El Presidente Díaz's disappearance has finally been cleared up. He has materialized at his palace with investors, whom Díaz says are critically important to the future of Mexico—the ultrawealthy British magnate, James P. Sutherland; his friend and fellow tycoon, Judith McKillian of the New York McKillians; and Mexico's own legendary mining mogul, the ever-attractive Señorita Dolorosa. They had been in a clandestine conference in a secret location, in which they were hammering out a series of financial covenants, arranging for several vast, much-needed investments in Méjico's mining, energy, and agricultural sectors. The conference was interrupted when the four friends experienced a boating explosion in the Sonoran River, during which they almost drowned. All's well that ends well, however. El Presidente Díaz says he knows the people who were responsible for the blast, and he assures the world that retribution will be harsh and swift. He is convinced that the saboteurs are hiding out north of the Rio Grande, and El Presidente wants them to know: Nothing will stop him in his

*quest for revenge. Díaz and his private army of rurales are
coming after them. El Presidente says to them:*

*   "We will hunt you down anywhere you go—in Méjico, in
the United States, anywhere. You cannot hide."*

"Maybe Mom and Dad are right," Richard said. "Maybe keeping your old name isn't such a hot idea."

"Maybe," Slater said.

But the next morning when Katherine got up, Slater was gone. All that remained of him was a note, which Katherine found next to the coffeepot. His new identification papers lay beside it. The note read:

*I have to thank you, Kate, for the papers and your
kind offer. I have to think about it though. Robbing
banks and trains, it's all I ever done. I stopped doing
that, I wouldn't know who I was. When I looked in a
mirror in the morning, I wouldn't recognize myself.
I'm not saying I won't take you up on it one day. I'm
getting older, and as Calamity used to tell me all the
time: "Torn, cards and guns, robbin' banks and
trains, that ain't no life for a grown man."*

*   So in the meantime, I'm leaving those papers with
you. I got me a hundred and fifty grand in fresh-
minted, fresh-printed yanqui dollars, buried down in
Madre Méjico and I'm heading back to reclaim it. It
ought to be cooled down some now. Maybe I can
spend some of it up here—before I spend most of it on
bad cards, hard liquor, fast women, and slow
horses . . . and waste the rest. Still that cash ought to
hold me over for a while, and who knows? Maybe I'll*

*make it back up to El Rancho del Cielo one day just
to say hi. Maybe I'll even ask you for those papers.*

*But right now I'm heading back across the Rio.
I can't let what Díaz said slide. I'm calling on him
and Sutherland, McKillian, and the Señorita—
letting them know I really don't want them messing
with my friends. Put it to them straight up—coldcock
and country simple . . . plain as the balls on a tall
dog, if you catch my drift.*

*Because, Katherine, you are mi amiga. You
always were, always will be. Or as the Chiricahuas
used to say in their sign-talk: Time-when and for-all-
tomorrows.*

*But right now I got to get kicking . . . toward that
borderline.*

So it's muchas gracias and hasta luego.

> *Tu amigo siempre* [your friend forever],
> *Torn Slater*

Katherine put the letter down and stared east out
the window. Dawn was rising above the rimrock,
throwing off brilliant shafts of yellow, orange, and
pure shimmering gold. It was a new day. It looked to
be a goddamn good day. Her kids were home, Frank
was doing great—at least, his cancer was in remission
and he had all his energy back. Slater claimed to have
even discovered a fortune in silver for them in that
old mine, and it looked like it was going to be a beautiful, prosperous, sunny morning at the Rancho of
Heaven. What more could Katherine ask for? Once
again, Torn Slater had given her her life back, had

given her a reason to live—a reason to . . . *believe.*
Katherine Jane Ryan now had everything in the world
to hope for.

Still she couldn't help herself. Her jaw quivering
and her shoulders shaking, she pressed her hands to
her face and . . . *cried.*

AFTERWORD
Slavery in the Age of Porfirio Díaz

Why dost thou beat my people to pieces
and grind the faces of my poor?
—Isaiah 3:15

Several writers and editors who read early drafts of *Dead Men Don't Lie* asked me whether slavery under Díaz was as horrific as I've portrayed it here. The answer is yes. Throughout Díaz's thirty-one-year regime, from 1880 to 1911, Mexico was a true hell on earth. That question is also interesting, however, because it indicates how little people today know about Díaz's Mexico. Few—if any—serious books are available on Díaz and his thirty-year reign of terror. People subsequently don't appreciate how brutally he ran Mexico and the extent to which he built and based its economy on slavery, which is largely why I've written this afterword.

Slavery became illegal in Mexico in 1829, but since the wealthy essentially appointed the law enforcement officials, there were no serious legal objections to the policy and the practice. And it was slavery. As in the American South, Mexican slaveholders effectively owned their workers, and their workers had no rights under the law. Concealing their proprietorship behind euphemisms such as "forced service," "contract labor," and "peonage," the owners often worked their chattels to death. Nor was escape a viable option. Typically if anyone ran off, the populace informed on them for the substantial price on their heads or out of fear that, if they did not inform, they might be accused later on of having abetted the escape. In that case they'd face imprisonment and enslavement themselves. Furthermore, Mexico was so destitute that living off the land, after escaping, was onerously difficult. Lastly, observers reported at the time that runaway slaves were almost always caught, and upon their return, faced ferocious floggings and starvation rations. Consequently, only the most recklessly brave or desperately foolhardy ever attempted to escape.

Physical chastisement of slaves was universal. Overseers beat them routinely in order to force more labor out of them. Their overseers called their daily whippings *cleanups*. They were administered in the morning at roll call and during the evening roll call, after the workers returned from the fields or the mines. The beatings were also administered during the day. The overseers beat the prisoners with canes and with knotted hemp ropes, soaked in brine.

The owners habitually starved their peons as well. Chronic hunger tended to fatigue the slaves, making them more malleable. The overseers also believed hunger forced their slaves to work harder in the hope of obtaining extra rations—or for fear of having their rations cut. And of course feeding them inadequately padded the owners' bottom line.

In his extraordinary first-person report on the lives of Mexican slaves, *Barbarous Mexico,* John Kenneth Turner argued that the chief difference between U.S. slavery and Mexican slavery under Díaz was that in the U.S., individual slaves had significant financial value. In fact, recent studies indicate that the value of an average slave came to $900 per person. Since that was an average figure, healthy slaves in the prime of life would have obviously brought much more. Turner argued that Southern slave owners, therefore, had a financial incentive to keep their slaves alive—at least long enough for them to breed replacement slaves. No such incentive existed in Díaz's Mexico. There, the potential slave-labor pool was virtually limitless, and the slaves were, consequently, worth almost nothing. Labor agents received as little as $45 for a slave.

Historians have pointed out that the reason Mexico imported so few African slaves—relative to the American South—was that those who sold the Africans forced-laborers could not compete in a market where slave owners could obtain *indios* and indigent mestizos for next to nothing. Nor did Spain's rulers believe in paying for slaves. It had been their policy in Europe first and then in New Spain to enslave their subjugated peoples.

I don't mean to suggest that slaves in the American South were well treated. Quite the contrary. After 1840, when the British brought their steam-powered spinning mills on line and discovered that the American South's domesticated Native American cotton— with its longer, stronger fibers—was especially desirable for mechanized processing, Southern cotton became explosively profitable. In fact, between 1840 and 1860, Southern cotton was as financially formidable worldwide as Big Oil would become in the twenty-first century. In 1860, American slaves, in aggregate, were worth more than the combined assets of both the country's manufacturing sector and shipping lines. Consequently, the U.S. cotton plantation owners began buying up every additional slave they could get their hands on and working them as hard as they knew how. More work out of their slaves meant more cotton for the mechanized mills in England and the North and more money for the planters. Moreover, the planters' profligate lifestyles exacerbated their obsessive need for constant cash infusions. They were continually borrowing money from the New York banks against future cotton crops in order to finance their prodigal spending and outrageous ostentation. A slave's failure to meet his or her cotton-sack quota at the end of the day could result in savage whippings.

All I'm suggesting is that Díaz's slaveholders found it easier and cheaper to replace their deceased slaves than America's slave owners did.

Díaz's slave owners had three different methods for conscripting men, women, and children from the general population of impoverished, illiterate *indios* and mestizos. Since Mexico had no middle class, the disempowered poor constituted between 80 to 90 percent of the country, and Mexico's jails contained a bottomless reservoir of potential slaves. Labor agents often paid jailers to consign their prisoners to them. Since most of these inmates had never appeared before a judge, the labor agents could charge the inmates with any crime they wanted and sentence them to their mines or plantations for as long as they wanted them to work.

The agents, or their subagents, could also often convince their prospects to sign bogus contracts for allegedly legitimate labor. Since, during the time of this book, virtually all of Mexico's poor were illiterate, bogus bond-labor agreements were easy to fabricate, falsify, and enforce.

Lastly, slaves could be conscripted through the age-old tactic of kidnapping. Because slaves were held incommunicado, once a person was in bondage, friends and relatives would discover it was almost impossible to track that person down. And even if they had succeeded in locating their loved one, finding a way to obtain the person's release would inevitably prove to be a lost cause. As I said before, Mexico's judges and officials were for all intents and purposes appointed by Díaz's plutocrats.

At one point in *Dead Men Don't Lie*, I incarcerate Richard Ryan in an especially atrocious slave-labor mine, and life for miners during the Porfiriato was truly nightmarish. All nineteenth-century mine tunnels were intrinsically dangerous places, but Mexico's were worse. Known as *ratholes*, they followed the veins of ore, regardless of how they twisted or corkscrewed, no matter how fragile the part of the mountain through which they wound. These shafts required meticulous maintenance, which they seldom got. Ore extraction took precedence over everything else. Cave-ins were a constant danger, and since Díaz's mines were torch-, candle-, and lamplit, and since dust and flammable gas were everywhere, mine fires were a continual threat. Moreover, the smelters, which surrounded the mountains, tended to cannibalize the mine's stock of shoring timbers, which were needed to prop up the tunnels. After all, the ore, which the mines produced, had incalculable value—and therefore the wood used to smelt the ore had value as well. The miners' lives were worth relatively little to the mine owners.

Still, mining requires some work skills—hacienda field labor less so—consequently, a miner was not quite as economically valueless to a mine owner as a plantation slave was to a *hacendado*. Often, miners received wages, but the expenses deducted from those wages kept the miner perpetually indebted to the mine owners . . . hence, keeping him perpetually enslaved. He could not quit his job legally, and if he attempted to flee, he was, as usual, informed on, apprehended, returned, then flogged and starved half to death.

On the whole, hacienda slaves probably had it worse than the miners. On some plantations, a slave's average life expectancy was as little as eight months.

The enslavement of women and children was common on the plantations. If the owners held entire families in bondage, their husbands and fathers were less likely to rebel, and even if they did rebel, long-term hunger and frequent floggings soon broke them of their rebelliousness. Díaz even brought the Yaquis to their knees. A relatively sophisticated agrarian people, the men proved themselves to be fierce warriors when they were threatened. In fact, those Yaqui warriors had been so tough, independent, and strong willed that Spain had never brought them to heel. With his advanced military technology, however, Díaz waged a war of extermination against them, then relocated the survivors to slave-labor plantations in the sweltering Yucatan, which was far away from their home in northern Mexico as Díaz could productively move them. The overseers invariably broke even the bravest of the Yaquis within a week or two through the twin scourges of starvation and the lash. If the slaves did not break, the slave owners had them publicly flogged to death or simply killed. After all, the deaths cost them relatively little. In the sugar plantations in Mexico's more tropical regions, the owners sometimes threw their dead slaves' remains into their crocodile-infested swamps.

Both the Maya-Azteca religion and the Christian faith taught fatalism, and Mexican people had come to accept and absorb it implicitly. Turner says in his book that Mexico's slaves endured the unspeakable horror of their existence with incomprehensible fortitude. Still while they were uncomplaining, he said he had never heard a Mexican slave sing or burst into joyful laughter.

Another factor that made Mexico's slavery unusually pernicious was the foreign ownership of so many of the country's mines and plantations. A significant number of wealthy Mexicans—I have one in this book—owned such operations, but, under Díaz, countless numbers of these enterprises were sold to foreign businessmen, often to wealthy Americans.

While these owners might occasionally visit Mexico, they were mostly concerned with the revenue their overseers could squeeze out of their haciendas, businesses, and workers. These financial moguls paid no Mexican taxes on their profits, and if they did not visit their vast holdings or did not look too closely into their day-to-day operations, they could claim ignorance of the ghastly violence that their overseers inflicted on their slaves.

Slave exploitation tended to be worse on the enterprises owned by absentee magnates.

Which brings us to the attitudes of men like Díaz and the attitudes of the owners of his slave-labor enterprises. That particular topic is so ugly that in this novel I employ considerable dark humor in depicting the plutocrats'—and Díaz's—views of the poor in general and Mexico's peons in particular. I am pleased that most readers find these sections hilarious. In point of fact, the reality was much more depressing. These people viewed their slaves as dumb engines of human flesh who existed solely to enrich the avariciously affluent and imperiously powerful, namely themselves. Even the Catholic Church, in the days when it owned so many of Mexico's largest haciendas, argued that peons were so inherently stupid and so intractably childlike that they responded only to and were improved only by the whip and the rod. So I made the slave owners in my novel personally sadistic and at the same time tried to make their cruelty comical—even though these people could not have been more unfunny.

Brutality in the nineteenth century was common.

Slavery existed throughout the American South for much of that period, and the nineteenth-century Western world, on a personal level, was far more vicious than our own present-day one. The beating of women, young people, and even employees, including child laborers, was widespread. In more barbaric countries, it was worse. In Russia, according to Dostoyevsky's prison memoir, *The House of the Dead*, prisoners were sentenced to as many as a thousand lashes in their Siberian camps.

Even in the twentieth century, Henry Ford's "labor pushers" punished "slow" or "insubordinate" workers with nightsticks, and corporal punishment of inmates was an everyday occurrence in many prisons.

Nor in the nineteenth and twentieth centuries were the upper classes immune from institutional sadism. The British public schools, which produced luminaries such as Winston Churchill, Robert Graves, Roald Dahl, and David Niven, were infamous for the perversity of their punishments. These men later wrote and talked about the harrowing physical abuse that they suffered, including floggings and child rape. Furthermore, the masters of these institutions were torturing the scions of England's elites. One can only imagine what little compunction or restraint they might have felt had they had the opportunity to torture the weak and powerless—the true wretched of the earth.

So, yes, on a personal, day-to-day level, the nineteenth-century world was more violent than our own, but even so, Mexico under Díaz was unique among the Western nations. When it came to physical coercion, Mexico was in a class by itself.

As to the attitudes of mine and plantation owners toward their slaves, again, I would refer the reader to John Kenneth Turner's *Barbarous Mexico*. His descriptions of the slave owners' comments on the flogging of their chattels is instructive. These men brag and gloat openly over their use of physical violence, saying that their workers are so lazy, stupid, and recalcitrant and that to elicit productive labor from them, constant whippings are mandatory. One such owner boasts that his women slaves *want* the owners to whip them at least once a day whether they deserve it or not. Another plantation owner likes to observe his roll call "cleanup" floggings, personally, dressed in fine attire, sitting sublimely on his horse. While he watches the men whipped, he smokes a cigar with languid, lordly hauteur, supremely indifferent to the agony of the men being beaten bloody. Only after he tires of his cigar, tosses it to the ground, and rides back to his hacienda does the flogging cease. One of the more iniquitous slave-labor procurers promises Turner, who is posing as an American investor, that he can supply Turner's enterprises with as many as twelve thousand child slaves a year and that once Turner takes possession of them, he can do . . . *anything he wants with them.*

While Díaz's regime was much wickeder than anything that had come before or after it, he did not create the world or the customs into which the Porfiriato came to be. Spain's mistreatment of the Mexican people set the precedent for his monstrous misbehavior.

When Cortés landed at what is now Veracruz in 1519, there were approximately 25 million indigenes living in Mexico. By 1650, there were 1.2 million. So Spain's rulers were responsible for the extermination of 90 to 98 percent of Mexico's *indio* population.

The situation actually became even worse in 1565, when Juan de Tolosa made a spectacular silver strike in Zacatecas at La Bufa, and Spain realized that Mexico was one gigantic mountain of silver. The king quickly understood that he could wrest illimitable riches from Mexico's mountains, but to do so the country needed a massive pool of slave labor. At that point, Spain's exploitation of the Mexican people became genocidally aggressive, and they began conscripting slaves in colossal quantities—as rapidly and ruthlessly as they could—destitute mestizos, in particular. After all, they'd killed off most of Mexico's indigenous population.

At times, Church and Crown did attempt to intervene on behalf of the beleaguered *indios*. There was too much money to be made, however, and the mines were too far away for Spain's royal and religious elites to monitor, let alone police.

Mexico's Spanish governors also institutionalized systematic and systemic legal corruption—known today as the *mordida*—that plagued Díaz's Mexico and still haunts the country today. Some historians believe that of all the abominable crimes that Spain committed against the Mexican people, their system of institutional bribery was the most ruinous, incorrigible, and long-lasting.

The Spaniards in Mexico were racist to a degree

that was not equaled until that of the Third Reich. A citizen's legal rights were defined by the percentage of "Spanish blood" flowing through their veins. This legal criterion was clearly preposterous, but many of Mexico's vilest laws under Spanish occupation were based on it.

The Spaniards originated the system, under which a foreign power—namely Spain—commandeered virtually all of Mexico's annual GDP, most of it obtained through inhuman exploitation of the Mexican people.

Under the Spanish rule, the Catholic Church had acquired amounts of land so vast as to be almost immeasurable. When the Mexican government, during the administration of President Ignacio Comonfort, finally confiscated the Church's holdings, some historians estimate that the Church owned a third of all of Mexico's arable acreage. (Some estimates go as high as two thirds.) When Díaz came to power, he continued this policy of land expropriation, dispossessing countless peons. He sold the bulk of these vast tracts to large hacienda-owners and foreign investors. Some of these plantations, which he sold off, encompassed millions of acres.

Since these landowners wanted to wring as much revenue as possible from their investments, they specialized almost exclusively in high-profit crops, which they could sell abroad. For the most part, they produced sugar, tobacco, coffee, cotton, bananas, and sisal for hemp manufacturing and blue agave for the distillation of alcoholic spirits. Since the Anglo-American-European countries were more prosperous than

Mexico, the demand for these goods over there was financially greater. Also their currencies were worth more than the peso. These *hacendados* were so avaricious they did not even produce sufficient corn and beans to feed the Mexican people, so Díaz had to import those foodstuffs from America. As a result, his starving peons paid more than their more prosperous American counterparts in the north did for the same quantities of corn and beans.

So as rapacious as Spain's exploitation of Mexico had been, the carnage and the suffering that Díaz unleashed on the Mexican people was infinitely worse than anything the Spanish had ever imagined. Among other things, Díaz possessed recently developed weaponry, railroads and telegraph communications that enabled him to conquer regions, enslave people, and seize lands that had been beyond the reach of previous Mexican rulers. His military power was unprecedented.

The epigraph under this afterword's title—"Why dost thou beat my people to pieces and grind the faces of my poor?"—asks, by implication, why Díaz wreaked so much death and destruction on his people. After all, he was not a foreigner—one of the groups he so shamelessly and lavishly enriched at the expense of those whom he'd sworn to serve. Díaz was one of the Mexican people. He should have understood and identified with their misery.

An examination of how Díaz rose to power and then maintained his hold over his country might contain the answer. Early in his political career, when Mexico was screaming for justice and more progressive government, Díaz allied himself with two great liberal presidents—first Benito Juárez, then Sebastián Lerdo. He quickly attempted coups against each of them in turn. His coup against Lerdo succeeded, and after taking office, he quickly betrayed Juárez's and Lerdo's liberal ideals, which he'd once agreed to uphold. When he finally ran for the presidency, he campaigned on the platform that he would not seek a second term, a promise he repeatedly reneged on. Once in office, he subjugated Mexico's judiciary and its press. If political rivals posed a serious threat, he imprisoned them. When he sold 90 percent of Mexico's economy to the ultrarich, many of them foreigners, he also increased his hold on power. In order to protect their investments, these tycoons backed Díaz politically and financially and by throwing the peasantry off their land and forcing them into hacienda debt-peonage, he so impoverished and debilitated them that they lacked the fiscal and physical means to oppose him. He even reduced the size of the army and the power of its generals so they could not defy him. He relied instead on the marauding, corrupt, and largely privatized bands of rurales, which he used as his own personal mercenary army. And he lined his own pockets in the process. At the end of his life, he could flee to Paris and retire in luxury.

So why did Díaz "beat his people to pieces and grind the faces of his poor"? He did virtually nothing in his entire career that did not expand his personal and political power; even at the age of eighty he still sought another presidential term. He was willing to embrace almost any and all actions that strengthened his grip on the country—no matter how catastrophic the consequences were to the Mexican people. Power in perpetuity was his sole raison d'être, his only driving dream.

And the havoc he wreaked was horrendous.

Did Díaz's oppression change the Mexican people in any way—then and today? These are difficult, complicated, and perhaps unanswerable questions. Still it is important to our understanding of Díaz's Mexico to consider how the Porfiriato affected—and to some extent might have forged—the character of today's Mexican people.

A good place to start might be the chapters in which I dramatize Mexico's Fiesta of the Dead. Originally a Maya-Azteca festival, the Catholic Church had outlawed it because of its heretical nature. During the Porfiriato, however, the Mexican people had become so depressed and beaten down that Díaz reinstated it, believing the people needed a holiday during which they could let off steam. (Díaz's slaves obviously did not participate in these celebrations, which occurred essentially in towns, cities, and villages.)

In many respects the Maya-Azteca religion had been a celebration of death. This life was a hell on earth, and people were better off departing it as quickly as possible. In their afterlife, a suicide and a noble warrior were, therefore, treated equally. After all, they both inflicted death—albeit on different kinds of victims—hastening that persons' departure from this veil of tears. Death was the supreme gift, and they were both dispensers of that lethal largesse. Nonetheless, even for killers and self-murderers, the afterlife was an ordeal. A heavenly Christian paradise was not in the offing. The gods did not think humanity deserved it. Human beings were born to suffer, sacrifice, and serve. The only hope in the afterlife that the dead could aspire to was to progress through the eight earlier hellworlds to the Ninth Level, in which the dead might conceivably find . . . *oblivion.*

Historians have also noted that the great dying off of the indigenous Mexicans between 1519 and 1650 further hammered this obsession with death even more deeply into that dark Maya-Azteca soul. Robert Jay Lifton described the Hiroshima survivors as suffering from "death immersion" and "death-in-life." The Mexican people experienced 130 years of Hiroshima, the Gulag Archipelago, and the Black Death. Some people believe that 370 years later the hell of that apocalypse is still emblazoned in Mexico's collective psyche.

Yet despite serious, critical differences between Christianity and the Maya-Azteca faith, Mexico's *indios* quickly and instinctively embraced the Catholic Church—to a degree that genuinely amazed Mexico's Spanish priests at the time—and during the Porfiriato, the Fiesta of the Dead began incorporating Christian rituals into the festival. In Díaz's day, the celebrants often ended the festival with a mock crucifixion of a Christ figure, which I dramatize in the novel.

One reason for the Mexican peoples' rapid and sincere conversion to Christianity was their intense identification with Christ's crucifixion. The Mexican people saw stark similarities between Jesus Christ and their own uniquely popular god, Quetzalcoatl, who they believed, like Christ, had once walked among them and truly cared about them. The other Maya-Azteca gods were openly hostile to humanity, and to placate these vindictive deities, the Mexican people had to offer up innumerable human sacrifices annually. Some eyewitnesses claim that their priests ripped the hearts out of victims on the top of their pyramids by the tens of thousands each year. But Christ and Quetzalcoatl cared about humankind. So in their own way, Christ's bloody sacrifice was to the indigenous Mexican people intensely Maya-Azteca, and they commiserated strongly with it. That their own god, their hybrid of Christ and Quetzalcoatl, had sacrificed himself in such an agonizing way in order to save them from a hateful universe's eternal damnation was to the Mexican people profoundly, overpoweringly moving. None of their previous gods had ever contemplated such an act, hadn't really liked humanity all that much, and so the sacrifice of Christ/Quetzalcoatl meant a lot to them. The *indios* and the first mestizos were passionate about Christ's crucifixion in a way that rivaled that of the most devout European Catholics.

So the fiesta was also dedicated to death and featured candies shaped like skulls, bread of the dead, skeletal costumes, posters advertising that all people were ultimately skeletons and food for worms— symbols and images that appeared ubiquitously throughout the pageant. Similarly, the Catholic Church had promoted the memento mori, which admonished Catholics to constantly "remember death" and to always remind oneself that this life was transitory— that a more important dispensation awaited us later on. The Fiesta of the Dead also promoted that precept. It exhorted the Mexican people to focus on the afterlife to come and never, ever to fear death—instead to exult in it and to celebrate it. In fact, the festival is filled with immense amounts of black humor, as if Death itself were a joke. The fiesta seems to say that if we do not fear Death, then why should we fear anything at all?

The Spaniards also brought the cult of machismo to Mexico. A code that revered physical courage, swordsmanship, skill with firearms, horsemanship, sexual promiscuity—in some cases even countenancing rape—and an eagerness to engage in duels, that code also disparaged book learning, science, mathematics, engineering, and hard work. In the end, this intensely Spanish code helped turn Spain from a great power into one of the poorer nations of Europe. While the Enlightenment, the Reformation, and the Industrial Revolution were transforming the rest of Europe, Spain sought to turn the clock back to an earlier, almost violently medieval epoch, and waged continual war on the modernizing nations. In the end Spain lost everything, including Mexico.

Cortés was an extreme exemplar of Spain's machismo code—particularly in his utter willingness to risk almost certain death and to kill people en masse, as demonstrated by his slaughter of countless thousands of Mexicans.

Díaz, who began his career as a military officer, was another example of the new, intrinsically Mexican machismo. In a sense, the Spanish code of machismo had honored violence, even homicidal violence, and the Maya-Azteca code had honored . . . *death*. Violence and death, the killing and enslaving of people nationwide, meant nothing to Díaz, and consequently, he represented the worst, most nihilistic aspects of both codes. Mexican lives were worth nothing to Díaz, not if there was a peso to be made. Unlike Cortés's conquests, there was nothing heroic about Díaz's achievements or his machismo. That he was a *mestizo*—a so-called mixed blood and part *indio* himself—made the plundering, mass murdering, and enslavement of his own people all the more heinous.

As many people have suggested, fatalism was always part of the Mexican people's essential mindset—as it was in both their Maya-Azteca and Christian worlds—but their forbearance was neither infinite nor eternal. They did rise up, forcing Díaz into his Parisian exile, where he died. Igniting a revolution that blazed with cataclysmic violence for over ten years, from 1910 to 1920, their rebellion became a fiery purgation for the Mexican people, one of those rare grassroots conflicts between the dispossessed against the elites—who, in many instances, resided abroad. Two of their most notable *revolucionarios*, Pancho Villa and Emiliano Zapata, led genuine people's uprisings, as did Father Hidalgo and José Morelos before them.

How do historians, in general, view Díaz? During the last hundred years, scholars have written almost no serious biographies of him, and only a couple of reporters did enough research to attempt his life's story. Nor were any good biographies written while he was alive, which is understandable. During his successive administrations, Díaz quashed most critical reportage, reputedly jailing, killing, and even blinding investigative journalists. Hence, the first, early biographies, written during his lifetime, tended to be uncritical, even fawning and sycophantic; worse, they sometimes treated the Mexican people with condescension, as if they deserved no better than Díaz, as if it took a tyrant to elicit profitable labor from them. The only recent book about him is a short, slim volume that also attempts to extenuate his misdeeds and paint him in a more approving, appreciative light. Most articles, short bios, and other writings about the Porfiriato handle Díaz's atrocities and triumphs the same way.

Díaz himself seems to be too big, challenging, and perhaps embarrassing a subject for professional historians. Consequently, there are almost no serious biographies of him available, especially in English, which, as I said before, is one of the reasons I have written this essay.

The dearth of significant books on Díaz is surprising but not the historians' urge to focus on his material accomplishments and to ignore the crimes he perpetrated against his people. After all, history is, in the main, a polemic of power—a story of nations that rise and of the nations around them that fall—and thus, it is a narrative written by the victors. In the histories of World War II, for instance, there may be a chapter or two on the Holocaust or the Stalinist labor camps, but such works are primarily about how the war was won or lost. A. J. P. Taylor thought history was largely a story of how, when the balance of power swung too far in one direction, the country that attained too much power would begin to bully its neighbors and then eventually invade them. Taylor believed, like Thucydides, that love of money and lust for power caused most wars. Moral issues in such histories take up relatively few pages. Toynbee's view of history is a rare exception to this axiom. Consequently, many historians have argued that Mexico, before Díaz, was, in the minds of foreign financiers, a hotbed of violence, banditry, and anarchy and no one would invest money in that country. Only because Díaz had pacified and stabilized that previously lawless and chaotic land did investors finally pump huge sums into that nation's infrastructure—into its mining, agriculture, industry, communications, and transportation systems. Hence, many historians argue that Díaz brought Mexico into the twentieth century and that without his foreign investors Mexico's economy would have stagnated, even deteriorated. These scholars argue that—Díaz's depredations notwithstanding—Mexico became a better place because of those investments and the infrastructure they created. That the Mexican people never profited from those ventures does not enter into that calculus.

Given the extreme excesses of Díaz's atrocities, however, and the violence of the ten-year revolution that they provoked, such arguments on behalf of Díaz's reign will not have much staying power. Furthermore, there are two simple, fundamental criteria by which history can judge the success of Díaz's thirty-year regime: (a) How well did his people eat? and (b) How much did the population grow during his presidency? The Porfiriato had been relatively stable. He should have been able to at least provide his people with sustenance. After all, the Aztecs, under Montezuma, were well fed—better fed than the European peasants of that period—and back then, Mexico had a population of approximately twenty-five million people. Some estimates suggest over thirty million. Under Díaz, however, the population never topped fifteen million, and yet, unlike Montezuma, he'd had to import his corn and beans in order to keep his people from starving to death. During Díaz's thirty years in office, Mexico's population grew by 50 percent, and only after Díaz was forced from office did the Mexican population surpass that of the Aztecs. In fact, in the seventy-five-year period following Díaz's presidency, Mexico's population grew by 500 percent—six times faster than it had grown under Díaz—and Mexico was once again able to raise enough food to feed its people.

So, while some historians will always genuflect before the altar of power—descanting about the enemies Díaz defeated, the miles of train rail that his oligarchs laid, the telegraph wire they strung, and the mine tunnels they dug—history must not overlook the radical evil Díaz engendered. The lands he seized and sold abroad, the peasants he enslaved and killed, the courts he corrupted, the political opponents he jailed, and the journalists he suppressed—those crimes against humanity will not be forgotten. The harm he did to his citizenry was almost unfathomable in its sheer hideousness and devastation; it will always be historically unforgivable. At the very least, the Mexican people will never forgive him.

The Mexican people have evolved enormously since the days of Díaz and Villa. In the Mexican community their sense of family loyalty—particularly extended family loyalty—are marvels to behold. In his extraordinary history of Mexico, *Fire and Blood*, T. R. Fehrenbach suggests that the Mexican peoples' calamitous history created their love of family and of extended families. To survive they needed the support of one another, and the most basic societal tribe—the group of people who band together for purposes of survival—is the family. Under Díaz, family was the most reliable group that a person could turn to for help and support. Family life was, therefore, integral—often indispensable—to one's own survival.

Also despite the many negative features of the Spanish and Mexican machismo, both codes exalted courage as the preeminent virtue. Without the courage to go on, there could be no perseverance or even endurance. Lord knows, the Mexican people under Díaz—and during their entire five-hundred-year history—have needed all the courage in the world.

Viktor Frankl in his landmark memoir of his experiences in the Nazi camps, *Man's Search for Meaning*, argued that for those living in extremity, loyalty has survival value. At Auschwitz he wrote that only those who systematically helped the fellow prisoners within their own small personal group survived. Solzhenitsyn in the second volume of *The Gulag Archipelago* in the chapter entitled "The Ascent" made the same observation. Writer James Clavell survived four years in Japanese POW camps, and he stressed the same point.

Ironically, Díaz's attempts to shatter the Mexican people—in order to enrich a relative handful of financial predators and to consolidate and enlarge his own political power—may have only made his people's sense of family unity . . . *stronger*.

People sometimes ask me where my interest in that country came from. After all, I have written or co-written seventeen novels, ten of which were set largely or entirely in Mexico, including *Dead Men Don't Lie*; and I've spent a lot of time in that country—in fact, in all of Central America. Initially, it came out of my interest in Mexico's revolutionary spirit and struggles. Mexico seemed to me a very dramatic place in which to set my novels.

Then two other people stimulated my interest in that nation. Gary Jennings, the author of the classic novels *Aztec* and *Aztec Autumn*, had admired my writing, and so I was invited to work on the last five novels in his fictional Aztec series, bringing his oeuvre up into the nineteenth century. To do that, however, I needed to do a staggering amount of research into Mexico's history, going all the way back through the Aztecs and the Maya. It was a peregrination worthy of Odysseus's odyssey.

Then, as I was beginning that journey, something else happened. I was close to an old woman who was widowed and living by herself in North Hollywood, California. Her small apartment building allowed pets, but the larger neighboring buildings didn't, and the old woman happened to have a grayish thirty-three-pound cat named Timmy. He looked more like a large lion cub than a cat.

Her neighborhood was almost entirely Mexican, and she was one of the very few Anglos living there. Timmy fascinated the innumerable Mexican children in her neighborhood and drew them to him like a lodestone. Among other things, there were almost no other animals around, and they would stare at him as if he were an exotic animal in a zoo. The old woman loved children as well as animals and let the kids into her apartment so they could play with and pet her cat. After all, he was the only animal available to them, and he was a true prodigy. The kids were so nice that she began baking cookies for them and serving them lemonade.

Their Timmy visits became ritualized so that the kids getting out of school could join the group that played with Timmy. Every afternoon at three p.m., children from all over the barrio poured into her apartment.

When the kids' parents found out, they began sending burritos and enchiladas with their children to give to the old woman. When the parents learned she loved their cooking, they invited her to their apartments for dinner. None of the parents spoke English, and most of them had never had an Anglo break bread with them before. The kids translated, and the dinners were so successful that the neighbors began visiting her, dragging their kids along as translators. The old woman had suddenly become part of an extended Mexican community consisting of hundreds upon hundreds of people.

Unfortunately, the old woman's memory began to go and a lifelong cigarette habit was destroying her lungs. Alzheimer's and emphysema had taken hold. When her son visited her and realized she could no longer take care of herself, he talked to her neighbors, saying that he was confused about what to do. A very young couple who lived next door to the old woman told him not to worry about his mother, that she was *nuestra familia* [our family], and that they would look after her, keep her clean, and feed her. He asked them what would happen if she walked out of her apartment and wandered the streets. The husband said he'd thought of it. He was a journeyman carpenter, and, with the son's permission, he would install a doorbell that would ring in his apartment if the old woman left hers.

Nursing homes can be miserable places for elderly patients with Alzheimer's, since they are aggravating to take care of and are at the same time utterly defenseless. After all, if they are abused, they can't remember it. The son didn't want to send his mother to a home and liked the couple next door. He trusted them. When they refused to accept money for their help—on the grounds that the old woman was *nuestra familia*—he forced it on them with the threat that if they didn't take it, he'd put the old woman in a state home.

The husband worked long hours. For a three-year stretch, he worked 110 hours a week, which also required a three-hour drive. He'd be so tired that he'd fall asleep standing up in the shower, but he made enough money to make the down payment on a large home in the same neighborhood. He and his wife told the son that they wanted his mother to move in with them.

She joined them, bringing Timmy and all her furniture. When the son visited, he would meet all of his mother's new extended family. The new house was constantly filled with relatives and close friends and had the greatest food and joy and love that he'd ever seen in his life. He came to believe that his mother was happier there than she'd ever been. He found a doctor and two nurses who made house calls. They always found his mother cheerful and they never found a bedsore. Given the severity of her aliments, the doctor and nurses had believed a full-service nursing home had been inevitable. They told the son he'd performed a miracle.

"It wasn't me," he said simply.

When his mother finally died, he took the young woman who'd taken care of his mother for seven years out for lunch. Driving her back to her house, he tried to give her an envelope filled with four figures in cash since the young woman was now officially out of work. It was his way of saying thanks.

She threw the cash envelope on the car seat and shouted at him:

"Don't you understand . . . *anything*? It was never about the money!"

Slamming the car door, she stamped off and entered her house without looking back.

They, nonetheless, stayed close friends. They are still close friends.

In case you haven't guessed, the old woman was

my mother. I owe her for many things, but not least of all for introducing me to so many amazing and marvelous *mejicanos*. Mom, I couldn't have written this book without you. You made it possible. So to you and to our magnificent *mejicanos* compadres this book is dedicated.

Tu hijo y amigo con amor . . . siempre.